Forced Attrition

A Novel By:

Jeffrey Williams

Forward

All heads turned as Angela Sarcosie walked through the door of the penthouse on the top floor of her father's office building. Angela often held business meetings in the penthouse when her father was away on business. This week Antonio Sarcosie was in Singapore meeting with a member of the International Trade Union.

Angela could best be described as an ambitious svelte seductress with tan, long legs extending from her tight black leather miniskirt. Her wavy brown hair and large glasses made her look like a harmless, sexy secretary. That look only fooled the people who didn't know her. Her daddy called her "Angel," but she was not even close to an Angel and she certainly did not deserve wings. In fact, a pitchfork, tail and horns would have been more fitting. Her smile could warm your heart and her soft lips could melt your soul as she slid a knife in your back and twisted. The women in the room envied Angela for the power she possessed and the men either feared her or wanted to get her in bed. What they all had in common was no one had the guts to cross her because they knew the consequences would be death and not a pleasant one.

The room fell silent by the time Angela reached the head of the long conference table where a single blood red rose was placed signifying that the meeting was held in subrosa. Angela was good at shock and awe. The group never knew what to expect at one of the meetings but they knew it would be illegal and highly profitable. Angela scanned the faces of the people seated at the table with her intense green eyes and got straight to the point.

"We missed our projected profit margin this year by fifty percent. I don't need or want any excuses. I know exactly what the problem is. Because I don't believe we can completely eradicate the problem I have devised a way to capitalize on the situation. Some of you will undoubtedly think my idea bold, cruel and risky. To you I say, where is your sense of adventure. We did not get this far and make this kind of money without serious risks.

Angela smiled and the whole room smiled with her, even though they did not yet know what she was talking about. Her smile and earnest expression exuded trust and made everybody feel comfortable. She was just getting warmed up and in the flow of things. Only one man in the room knew what Angela was about to explain. If the others knew a few of them would have skipped this meeting and likely cashed in all together. Angela hoped to win them over with her presentation. Now that they were there it was too late to back out without looking weak. Plus, their curiosity was up about the possibility of capitalizing on the problem. After all, money does grease the wheels that make the world go 'round. The exclusive people in that penthouse knew exactly why they were sustaining heavy losses. They just didn't know how to correct the situation.

"Although we made a sizable profit last year," Angela continued, "it is my estimation that we lost approximately three billion in products, cash, assets, man power and other related costs, such as legal expenses."

The group was looking gloomy at the thought of losing three billion. Some more than others because they knew it was some of their people who caused a substantial portion of the recent losses.

"In order to help recoup our losses and to send a serious message to the individuals who are directly responsible for causing those losses, we will be sponsoring and hosting gladiator events. Don't look so skeptical. This idea is innovative and lucrative. We will make our money by taking bets on the odds similar to boxing, and in the long run, from the blood and painful nature of the events. The prospect of our lesser, low level associates suffering an excruciatingly painful death should deter many of them from using such poor judgment. I estimate that, within five years our profits from the gambling proceeds that we derive from the gladiator events will offset our losses and even surpass them."

"Angela, this is all very interesting. I trust that you have worked out all of the logistics. I am curious how these gladiator events will proceed and I must say that I am intrigued by the prospects. You have my full support. Let me know what you need from me and my people. I believe that I speak for everyone here when I say that we all appreciate your efforts and ideas."

"Thank you, Edward. I have packets ready for everyone explaining the details. Each packet also contains your personal access code that will be changed after each event. You will be able to view the statistics of each opponent, place your bets, and view the matches via a scrambled computer link. Isn't technology wonderful? Of course, our exclusive members will be able to view the matches in person, complete with all the amenities your finest clubs offer, plus some." Angela said with a vivacious smile.

The meeting was adjourned and everyone shook hands and said their goodbyes. Some of the people in the meeting only had a vague idea what a "gladiator event" truly was. They associated the concept with the movie Gladiator with Russell Crowe. The movie was romantic and made the fighting look fun and exciting. They were about to discover that it takes a strong stomach just to watch a gladiator event.

Edward was the only person attending the meeting that knew exactly what was about to transpire. He had helped plan the whole thing. Edward was also known as "Big Eddie" by his close friends. Big Eddie ran his empire from a wheelchair. He was respected by most and feared by many. Not only did he know what a gladiator event was, he was ready to get them underway. It wasn't just the money that drove Big Eddie. He wanted to bring integrity back to organized crime. Power is intoxicating and Big Eddie was ready to get drunk.

Chapter 1

William Bracket was a recent transplant to sunny California, all the way from New York City. He had dreamed of moving to California since he was a kid, but it was a heart-wrenching breakup with his long-time fiancée that opened the door for the move. Coming from two neighboring affluent families, William and his ex-fiancée had been together since they were in high school. William was still struggling with the fact that the love of his life could have sex with another man then calmly try to convince him that it was nothing. William knew a lot of men whose wives had cheated on them, but he felt that the men deserved it based on the way they treated their wives. William had been faithful and loving. He had no idea what he had done to make his fiancée stray, but he was certain that it must be his fault. It was easier to blame himself than it was to accept that it was a character flaw in his fiancée that caused her infidelity.

William's mother had encouraged the move to California. She knew that a change of scenery would do him good. As William was preparing to leave his mother reminded him, once again, that it wasn't his fault and that denial was not a river in Egypt. She wanted her son to be happy. In his current state he certainly wasn't. He had his entire life planned out all the way down to two children and which schools they would attend. Finding his wife in bed with another man was as unexpected as a plane crash and just about as devastating to his heart.

This was William's first day as an agent with the Los Angeles Police Department (LAPD) Missing Persons Division. His previous job had been with Missing Person at the NYPD. Finding people, especially children and reuniting them with their families was fulfilling, even though many of the cases were ultimately homicides. People need to know what happened to their loved ones even if it was often bad news.

When William walked into the precinct his first impression was that the place was not near as big as the precinct he worked out of in New York. He asked the duty sergeant where he could find detective Holiday.

"Take the elevator to the third floor. Turn right and go to the last door on the left and ask for Doc."

William thanked the sergeant and walked off thinking that it was just his luck to get partnered with some cowboy who thought he was Doc Holiday. When William arrived at his destination he noticed that there were eight small offices, four on each side of the room, with big glass windows so you could see into all of them. There were two rows of desks running down the center of the room in front of offices. The place looked like something William had seen in an old movie. It had a comfortable feel to it, with a busy buzz of people working and talking on the phones. He was smiling when he asked the first person he came to where he could find Doc Holiday. Using hand gestures, the person told him to go all the way to the back office on the left.

William continued to survey the room as he slowly walked down the center aisle. When he approached the office in question he could see a beautiful raven-haired woman dressed in a classy beige outfit standing next to a desk animatedly talking on the phone. She was punctuating and chopping the air with her right hand as she shook her head back and forth. It was obvious that she was not pleased with someone. When she looked up and saw William looking at her with a smile on his face she held the phone out, glanced at it, hit the end button and tossed it on the desk. She then stepped over to the already open door and said, "I can tell by that gun you're packing that you are not the pizza delivery guy. What can I do for you?"

"I'm looking for Doc Holiday," William exclaimed in a jovial manner.

"And why do you think that is funny?"

"Pardon me, ma'am. I was just picturing a guy with a black cowboy hat, a six-shooter and a handlebar mustache."

"I can't believe you called me ma'am. I am sorry to disappoint you. I'm Doc Holiday. They call me Doc because I have a doctorate in behavioral science. My name is Gloria, but my friends and colleagues affectionately call me Doc, because they don't want to slip up and mistakenly call me Glory. That really pisses me off. I'm guessing you're my new partner, William Bracket, from New York City. The guys around here will have fun with that. New York City!"

"Yes, ma'am. I mean Doc. I am your new partner. I apologize if we got off on the wrong foot. I was hoping to make a good first impression and it looks like I blew it."

"I'm impressed by abilities, Mr. Bracket. That sounds too much like Inspector Gadget."

"Call me Will."

"Okay, Will. Your performance will determine how impressed I am. Right now, our office has twenty-three active missing persons cases. They stay active for one-year. If they are not solved within that year they are no longer priority and are bumped back to open-unsolved. Obviously, the cases that are less than one-year old have a higher priority. Your deck is the one in front of my office. That's how each team works. I have taken the liberty of putting a copy of the case files for all twenty-three active cases on your desk. I would like you to go over each file, working backwards from the most recent case and complete the background checks on the missing persons. I want to know who these people are. You will notice that the files are pathetically thin. We are expected to work miracles and find these people with little or nothing to work with. Other teams are doing backgrounds on family, friends and so on. I need you to create a profile on each victim."

"No problem. Do I need a computer access code to get started?"

"It's on your desk, along with your phone extension and fax numbers. Anything else?"

"I think that will take care of everything, for now. I'll get busy then. It was nice meeting you. I am looking forward to working with you and I will let you know when I'm done."

As William logged on to his antiquated computer to begin the necessary research on the missing people, he was thinking about how lovely his new partner was and wondering whether it would have an impact on their working relationship. By noon William had worked his way through eleven of the most recent cases and compiled a short biography on each of the eleven. William found it odd that six of the eleven had some striking similarities.

When William noticed it was a few minutes after 12:00 he logged off his computer, closed his case files and stepped over to Doc's open office door. Doc waived him in when she noticed him approaching and asked if he was ready for lunch.

"There's a nice little deli close to here. Let's go there and discuss your progress," Doc stated.

On the way to the deli William wasn't just thinking about the similarities in the six cases in Los Angeles, he was also remembering that there were some missing persons cases back in New York that fit the same profile. He also couldn't believe that he was walking down a sidewalk with a woman so gorgeous that men and women were turning their heads to look at her.

Doc noticed Will looking at all the people and smiling, and said, "What?"

"Do you get this all the time?" asked Will.

"What?"

"All these people staring at you like you are a movie star?"

"They are not staring at me. There're staring at you and wondering why I'm with such a dork." Doc smile and walked a little faster.

They arrived at the deli and after ordering Will proceeded to tell Doc about his discoveries.

"Finding six cases that involve males from the ages of twenty to thirty-five is a little odd because most of your run of the mill missing persons cases are female and younger, but I don't see what the fuss is about."

William smiled and said, "How about the fact that all six were informants on high profile drug conspiracy cases and the fact that there are some very similar cases in New York? Oh, and I solved one of the cases already. The guy is in jail."

"Well, you're not just a pretty face after all," said Doc with a smile and a wink.

Chapter 2

Rakemb Jamar Wilson had only been out of jail for a few days when the phone in his mother's tiny apartment interrupted his slumber. The call had royally pissed him off until he heard the sexy voice of Kanesha coming through the line. Kanesha was one of the sexiest hood-boogers in the project. Rakemb had wanted to tap her for a long time. Only Kanesha knew she had it going on. She thought she was special and would not come off any of that pussy.

"Hey bad boy. Kanesha is lonely. Get over here and take care of business. You been locked-up a while and I'm hot and wet. That's a good combination," said Kanesha.

Rakemb told Kanesha he would be right there, then threw on some clothes, brushed his teeth and ran out the door without giving it a second thought as to why she called him. He never even paused to consider that things might be amiss. It wasn't far to Kanesha's apartment and it was all he could do to keep from running the whole way. Rakemb had dreamed of doing Kanesha and every time he laid eyes on her he knew that getting her in bed would be nothing short of bliss. When he rounded the corner to Kanesha's place she opened the door before Rakemb could knock. As he walked into the dark apartment he noticed that it was lit only by candle light and music was playing softly. She handed him a glass of wine and told him to drink it down. He obeyed in an instant and she refilled his glass. Rakemb couldn't believe his good fortune and he didn't even think to question her motive. Kanesha was practically naked, rubbing against him and strutting around the room. She told him to have a seat then excused herself to the restroom with a sexy shake of her perfect little round ass as she walked away down the hall. Rakemb didn't know whether to take his clothes off or play it cool until she returned. He quickly decided to just sit there and listen to the bump and grind. For some reason, he was feeling a little dizzy. He must have drank the wine too fast and with all the excitement and not drinking in a while he was feeling pretty light headed. He shook it off and took another drink. After all, he was a player and that's how players roll.

A moment later Kanesha heard Rakemb fall out of the chair and hit the floor. The carpet softened his fall. Kanesha had moved the coffee table so Rakemb didn't hit his head like the last one. The fast acting barbiturate did its job. Kanesha put on her robe and cautiously looked out the bathroom door to make sure Rakemb was down, then she tapped on the bedroom door. Two casually dressed men came out of the bedroom with one pushing an empty washing machine box that was strapped to a furniture dolly. The smaller of the two men bent over Rakemb and injected a hefty dose of Ketamine in his butt cheek right through his jeans. After duck tapping his hands and feet they carefully placed Rakemb into the washing machine box.

The men paid Kanesha for her services then calmly wheeled their load out to a delivery van that was waiting in the parking lot. It was easy money for Kanesha and she didn't even get her hands dirty. She didn't have to worry about the police tracing anything back to her because she had used one of the goons' phones to call Rakemb just like the time before. It didn't matter to her what happened to Rakemb. She didn't care and didn't want to know. It was better that way, for everyone. When Rakemb got her friends busted and testified against them it had cut off her extra money. It was payback, baby.

On the drive to the ranch the two guys were laughing about how easy these rats kept falling into their trap. It was like putting out a little cheese to catch a mouse only it was pussy to catch a rat. It was the easiest money they had ever made. They were being paid five-thousand for each rat and were scheduled to pick up at least one a week. That was two-thousand each and a thousand for Kanesha. They were provided with the informants' current addresses, telephone numbers and current pictures. The rats were so dumb they would fall for anything. Kanesha could pick them up anywhere. They would follow her around like little dogs. It only took a few hours a week and working with Kanesha was nice because she was pretty and funny. She never asked questions, just did her job. All they had to do was pick them up and drop them off. Life was good.

The drive back to the ranch was usually pleasant. They alternated routes every time and stopped to eat at nice places on the way. There wasn't any hurry because their charge would be asleep for about twelve hours. The ranch was in the foothills not too far from Reno, Nevada. They took the guys to the barn and turned them over to the girls who ran the horse ranch and they were on their way. What they didn't know was that the horse ranch was just a front. It was ran by two aging Las Vegas showgirls who happened to love horses. They did all the cooking and cleaning and general upkeep to the place. Under the barn, hidden from view, was a small prison with only twenty cells. The girls, who had maintained their looks remarkably well, had to feed the prisoners three times a day, wash their clothes twice a week and keep them supplied with basic necessities. It was simple because they never had direct contact with the prisoners. The prisoners were locked into the cells by a man who showed up when prisoners were being delivered or moved. The girls didn't even have a key to the cell doors. All they had was a key to open the bean-hole to feed the prisoners, do their laundry and hand them hygiene supplies. The girls enjoyed working with each other and they wouldn't dream of changing jobs because the money was too good. There was usually around ten other ex-showgirls working around the ranch and training horses but they were not directly involved with anything related to the prisoners. Most of their supplies were delivered so they didn't need to go into town often. It was a perfect job for someone who had seen all the excitement they wanted to see in life. As a precaution, all of the women who worked there signed contracts that included a signing bonus and a bonus if they stayed with the company ten-years, which would allow them to retire in comfort. Of course, the contract also included a non-disclosure clause that prohibited the women from discussing any matters involving the ranch. The two girls who ran the ranch had no idea what actually happened to the prisoners. They did their job and kept their mouths shut. They had been around the block a few times and knew how to keep quiet. Based on what they knew about the people who wrote their paychecks they knew it was in their best interest to go by the rules.

Rakemb woke-up with his mouth dry, his vision blurred and one hell of a headache. When he could finally focus he looked around and realized that, shit, he was back in jail. Only it was a new jail unlike any he'd been in before. It had the same kind of stainless-steel sink and toilet combination, but it also had a small shower like you would find in a segregation cell for maximum security or protective custody. The real interesting thing was the recessed portion of the wall that held a small flat screen television with a plexiglass cover. Obviously, whoever put him in the cell did not want him changing the channel. On closer inspection, he realized that it was a computer screen. That was odd. He had heard about super-max security federal prisons having a setup like that but he'd never seen one, until now. Rakemb had no window in his cell so he couldn't tell if it was night or day. He was surrounded by four concrete walls and held captive by a solid steel door that had a four-inch wide and ten-inch tall window set at eye level. When he looked through the tiny, thick glass window all he could see was a hallway separating him from another row of cells. It was impossible to determine where he was or how many more cells there might be. He tried banging on the door and yelling to get attention. That didn't work so he drank some water from the sink, laid back down and started thinking about how he got there and how he might get out.

Rakemb had at least twenty questions on his mind when he heard a key go into the lock. At first, he thought it was the door opening then he realized it was only the bean-hole slot that was positioned in the lower portion of the door. Before he could ask any questions, a plastic tray came through the open slot and he was stunned by how good the food looked and smelled. The bean-hole was closed and locked before he could say anything. He was hungry. One thing he could tell for sure was this placed fed good, which was unusual for a jail.

After Rakemb finished his surprisingly good meal he was looking out the little window in the door when he heard someone behind him say, "Excuse me." He almost pissed his pants as he spun around looking for the source of the voice. There was a man's face on the computer screen.

The face said, "Please take a seat and face the monitor. You are Rakemb Jamar Wilson?"

"Hell, yes. What the fuck's going on? Why am I in jail?" Rakemb yelled as he took a seat at the small desk that was bolted to the wall with a little stool bolted to the floor in front of it.

"It would be best if you held your questions until I have completed your orientation. If you exhibit disruptive behavior I will terminate this conference. I am certain that my explanation will satisfy all of your questions so bear with me until I am finished. Our newly formed International Court ordered you picked up for being maleficent."

"What the fuck is maleficent?" asked Rakemb with a sneer.

"A maleficent is someone who knowingly engages in harmful or evil conduct for his own benefit and to the detriment of others," said the smiling face.

"Man, I just got out of jail. I haven't done anything harmful or evil. You got the wrong guy. I want to talk to my lawyer."

"Under this tribunal, Mr. Wilson, you are not entitled to an attorney. I was assigned as your case agent or representative, if you will. The evidence against you is overwhelming, irrefutable and conclusive. You have been nothing but a drain on the economy, a burden to our judicial system, a disgrace to your family and a Judas to your friends. The FBI-302s and DEA-6s: those are the signed statements you made against your friends and colleagues in Federal Case Number 4:14-CR-3729, together with the trial and sentencing transcripts for that case, all prove that you made incriminating statements against several people and testified against them at trial and sentencing. You cannot dispute those facts. The decision is final and there is no appeal," said the solemn face on the screen.

Rakemb was despondent and lost for words. There wasn't any denying it. He had done those things but nobody told him that he could be arrested for it. All he did was "get down" on his friends before they could "get down" on him. Hell, everyone was doing it.

"Based on the undisputable, conclusive facts in the record, the International Court has found you guilty of being maleficent and sentenced you to attrition."

"This is crazy. I don't even know what maleficent and attrition is."

The face continued, "I will be doing a group orientation soon and I will explain all the facts, your rights and responsibilities and what will be expected of you in the future. Until then just relax and enjoy the nice food."

After the screen went blank Rakemb sat on his bed and figured that whatever was in store for him couldn't be too bad. He hadn't killed anyone.

Chapter 3

Big Eddie didn't know a lot about computers and he didn't trust them. He didn't know a mainframe from a bedframe but he wanted to know all the details in case something went wrong. It was always important to know the facts so you can find the responsible party to ensure that you put the correct head on the ol' metaphorical chopping block. Big Eddie was speaking with his computer expert, Raymond Charleston, III. His friends jokingly called him Ray Charles because he was known for predominantly wearing dark Blues Brothers sunglasses. Being twenty, tall, skinny and white made him anything but a Ray Charles.

"Mr. Charleston, you seem very young to be an expert in your field," said Big Eddie.

"Yeah, I get that a lot. Most of the old geeks can't keep up with the fast-moving pace of computer advancements. It takes a young, snappy, innovative mind to get the job done in today's work place."

"I would like to know how the system you have created works, in layman's terms if you please, from start to finish. I find it most fascinating."

"From start to finish, okay, wow. Here we go, at the ring the digital cameras are set up just like any other fighting ring. There are six stationary, unmanned cameras that feed through a central control booth. The signal is scrambled at that point then relayed through seven microwave towers that have our own boosters and hardware so there is no record of the transmission on the tower system.

"We are not using a satellite link because that would make it too easy to trace the source. The live scrambled feed leaves the control booth through a land-line to the first tower then relayed it through the other towers where it is once again sent through a telephone line to New York. If the signal is hacked it will be from its destination point and then it can only go back as far as the super computer owned by the communications company where I have hidden our program. The company doesn't know that our program exists in its system and it will only be running for a short time at night so it will likely go undetected.

"If the system is hacked, not only will they get a scrambled transmission, my program will identify the exact location of the hacker and notify me. The communications company's computer system is so huge they will likely never notice the hidden program. If one department does happen to notice they won't know what it is and will probably think it is part of another departments program. The scrambled signal will only go out twice a month for four hours each time. That will give anyone that might be looking a hard time if they are trying to trace or descramble. Of course, they could record the scrambled signal but by the time they could get it descrambled the transmission would be gone and the access code changed.

"The signal remains scrambled until it reaches its final destinations and then it can only be descrambled by those who have the correct program and the proper access code at the other end. The authorized people will be able to view fighter statistics and place bets for three hours before the actual fights. The fights will be viewed in real time with a .139 millisecond delay. If my program detects a hacker we will be able to determine who it is and remove all our equipment from the microwave towers, if necessary, before any hacker can get past the super computer in New York. The fight broadcast is so they cannot trace that backwards unless they do it during the actual broadcast.

"The only interactive portion of the program is betting with the house. Those bets are scrambled and routed to a separate location. That location is manned only by computers and if those computers are tampered with they will notify me, crash and self-destruct. If I have forgotten anything feel free to ask questions.

"I am most impressed. Do you consider the system foolproof?"

"Nothing is foolproof. Your primary concern is keeping the location of the fights secret. I am confident that we have accomplished that. There isn't much between those microwave towers and if the signal is discovered between towers it would be by chance and even then, it is scrambled. My early warning system will alert us to any interference there, as well. I will be monitoring everything during the broadcasts. If the program is discovered in New York on the super computer it can only be traced back to the first microwave tower because of the land-line connection. I have also taken precautions at that tower and there is no record of that particular line. They won't be able to trace where the scrambled signal is going because it is going everywhere on the internet. Only the people with the correct program and access code can descramble the program. To a hacker it will look like many other scrambled sporting events and most hacker won't be interested. Most hackers are interested in things like national security, stealing money or porn, not sports."

"Will you be viewing the events, Mr. Charleston?"

"I might look in from time to time but I'm not interested in sports. I'm into interactive video games. I'll be keeping an eye on the computers in case of trouble, but mostly I will probably be writing new programs for games. That's where the money is right now."

Big Eddie said, "I want to remind you of the confidential nature of this adventure. You know that the gambling portion of these events is illegal and if there is anything about the matches themselves that disturb you I want you to discuss it with me and no one else. Is that understood?"

"Yes, sir. You're the boss. Oh, and if there are any glitches in the program let me know and I will correct them immediately. I have run the program from start to finish several times and haven't discovered any problems. Let me know if something pops up," said Raymond with a cocky smile.

"Thank you, Mr. Charleston. You have done a great job. I'll have an outline for the other projects we discussed sent to you right away," declared Big Eddie.

Big Eddie wanted a program designed where he could access the computer cameras at each location where the fights were being viewed so he could gauge the spectators' reactions and observe who was watching from the other end. It would make it a lot easier to avoid potential problem early on.

Ray left thinking that the boss went a little overboard on the secrecy end of things. It wasn't like they would be airing dog fights. It was probably some kind of full contact boxing or karate without gloves or pads, which was illegal in the United States. Hell, for the kind of money they were paying him he didn't care if they killed each other.

Big Eddie liked this Ray kid. He hoped the kid was smart enough to just do his job and not have some sort of moral calamity that could end bad for him. The first fight was coming up quick. It was going out to over three-thousand locations and hopefully twice that many by the next broadcast. Each location had to pay five-thousand just to receive the program and access code but they stood to win hundreds of thousands if the betting went well. Although this business adventure had cost a bundle to setup, it had the potential to make a fortune if things went well. It was an elaborate setup with plenty of room for errors. Like the kid said, nothing is foolproof. Big Eddie hoped that he had distanced himself far enough from the project that he didn't get covered in crap when the shit hit the fan. He knew it would at some point. Nothing lasts forever. He had people standing by for damage control.

Big Eddie wasn't naïve and he knew this thing would not go off without a hitch. Most worthwhile business adventures were risky and had to have some bugs worked out. The fight business would not be any riskier then the drug and firearm trade or any other illegal venture he was involved with. There were plenty of rats right here in the United States and they were easy to find so there would not be a shortage of gladiators.

Chapter 4

It had been a productive week, so far. Agent Bracket had finished compiling the profiles on all twenty-three missing persons and solved three more cases. He had found another missing person in jail and two in the morgue. He would have preferred happy endings in those cases but any ending was progress. One of the deaths was probably an accident and the other was clearly a murder so he turned them over to the homicide division. Hospitals have a policy of notifying the police anytime they have an unidentified victim and Will was checking those records when Doc stepped out of her office.

"Saddle up. It's time to ride. We've got another one," Doc proclaimed.

"I love it when you talk cowboy slang. It sounds kind of Mae Westy and it makes me want to climb on a horse and embark on an epic journey across the lone prairie. Of course, I have never been on a horse and have only seen cowboys on television. However, if they don't bite I would love to try one," said Will excitedly.

"They are not candy," Doc said. "You don't try them you ride them. If you like I'll take you riding sometime."

"You ride? I would like that," replied Will.

After a chuckle and a shake of her head, Doc said, "Will, you sound like you are sexually frustrated. Maybe a change of scenery will do you some good. Come on, we're headed for the jungle."

"A safari! I love this job," said Will with a smile.

Maybe Will was sexually frustrated but the fact that his new partner had noticed it was not a comfort. Just looking at her made him fantasize about taking their relationship to the next level. However, that was not what was bothering him. Today would have been his wedding day. If things hadn't fallen apart he would be getting ready to walk down the aisle to marry the woman he loved. They had planned a two week honeymoon in France. He started to go to France anyway but changed his mind because he knew it would just remind him of how things could have been. Submersing himself in work was a better idea. Staying busy would help him forget or at least keep him from thinking about this to the point of depression. His only solace was that it was better to find out now, rather than several years down the road, that the woman he loved was a slut. Will often resorted to humor to combat depression and witticism as a first line of defense.

After checking out an unmarked sedan from the LAPD motor pool Doc started navigating through the traffic towards their destination.

"Okay, Will what is it? I know something is wrong. Did someone steal your puppy? Is it the sexual tension between us? If it is we have to get that worked out."

Will smiled and said, "Oh, there is some sexual tension and I am all for getting it worked out. That's not what's bothering me. Today would have been my wedding day. If my fiancée wouldn't have screwed one of her co-workers, in our bed, I would be getting married this evening."

"So, you caught them in bed. That had to suck."

"It was the first time I can remember ever being lost for words and it did suck. She was my high school sweetheart and we'd been together a long time. Saying something like, 'What are you doing?' seemed pretty stupid so I just walked out. I'm worried that the extremely negative experience has messed up my ability to trust and every time I see a pretty woman I automatically wonder who all she's screwing."

"Some woman can be cruel and just plain stupid. Obviously, you should already know that. Surely she's not the only woman you've ever been with." After receiving an affirmative nod, Doc said, "Well that was awkward. Wow, in this day and age that makes you practically a virgin. You need to get laid.

"I'm not totally against that and it's not the furthest thing from my mind," said Will as he smiled and raised his eyebrows.

"Not with me. We have to work together and I don't think having a personal relationship is a good idea."

"So, you have thought about it?"

"Of course, I've thought about it. You have that cute muscle bound college boy thing going on. I'm sure that every woman who sees you thinks about it."

That made Will feel better about life and gave him something to think on. To change the subject Will started telling Doc about his progress with the missing persons cases that involved informants. Will's contact in New York had confirmed the fact that he had three missing informants. He was conducting a further investigation into the matter because it was an area they hadn't previously concentrated on and he would get back to Will right away. If something more came up Will was going to expand his inquiries nationwide. It was obvious to Will that something unusual was happening. He could feel it in his gut and he knew it wasn't indigestion.

"Why do they call this part of LA the jungle," Will asked. It didn't look like what they called the jungle in New York.

"These apartment complexes being so close together and built at different times create a maze. China town has nothing on this place. If you are not careful you can get lost in there while on foot pursuit. You never know what you might run into when you round a corner. It is a good place to get killed.

"The dope heads and the crack dealers have learned to stay off the front streets where it is too open and patrolled by cops. Crack dealers have setup shop in many of these apartments so every time we go in we run the risk of getting shot just for being there, even if we are there on a call for help."

"That's a comforting thought. Show up to help and get blasted by a crack head for your trouble," stated Will.

They pulled to the curb and got out of the car like they belonged there and headed into a four story low-income housing project. After walking through the surprisingly well kept courtyard they located the apartment they were looking for at the rear of the complex on the fourth floor. The front of the apartments all faced the inside of the courtyard with wide sidewalks all the way around on each floor. You could tell it had been a nice roomy place in its day. Time and lack of proper maintenance had left the place looking old, rundown, weathered and somewhat rustic.

When agent Bracket knocked on the door of apartment 437 an aging, distraught mother answered the door. She looked like she had lived a long, hard life. After identifying themselves they were invited inside and offered coffee, which they politely declined.

"Mrs. Wilson," said Doc, "When you called you sounded certain that your son is missing and that something bad has happened to him. Couldn't he simply be away with friends?"

Mrs. Willamae Wilson (Mae to her friends) was openly crying and wringing a piece of tissue with her fingers. Her husband had been killed by a hopped up dope head during a robbery and she had been a widow and single parent for many years. She informed them that a mother knows her son. As the facts came out they discovered that her son Rakemb had spent some time in jail but was recently released and had only been home a few days. Rakemb had always been good about checking in with her. The last time she saw him he was asleep in his room. She looked in on him before she left for work. She knew he would not have missed his weekly check in visit with his probation officer unless something really bad happened. The probation officer had already called trying to find Rakemb because he missed his scheduled visit.

Mrs. Wilson provided them with a list of Rakemb's old friends and the likely places he might go but she had checked them all before she called missing persons. The only person she hadn't talked to was a girl named Kanesha who called Rakemb the day he went missing. When asked how she knew that Kanesha called, Mrs. Wilson explained that her answering machine didn't work right. It would come on every time someone called and record part of the conversation. The machine didn't tell you to leave a message at the beep it just came on and started recording. She played the recording for them and it started at: "Kanesha is lonely," and went on to invite Rakemb to her place for a roll in the hay. Mrs. Wilson didn't seem bothered by the short conversation between her son and Kanesha. She told them which apartment building that Kanesha lived in. She didn't know which apartment or her last name.

Doc and Will thanked Mrs. Wilson for her time and assured her that they would check things out and get with her. As they were walking back to the car Will told Doc that he was certain there was a Kanesha mentioned in one of the other missing persons cases. Since they were in the neighborhood they decided to stop at Kanesha's apartment building and try to find her. They didn't have to go far. The building they were looking for was just in the next block. While Doc was parking the car in a no parking zone Will said, "Rakemb fits the same profile as the missing informants. When we get back to the office I'll do a criminal record check on him to see if he was an informant. If he was, that means we have seven missing informants just her in LA. You can't tell me that's a coincidence."

The superintendent of Kanesha's apartment building told them that the only Kanesha he had was Kanesha Sims. He assured them that Kanesha was never any trouble, and because they were cops, he gave them her apartment number.

Kanesha opened the door like she was expecting someone, other than cops. The smile on her face was quickly replaces by a look of confusion.

"What?" Kanesha said impatiently.

"I'm agent Bracket and this is detective Holiday. Are you Kanesha Sims."

"Yes, but I ain't done nothin'."

"We're not implying you did ma'am. We just stopped by to ask you some questions about your visit from Rakemb Jamar Wilson day before yesterday."

"What makes you think he came here?"

"Are you saying that he didn't come here?" asked Will.

Kanesha's pause was a telltale sign of deception. Before Kanesha could respond Will said, "Is he here now? We would like to speak with him."

"No!" Kanesha said too quickly.

"Would that be 'no' he isn't here now, or 'no' he didn't come by the day before yesterday?" Will asked.

"He's not here now."

"So, he was here the day before yesterday?"

"No," Kanesha said hesitantly.

Will kept doing the talking while Doc stood there expressionless. "I find that odd. Young men usually jump at an invitation to spend time with a beautiful woman. When you called and invited him over I would think he dropped whatever he was doing and came right over."

"I didn't call him," Kanesha declared with some panic in her voice.

"You sound like the same Kanesha I just heard on Rakemb's mother's answering machine inviting Rakemb over for a little one-on-one and I'm not referring to basketball here," agent Bracket said solemnly.

Realizing she was caught Kanesha said, "Oh, that right. I did call Rakemb the other mornin'. Yeah, he did come by for a few minutes. I haven't seen him since."

"Do you know where we might find him?"

"No," Kanesha said.

When Doc finally decided to speak she handed Kanesha a card and said, "If you see him or have any information regarding his whereabouts please give us a call."

Will took that as his cue to smile and say "Have a nice day," as he walked away.

On the way back to the car they both agreed that Kanesha couldn't tell the truth if her life depended on it. They didn't believe anything she said and were certain that she knew something.

Doc said, "I'm impressed by the way you handled that interview, but you should have asked her if we could come in so we could have a look around."

"I didn't want her to feel threatened. I'm sure we will be back and the next time we come, if she doesn't let us in, we'll have enough probable cause to bring her in for questioning. I know I saw her name in at least one of the other missing persons files. I'll check the files when we get back and do a check on her. She didn't strike me as a serial killer but stranger things have happened."

"You New York boys are slick," Doc said flirtatiously.

"Have dinner with me tonight and I will try to impress you with how slick I handle other things."

"Only dinner. Pick me up at 7:00."

Chapter 5

When the face appeared on the computer monitor this time is appeared in eighteen of the twenty cells. Only two of the secret underground prison cells were unoccupied.

"Gentleman, if I could have your attention please. I am speaking to you all in a group because this concerns every one of you. You have each been found guilty of being a maleficent and sentenced to attrition."

"Listen motherfucker, I don't know who you think you are, but when I get my hands on you I'm goin' ta fuck you up."

"I'm the person who has the key to that tiny little jail cell you are locked up in Mr. Michael Tyron Davis. I am going to suggest that you listen very carefully to what I am about to tell you because your life depends on it. You gentleman have been blessed with a unique opportunity. Whether you live or die is completely up to you. Not only can you come out of this alive, if you are the winner of the contest you get five-thousand dollars, a five star dinner with a beautiful woman and a night of wild sex with her. You will also be forgiven for being an informant and allowed to live and move on with your lives without fear of reprisal. However, if you refuse to cooperate you will be terminated in a most unpleasant and painful manner," said the face.

"Man, fuck that. I'm not cooperating with shit. You can kiss my ass."

"Judging from your outburst, Mr. Davis, it appears that you are refusing to cooperate. Is that correct?"

"Is that correct? Fuck yeah it's correct, motherfucker. I ain't done nothin' and I'm not cooperating with shit."

Some of the other prisoners were agreeing and making similar protests but it was clear that Mr. Davis was leading the pack.

The face continued, "Let's see Mr. Michael Tyron Davis, formally of Los Angeles, California. The city of angels. You are far from an angel Mr. Davis. You have a colorful past. Your first conviction was at age 15. It was a juvenile carjacking conviction where a woman was dragged from her car and you beat her in the head with a pistol. The unfortunate lady spent five days in the hospital. You told on your friend and received probation. At 17 you were arrested for being a felon in possession of a firearm; possession of a firearm while trafficking in a controlled dangerous substance, crack cocaine; possession with intent to distribute cocaine; and three unlawful deliveries of crack cocaine, where you sold directly to an undercover cop. You ratted on your dealer and friends, helped setup some undercover cover deal, and for that you got five-years probation when you should have gotten twenty-years in federal prison. That brings us to the most recent case. At age 20 you were again caught red-handed with a firearm and crack cocaine. Because of your prior criminal history, you were facing twenty-years to life in prison. To get out of that mess you agreed to cooperate with the government and setup some large scale drug distributors. Once again you managed to avoid prison and get probation and you were allowed to remain a free man.

"What you have done Sir, is repeatedly break the law and cause misery to others. Yet you have the nerve to claim you have done nothing wrong. You are nothing but a parasite, a leach sucking the life from the people who trusted you. You don't even deserve this one-time opportunity to atone for your crimes. You should have been locked away a long time ago or someone should have done the world a favor and put a little lead bullet in your head. This is your last chance. What's it going to be Mr. Davis?"

In a far less enthusiastic voice, Mr. Davis said, "Fuck you, "which soon proved to be the wrong answer.

The face was left with no other choice. He had to make an example out of someone and Mr. Davis had effectively volunteered. This was going to be the demonstration of what happened to a prisoner who refused to cooperate. He gave the prearranged signal to the men waiting to carry out the nasty task of torturing and informant to death. They were actually excited and looking forward to it. A moment later the two men who had been watching the exchange on a monitor put on their face masks and helmets and walked out the door of their small office. They were dressed in black and wearing jackboots. Each wore a utility belt that sported handcuffs, a 9mm Glock and a police nightstick. They looked formidable as they walked side-by-side down the short corridor between the cells. The other prisoners were looking out the little window in their doors at the two imposing figures. The only person making any noise was Mr. Davis, because he feared the unknown. Had he known that hell was coming for him he would have been trying to make amends.

Mr. Davis was cussing the two men and taunting them when they approached his cell door. He still though that the men could not violate his civil rights. Rather than open the door they opened the bean-hole and quickly shot Mr. Davis in the stomach with a taser. When the two small leads hit the prisoner, high voltage dropped him to his knees. By the time the cell door was opened Mr. Davis was curled up on the floor shaking and jerking with drool and blood oozing from between his lips. He'd bitten his tongue when they shocked him. The two black clad men cuffed his hands behind him and shackled his feet together. Then they each grabbed an arm and dragged their prisoner out of the cell and down the corridor in front of the other prisoners. Only a few prisoners on the far end were unable to see the men dragging Mr. Davis away, but they had a pretty good idea what was happening.

The next thing that came on the monitor in the cells was a live video feed showing a black man strapped to an autopsy table, complete with blood drains. The man the prisoners knew as the "face" stepped into the picture wearing an impeccably tailored suit like a game show host.

"Gentlemen," announced the face, "I would like you to meet Michael Tyron Davis. As you heard during the earlier exchange, Mr. Davis, for lack of better wording, has not too graciously refused my generous offer. What you are about to witness is the result of his lack of cooperation. The steel table is the ground. Those six cables you see dangling above Mr. Davis are the leads that carry a positive current. I am going to leave because I don't want to see what comes next. You, on the other hand, should watch closely because this is what will happen to all prisoners who refuse to participate. The sad part is, Mr. Davis chose not to participate before he knew all the details and the consequences of his actions. Once this execution is over I will be back to explain your rights and responsibilities. I am confident that once you fully understand your predicament and this unusual situation you will recognize the benefit of cooperating."

With that said, the face walked out of the picture and the camera zoomed in closer. All the prisoners could see that Mr. Davis was gagged and his eyes were wide with panic. The two men in masks and helmets came into the picture and positioned themselves on opposite side of the menacing autopsy table. They both reach up and each selected an electrical cable. The cables had nasty looking four-inch spikes on the ends. The men placed the spikes on the tops of Mr. Davis's legs and pushed them into his thighs. Mr. Davis's screams were muffled by the gag. It was obvious that he was suffering extreme pain and that was only the beginning. His head was shaking back and forth, snot and sweat was slinging from side-to-side. There was very little blood because the spikes were plugging the holes. The two men each selected another cable and quickly forced the tip of the spikes into Mr. Davis's sides, just below the ribs and far enough out to the edge so they would not hit any vital organs. Their prisoner was hyperventilating and trying to beg through the gag, to no avail. The men took hold of the last two cables and jabbed the spikes into Mr. Davis's shoulders. They had planned this well to produce the most dramatic effects. The ill-fated prisoner looked like something you might see in a modern day Frankenstein movie.

The two executioners/torturers stepped out of the picture and a moment later sparks flew from the prisoner's right leg, smoke poured from the wound and pathetic looking Mr. Davis went into convulsions and vomited into his gag. One of the men hurried back into the picture and cut the gag free. The prisoner expelled vomit in a choking scream and gasped for breath. No sooner than he cleared his throat, sparks flew from his other leg and it began to smoke, as well.

The high voltage was administered in controlled bursts and had the same effect as lightening. The electricity would arc from the spike on the end of the cable carrying the positive current through the remaining portion of muscle and skin to the table that acted as the ground. It instantly blew a dime size hole all the way through to the table without going through the heart, which would be fatal. The cauterization caused by the electrical burn slowed the bleeding and prolonged the torture. It was actually an ingenious, slow, painful death that made for a spectacular demonstration.

When the electrical charge passed through the prisoner's side it was easy to see that he was not long for this world. His screams were reduced to wide mouthed exhalations of air. His vocal cords were damaged. Somehow, he lived through his other side being blown open but he gave up the ghost when his left shoulder exploded in sparks. There is only so much the human body can take before the heart quits. It was so deathly quiet that you could hear the blood and urine dripping into the bucket at the end of the autopsy table. The quiet was broken by one of the masked men shockingly saying, "We're going to need better ventilation in here."

The face didn't appear again until after the evening meal. He wanted to give the prisoners time to think about what they'd seen.

"Gentlemen, as you saw by our little exhibition, you are all in a grave situation. Pardon the pun. I am sure you cannot see the humor in it. I certainly wouldn't if I were in your shoes. However, what you should be concentrating on is the alternative. You can leave here with money in your pockets and no fear of retaliation for what you have done in the past. All you have to do is participate in one fight. Just one and if you win you walk away a free man. The only other way out is feet first after you visit that room with the cold steel table and poor ventilation. The right way out of this is to fight and live with your pride and dignity intact and a new lease on life. It certainly beats a ride with the ferryman.

"Here are your rights and responsibilities. If you choose to participate, you have the right to eat well while you are here, which you have already experienced. That comes with the responsibility to fight well when the time comes and it will come soon. Either way your stay here will be short. You have the right to be treated with respect and to be matched with an opponent of your size, stature and capability. That comes with the responsibility to fight to the death. You must kill your adversary. You will be provided with a shield and a knife to fight with. Only one person leaves the ring alive gentlemen and that is the winner.

"If you stop fighting and try to run without finishing the task you will die the same way the most unfortunate Mr. Davis did today. That is a guarantee. Fight or die. Or should I say fight and live. Is there any of you who wish to refuse this offer of life? If so, please speak up so you can be our next example."

Some of the prisoners were jubilant at the prospect of getting to live and go free after only one fight. Others were gloomy and frightened, but none spoke.

"Based on your silence," said the face, "I trust that you have carefully considered your options and decided to fight and live rather than die like cowards. Gentlemen, you are now modern day gladiators. I hope you fight with honor. Good luck."

Chapter 6

Precisely at 7:00 o'clock, agent Bracket knocked on the door of Doc's humble little brick two bedroom house with its connecting one car garage. The home was in a nice middle class neighborhood. There were a lot of trees up and down the block that were not much taller than the homes. All the homes in that area had been built in the 60s when space was a personal requirement not a luxury. The homes were remarkably well kept. Doc's lawn had recently been mowed and edged. The flower beds were nicely weeded and colorful and there was fresh paint on the house's trim. Being new to LA, it had taken Will some time to find the place. He felt good that he'd managed to be on time.

When Doc opened the door, she was a vision of loveliness. Her tight fitting low back emerald dress showed just the right amount of cleavage. Her tasteful emerald neckless and small emerald earrings accented her captivating green eyes. Will wasn't dressed like a slouch, himself. With his loafers, slacks, tie and camel hair jacket he looked quite dapper.

"You look stunning," said Will.

"Thank you handsome. I figured we were probably going some place nice and I wanted to look good."

"Good is a serious understatement. With you dressed like that we most certainly won't be going to McDonalds."

Doc closed and locked her door. Will, being the chivalrous well mannered individual that he is, opened the car door for her like a perfect gentleman, which was a testament to his upbringing. Will's thoughts weren't nearly as pure and noble as his actions. He wanted to kiss her and get her out of that sexy little dress.

Getting a last minute reservation was not an easy task. William had to settle for his third choice. In New York he wouldn't have had that problem. From now on he would make sure to plan ahead. He was pleasantly surprised when they arrived at the restaurant. The valet was polite, the hostess promptly escorted them to a cozy corner table and provided them with a wine list. The lighting was low and the table was lit by a candle. The setting was romantic and just what Will needed to get his mind off of his failed relationship. Things were going great until a man walked in with a gun and tried to rob the place.

Will had seen the man come through the door and thought he looked out of place as he walked to the bar where the old fashion cash register sat. When the man's gun came out Will pulled his gun from his shoulder holster, jumped up and yelled, "Freeze, police," as he took aim. When the man turned he fired a shot that went wild and shattered one of the restaurant's front windows. Will fired and dropped the would be robber with two well placed shots to the heart. It was over so fast that nobody had a chance to take cover. Will hurried to the body, secured the gun and checked for a pulse. There wasn't one. The man was dead by the time he hit the ground.

Doc got up and told everyone to remain calm, it was all over, as she dialed dispatch on her cell phone to report the officer involved shooting.

Will walked back over to Doc and said, "This would make for a good episode of Hell Date. Shooting a guy takes all the fun out of a date. It is the first time I shot someone while on a date in a crowded restaurant. Hell, it's the first time I shot someone."

"You have officially graduated to cowboy status. Are you okay Will? 'Cause you look a little shook."

"Actually, no I am not alright. This pretty much sucks. It's definitely not what I had in mind for our first date. Dinner was shot to hell. That was not intended as a pun."

"You did good Will. Nobody can fault you on this one. It's a clean shot. Everyone here will back you, but I think our chances of getting dinner to go were blown out the window. HA! We're just full of puns tonight."

They both shared a strained, humorless laugh. It took three hours of repeat interviews and explanations to get Will and Doc out of the restaurant. Will had to turn over his firearm to the Special Investigation Division (SID) officer that would investigate the shooting. He didn't mind, he kept a spare gun in the car. By the time they left the restaurant they were famished and the only thing open that was close to home was an all-night pancake house. They were over dressed but that really doesn't matter when you are overly hungry.

After giving Will directions to the pancake house, Doc said, "This is a nice car. They must pay good at the NYPD. What's a Beamer like this cost, eighty grand? That's more than my house cost."

"It was a birthday present."

"Damn, what did you get for Christmas?"

They both laughed again, helping to break the tension. The all-night diner served a good breakfast and it was one of the few places you still get a regular, normal cup of coffee, rather than a fancy chocomocalatte, something or other. During their meal Doc listened to Will ramble about his progress on the seven missing informants. She thought it was therapeutic for him to talk about something other than blowing a guy away for dinner.

Will reported that his contact in New York had discovered nine missing male informants in the same age range as the LA informants that were reported within the same time frame as the missing LA informants. He also found one informant missing in Lafayette, Louisiana and one from Oklahoma City, Oklahoma. Brining the grand total to eighteen missing informants. The number was far too high to be a coincidence. Informants were frequently killed, which was the nature of the beast and a simple fact of life. You cannot rat on someone without some type of consequence. But there was usually a body discovered almost immediately. To have eighteen missing bodies was unprecedented.

Because of the multi-jurisdictional problem and the fact that all of the missing informants were involved in high profile federal cases, Will knew he was required to notify the FBI. However, because Kanesha Sims name came up in not one, but two of the other missing persons case files, Will planned on talking to her at least one more time before bringing in the Feds. Her name popping up in three cases was another thing that was too much to be considered a coincidence. With Doc's help Will intended to knock on some doors and ask Kaneshas' neighbors a few questions before having a sit-down with Kanesha.

When Will pulled up in front of Doc's house Doc leaned across the console of Will's BMW and kissed him slowly and softly.

"Come in with me virgin boy. I don't think either one of us wants to be alone tonight. We have only known each other a week, so don't get all serious on me. Having sex will either make our professional relationship better or worse. We can examine the results tomorrow."

Will didn't say anything. He just got out of the car trying his best not to show his excitement. The prospect of sex with this exquisite woman, whom he'd grown to love and respect in only a week, had pushed all thoughts of the earlier shooting away. He couldn't get in the house fast enough. That old saying that men have a brain and a penis but only enough blood to run one at a time is certainly true. If Will would have known that shooting someone would get him in bed with Doc he would have shot someone the first day on the job. It takes a lot of willpower to turn down a beautiful woman and Will didn't have that kind of power with Doc. Hell, even if he did have that kind of willpower he wouldn't have turned her down.

Will followed Doc into her home like a puppy, where they engaged in a hot, passionate kiss behind the closed door. Doc took Will by the hand and led him to her bedroom where they helped each other undress by the light coming through the bedroom window. Will didn't need any coxing to get hard, but he did require a little guidance on how to get started. Doc took charge, flipped the peach colored comforter back and laid down on the cool sheets with her legs invitingly spread. She had been thinking about this moment all evening and her juices were flowing. Using both hands she held herself open so Will could work his way inside her. Will tried to pace himself, but with Doc prompting him to go faster and harder Will was soon sweating in a mindless frenzy seeking climax. They came together with orgasms so intense that they were squeezing each other with their arms and legs so tight it was almost painful, in a glorious way. Before Will could lose his erection, Doc rolled over on her hands and knees, with her ass in the air and told Will to do her from behind. Will recovered instantly and enthusiastically obliged. When they both came together the second time they were glistening with sweat. Will held himself inside her until the last drop was expelled, then he collapsed on the bed next to Doc.

As they caught their breath Will said, "Shit! I didn't know sex could be that great."

Doc laughed and said, "It certainly was great. Give me a minute and I'll get us a towel."

"No, I'll get it." When Will returned from the restroom he had a warm wet washcloth and a towel.

"That was thoughtful of you. Thank you."

"That's me, Mr. Thoughtful," said Will, as they slipped into an exhausted sex induced sleep.

When the alarm went off a few hours later they were both momentarily startled to discover another person in the bed. They climbed into the shower together, had sex standing up in the warm spray of water, then had coffee and toast.

"This seems very domestic. I hope you're okay with this, because we have to go to work and act like nothing happened and everything is normal," said Doc.

"You got it boss. Nothing happened. I hope nothing happens again soon in that same normal way. Everything is normal. Well, other than the fact that I shot someone on our first date. We can tell everyone that we were on a stakeout together looking for a missing person."

"Don't call me boss. We are partners," said Doc.

"Okay boss. I mean partner."

Will thought that was pretty funny and they both laughed. Doc was trying not to get too close too fast. She had been hurt so many times she could no longer count them. She was constantly making poor choices with men. Will was still grieving and on the rebound. Doc didn't want to be a throw-pillow, tossed around for decoration and temporary comfort, but she started it, so she would have to deal with the consequences.

They drove to work in separate cars and rendezvoused at the office. When Will walked through the door one of the desk jockeys yelled, "Hey, New York, you shot any bad guys today?"

"Not yet, I just got here. Generally, I only shoot bad guys on my time off."

On the way to his desk Will was patted on the back several times and congratulated on his efforts to stop crime in their fair city. Will thought it seemed somewhat morbid to be congratulated for killing a man, but he appreciated the acceptance and encouragement. The commander came in and shook Will's hand and informed him that he would remain on active duty during the routine investigation of the shooting. Will thanked the commander as he left. It took an hour for Will and Doc to give their official statements about the shooting then they were allowed to proceed with their investigation.

On the elevator ride down to the garage Will and Doc were accompanied by another officer, Brian Scofield, who happened to be Doc's ex-boyfriend.

Brian said, "Hey, Doc. I hear your new partner shot a robber while having dinner with you last night."

"It was actually before dinner. Brian Scofield, meet William Bracket, my new partner."

"Nice to meet you William," said Brian as he tried to crush Will's hand with his handshake. "What have you two been up to?"

"Not sex, because we are two responsible professionals. Everything is normal," said Will with a cocky smile.

The elevator stopped on the first floor and Brian stepped out when the doors opened and with a curt nod, said, "Hope to see you later Doc."

When the doors closed Doc laughed and Will said, "Old boyfriend?"

"Oh, yeah, old," Doc exhaled

"Why did you breakup? Except for that finger breaking handshake he seemed like a nice guy."

"He is a nice guy. Other than being an asshole and married. That's why we broke up."

"Those are good reasons," Will stated as he dropped the subject.

The car they checked out of the motor-pool would not have qualified as dilapidated, but it fell short of top-notch. In fact, it may have been possessed by an evil spirit. The passenger window wouldn't go down and it was lodged crooked in the frame so wind whistled through a small gap as they drove. The driver's safety belt would not latch and the radio mic was taped together. At least the air conditioner worked, even though the fan motor would squeal from time to time then stop when they hit a bump in the road. Will wasn't sure if it was possessed or cursed.

The drive to Kanesha's apartment complex didn't take long. The rush hour traffic had cleared. They spent over an hour interviewing Kanesha's neighbors where they discovered some interesting information. They decided to have lunch and organize their notes before talking with Kanesha.

By the time they knocked on Kanesha's door they had a solid plan.

Kanesha opened the door right away and said through the crack, "Why you keep botherin' me? I ain't done nothin'."

"We would like to come in and ask you a few questions," said Will.

"I got company and I ain't answerin' no mo questions. I know my rights."

"That's good," said Will. "It's important to know your rights. However, if you don't let us in, I get to read them to you anyway as I arrest you and take you downtown. Now tell your company to come back another time so we can have a chat or my partner is going to handcuff you while I call in to get a warrant for your place, because I happen to smell marijuana."

The door opened further and a young man buttoning his shirt excused himself and walked out. Doc asked to see his identification before he left.

Sitting at Kanesha's kitchen table, which was fortunately clean, Kanesha was visibly nervous.

"Kanesha, you need to come clean with us and tell us everything you know about Rakemb Jamar Wilson."

"I tol' you everything I know. I seen him that day and I ain't seen him since."

"I believe that part. The part I don't believe is that you don't know what happened to Rakemb. In fact, I'm sure you know more than you are telling me."

Kanesha was sort of telling the truth when she said she didn't know what happened to Rakemb, so she stuck with her story.

"How about Leroy Dwayne Walker. What happened to him?" asked Will.

"I don't know who that is."

"That's odd. He was reported missing a few weeks ago and your name is in his file as a person of interest."

"What about Michael Tyron Davis? Your name is also mentioned in his file. He was reported missing too. That is three people Kanesha. You can't tell me that is a coincidence. What's going on here Kanesha?"

"I know Tyron. I ain't seen him in a long time and I don't know where he is or what happened to him neither."

Will changed strategies and asked, "How often do you do laundry?"

"Once a week. Every Saturday."

"What laundry do you use?" asked Will.

"The one here. Me and my girlfriend Tosa go early while it ain't busy."

"So, if you don't have your own washer and dryer why do two men keep bringing a washing machine box out of here? One of your neighbors saw the same two men wheel out a large washing machine box three or four times over the past few weeks. Once on the day Rakemb came to visit you and went missing. What can you tell us about that?"

"That ain't right," said Kanesha, but the conviction had left her voice. "Ain't no men been here with a washin' machine box."

"Kanesha, you are in over your head. We know too much and we will put it all together. The only way you can save yourself is to tell us everything you know," said Will.

Kanesha didn't really know what was happening to the informants she was helping round up, but she knew it wasn't good. There was no way she was going to end up in a washing machine box. She quickly decided to keep her mouth shut no matter what these cops did.

Doc said, "Even if you don't help us we will figure it out on our own, then there will be no deal for you. We think you lured these young men over here and those two men hauled them away in a washing machine box. We want to know three things: who the men are, why they took the boys and where did they take them? You either help us or we will find a way to put you in prison for a long time."

"I don't know nothin'," Kanesha declared.

It was obvious that Kanesha was lying, but Will and Doc didn't want to arrest her at this point. Kanesha needed some time to think things through and they needed some time to gather more facts. They assured Kanesha that they would be back and left the apartment.

"I would certainly like to know who she called after we left her apartment. Let's get a copy of her telephone records. I bet we find something helpful there," said Will.

Chapter 7

The fight was scheduled to take place in Reno, Nevada. Earlier that day the two executioners, dressed in black, put on their masks, helmets and other gear and went to fetch the two prisoners who had been there the longest. Taking one at a time, the two men instructed the prisoner to turn around with his hands behind his back and extend them through the bean-hole in the prison cell door. The prisoners had all been to jail before and knew the protocol. Once the hands were cuffed, one of the guards placed a long nightstick between the wrist to pin the arms in the bean-hole, then the other guard opened the door and placed shackles on the prisoner's legs.

When the prisoner was secured the nightstick was removed so the prisoner could be slowly walked down the hallway, past the autopsy table, to a flight of stairs that led up to a small sallyport where a van was waiting. The van had no side or rear windows and the cargo area was sectioned off into two cages made of aluminum diamond plate, fashioned so the prisoners could not see each other or see out of the van's front window.

When the two prisoners were loaded the barn doors opened and the van pulled out and proceeded on its fifty mile journey to a warehouse in Reno, Nevada. They were not too far from Lake Tahoe and at that time of year the Sierra Nevada mountains were exceptionally beautiful. It was a short and pleasant drive.

The automatic garage door opened when they arrived and they drove the van into the rear entrance of the warehouse. Two small corner offices had been prepared for holding the prisoners prior to the gladiator fight. One office was decorated in red and the other in blue. A coin toss determined which prisoner got which color. From that point forward names didn't matter. The prisoners were known as Red and Blue. A monitor and camera were setup in each office area and a large American flag was hanging on the back walls. Four other masked guards joined the original two to assist in removing the restraints and placing the prisoners in their rooms. Each of the four new guards carried five shot 12 gauge pistol-grip riot guns. After seeing the torture and execution of Mr. Davis these two prisoners were not going to cause any trouble, but the riot guns sealed the deal.

The face came on the monitors in each room moments after the two prisoners, Red and Blue, were turned loose in their rooms.

"Gentlemen, your incarceration has come to a conclusion. Tonight one of you will be a free man, enjoying a wonderful meal, having sex with a beautiful woman, with money in your pocket. The unfortunate consequence is the other will be dead. A life for a life. Ironic, isn't it? One of you must die so the other can live. I want to warn you again, if you give us any trouble or refuse to fight to the death, as previously instructed, you will suffer the same fate as Mr. Davis. You will be strapped to that cold steel table and electrocuted by those same two masked men who love their jobs, until you die. As I am certain you remember, it is a slow and very painful death. If you attempt to run and leave the ring without completely finishing off your opponent you will be transported back to the prison and placed on that table. We will not tolerate cowardliness. You have been provided fighting trunks and matching boots like boxers' wear. Put them on and prepare to have your pictures taken in a fighting stance in front of the American flag. I will be with you shortly, when the pictures are taken, with additional instructions. Meanwhile, help yourselves to a beverage from the mini-fridge."

The prisoner, now designated as Blue, was from New York. He had resigned to his fate, but wasn't happy about it. In fact, he was downright pissed. So pissed that he was mad and worked-up, ready to kill someone. He planned to climb into the ring, kill that punk he was fighting, get the fancy meal, sex and money and get the hell out.

The prisoner designated as Red was in a different state of mind. Ever since he woke up in that crazy prison and especially since Mr. Davis was murdered, he was so scared that it was all he could do to keep from wetting his britches. He didn't want to fight, but by God he was going to rather than be killed. Getting food, sex and money was secondary to his life and freedom. He got dressed to fight, selected a Coke from the icebox and sat down to wait on the face to appear on the monitor.

The idea was to fight two prisoners from different areas. That way there was less chance of them knowing each other and it would help the house odds. Just like any sport, people tend to bet on their home team, no matter what the odds were. The bettors could bet on many things. They expected the most common bets would be a bet to win and who drew first blood. The higher odd bets included things like a bet that one of the fighters would attempt to flee the arena, thereby forfeiting the match. A person could bet that both fighters died. It was possible that the winner could suffer a mortal wound and die within minutes of winning, but every effort would be made to keep the winner alive because the house did not want to lose a high odds bet. Also, they needed living winners for promotional videos.

When the face came back on the monitor he had each prisoner stand in front of the American flag in their rooms so their pictures could be taken. One picture was taken of them standing straight facing the camera with their arms at their sides. Then another picture was taken with their hands help up in a fighter's pose so they could show off their muscles. Their pictures and statistics would go out on the scrambled, secure web-site three hours prior to the fight. Bets could be placed until the fighters stepped into the ring.

"Gentlemen," said the face, "you will each be escorted to the ring by two armed guards. I advise you not to test them, because you do not want to go into that ring injured. That would be a disadvantage to you. There are many people here tonight to watch this event. They are all expecting a bloody fight to the death, so cries for help would be futile. The better you impress these people the better chance you have of possible business opportunities. My point is, if someone in the crowd is impressed with your fighting you may land a very good job. Therefore, it would behoove you to put on a good show out there so these people can see that you are not a coward. I realize that all of this has been dumped on you on short notice, but you have an opportunity here and it would be wise to take advantage of it."

For dinner the prisoners were served a medium-well steak and a hefty baked potato with butter and sour cream. There was corn, green beans, hot rolls and apple pie, with iced tea to wash it all down. It was a great last or first meal, depending on how you looked at it and whether you were the winner or loser.

At the appointed hour, three masked guards dressed like futuristic combat soldiers, escorted Blue down a hallway towards the ring. With one guard on each side and another close behind there was no chance of escape. As Blue walked into sight of the spectators the crowd cheered and clapped. Some were yelling Blue-Blue-Blue. It was electrifying. Blue went from nervous to awed. These people were cheering him. He held up both arms, pumped them in the air and started prancing like a boxer as the crowd cheered louder. There were at least three-hundred people seated around the ring. The smell of perfume, cologne, expensive alcohol and cigars filled that portion of the warehouse with the aromas of the rich and powerful. This was indeed a choice crowd.

The classical music that had been playing somewhere in the building had helped to soothe Red. It sounded peaceful. When the unseen crowd started cheering for Blue, Red began shaking more than he already was. He knew the time was quickly approaching. The door to his temporary sanctuary opened and three guards beckoned him to come with them. He had a hard time getting to his feet on shaky legs. The crowd erupted with cheers as Red walked between the rows of people towards the ring. Some were yelling Red-Red-Red. Suddenly the shakes stopped. He thought, "This must be how movie stars felt. These people are cheering me." He couldn't help but smile and raise his hands.

After Red stepped into the ring he felt even better about his chances. The other guy, Blue, looked scrawny compared to him. It was like the guy had never worked out in his life and he was even a little fat in the middle. This gave Red a renewed sense of confidence. He raised his hands to the delighted cheers of the crowd and started bouncing around like Blue who was in the opposite corner of the ring. They still didn't fully understand the seriousness of their situation.

Big Eddie was in the control booth sitting in his wheelchair looking at the live feed from all six cameras.

"I thought we would have to drag those bastards into the ring kicking and screaming and force them to fight at gun point. This is far better than I expected," said Eddie.

The director and video techs all agreed. They were busy switching the live feed from camera to camera, getting the best effects, moment to moment. The camera featured Blue when he came into the ring, then switched to Red. Now it was a wide angle view taking in the announcer and both fighters as the announcer began his introductions.

"Ladies and gentlemen, from New York City, New York, at 176 pounds, standing there with a charming smile on his face, I introduce Blue."

"From Los Angeles, California, at 182 pounds and looking fit and ready to fight, I introduce Red."

The crowd cheered as Red shook his head and rolled his shoulders, then slammed his right fist into the open palm of his left hand.

When the announcer left the ring, two men stepped into the ring, one at each fighter's corner. They both held a small shield in one hand and a wicked looking knife in the other. They held them in the air and turned around so the spectators could see, and once again, the crowd went nuts with yells and cheering.

The shield looked like a large forearm with a fist to cover the fighter's hand. It was not a conventional round shield like you see in the movies. It was long and narrow, about four inches wider than the fighters actual forearm and the fist on the end of the shield was only slightly larger than the fighter's fist. Once the shield was firmly in place the men handed the two fighters their knives. The knives looked evil and satanic with a skull on the end of the handle and bat wings for a finger guard and the blade tapering down to a fine point like a huge dagger.

Each man told their fighter to run out to the center of the ring as soon as the bell rang and to finish their opponent quickly before he got too tired. The two men also informed the fighters that they would be in the corner coaching them and yelling advice. It was a prearranged script. Then they both climbed out of the ring.

Blue had already made up his mind to attack his opponent and kill him quick. There was no doubt in his mind that he could do it. Blue yelled across the ring telling Red, "I'm comin' for ya motherfucker. I'm gona kill your ass."

Red was feeling more confident just looking at the smaller weaker looking Blue. "Fuck you," yelled Red. "You a dead man."

When the bell rang Red and Blue hurried to the center of the ring and circled each other waving and pointing their knives. When they rushed each other they both blocked the knives with their shield and knocked the knives out of each other's hands. In a panic, they both dashed to pick up their knives. Blue was a little slower and as he was turning back around to attack Red, Red was already there. Blue was late getting his shield up and only managed to partially block Red's knife. The knife slashed across the top of Blue's left shoulder. It hurt and Blue jumped back, but the pain was held in check by the amount of adrenaline and endorphin pumping through his body, so the cut just made him crazy. He ran at Red swinging with his shield and trying to stab Red around his shield. Blue was concentrating so intensely on stabbing Red that he raised his shield too high and Red stabbed Blue in the left side, just below the ribs.

Blue jumped back, stumbled, slipped in his own blood and went down to one knee. He slashed out and caught Red in the leg, just as Red cut a gash across Blue's left cheek. They both backed up, leaving footprints in the blood. As the crowd yelled and cheered them on Red and Blue were screaming and cussing each other. They were both focused on surviving, not the noise of the crowd.

Angela Sarcosie was perched on the edge of her seat with a faint smile on her face. Her heart was racing as she watched and listened to the roar of the crowd. Her plan was coming to fruition in a spectacular manner. Some of the other women with Angela and others she could see in the audience were averting their eyes. The fight was too gruesome for the weak at heart, but not for Angela and her lesbian lover, Kera. The violence and blood had them so hot they were having a hard time keeping their hands off each other. Kera had already finger-fucked herself into an orgasm, then held her hand up for Angela to lick and suck the juices from her wet fingers.

Red was limping from the cut on his left leg and Blue was doing poorly, with blood coming from his shoulder, face and side. The blood leaking from both opponents almost covered the center ring and they were tracking it all over with every step they took. Seeing that Blue was favoring his left side, badly bleeding and looking weak, Red tried to run at him but slipped in the blood and fell. Blue, seeing an opportunity, rushed him and fell on top of him, stabbing Red twice in the left shoulder. At the same time, Red was stabbing Blue in the ribs under his shield. They jerked apart and rolled away from each other screaming and cussing and covered in blood.

Blue couldn't get up. He was starting to lose his cocky attitude. He was on his hands and knees trying to get his footing on the blood soaked mat. Red slipped trying to get up but finally made it to his feet. When Blue saw Red coming he rolled onto his back and attempted to kick Red. All that did was allow Red to slash Blue's legs with his knife. Blue let out a choked yell as Red fell on him stabbing him in the neck and chest. Red did not stop until Red was limp on the mat. He then rolled off of Blue crying and getting to his knees as he gasped for breath.

The crowd got quiet during the last few seconds of the fight, but as Red got to his knees they erupted with cheers and chants of Red-Red-Red. A medic climbed into the ring with a helper and quickly wrapped Red's cuts to slow the bleeding as they started an IV. As Red was being carried from the ring the announcer climbed into the ring and proclaimed Red the winner. The ring lights dimmed when two men came into the ring to collect Blue's body as the spectators exited the building. Nothing was left to see or do but to patch up Red and clean up the mess.

The medic knocked Red out with a sedative, administered Novocain locals to each cut then stitched him up.

When Red woke an hour later he was back in the room with the American flag on the wall. He was clean, covered up nicely, with the IV drip still running. The IV contained glucose, an antibiotic and a pain reliever. Red was feeling no pain. A video camera was monitoring Red and recording everything he did. Moments after he woke the door opened and a gorgeous scantily clad black beauty came into the room pushing a cart. She bent over and kissed him lightly on the lips then helped him sit up. That is when he noticed that he was wearing a nice robe with a sleeve pushed up to accommodate the IV.

The woman removed the silver warmer covers from the food and set them aside, then popped a cork in a bottle of wine. She handed Red a glass of wine then reached beneath a towel, retrieved a stack of hundred dollar bills and fanned them for the camera. She then handed the money to Red who was so doped up on pain medication he did not realize the extent of his injuries. Red kissed the money and waived it back and forth for the camera.

"That's what I'm talkin' about," said Red.

After they both ate a little of the wonderfully prepared food, the woman carefully removed the IV from Red's arm then positioned him in a chair so the camera could record her giving Red a blow job and film him fucking her until he was played out.

When the fun was over the face turned off the video feed from the camera. The girl wheeled the cart out and a medic stepped into the room asking Red how he was feeling and congratulating him on his magnificent fight. The medic told Red that he was going to give him a shot of an antibiotic to stop any possible infection. The medic gave Red the shot then stepped back as Red went into convulsions and died. Then the medic opened the door and told the two waiting guards to bury Red's body with the other rat.

They never intended to let the winners live to go tell it again. They just needed them to believe they were going free so they would have an incentive to fight. They would show the video of the fight and the reward to the other prisoners. It should have the desired effect of helping the prisoners make the decision to fight for their lives.

Showing the fight live to the prisoners had some of them cheering with excitement. However, it had the opposite effect on one. He made a crude rope from a strip of a sheet and hung himself while everyone was occupied watching the fight. If he would have waited until after he had a chance to see Red receive his reward he may not have hung himself, but it was good to get the weak ones out of the way. They probably wouldn't fight well anyway.

Angela and Big Eddie learned a lot from the first fight. They agreed that the ring needed sand spread on it to help soak up the blood and reduce the slippage. It would help the fighters get better traction. The knives would be modified with a leather strap to fasten around the fighters' wrists so they could not drop the knives. They planned to dull the blade and point of the knives so the cuts and stab wounds would not be so deep. That way the fights would last longer and make for a better show.

Chapter 8

Doc was of the firm belief that FBI stood for "Fucking Bureaucratic Idiots." If you wanted something screwed up and bogged down in red tape all you had to do was involve a government agency like the FBI.

Will didn't want to contact the FBI, but he knew he was required to because it involved the possible kidnapping/abduction of at least eighteen federal informants from multiple jurisdictions. Rather than send copies of each case file, Will typed a twenty-six page memorandum that outlined his and Doc's discoveries and the information related to their investigation. He included copies of the short profiles he compiled on each of the eighteen missing informants and a copy of Kanesha's phone records.

Doc had a friend, Cody Daniels, who was a local FBI field office operative, which was just a fancy name for agent. The only difference between a cop and an FBI agent is: a cop sits on his ass and looks at a file and an FBI agent sits on his derriere and peruses a dossier. The name Cody struck a chord with Will and all he wanted to know was whether his friends called him "Wild Bill?" Of course, Will thought that was absolutely hilarious. Doc Holiday and Wild Bill Cody. How funny was that. He was in the wild, wild west for sure.

"You are confusing Cody with Wild Bill Hickok," Doc corrected. Cody was Buffalo Bill Cody."

"My bad," said Will. "That is a lot of Bills to remember. You must know your western history well, or you have a cowboy fixation. Should I get a cowboy hat and boots?"

"Will, I think a cowboy hat, boots and even a six-shooter would only take away from your New York City pretty boy image. I like you just the way you are. In fact, I was hoping you would come by my place for dinner tonight. There won't be anyone there for you to shoot, but I could play with your other gun and we can keep each other occupied."

"Occupied is good," said Will. "I like occupied."

They agreed on a time and Will promised to bring the wine. He brought a case of his favorite cabernet sauvignon with him from New York. It was a delicate, dry red wine from Italy that was easy on the palate. He was looking forward to sharing a bottle with Doc.

Rather than waste time talking on the phone, Doc typed a note to agent Cody Daniels and Will included it with the memorandum he prepared and the profiles, then sent the package by departmental courier to FBI headquarters for Daniels. By policy they were required to notify the FBI of their findings, but that didn't mandate an email or personally going to the FBI building and kissing someone's ass. Doc and Will had been to FBI offices before and having to wait in an outer office for hours was not their idea of fun.

Will and Doc ordered Chinese delivery for lunch and it was actually delivered by a Chinese guy, making it seem more authentic. The sesame chicken and egg rolls were among the best Will had ever eaten. With the food cooked in soybean oil, with no trans-fat, it wasn't even that bad for them and the taste outweighed any possible adverse health consequences.

They were putting away the empty cartons and throwing away their trash when two suits walked into Doc's small office.

"Hello detective Holiday," said the first suit.

"Agent Daniels. You must have received our package. This is William Bracket, my partner, who put it all together."

Cody stuck out his hand and said, "Officer Bracket, nice to meet you. "I'm agent Cody Daniels with the FBI. Thank you for sending us the information you compiled. I can't stress how important it is for us to keep this matter confidential. We have to protect our assets."

Will looked at Doc and asked, "Did he say asses?"

Doc shook her head and smiled.

"I believe you know I said assets, officer Bracket," said agent Daniels.

"It sounded like asses and just for the record, in case you didn't notice, you didn't find out about this on the six o'clock news. We sent you a confidential memorandum by way of departmental courier. We keep everything confidential. It's our job and I resent the implication that you don't think we do our jobs. We kept it confidential up to this point, so if it happens to get out now you might want to look in your office for a leak, not ours," Will proclaimed.

"That went well," said Doc. "Cody, why don't you tell us why you stopped by. That would be good." Doc was trying to defuse the situation and get Cody out of her office as fast as possible.

Turning away from Will, agent Daniels said, "I would like to have copies of all the case files. If you don't mind."

"We thought you might. We requested copies of the case files from New York, Oklahoma and Louisiana. It was Will who figured this out. He knows the case agent in New York. We copied everything for you and it is on this flash drive."

"That should do it. We'll take everything from here," said Daniels.

"Until we find the seven missing persons from our jurisdiction we will be actively pursuing our investigation," Will said. "Detective Holiday and I will keep you informed of our progress. If you happen to find any of them before we do we would appreciate a courtesy call notifying us of such."

The implication was crystal clear. Will might as well have said, "If you can keep from stepping on your over inflated dicks."

Agent Daniels pointed to the flash drive like it was dirty and the unintroduced agent picked it up and walked out the door with Daniels hot on his heels.

"Arrogant asshole," Will declared. "How well do you know him?"

"We dated briefly," Doc Answered. "You're right. He is an arrogant asshole. I haven't had very good luck with men. I hope that's changed."

The day went smoothly. Will felt like he'd made some progress on locating the man who left Kaneshas' apartment. The basic background check showed that the man had a long record of assaults and petty crimes, which did not surprise Will. Will decided to follow up on it in the morning. Dinner with Doc was the only thing on his mind at the moment.

Just before 5:00 p.m. agent Daniels and his sidekick came waltzing back in the door and smugly strutted across the department. Will stayed at his desk as Daniels walked by and into Doc's office. A moment later Doc came to her door and asked Will to join them.

"Kanesha Sims is dead," Doc said.

"We went to her apartment to follow up on your investigation," Daniels said. Kanesha's friend Tosha was just letting herself in with a key when we arrived. We introduced ourselves and followed her in to find Kanesha dead on the living room floor. Apparent strangulation, judging from the wire around her neck. I'm guessing, but I would say it was a professional hit. The wire garrote was similar to those used by the Army Special Forces and it was twisted at the back of the neck in the same style taught by the military. Very effective."

Will's mind was racing. Whatever and whoever Kanesha had been involved with was seriously dangerous for them to have killed her to keep her quiet. She must have known a lot more than she was willing to share with him and Doc. Kanesha being murdered was a pretty good indication that the missing informants were either dead or in some deep trouble. Since Kanesha's phone records didn't show any calls to anyone other than immediate family after their visit to her apartment, either one of her family members were involved or she used another phone to contact whoever killed her. In that case there might be a phone number in her effects. Maybe her apartment was bugged or someone was watching her very close. For a moment Will thought that he may have lost his only solid lead, but then he remembered that he was doing a check on the man who left Kanesha's apartment. Will hoped that Doc would keep that to herself so they could pursue that lead together.

After visiting about the case for a few minutes, the caped crusader and boy wonder excused themselves and left in their FBI suits to fight crime and protect the American way. Will thought that it would be pure luck if either of them could find their own asses with both hands.

When they left their office, Will went to a gym where he put in a vigorous one hour on an upper body workout. Kaneshas' murder had disturbed him. He needed to focus and get his mind right. A good workout usually did the trick. It had even helped when he caught his fiancée in bed with another man. After his workout, he spent twenty minutes in a steam room, showered then headed home to change and grab that bottle of wine. By the time Will reached Doc's all he was thinking about was their previous sexual encounter and he was hoping for a repeat performance.

Doc surprised him when she opened her front door. Her hair was in a sexy, sassy ponytail, high on the back of her head. She was wearing a sports bra, tank-top, spandex shorts and running shoes. She looked super sexy after her run. They kissed at the door. Doc took Will's hand and said, "Dinner is in the oven and on the stove. We have twenty minutes. Come take a shower with me."

There is nothing like a quickie in the shower to start an evening rolling. It removes the tension and urgency for sex and allows a couple to truly enjoy a meal and friendly conversation before the next round.

Sex and a sandwich would have been fine with Will, but Doc had cooked a fabulous pot roast that was so tender Will could cut it with a fork. The roast went great with the excellent red wine. There were no thoughts of work, missing people or Kanesha. The only thing that kept them from diving to the floor and pulling their clothes off was the wonderful food and wine and the fact that they thoroughly enjoyed playing footsies and making goo-goo eyes at each other.

After the delicious meal, with a little wine buzz going on, they cleared the table and hand washed the dishes together as they flirted and rubbed against one another.

"This is so domestic," Doc said with a smile.

"I like it," answered Will.

They embraced for a long, soft kiss. Doc feels Will's hardness pressed against her. With a mischievous grin, Doc unbuckled Will's belt, undid his pants then slides down his body onto her knees, taking Will's rock hard member into her mouth. Will was overwhelmed with sensation. Her hot, wet, soft lips wrapped around him was more than he could take. Will soon erupted in her mouth and she sucked out every drop. Pleased with herself, Doc took Will by the hand and led him into the bedroom with Will holding up his pants. Doc was having fun showing Will her wild side.

Will wasn't very experienced in oral sex. He'd only been with one woman and oral sex wasn't an area they had delved into much. Doc was looking forward to showing and explaining the fine art of oral sex to Will. With Doc's gentle coaxing and instructions, Will used his tongue, lips and fingers to lick, suck and probe Doc into a magnificent orgasm. Watching Doc enthralled with pleasure as she came gave Will an intoxicating sense of power. Will was worked up and so hard a cat couldn't scratch him, when Doc gasped for air and said, "Fuck me," in a breathless, seductive manner that made Will jump on the task like a starved dog on a pork chop. The sex was hard, fast and intense. Will remembered how she liked it, so as soon as they came together he told Doc to roll over where he took her from behind like a wild man on a mission.

The next morning when Doc woke-up in bed she could smell coffee, toast and sausage. Will was cooking breakfast and it was a good feeling. Doc quickly showered and met Will in the kitchen. Will was already dressed for work, all clean and smelling fine. After a soft kiss, they shared a heavy breakfast that included scrambled eggs. Will left before Doc because he needed to stop by his place on the way to work and pick up a few things. The night was wonderful and the day was starting great.

At the office Will resumed his search for Kaneshas' man friend, Derick Jerome Aguilar. The man they'd seen leaving Kaneshas' apartment. It was obvious, not only from the name, but from his features and complexion, as well, that Derick's father was either Mexican or Puerto Rican. Will had already completed a basic background search and determined that Derick has a record, but no outstanding wants or warrants. Upon closer examination Will discovered that Derick was on probation. Will called the probation department and was transferred around some until he was connected with Derick's probation officer. After the necessary preliminary identification issues the probation officer provided Will with Derick's home and work addresses. Since Derick worked nights Will and Doc headed for Derick's house.

The neighborhood where Derick lived, as they expected, was full of small seedy, dilapidated clapboard houses. The closer they came to Derick's house the more run down the homes became. Most of the tiny yards hadn't seen enough water in their life to grow grass. Many of the matchbox yards were fenced with chain-link and had a Pit Bull or Rottweiler laying in the hot, hard packed dirt under whatever they could find for shade. It was a pitiful example of a dog surviving its domain no matter what sorry condition its owner kept it in. It was obvious that even the dogs didn't want to be there. A simple look around told them that it was a typical low-income housing project that was riddled with crack houses and wanna-be gang bangers. Not a great place for two police officers to spend their morning.

Derick's house was no exception. The long years and Southern California heat had dried the old house out and it was sagging at the corners to the point that it looked like it was tired, frowning and sad. There was no activity and no dog so Doc and Will walked through the open, broken gate and knocked on the door. A car registered to Derick was parked in the driveway. It looked far too new to be sitting in this place, where most normal people would not venture.

When Will knocked on the door they heard a man's voice yell, "What? Damn it, this better be good."

They heard the man in the house walk up to the inside of the door and say, "Shit." Then they heard him take off running through the house towards the back door. Will kicked the door in and Doc was already running around the house. Will was slowed down because he had to check every room on his way to the back door. Will burst through the back door just in time to see Derick slam through a tall wooden gate at the side of the yard, leading into the alley, where a six foot high plank fence ran around the back yard. He heard Doc yell and spit out a string of expletives. When Will ran through the gate Doc was getting up from a pile of trash, cussing a blue streak and pointing in the direction Derick ran. Without hesitation Will turned on the speed and took off in pursuit. Doc was hot on Will's trail when she saw Will round the corner of another tall wooden fence. Then she heard four gunshots fired in quick succession. From experience Doc knew they were pistol shots. Doc carefully peeked around the corner and saw Will laying on the ground, struggling to get to his feet while holding his left hand to his bloody side. Will was shot. Doc panicked and ran to Will's side fumbling for her phone to call for backup and an ambulance. At that point Doc could see Derick laying on the ground, motionless, less than fifty feet away at the end of the fence line. Doc told Will to lay still as she barked orders into her phone then ran to Derick. Derick was gasping for air as a huge puddle of blood grew beneath him. His throat was blown out and he'd taken a hit in his right shoulder. Doc knew the small bullet hole in the front of Derick's neck was nothing compared to what the exit wound would look like. There was nothing she could do for him. He would be dead long before help arrived. Doc secured his weapon. Using one finger through the trigger guard, she carried it back to where Will was laying on the ground.

The scenes you see in the movies where the cops leaves the gun where it fell just isn't practical in the real world. A cop never leaves a gun unattended. There is far too big a risk that a spectator might pick it up and run off with it before backup arrives, or God forbid, the shooter recovers enough to get the gun and start shooting again.

When Doc kneeled down next to Will to check his wound, Will, with obvious pain on his face, was laughing.

Doc said, "Okay cowboy. What the hell's so funny?"

"He's dead, isn't he?" asked Will.

"Pretty much. He took one in the neck and one in the shoulder."

"We don't seem to be able to go anyplace together without me killing someone. Last time I killed a guy before dinner. Today I kill one before lunch. I think the missing persons business is getting pretty tough," Will said as he grimaced from the pain and stifled a laugh.

"You're making me all misty. Shut-up and lay still you big shit. If you get yourself killed on me I am going to be pissed. I may write off men and become a lesbian," said Doc, as tears ran down her cheeks.

Will was lucky. The gun shot hole in his side wasn't bleeding bad so the bullet hadn't hit anything vital, Doc hoped. The bullet hit Will in that narrow place between the bottom of the ribs and just above the hip bone. A little higher or lower and the bullet could have caused a lot of damage. Most of the area was skin and muscle and the 9mm bullet had passed through, ruining a good shirt and a nice jacket, while taking a huge chunk out of Will's ego and pride. Not a good thing for an alpha male.

Sirens came from every direction as other units converged on their location. Doc was back on the phone telling dispatch that the scene was secure and that the shooter was down. She didn't want the other officers coming in hot like they usually do when a fellow officer is down.

Doc was going to have to play this cool. It was all going to come out and it would get sticky. Sure, the recently deceased, very recently, was technically a person of interest in a string of missing person cases, but upon Keneshas' death he'd also become a murder suspect. A fact that required Will and Doc to provide that information to the homicide division. If they had, there would have been more backup and the back of the residence would have been properly covered by a tactical team. Ergo, the sticky situation. One man dead and her partner wounded. The situation sucked.

When Doc's supervisor arrived, a man known for his hard line on proper police procedures, Will was being loaded into an ambulance. Her boss pointed at Will and said, "Can't you keep your partner out of trouble? He hasn't been here a month and he has shot more people than I have in my whole career. What the hell's going on? You people work in missing persons, for Christ sake. How am I going to explain this?" he said, pointing at the dead guy who was having his picture taken for the last time.

"I think it went pretty well," said Doc. "No cars got wrecked. No houses got shot-up and no innocent bystanders were injured. I believe that's a damn good morning, boss."

He looked at Doc a second then laughed and said, "Point taken Doc. Now what the hell is going on?"

It didn't take Doc long to lay all the facts out for her boss in a manner that justified not calling in homicide before they went to visit with Derick.

When Doc got to the hospital she was just in time to hear Will telling the doctor that he was not spending the night in the hospital over a flesh wound and a pint of blood.

Doc spoke with the doctor and convinced him that she would take Will home and put him to bed. The doctor said something about macho cops then explained to both of them that "officer Bracket" was a stubborn man. He explained that Will would suffer a bad bruise and be sore as hell once the local anesthetic wore off.

As they were leaving the hospital Will said, “I killed our only lead.”

“Don’t beat yourself up over it. He meant to kill you and his actions are a fairly good indication that he killed Kanesha or knew who did. When we get to my place I will call agent Daniels and fill him in on what happened and get him working on Derick’s phone records. By the time the Crime Scene Investigators get through with Derick’s house they may turn up something we can use. Look on the bright side, you get the rest of the day off. I’ll go in and get the reports filled out then come back and make my cowboy dinner.”

Will was smiling as they drove towards Doc’s house. He liked the idea of being a cowboy. The old song playing on the radio went: “I think I’m gonna love you, for a long-long time.” Will and Doc looked at each other and smiled. The music said it all.

Later that evening they learned that the search of Derick’s home had turned up cocaine, marijuana, money and firearms. It was obvious that Derick was a mid-level drug and firearms dealer. That fact would certainly help to justify the shooting.

“I need more guns,” Will proclaimed.

With his regular pistol and his spare backup gun being held by Internal Affairs during the investigation Will was gunless and felt naked.

Doc replied, “I got you covered.”

Doc went to her bedroom closet and retrieved a large gun case and placed it on the bed. Will was amazed when she opened it and it was full of nice, new handguns. He picked a thirteen shot SIG 9mm and smiled.

I have got to get me one of these," said Will, referring to the case full of guns as Doc closed the case and returned it to its place in the closet.

Chapter 9

Angela Sarcosie and her long legged sexy companion Kera arrived at Big Eddie's for the party ahead of the other guests. They had some business they were anxious to discuss before the fun began.

The door was opened by the time Angela and Kera reached the top of the steps leading into Big Eddie's sprawling beach front hideaway. The butler, in a freshly pressed tux, led them to the library where Big Eddie was parked behind a massive, ornate teak desk that was fit for a king. In fact, the desk had been designed for a Saudi prince who didn't live long enough to take delivery. Early death was one of the unfortunate downfalls of trying to assume control of an unstable country. Big Eddie and some of his close friends were picking up a lot of great deals in the Middle East with all the civil unrest caused by Bin Laden and his merry band of terrorists. The raw heroin and arms trade had never been better.

Angela walked around the huge desk, that was so big it made Eddie look small and kissed him on the cheek. Kera went to the wet bar to fix drinks.

"The numbers are in," announced Angela. "After all expenses, including that three-hundred-thousand dollar miniature prison you built, of the fourteen point seven million in bets that were placed on the fight we cleared two point five mil. That is better than I figured we would take in on the first fight. But, not near what I project for the future. I think we will average ten million a fight. Do the math. That is twenty mil a month. Two-hundred and forty mil a year. We are already starting similar operations in the UK, China and Russia. We could bring in a billion a year on these gladiator fights. That covers a third of our last year's losses. At two fights a month we will be eliminating forty-eight rats a year right here in the old U.S. of A. Worldwide that will be at least one-hundred and ninety-two rats a year, or more. That, my friend, is a lot of blood and gut entertainment for your viewing pleasure. It will send one hell of a message to potential informants around the globe, which should also reduce our losses. Of course, nothing lasts forever, but if we can get our projected ten years out of this each partner will clear an extra billion. That is one hell of a return on the small investment we all started with."

Under all that class Angela was a cold hearted, crude bitch, motivated by money and power.

"That, my sweet Angela is cause for celebration, worthy of a toast to our success," Big Eddie said.

Kera handed Big Eddie and Angela their drinks, with a sexy smile and seductive display that caused them both to lust after her even more. Kera was ready to get the party started so she could dance the night away.

Guest were due to arrive within the hour. It was going to be a relatively small affair with only about one-hundred people in attendance. Most of them were investors, customers and very wealthy people interested in expanding their fortunes in the illegal fighting and gambling business. In the criminal world, greed and excitement breed and no matter how much money and excitement you generate you have to have more. It's an addiction that can only be placated by new and exciting adventures that net more money. It is all about calculated risks, money, sex, drugs and rock-n-roll. Fun, fun, fun, 'till our daddy takes our T-bird away. Most of the hardcore tough guys and gals lived by the philosophy that there would be plenty of time for sleep once they were dead.

They planned on enjoying themselves to the fullest until that final day arrived. For some, life is a party and it would be best for everyone to stay out of their way while they indulged.

It wasn't long and the front of Big Eddie's beach front home was looking like a high-end exotic car dealership. The party was heating up around back where a spectacular view of a California sunset was displaying itself for the guests.

The live band that was softly playing oldies rock, the two full bars outside and one inside, the many catered foods, the dancing and even the location were all carefully selected to give the appearance of legitimacy to the event, when in fact, it was just the opposite. It was a celebration of their illicit success and a new and exciting promotional gig for their illegal enterprise. Private viewings of the fight tape, along with the tape of the winner receiving his prize, were being conducted with select members of the party. The tapes were well edited and short and it didn't take long to show them and explain how the live viewing and betting worked. The video of the fight was on a professional level that would rival any boxing match or sporting event.

Before the night was over Big Eddie planned to have at least thirty more people participating that would each have a minimum of ten locations set up to view and bet on the fights. The party was a huge event and to Big Eddie's delight it was moving along without a hitch.

The party was semi-formal. The men were wearing expensive tailored suits and the women looked like a cross between Charlie's Angels and Playboy Bunnies. You couldn't tell the difference between the regular female guests and the dozen or so high class hookers Big Eddie had brought in from Vegas to help liven up the festivities. Angela and Kera wore matching black leather miniskirts with spike heels and black nylons with a seam running up the back. A man's imagination automatically said: "Garter belt, no panties." Angela wore a green silk blouse that matched her emerald eyes and Kera was wearing a ruby-red blouse that set off her short red hair. They made it obvious that they were together which kept the men and other women at bay while still grabbing the attention of the crowd.

The sun had dropped below the horizon and the sky to the west was filled with colors ranging from deep orange, red and purple. There was a huge yacht anchored about a quarter mile off shore. One of Big Eddie's toys that added to the rich, luxurious atmosphere of the party. The yacht was another one of those good deals Big Eddie picked up from a wannabe Sheik. The yacht looked fancy and all lit up out there on the water with the aftermath of the sunset as a backdrop. It was romantic and tantalizing. Everyone at the party wanted to be rich like that and some were getting close.

Ray, the computer geek, was milling around the party trying to get better acquainted with the woman Big Eddie had put on his tail to watch over him and keep him happy. The young computer guru was an important part of the plan and Eddie intended to pacify him, if possible. After watching the first fight Ray had contacted Big Eddie about the ending of the fight. The violent death had shaken up Ray to the point he was almost ill. To put it bluntly, it scared the shit out of poor Ray. Initially, Ray had no idea what he was mixed up in, but that fight had painted a pretty gruesome picture for him. Big Eddie didn't want to involve another computer expert so he was going out of his way to dazzle the kid. Eddie liked Ray and he didn't want to have to feed him to the sea. But, that's where things were headed if Ray didn't get on board, all the way. A little extra money, wine, women and song had worked wonders so far. Eddie was monitoring Ray closely. If he had a bout of conscious, or even farted too loud, Big Eddie would initiate damage control and either lock the kid down or take him on a short sea voyage. Business is business, after all.

Two hours into the party Eddie called a small meeting that included Ray. Eddie wanted Ray to feel like he was an intricate part of the operation. Angela and Eddie had discussed the matter and they planned on making Ray feel important by including him on a few decisions about the up-coming fight.

"Angela, Bob, you've met Raymond," said Big Eddie. "I've brought him in because he has a sharp mind and may have some input that will help on the next fight."

"Wonderful," Angela replied as she walked over to Ray and kissed him on the cheek. Ray blushed and Angela smiled like one of those vampires you see in the movies right before they bare their teeth and bite you on the neck.

Robert (Bob) Rynalds was an enforcer that took care of Big Eddie's day-to-day affairs. Through Eddie, Bob had connections all over the world. Bob was the go-to guy for anything Eddie needed done. Bob was there to give them an update on the progress and planning for the next fight. They decided that sand on the mat would not be a good idea. A thin layer of saw dust would be applied to help stop slippage from the blood. The knives would be dulled just a little and a wrist strap would be added to the handles. The fights would last longer and the fighters would not be dropping their knives so easily. There was some lighting issues to discuss and Ray agreed with all the changes. They all further agreed that the next two fighters would be white. It would prevent any racial questions. Ray, who was a little drunk and in awe of his surroundings, thought that was a great idea.

Bob brought up the point that one of the informant prisoners was a small Mexican man and they didn't have another Mexican or anyone small enough to fight him. Ray, now in the swing of things, suggested that they pair the little Mexican with an oriental informant of the same build.

They all agreed that that would be an outstanding idea. Bob said he would get right on it. It was obvious to everyone but Ray that Ray didn't realize just how deep he was in. At that point, it was either sink or swim. Saying Ray was in over his head was an understatement and it was far too late to turn back. Turning back would come with serious repercussions that might cause Ray to drown, literally, but he didn't need to know that as long as he played the game.

After Ray returned to the party Big Eddie and Angela talked over a few other business details and Bob left to do what Bod did.

Angela pointed out the window to the party and asked who the guy was in the bright yellow zoot suit. He was kind of cute in a silly sort of way, with that bright colored suit that looked three sizes too big and a matching wide brim hat. The guy was strutting around the party saying hello to everyone with a great big, mean looking, monster of a man following him everywhere he went. It was funny just watching because some of the women guests would see the pair coming and start gracefully moving along ahead of them. They were scared of the big guy. The little one just looked like a dangerous joke.

"That is Carmine Antonellie," said Eddie. "His mother is French and his father Italian. He got his good looks from his momma and his ruthlessness from his pop. His father made a ton of money in the old days running a racket and booze. Back when being in the mob meant something. Junior, who liked to be called Pierre by the way, owns four up-scale clubs in LA that bring in a bundle and he has expanded into the cocaine, heroin and meth trade. He came up a little too fast and as you can see he is a little too flashy for my liking. I'm keeping an eye on him. He bought in and I don't mind taking his money. He acts like a Mafia kingpin but he wouldn't know a shylock from a padlock. The oversize lug following him around is his bodyguard, Serge Molisnikov. Pierre's daddy brought him over from Russia to look after Junior. I was told that they call the big man Hammer."

"Pierre and Mr. Hammer," Angela laughed. "This is starting to sound like a circus. Pierre looks like a canary being stalked by an ugly bulldog. If Pierre is going to make it without being eaten or busted he's going to need some advice and direction. I hope you're looking into that."

"No worries, sweet Angela. With a little guidance, our friend Pierre might just turn out to be bigger than he looks in that ridiculous suit," said Big Eddie.

Chapter 10

Wu Tran lived in a spacious studio apartment on the outskirts of New York. The building was originally an old three story warehouse. It had been divided into twelve tenements. Four on each floor. On the outside the building would best be described as plain or nondescript. The red brick edifice hid its interior extravagance. Mr. Tran had owned one of the apartments on the top floor for many years. It was one of many assets Tran had managed to conceal from the government after being arrested as part of a massive drug conspiracy involving the importation and distribution of heroin and ecstasy. After agreeing to cooperate with the government, Tran was now living in the lap of luxury with a new identity, while over thirty co-conspirators in the drug operation languished in jails and prisons from America to Japan. Over five million in narcotics had been seized and at least that much more in cash and assets. All thanks to Tran who was originally placed in protective custody then released into the witness protections program.

Tran was very well aware that some very powerful people wanted him dead. He had also heard stories about informants being kidnapped and forced to fight each other to the death. Greedy, sadistic Americans had even devised a way to bet on the fights. Tran was over forty, rich, intelligent and cautious. He planned to avoid death and abduction by laying low in his comfortable apartment for a year before he ventured out. He had no idea just how determined the people he crossed were and to what expense they were willing to incur to capture him. He was about to learn.

Tran kept one full time bodyguard, a cook and two women in the apartment with him. A man of his stature required protection, quality foods and extravagant sex. After all his years of hard work Tran felt he'd earned a lifestyle of his choosing. The two women and the old cook did all the shopping. Tran and his bodyguard never left the building. There were video cameras monitoring the hallway and front door of the apartment. Video surveillance is only as good as the people watching the monitor. Tran thought he was safe. He didn't realize that the people closest to him despised him for his treachery. Money cannot purchase loyalty and respect. These things must be earned. People who do not respect you are always subject to being bought by the highest bidder.

It had taken several days for Big Eddie's man Bob to locate the whereabouts of Mr. Tran. The plan was to attempt an extraction so Tran could be forced to participate in the gladiator fights. Or to just kill him, even if they had to blow-up the whole building. After the women and old cook came out of the building Bob and his men snatched them as they were crossing an intersection a block from the target location.

After determining the layout of the apartment and that there were only two people inside, Bob and his men executed a precision assault on the apartment that looked like a police SWAT operation. They smashed the door, ran in and neutralized the bodyguard with two quick shots in the chest with a silenced .9mm pistol, then commenced their search for Mr. Tran.

When Tran heard the front door burst open he knew what was happening. He immediately ran to the bedroom window, jerked it open and climbed through to the fire escape, fleeing for his life. As Tran reached the bottom landing Bob peaked out the open window and cursed. Bob probably could have shot Tran at that point but he still had hopes of catching him. Bob sent one man down the fire escape as he pulled out his phone and headed back out of the apartment. Bob barked orders into his phone as he ran telling his driver to converge on the alley and stop Tran.

By the time Tran reached the end of the alley Bob's man had reached the bottom of the fire escape and was in foot pursuit. Half a block away a car came screeching around the corner heading towards Tran. Tran didn't have a lot of options so he kept running across the road and into the next alley. The driver paused at the mouth of the alley just long enough for his partner to jump in the passenger side door then he took off down the alley after Tran. The pause gave Tran the short lead he needed to make the corner at the far end of the alley and head towards a small park.

When the men in the car turned the corner following Tran they were just in time to see Tran run through some bushes into the park. Tran could hear the car accelerating behind him and he expected to hear tires squeal as the car braked to a halt outside the park. To Tran's surprise, the car crashed through the hedgerow like an angry monster on methamphetamine, with its headlights gleaming like fiery eyes. The engine was roaring as the car appeared in midair then crashed to the ground in a cloud of dust, sliding to a stop with a rocking motion. Both doors flew open and the men jumped out of the car looking for Tran. The whole scene radiated the theme of: I'm coming to gettcha. It was too late. Tran had already made it into the denser trees and was out of sight.

Tran went directly across the park into a business district where most of the businesses were already closed for the day. The only thing open within sight was a liquor store and a combination convenience store/gas station. He headed for a bank of payphones at the brightly lit convenience store while he looked over his shoulder. Tran dug out his wallet and removed a business card then fed change into the phone and punched in a number he'd hoped never to use.

Agent Thomas Dean, Tran's case agent at FBI headquarters in New York answered his phone on the forth ring with a curt, "You got me."

Tran, in an almost hysterical utterance said, "You must help me. They broke into my apartment. Chased me down fire escape into park. They try to catch me. Make me fight."

"Whoa, calm down. Who is this? Where—"

"Wu Tran, Wu Tran. No calm down. You come quick. They catch me, make me fight."

"Tell me where you are."

Agent Dean then heard the unmistakable sound of a stun-gun, the phone bounce off the metal phone stand and a body hitting the ground. Then the phone went dead.

One of Bob's men spotted Tran heading to the phones at the convenience store. He called for backup and worked his way around to the side of the store closest to the phones. He then stepped around the corner and stunned Wu, then dragged him around the corner, cuffed and gagged him. When his partner drove up the man waved him to the side where they quickly placed Tran in the trunk and drove away. They didn't go far. A van was waiting at the rendezvous point where they transferred Mr. Tran into the van and he received an injection in his ass to keep him quiet for the long journey he was about to embark upon. Bob had a private jet waiting to transport their prized package. It would be Tran's last first class flight.

When Tran woke twelve hours later his first thought was of water. His head was fuzzy and he was beyond thirsty. He was on the floor and as his head cleared he realized he was in jail. Tran was relieved that the police had somehow rescued him from his abductors. Then he wondered why he was in a jail cell, in what must be protective custody, rather than a hospital. He slowly got to his feet and realized that he'd pissed his pants. He then made his way to the sink where water had never tasted so good.

After looking out the small window in the door to his cell and trying to raise the guards, Wu Tran turned his attention to his wet pants. He stripped down, washed himself and rinsed out his shorts and pants then hung them up on wall hooks to dry as he looked about the cell with a towel wrapped around his waist. Tran had no idea what time it was or where he was, but he was certainly getting hungry.

A short time later Tran heard the unmistakable sound of a food cart and trays being served. He was looking out the window in the door when a pretty lady appeared pushing a cart and another pretty lady opened the feeding slot in the door and handed in his tray. The little slot was closed and the ladies moved on before Tran could set down his tray and ask them questions. Tran ate his meal in quiet while he planned his next move. He figured he would have to give the FBI something more to get out of this predicament. He wasn't sure what it would be but he had plenty to choose from. He was looking at the enclosed computer screen mounted in the wall when it came on. Tran's heart almost stopped, because he knew that face on the screen. He instantly realized that he was not in jail. He was in deep shit.

The face said, "Good afternoon Mr. Tran. It is a pleasure to see you again. Nice of you to join us. You have been quite troublesome. Haven't you heard that saying: 'You can run but you can't hide?' Not for long anyway. After crossing as many people as you have and costing them such an absurd sum of money, surely you didn't expect to just walk away with no repercussions."

"What do you want from me," Tran demanded.

"It's rather simple really," said the face. "You are being given an opportunity to live. We call it 'Forced Attrition,' or retirement if you wish. All you have to do is win one fight. Of course, if you lose you'll be dead, so nothing will matter much at that point. You will be provided with a copy of the rules and your rights and responsibilities. Read them carefully. There is no room for error. Over the next few days I will be showing you videos of a winner receiving his prize. You will also be shown a video of what happens to the people who refuse to cooperate and fight. Remember this, if you win the fight you will no longer have to worry about reprisal. All will be forgiven. You will be able to move on with your life and put this ugly mess behind you."

"I can pay," Tran said.

"Mr. Tran, the few million you have stashed is nothing compared to the millions you have already cost us or the money we will make on the fight. Paying your way out of this is not an option. You are getting off easy as it is. In the old days, we would have slowly broken every bone in your body while you begged for your life and the lives of your family. Be thankful for your accommodations and start preparing yourself for the upcoming fight. You won't have long to wait."

When the screen went blank Wu Tran looked down at his feet as if he expected them to give him some answers. He could not believe his misfortune.

Chapter 11

Will walked into Doc's office, laid a folder on her desk and said, "We may have an interesting development in the informant kidnapping cases."

Will went on to explain how his contact in the New York missing persons department had called him with the details and faxed him the file. Wu Tran's women and the cook had returned to the apartment after being released by Bob's men to find the bodyguard dead and Mr. Tran missing. They immediately called 911 and reported everything to the responding officers.

Agent Dean had also called 911 to report the possible abduction of Wu Tran and to give them the phone number that had appeared on his caller ID.

All the facts fell together quickly. Agent Dean was getting in his car when he got the call back on the location of the phone Tran used. When he arrived on the scene the officers there informed him of the secondary location of the apartment where the bodyguard was dead and the chase apparently began.

The apartment was swarming with detectives from most every department from homicide to missing persons. When agent Dean walked in and introduced himself there was a moment of confusion until agent Dean explained why he was there. Then the pieces of the puzzle started coming together.

Another federal informant, a very high profile informant, had been kidnapped. Agent Dean purposely neglected to mention that Wu Tran had been in witness protection, but had slipped away just days after placement.

The number of missing informants was now up to nineteen. It was also now apparent that the people behind the abductions were willing to kill to keep them covered up and to accomplish the kidnappings. Those facts certainly didn't bode well for the kidnapped informants.

The new information provided by Will's contact in New York was disturbing but hopeful. The fact that Wu Tran was able to get away, albeit temporarily and place a call where he informed the FBI that someone was trying to catch him and make him fight left the possibility open that Tran and the others might still be alive. It made the investigation that much more urgent because a swift resolution might save some lives.

Doc and Will were hoping that the agents in New York would catch a break because they were running into dead ends. They decided to follow up on a few leads that were discovered in Kanesha Sims' boyfriend Derick's house. Maybe they would get lucky.

After lunch at a small Chinese place Doc favored, they started making the rounds interviewing the people Derick had been calling. They talked with Derick's mother and sister, leaving out the part that it was Will who shot Derick.

One of the people Derick had been calling was Silvestre Deveraux, who had a short rap sheet for drug possession. The address turned out to be an old mechanic shop with living quarters above it. The place was closed, but there were several vehicles parked in and around the place. Looking through the windows they could see that the lights were off and no activity. Will tried a door on the side of the building that opened to a stairway leading to a landing on the top floor. A strong chemical odor lingered in the entrance.

Doc and Will un-holstered their guns and slowly made their way to the top of the stairs. The chemical odor was much stronger and they could hear someone moving around inside. Will knocked on the door and purposely did not announce himself as a police officer. They heard what sounded like a metal pan hit the floor and an agitated male voice say: "Shit-fuck." Then the door was yanked open by a tall, skinny, scraggly looking white guy with four black teeth and a week old beard. The man's eyes were bugged out and his hair hadn't been washed that year. It was obvious that the man was on methamphetamine and had been up for several days. His eyes were glazed over and unfocused and he had a dirty paint respirator hanging around his neck. The chemical smell coming out the door was overwhelming and the room behind him was hazy with fumes.

The guy yelled, "W-who the h-hell are you?"

Will raised his gun and said, "Police! Put your hands on your head and get on your knees. Now!"

"Shit-fuck," was all the guy said as he complied. Then as an afterthought the man added, "D-don't shoot that gun in here, you'll b-blow us all to h-hell."

As Will cuffed him the guy's eyes rolled back in his head and he fell forward, passed out. He was snoring almost as soon as he hit the floor. Will pried the guy's wallet out of his back pocket and determined that the man was, in fact, Silvestre Deveraux. Will and Doc then each grabbed an arm, hoisted him up and dragged him down the stairs and out the door into the fresh air. As Doc watched Mr. Deveraux and called for backup Will did a fast walk through of the garage apartment to make sure no one else was in there. Then Will joined Doc outside where he told her that every room had chemical containers and laboratory equipment in them. There was money, guns and what appeared to be methamphetamine on the kitchen counters and table. They had inadvertently stumbled onto a working meth lab and caught the guy red handed with everything.

Other officers were showing up but they were all staying outside waiting on the Hazardous Waste Team to arrive. With the downstairs door open the chemical smell had reached the parking area.

Deveraux was asleep in the back of a patrol car and Doc and Will were busy talking to other investigators about how they discovered the lab when the Hazardous Waste Team got there. The three men and one woman team put on their cumbersome environmental suits, took their cameras and evidence bags and went up the stairs to start their search and gather evidence. It wasn't long before they were carrying out boxes and bags with red and yellow hazardous waste symbol on them and putting them in a trailer they'd brought for the task.

When Doc and Will's department supervisor arrived on the scene, after hearing all the facts, he congratulated them on a job well done. He then jokingly laughed and said that he was going to have to create a new department just for Will and Doc since they were getting into so many different areas of crime.

Things were moving along pretty smooth and quiet when all of the sudden one of the Hazardous Waste Team came crashing down the stairs and stumbled out the door pulling off his hood. He dropped to his knees, vomited on the parking lot and started coughing. Another team member came out behind her and pulled off his hood as he kneeled down beside his partner. He then yelled across the parking lot, "We need to get homicide down here. We've got a female body cut up and packed in a drum up there."

They all looked toward the police car where Deveraux was sleeping then started making calls. It went from a simple questioning about a kidnapping to a drug lab bust and a homicide all in less than an hour. It was a perfect definition of a cluster-fuck, which solidified their supervisor's comment that he needed to create a new department just for Will and Doc.

Will and Doc went back to the office to type up reports. When they arrived, they had a message to report to their commander. Before they started any paperwork, they trudged up the stairs to see their commander, Ted Lewis. Ted was a very large, imposing ex-marine who ran a tight ship. He was known to be a fair, no nonsense guy who wanted things done his way.

When they were ushered into his office by an equally no nonsense secretary, Commander Lewis stood and addressed "detective Holiday" and "agent Bracket," as they shook hands.

"Good news," Commander Lewis announced. "Agent Bracket has been cleared on both shootings."

Lewis reached into his desk drawer and removed two large plastic bags that contained Will's .9mm pistols that were held by Internal Affairs and gave them to Will.

"Thank you, commander," Will said with a smile.

"The other reason I summoned you both is to inform you that your main priority is now these missing informant cases. I'm delegating your case load to other teams, freeing you both to work on the informant cases, exclusively. I have received several calls from high-up and from the media asking questions about these cases. It is in our best interest to make them go away as fast as possible. You will be coordinating your efforts with FBI agent Cody Daniels here in LA, whom you already know, FBI agent Thomas Dean in New York and the Missing Persons Department in New York. I believe agent Bracket knows the agents there. Any problems? No. Any questions? No. Then get to work."

"Yes, sir," Doc and Will exclaimed together as they exited the office. In the elevator Doc said, "That went well."

"Better than I expected," Will replied. "I believe it is cause for a celebration. I thought we were in trouble. Maybe we could celebrate at my place tonight."

"Maybe," Doc said flirtatiously.

Back at his desk Will prepared his report on the Deveraux bust and updated the file on the missing informants before he checked his emails and sent his mother an email. Will had an email from agent Daniels, AKA Shithead, requesting an update on their progress. Will was determined not to do agent Daniels' job for him. Will also had an email from agent Dean in New York that included a copy of his report on the Wu Tran fiasco and a request for copies of the reports of the missing informants in LA. There was also an email from Will's contact in the New York Missing Persons Department and a copy of his report on Wu Tran. The most interesting email had just come in from deadserious@hotmail.com. The email simply read:

"Agent Bracket:

The informants are being held in Nevada. Exact location unknown. If they find out I contacted you I am seriously dead. Good luck."

There was no sign off name, just good luck. Will quickly sent an email to deadserious@hotmail.com asking for more information. While he waited for a reply Will printed a copy of the email and took it to Doc.

"This may be our break," Will said proudly.

Doc read the email, smiled and then said, "We need to know where this came from."

"I'm all over it like cream gravy on chicken fried steak," Will stated.

Doc laughed and asked, "Where did you hear that, some place in Oklahoma?"

"I thought it was a western saying, meaning that I have it covered," Will replied. Doc just laughed and smiled.

Will decided to email everyone on the case with the information to get them started on tracking the deadserious email from every direction. After he sent a letter outlining the situation, with a copy of the email, to Daniels, Dean and his person in the New York Missing Persons Department he called the computer techs there in the LAPD and asked them to pinpoint the origin of the email. He needed a location and fast.

There wasn't much more he could do other than wait on a response from this deadserious person. It was late in the day so Will returned the pistol he'd borrowed to Doc, with a polite thank you and asked her to a casual dinner.

When they left the department, they took Will's car. They were spending so much time together that driving two cars didn't make sense anymore. Will was hoping for another night of loving with Doc. What he didn't know was, Doc was hoping for the same thing.

During dinner, they decided to spend the night at Will's apartment because it was closer to the restaurant and to work. They were both falling into a comfortable routine and falling in love. Will was slowly forgetting his ex who did him wrong. Even though it hadn't been that long, it felt like old news. Will had more than enough to keep his mind off the past. He was thinking more about a future with Doc. Things were looking up.

Chapter 12

Christopher Dawsen, Chris to his friends, weighed 192 and stood an even six feet. He was built well but not in great shape. Dope use played a large role in his life and at twenty-eight he looked forty. His mother was an aging drug addicted prostitute and his father could have been anyone. Chris was pretty sure it wasn't the President. Chris was a typical product of his sorry environment. He'd been smoking, drinking and using drugs since he was in high school, which he didn't complete. He'd never had a real job. He lived off petty theft that had progressed into strong-arm robberies and selling drugs. He had been arrested so many times he'd lost count. By cooperating with the LAPD, he had avoided prosecution every time. It all caught up with him when this hot black chick, Kanesha, invited him to her apartment. Chris, being white, had never been with a gorgeous black woman so he jumped at the opportunity. Then he woke-up in a jail cell from hell faced with a fight or die situation. Life really sucked sometimes.

Just down the corridor in another cell, Jasen Krieg, also known as Boss Hog, was laying on his bunk all cried out. Jasen was only five feet ten, but he weighed 220, mostly fat. If there was an ounce of muscle under there some place it was well hidden by fat. He knew he was fucked. He didn't know anything about fighting. The only thing that made him want to fight was his fear of ending up on that autopsy table being electrocuted to death. Seeing the video of the man being tortured to death on that autopsy table had freaked Jasen out to the point that he would fight a bear to keep off that table.

Jasen had been convicted of having sex with a minor and child pornography. He was not a model citizen. He'd told on everyone involved and on some people in the illegal drug trade, which resulted in Jasen only spending a short time in prison. Everything he'd ever done had now caught up with him. The only thing that was keeping him sane and from killing himself was the prospect of winning the fight and receiving the reward. Jasen had watched the video of the other fight winner having sex with a beautiful young girl. The other things like the food, money and even his freedom were secondary to having sex with that young, tight girl. He was obsessed with sex to the point of dreaming about it and masturbating. Jasen didn't know that he was a sick pervert. But the people who captured him knew it and they were going to make sure that he paid for it with his life, but not until they had some fun with the self-proclaimed Boss Hog.

After the evening meal, the face came on the monitor in Chris and Jasen's cells and announced that the time had come for them to fight. The face once again advised them that failure to cooperate would result in a very slow and painful death. He further informed them that good showmanship would result in additional rewards of up to ten thousand dollars. Cowardice would not be tolerated. Plus, they had no other option. It was either fight or die on that scary damn autopsy table.

It wasn't long and the sound of the two big guards coming down the hall in full riot gear was loud and clear. They stopped at Jasen's cell door first, cuffed him through the bean-hole, opened the door and shackled his legs then escorted him back down the hallway past the dreadful autopsy table and up a flight of stairs to a waiting van. After Jasen (Boss Hogg) was secured in the back section of the van the two big guards went back for Chris.

Chris was scared but he didn't want to show it. He was trying to play tough guy, but was limited by the cuffs and leg restraints to simply being a smart ass. Because the guards were dressed exactly the same, all the way to identical face masks, Chris asked them if they were twins. That question did not generate a response. The only time the guards spoke was to issue commands. Chris told the guards that they might want to consider a diet because they were putting on some weight. Nothing Chris said got a rise out of the guards. Chris got very quiet when the guards walked him past the autopsy table. As the guards were putting him in the van, Chris informed them that after he won the fight he was coming back to kill them. The guards still didn't say anything, which was even more unnerving to Chris.

The drive to wherever they were going seemed like a long time to Chris and Jasen. Traveling in cuffs, leg irons and in a cage in the back of a dark van was so uncomfortable that it made the trip seem much longer. When they arrived at the warehouse the van pulled into the building and the large garage door was lowered behind them, sealing them off from the world beyond.

The two would-be fighters got another surprise when they were extracted from the van only to discover that any thought of escape would not be possible. Four more black-clad guards stood in a semicircle next to the van as each prisoner was removed from his cage. Each of the additional guards carried a 12 gauge pump shotgun. Jasen and Chris were escorted one at a time to their holding rooms.

Chris's room was done in neon green. He was instructed not to cause any trouble as the guards removed the chains. When the guards were backing out of the door a computer monitor instantly came on and the face appeared.

The face said, "Mr. Dawsen, from this point forward you will be known as Green. You need to disrobe and get into your matching fighting trunks and boots. I will be taking your picture in front of the American flag shortly. Be ready. You can help yourself to a soft-drink from the mini-fridge if you like, but be ready to fight in about four hours."

"And if I don't" asked Green.

"Mr. Dawsen, surely I don't need to go over this with you again. At the risk of repeating myself, at the first sign of trouble you will be stunned and whisked back to that cold steel table where you will be slowly electrocuted to death. I'll have another fighter here within the hour. And you sir, won't even make old news. Am I clear on that?"

"I'll fight," Chris said as he nodded his head in understanding.

Jasen, AKA Boss Hog, walked into a room done in bright yellow. No matter what he tried to think about he could not stop his uncontrollable shakes. He was shivering like a wet dog in a snow storm. But his fear of that table had overcome his fear of fighting. He was scared, sure. But he was going to fight to avoid that table. Jasen had been praying for his heart to stop and the way it was pounding he thought it surely would. It didn't though and he was too big a coward to try and kill himself.

The face appeared on the monitor and said, "I see you are struggling with your fears, Mr. Krieg. I hope you will not let them interfere with your ability to fight. Fear, when focused, can be a great stimulator. Use it to your benefit and advantage. Every soldier goes into war with fear, but he fights with courage and often wins the battle. The fight will commence in about four hours. Get dressed in the matching fighting trunks and boots I have provided. From this point on you will be known as Yellow. The color is incidental, of course. It has no reflection on your fear. I will be taking your picture in front of the American flag that I placed on the wall at the back of the room, as you can see. It would be best if you would try not to let your fear show in the picture or in the ring. Do you have any questions?"

"Will people be watching?"

"Oh, yes. There are many people here to watch in person and people will be watching and betting on the fights all over the world. This is a major event. This fight could make you famous. Win this fight and the possibilities are limitless. Show courage and you will be in a position to obtain anything your heart desires."

The face knew what Mr. Krieg needed to hear and he gave it to him. It was the fight that mattered, not Jasen Krieg. The face didn't give a damn about the so called "Boss Hog." He was nothing more than a bad joke who was about to pay for his sins. The face hoped that Jasen would quickly grow some balls and put on a good fight.

The face took pictures of the two fighters, now called Green and yellow, standing in fighting poses in front of the American flag and placed them on the scrambled computer link with a short bio of each fighter. The bios included their statistics and a brief outline of their crimes and who they ratted on to get themselves out of trouble. The informants' dilemma was a prime example of a man jumping out of a frying pan and into the fire. They were going to get burned no matter what. Big Eddie and his colleagues knew that this additional information would inflame the bettors. The information was relayed by the microwave towers to the super computer in New York where it was then broadcast in real time on the internet.

People all over the world would be reviewing the statistics, looking at the fighters and placing their bets. Most of the viewing locations were like party central, with their bars running full blast while they waited on the fight. In many locations, a limited menu was available where the viewers could enjoy a nice meal with wine or champagne while they waited for the fight to begin. By the time betting closed there was over thirty-two million in total bets placed.

Green was the first fighter to be escorted to the ring. He couldn't believe how many people were there to watch the fight. The cheering crowd pumped up Green's ego and had him ready to fight. Green was standing in the ring waving to the crowd and cameras, soaking up the enthusiasm, when Yellow came walking between the rows of chairs with his three armed guards close by his sides and rear.

A new round of applause and cheers erupted as Yellow came into view of the crowd. Yellow was momentarily mesmerized and his fear was forgotten as his thoughts were lost in the roar of the crowd. When Yellow paused to look around the guard behind him gently prodded him forward. The ropes were parted by an assistant and Yellow bent over and stepped through the ropes into the ring. When Yellow (Boss Hog) looked up and saw Green the fear rushed back in a wave that almost knocked him down. Yellow's sudden body language and the expression on his face exuded panic. He turned to flee but saw the guards there with their shotguns and stun-guns waiting for him. With no other acceptable alternative Yellow turned to face Green.

The announcer stepped to the center ring with a microphone and without delay started his spiel. "In this corner (pointing at Chris), weighing 192 pounds and standing six feet tall, from Los Angeles, California, we have Green," said the announcer.

Then he turned to the other corner and pointed at Jasen and said, "In this corner, weighing in at 220 and standing at five feet eleven inches, from Shreveport, Louisiana, we have Yellow."

The crowd went nuts again with whistles, catcalls and cheers. Before Green and Yellow had time to think, two assistants were helping them put on their shields and strapping on their knives. The knives clearly gave both fighters a renewed sense of confidence. The assistants told their charges to move to the center of the ring at the sound of the bell and to stay off the ropes.

Jasen, in his bright yellow trunks and boots, was hyperventilating and visibly sweating. His assistant told him to get out there and kill Green as fast as he could and not to stop until the job was done. Green was receiving similar instructions at the opposite corner of the ring, with the inclusion of "kill that fat fuck. He's a child molester."

When the bell rang both assistants yelled, "go-go-go," as Green and Yellow headed to center ring. Green could see the fear in Yellow's face and in his eyes. It gave Green a new sense of confidence. Yellow looked left and right and saw the guards with their shotguns ready. The fear was too much. Yellow bellowed a blood curdling scream and charged Green. Green started to hold his ground then side-stepped at the last moment, but it was too late. When Yellow ran into Green it knocked Green off balance, but not before he managed to inflict a shallow cut on Yellow's left shoulder. Yellow howled in pain, fear and frustration. He quickly turned and cut Green on the left shoulder before Green could right himself. The sight of blood issuing from both fighters had the crowed in a frenzy and both fighters freaked out.

Yellow was panting and yelling between breaths in a rhythm that sounded like a war chant. Green was caught by surprise. He hadn't seen this coming. Looking at Yellow, Green thought he would have to chase him down to stab him. He was wrong and this unexpected turn of events was shocking. The fat guy in yellow trunks was going crazy. He was frantic with fear and charging again. When Yellow crashed into Green the second time he went for Green's face with his knife. Yellow had left himself wide open for attack, but when Green saw the knife coming at his face he panicked and tried to duck under the knife as Yellow slammed into him, cutting a gash across Green's forehead and knocking him to the mat in the saw dust.

The blood came fast and was a copious flood into Green's eyes and all over his face and chest. Yellow fell on Green, pinning Green's knife hand to the mat as Yellow hacked and slashed at Green's face and neck. Yellow was screaming like a kamikaze pilot on a suicide run as he cried and gasped for breath. He sounded like an old record skipping on a bad spot.

When it was obvious that Green was dead, one of the assistants climbed in the ring and told Yellow to stop and lower the knife. The fight was clearly over. It took a few seconds for Yellow to register what was going on. He then stopped hacking and dropped his knife hand to the mat. The assistant moved in telling Yellow that he did good and removed the knife from his hand. A doctor came into the ring, gave Yellow a shot in his bleeding arm, as another assistant gave Yellow a drink of water.

After a temporary bandage was placed on Yellow's shoulder and the blood and sweat wiped from his face he was helped to his feet. The announcer proclaimed Yellow the winner and the crowd cheered his victory. Yellow (Jasen/Boss Hog), whatever he thought of himself, was in a daze as he was led from the ring. It all happened so fast it seemed unreal, like a bad dream. He didn't even remember the walk back to the room where he received another shot before he passed out and the doctor sewed up his shoulder. The fight hadn't lasted a full minute, but it was being replayed in slow motion for the viewers. A new added touch to keep the bettors feeling like they got their money's worth.

Later that evening when Jasen woke-up there was a beautiful blonde young girl looking down at him. She said, "Hello, sugar. You did good tonight."

Jasen smiled. He was feeling no pain because the IV drip was loaded with a pain killer. The girl wiped his face with a cool rag then helped him sit up. He was weak and a little shaky, but one look at the girl got him smiling and excited. She wasn't as young as he would have liked, but she was hot, with a body that rocked. She wheeled a table over and told him that he needed to eat because he would need his strength. Then she giggled like a school girl. The girl helped Jasen with his IV stand while he took a pee. Back at the table she poured him a glass of wine then sat down to eat with him. Before she started eating she reached over and picked up ten-thousand in hundreds, fanned them out and waived them for the camera. She handed the money to Jasen, informing him that he got a five-thousand dollar bonus for doing so well in the fight.

Jasen held the money up and waived it for the camera. He couldn't stop smiling. It took them close to an hour to finish the meal of steak, fried potatoes, corn, green beans and fresh baked rolls. When dinner was over the girl dramatically moved the cart away then slowly did a table dance to the music that was playing and stripped out of what little clothes she had on. She was scantily clad to begin with, so it didn't take long to shed her clothes.

She opened Jasen's robe so the camera could take it all in, then she took Jasen's hard cook in her mouth and worked it for the camera. After Jasen shot his wad into the air the girl climbed on him, being careful of the stitches in his shoulder and the IV line and slid his dick inside her before Jasen could lose his erection. The camera was positioned perfectly to get a clear shot of the girl going up and down on Jasen's dick. It was all well orchestrated and the show was fit for a porn queen. When Jasen came again she climbed off him, picked up her clothes and left the room.

The show was over, so the camera was turned off just before the doctor came into the room. The doctor was cheery when he asked Jasen how he was doing. He complimented Jasen on the fight. When the doctor pulled out the syringe filled with liquid Jasen didn't even ask what it was. The doctor told Jasen that it was an antibiotic and administered it into the IV port taped to the back of Jasen's hand. It only took about ten seconds before the high powered drug hit Jasen's heart and sent him into cardiac arrest. The shock of realization was mixed with the contorted pain etched on his face as he thrashed in a seizure clutching his chest. Of course, the other prisoners would never see that part of the reward. This poetic justice was appropriate for Boss Hog's misdeeds, but somehow seemed insufficient when considering the pain and suffering this boil on the ass of society had caused.

Chapter 13

Humboldt County Sheriff, Stanly A. Hall, had been sitting in his office in Winnemucca, Nevada all afternoon doing paperwork. It was one of the tedious, never-ending tasks that made him look forward to retirement. It had been an uneventful, easy day. He started with a pancake and sausage breakfast with his favorite thick maple syrup and a liberal amount of real butter. He knew it wasn't good for him, but good food was his only vice. He'd given up smoking, drinking and womanizing when he got married to the most wonderful woman he'd ever known. It was hard for him to believe that after ten years with her he was still happy and more in love every day. He knew he was a lucky man.

After breakfast, he'd escorted a prisoner to the courthouse for trial. He then took a short drive to a small home in the foot hills to serve a warrant on a drunk who had beaten his wife. After dropping the drunk off at the county jail, Sheriff Hall went to lunch where he enjoyed a quick burger and chocolate shake. It didn't take much to make him happy. A fair wind and a smooth day with few waves and good food were about all it took.

Just about the time Sheriff Hall was wishing he had another burger one of his deputies knocked on his door and poked his head into his office.

"Sir, I'm awful sorry to bother you, but we have a couple of young fellows in here that were hiking above the Summit Lake Indian Reservation and they believe they witnessed some suspicious activity. You might want to listen to what they have to say. It could be something."

The Sheriff got up and walked around his cheap metal desk and followed his deputy down the hall to an interview room.

As they both walked into the room the deputy told the two young men to explain what they saw to the sheriff.

The smaller of the two young men, who was about twenty, said, "Dude, we told you like three times. Two dudes in a white van dropped off two big bundles that looked like they might be bodies in the woods between High Rock Lake and the Summit Lake Indian Reservation."

The deputy said, "Okay, I know and I appreciate your cooperation with this. But why don't you start at the beginning and tell the sheriff what you told me. If it really is some bodies we need all the facts."

The bigger guy remained quiet while the little guy told the story, with only a few agreeing head shakes from the bigger guy. "We both took off work Friday so we could get an early jump on the weekend. We spent the night on Quinn River then went up to High Rock Lake Saturday morning. We messed around the lake and spent the night there. Sunday morning we were heading up to the Sheldon Wildlife Refuge when we saw some interesting hills and decided to take a hike. We were somewhere southwest of the Summit Lake Indian Reservation. We were sitting on a bluff overlooking a little valley having lunch when we saw a white van on the opposite side of the valley. It was about a half mile away. The van was out of place way out there and we both thought, 'Shit,' because it took away from the feeling of being alone in the middle of nowhere. Dude, all the sudden a van pulls up across the way, it was like, can we ever get away from civilization? Then the van pulls into the tree line and stops. Two guys get out and open the back doors, which happened to be facing our direction. Then they slid out a large bundle that was as big as a person and carried it into the trees. A few minutes later they came back and got another bundle and took it into the trees. They came back again and got what looked like shovels out of the van and went back into the trees. They were gone for like two hours then they came back and drove away. We don't know for sure if it was bodies they carried off into the trees but after we thought about it, we felt like it was best to come tell you about it. That's it. Here we are."

The Sheriff asked, "So you saw this about noon on Sunday. What took you so long to get here and report it? It's Monday afternoon."

"By the time we got back to the car it was late so we spent the night in the hills. It's a long way up there and we really didn't want to come down here and tell anyone, but we knew we had to, because it might be real important. So here we are," said the smaller guy.

"Did you manage to get a tag number?" asked the Sheriff.

"No, it was too far away."

The Sheriff asked, "How do I know that you two didn't dump a couple of bodies up there and are just trying to cover your asses?"

"Dude, we don't drive a white van. We drive a Toyota." Like that was all it took to explain things.

The bigger guy finally spoke up and said, "See, that is the reason we didn't want to come down here and tell you what we saw. You guys always think the wrong guy did it."

"I don't think you guys did anything and I appreciate you coming in to tell us what you saw. The problem I see now is, the only way we can find the exact location is for you two to show us. Can you do that?"

"Yeah, dude, but we need you to call our bosses and explain why we didn't come into work this afternoon," said the bigger guy.

The Sheriff took one deputy and the two young men in his Chevy Blazer with two additional deputies following in a county car. Driving ninety miles an hour it took less than two hours to get to the location. They found the old dirt path that the van had taken and followed it to where the boys said the van stopped. The sheriff and deputy got out of the Blazer to have a look while the witnesses waited in the back seat.

The van's tire tracks were distinct in the dry, sandy soil. It was obvious where the van pulled into the tree line then backed out and left the way it came. They were careful to keep their distance from the tracks just in case the area turned out to be a crime scene. They could see two sets of hiking boot prints leading from where the van had parked heading deeper into the tall pine trees. The foot prints led them to an area that had been recently dug in and mounded like graves. The odd thing was, there weren't just two mounds, there were six in all. Four that looked older then the two fresh mounds. The sheriff knew they had something, so he and the deputy walked back to the truck and retrieved two rolls of crime scene tape and started making a boundary to protect any possible evidence. The deputy then took a shovel and carefully dug up one end of the newest and closest mound. Sheriff Hall stood outside the crime scene tape while his deputy slowly moved the loose dirt to expose what was buried. The grave was shallow. Not more than a foot below ground level the deputy hit something that was wrapped in canvas. It looked like a piece of an old Army tent.

Sheriff Hall handed the deputy a pocket knife and told him to cut the canvas to see what they had. The deputy sliced open the canvas exposing a pair of bare human feet.

"We've got a body Sheriff!"

The deputy backed away and they both walked back to the Blazer. It was going to be a long night. It didn't take long to make the calls necessary to get the troupes rolling. The coroner would be coming from Winnemucca, but the Crime Scene Unit (CSU) was stationed in Reno. It would be dark by the time everyone got there, so the Sheriff called his office and got generators, lights and food coming. He sent two of his deputies back to town with the witnesses who would be placed in a motel until the homicide detectives questioned them. Then he sat back to wait, wishing he had another burger. He was an avid hunter and had run many crime scenes out in the middle of nowhere, so he kept a few candy bars and bottles of water stashed in his truck for just this type of situation.

By dusk his deputy arrived with the generators and lights. The food was cold and the coffee tepid, but what could you expect after a two hour drive. The Sheriff showed his deputy where to place the lights and the deputy got busy stringing extension cords. A short time later the coroner came driving up the dirt trail with an assistant driving another wagon close behind. The Sheriff and coroner took a walk around the perimeter of the crime scene. It didn't take long and they both agreed they had two fresh graves and what looked like four older ones.

The Crime Scene Unit arrived well after dark in a caravan of cars and trucks. The special agent in charge (SAC), Eugine Dawlrimple, did a preliminary assessment and established a grid. Two CSU men started taking pictures and making plaster casts of the tire imprints left by the van and the boot prints. Two more CSU team members started slowly excavating the first body, sifting through the dirt looking for evidence. Still others were establishing a command post in a tent that was attached to the side of a box van.

Once the body was removed from the hole the coroner finished cutting open the canvas cocoon and determined it contained a body of a white male approximately 25 years of age with multiple stab wounds, cuts and contusions to the face, neck and upper body. The cause of death was likely exsanguination, but a pathologist would make that call after an autopsy.

One of the CSU technicians fingerprinted the deceased with a laser scanner and sent the digital prints to the national fingerprint database. After he narrowed down the search with the known information, white male between the age of 20 to 30, hair color, approximate height and weight, they had a match in less than ten minutes. The man now in a body bag was one Christopher Dawsen from Los Angeles, California. He was flagged as a high priority missing person. The contact person was agent William Bracket with the LAPD.

Even though it was after midnight the CSU tech pulled out his phone and called Bracket's private number. Will had just dropped off to sleep after he and Doc had made love for the fourth time. Will grabbed the phone from the nightstand where he kept it and said, "Hello." When the CSU tech identified himself and explained the call Will came fully awake. The CSU tech told him that they had one body identified as Christopher Dawsen and they were in the process of excavating five more graves. Will wrote down the contact information and location and said that he and his partner were on the way.

As much as he didn't like agent Daniels it was the perfect time to wake him up and utilize his FBI resources. They needed one of those fancy FBI jets to fly them to Reno and a chopper to take them from Reno to High Rock Lake. Also, Will wanted to gloat and rub in the fact that it was his idea to flag the missing persons in the national fingerprint database. It was a feature many officers and agents didn't know the system offered.

Agent Daniels didn't appreciate the early morning call, but Will's excitement and enthusiasm quickly got Daniels out of bed and on the phone arranging for the jet and chopper. They knew this was probably the break they had been waiting for. Tracing the origin of the email that Will received was starting to look like a dead end. Whoever sent the email certainly knew how to cover his tracks. Even if they determined where the email originated it would likely be an inane location like an internet café with no way to verify the sender. The email had pointed them to Nevada. Now they had at least one body, possibly six, in Nevada. It was clear to Will that Nevada would be the hot zone for the missing informants.

An hour and a half after Will received the call from Nevada, Will, Doc and agent Daniels, along with three other FBI gurus were climbing aboard a sleek twelve passenger Lear jet. As they were boarding agent Daniels unexpectedly shook Will's hand and told him, "Great job." Will appreciated the accolade, but it didn't seem to mean as much coming from agent "Shithead."

When Doc came on the plane, agent Daniels said, "Hell Doc. You look positively radiant."

With raised eyebrows and the look and sound of indignation, Doc said, "Can it Daniels."

The others may not have understood her attitude, but Doc felt that her and Daniels history warranted and even justified her anger. Doc wanted it damn clear that Daniels better not ask her to bring him his coffee.

During the short flight to Reno Will received another call on his cell phone from the CSU tech informing him that the second body, who was also flagged for notification, was identified as Jasen Krieg, cause of death unknown, at that time.

That news was a good indication that the other four graves probably contained more missing informants. Will relayed that information to the CSU tech and told him how to access the file on the missing nineteen informants. The number "nineteen" shocked the CSU guy. Will had to repeat it twice. Will asked the man to try and keep a lid on that fact as long as possible.

The fact that they probably had six informants in the ground, although disturbing, started another round of discussion and gave them hope that they would find clues that would lead them to the remaining thirteen informants while they were still above ground. They all knew a shit storm was coming when the media discovered that six informants were found buried together in a remote spot in Nevada. It wouldn't take the media long, once they started digging, to unearth the actual number of missing informants. People would want to know why the federal government could not protect their informants. Confidence in the justice system would waver and dwindle fast. It would be big news that would come with a lot of heat. Will and Doc were the only two on the jet that didn't care about making a good impression. All they wanted to do was find the missing informants and solve the case. Saving lives was more important to them than pats on the back.

A helicopter was waiting to fly Will, Doc and Daniels to Winnemucca and then on to the site. The other three agents were driving from Reno because they were going to be there gathering evidence and writing reports during the whole event.

When they landed in Winnemucca an SUV was waiting for them. They drove to the Sheriff's office to get an update on the progress. After meeting with a deputy and learning that Sheriff Hall was still on location they went to a recommended diner for breakfast. It was just getting daylight when they got back in the helicopter.

When they arrived on site they were met by Sheriff Hall who was unshaved and looked a little ragged. He'd slept a few hours in his truck. He was very thankful that the CSU team had a coffee maker in their van and glad to see that the chopper had also delivered four large boxes of assorted doughnuts.

After introductions all around and thanks for the doughnuts, the Sheriff informed the new arrivals that they had two more bodies out of the ground. All he knew at that point was they were adult males who had been in the ground for a couple of weeks. The bodies were in various stages of decomposing. The worms and maggots had done a pretty rough job on them, but they worked on the softer tissue first. They would probably be able to get their prints, or at least they had a narrow group to look at first if the task required dental records. One of the crime scene guys had carefully removed the tips of one finger on the right hands of each of the bodies and had it soaking in a special solution used to soften and clean the skin. He was in the process of placing each print between slides so he could scan them. Will explained to Sheriff Hall that there was a strong possibility that the other four bodies would also be from the pool of nineteen missing informants.

"At least we have a good idea who we are looking for," said Hall.

Later that afternoon the four partially decomposed bodies were identified as Michael Tyron Davis from Los Angeles (who died of electrocution on the autopsy table); Maliek Sharon Taylor from New York (known as Red in the first fight); Exavier Leon Washington from Los Angeles (known as Blue in the first fight); and Alphonso Deon Lere from New York (who hung himself in his cell). All were part of the group of missing informants.

The one point that was extremely clear and they all agreed upon was, that if they didn't solve the puzzle quickly they were going to have a lot of dead informants on their hands.

Chapter 14

In the back of a restaurant belonging to one of the "partners," was an exquisitely done private dining area that was primarily used for corporate events. Some of the largest and most prestigious companies and firms in Los Angeles frequently utilized the dining room because of its wealthy atmosphere, outstanding service, superb cuisine and extensive wine list. It was one of the few places that not only allowed smoking in the private dining area, but also carried a wide variety of the finest cigars available in the world. The owner took great pride in his wine and cigar list.

Today the original ten "partners" were joined together enjoying a fine meal of rare roast beef. One cute little waitress was making her way around the table slicing liberal amounts of meat from a tender rump roast as other waitresses followed the entrée with a variety of assorted dishes. It was a feast fit for royalty.

Even though Big Eddie was pretty much the brains behind the whole operation he liked to have Angela do the speaking. Of course, he always made Angela think it was her idea. She was so enthusiastic, energetic and sexy. She was fun to watch and listen to as she stood there making her presentation. That and she could stand and take control of the audience, while Eddie was stuck in that damn wheelchair. He could stand and walk some but it was very uncomfortable. The wheelchair was arduous and it drove Eddie that much harder to be a successful business man. But he still didn't like giving speeches when he was the object of everyone's curiosity and stares. It made him feel uncomfortable and pissed him off. It made him want to pull out a gun and shoot everyone in the room. That would wipe those fake smiles from their faces. It was less stressful and more fun to watch Angela.

Eddie was at one end of the banquet table with Angela at the other, with eight partners, four on each side of the table. It was hard to tell who was at the head of the table, Big Eddie or Angela. At the conclusion of the meal, Angela stood and made a toast to their success and a profitable future. Then she got down to business. Eddie sat back and enjoyed the show.

"Ladies and gentlemen – friends," Angela began, "for security purposes this will be our last meeting for a while. Your earnings will be deposited in your accounts, as usual, but with the recent media coverage about the missing informants and our overseas expansion in progress we should exercise caution. It would be a great time to take vacations and spend some quality family time. The wheels of progress are in motion and they will roll right along with minimal supervision. Edward and I will see to any little hiccups we may experience. Thank you for coming and I hope you enjoyed the meal. Edward?"

"I just wanted to add that the national media coverage the missing informants are currently receiving will fade over time. The illegal drug trade generates its share of coverage and that certainly hasn't stopped progress. What it has done is make drug dealers more cautious and inventive. The same thing will happen with the gladiator events. We will continue to distance ourselves from the fray, while we erect new and better security systems to fit any situation that may occur. The one immediate benefit is the impact it will have on future informants. Once all the facts come out about the six dead informants they found in Nevada, the public will know that informants are being kidnapped and forced to fight each other to the death. That, in turn, will make a lot of people think twice before becoming an informant. The long terms results will be far less lose in other areas. My point is, the media frenzy, although a little sooner than expected, is actually good. Another point I would like to make is, don't panic when the media discovers that informants are missing worldwide not just in the United States. It is going global. That will take the focus off the United States. The government will think it is terrorist related. Soon the whole world will know that informants are not safe anywhere in the world," concluded Big Eddie.

The quiet in the room didn't last long. Angela stood, clapping her hands and the other "partners" followed suit. They all shook hands, exchanged some pleasantries and excused themselves. Angela hugged Big Eddie and planted a kiss on his cheek before she bade fare well and left to join Kera in a waiting limousine.

Big Eddie's only real concern was internal security. Only a small handful of people actually knew of his and Angela's involvement. Those people didn't know about the other partners, so Eddie and Angela were the only ones in vulnerable positions. Eddie was confident in his immediate subordinates, except for one. Ray the computer genius was too close and knew too much. Eddie had been very impressed by Ray's computer abilities long before he decided to have Ray create the fight and betting programs. Now Ray's basic program design was being used by all the other branches in other countries. Ray's knowledge was limited to the computer programming just in the United States. Ray didn't know any of the underlying facts like who was doing the kidnapping or where the informants were being kept. Even though Ray had setup the betting program he didn't know where the money went from there or to whom. But Ray was still too close.

Money is a powerful aphrodisiac that can assuage not only man's sexual appetite, but his guilty conscious, as well. In Ray's case it was becoming obvious, because of Ray's excessive weight loss. It was very noticeable on Ray's already skinny body, which certainly didn't look good and by his increasing paranoia, that young Ray was falling apart under the stress. Big Eddie had grown to like the kid, whose father had been a close friend of Eddie's until the silent killer called cancer had painfully taken his life. Eddie felt like he owed Ray's dad and he was hoping that Ray would follow in his father's footsteps. Things weren't looking good for Ray. Few people could handle the kind of pressure brought on by knowing they are involved in the deaths of others and knowing that knowledge could result in their own death. It was a lot to expect from anyone. Eddie decided to give Ray a vacation. When Ray arrived at Big Eddie's office he was looking terrible and his fear was evident. He looked gaunt, shaky and nervous.

Big Eddie thanked Ray for coming and got right to the point. "I know this whole ugly business has been very disturbing for you. I won't go into a long explanation of why it is all necessary, but I want you to know that it is not only necessary but essential to running and carrying on my business. We live in a cruel world. There are a lot of different kinds of cruel. The people you have seen in those fights are cruel and bad people. Trust me, they deserve everything they get. Each and every one of them are nothing more than terrorists who are trying to undermine everything we believe in. So, I don't want you to feel sorry for them or care what happens to them. I want two things from you. I want you to forget about the fights and keep your mouth shut. You can do that. No more worries. None of this was you're doing, so just forget about it, okay? I'm sending you on vacation with that good looking gal that's been keeping you company. I know you like her. You're going to spend a week on my yacht. Then it's off to Spain, Italy, Rome and France. I like the French, they are peaceful people. Forget about computers and bad things and just have fun. Have sex with that beautiful girl all over the world. It will be good for you. Start eating and put on some weight. If you like one of those countries you can stay and make it your home. Or, you can come back here and work for me, all perfectly legal, if that's what you want. You know your dad and I were close. God rest his soul. He would want me to look out for you. Frankly, he would probably be upset if he knew I involved you in any of this. But if you will remember, I told you it was illegal when I offered you all that money to write the program. At that time you didn't have a problem with it. So now, I want you to go have a good time and forget about this. If anyone ever asks you about it you tell them you don't know what they are talking about. Understand?"

"Yes, sir," replied Ray with a forced smile.

"Good! Now get out of here. See my secretary, she has your itinerary. Have a nice time Raymond."

Raymond Charleston, III was scared shitless. There was no doubt in his mind that Big Eddie was having him watched at every turn. It was like Big Eddie wanted him to know that the whole world was his prison and Ray was on a short leash. The questions in Ray's mind were driving him crazy. Did Big Eddie know that he'd sent an email to that cop that was working the missing persons cases? Was Big Eddie sending him on vacation to make him disappear? Ray wanted to run but he knew there were people watching him and he didn't know where to go or how he would get there if he had a place to go. All he could do was play along and hope for the best until he figured a way out.

Big Eddie had things set-up where the phones and computers on his yacht and every place Ray would be staying, were monitored. If Ray started acting too crazy the girl with him would report it to Bob. Eddie hoped that, in time, Ray would get over his paranoia and fear. Hopefully, the kid would get his shit together before Eddie got tired of his crap and put a permanent end to it, which would be the far easier thing to do.

With Ray safely out of the way Big Eddie turned to more pressing matters. He had two tons of cocaine coming in from Columbia, a ton of heroin coming in from Afghanistan and a ton of hashish on the way from Turkey. All of which had to be warehoused and distributed under the watchful eyes of a rat that was lurking in the wood pile. Eddie had narrowed it down to two possibilities and the day of truth had come. Eddie had secretly rerouted the actual shipments to secure locations in other harbors. Each of the two possible informants were given false information about the shipments.

Each believed that certain ships would be arriving with the loads and each were assigned a different warehouse for storage of the shipping containers. Neither was aware that their containers actually held legitimate merchandise. It was a ruse to flush out the informant. Eddie had the ships, warehouses and men being watched. Both ships were just coming into port and scheduled to unload that afternoon. Eddie had paid his man in the port authority not to inspect the containers in question, as usual and they should be in the warehouses by late afternoon.

Big Eddie received a call from his man Bob while he was having dinner. A federal drug task force had gathered in an empty warehouse on the dock. It was obvious they were about to execute a strike, but to which warehouse was not yet clear. Eddie told Bob to move on their plan the moment the task force entered one of the warehouses.Bob had teams watching and ready. It wasn't long before four new black SUVs came rolling out of the old warehouse with three black clad agents standing on the running boards on both sides of all four trucks. When they arrived at the target warehouse they blew the side door and entered in full assault formation.

As the task force agents were going in the warehouse, Eddie had his own assault team raiding the home of Harald Butkus, the rat. The two FBI agents who were babysitting Butkus were taken out before they could get off a shot, or even get their guns unholstered. Butkus was in the van and moving in less than two minutes. For years Butkus had acted like a tough guy, but all it did was show people how much of an asshole he was. He did a good job of keeping people in line, but he had no friends. The few people who tolerated him called him Harry behind his back. They all thought it was rather funny, Harry Butkus. In his day Butkus was a dangerous man. But for some reason he broke weak and started cooperating with the feds. This was not going to be a good day for Harry Butkus. First, Big Eddie needed to know what Butkus had told the authorities. Second, old Harry was going to be shipped off to a little prison where he would be forced to await the fight of his life. Bob would see to the interrogation personally then report back to Eddie.

Snatching Butkus without losing a shipment and before he had a chance to testify before the grand jury wasn't just dumb luck. It was part of a risk management program designed by young Raymond that included GPS tracking, phone taps and surveillance on key personnel. Those key people were expected to track and monitor their subordinates. It was somewhat costly, but not near as costly as losing a ton of heroin, or a load of ten thousand machine guns headed for Ireland to the IRA, or to the PLO in the middle east.

By morning Bob had all the information he needed from Butkus, including the names of the other lower level informants involved and Mr. Butkus was on his way to the secret prison in Nevada to await his fate. To avoid undue pain and suffering Butkus had simply told Bob everything. He knew he was a dead man the minute Bob's men killed the two FBI agents and grabbed him. There was no point in refusing to cooperate and getting tortured before they killed him, so Butkus just told Bob what he wanted to know. Butkus thought he was holding on to his dignity by not begging for his life, when in all actuality he lost any aspect of dignity when he agreed to cooperate with the government.

When a person knowingly engages in criminal activity, being a man requires that person to take responsibility for his own actions. Butkus, if he ever knew, had forgotten that fact. He had also forgotten his childhood Bible teachings where in John 15:13, it states: "Greater love hath no man than this, that a man lay down his life for his friends." Butkus was far too big a coward to lay down his life for anyone and he was too selfish to sacrifice his freedom for his friends who had stuck by him for years and made him rich. He was about to learn that a prison sentence would be much better than a death sentence based on his betrayal.

When Butkus woke he was in a jail cell alone, he didn't think much about it until the face came on the computer screen and explained his dire situation. Even then it didn't really sink in until the face showed him the videos of the electrocution, two fights and the rewards. Oddly, Butkus thought it was rather funny that he still had a chance to come out of his predicament alive. He had felt bad ever since he agreed to cooperate with the government. Now was his chance to make things right.

Chapter 15

It didn't take long for Big Eddie's predictions to come to fruition. Within days the media attention in the United States, which was largely focused on, "How could our government let this happen?" spawned many wild hypothetical responses. Law enforcement agencies around the world started contacting Interpol, the CIA and FBI with reports of dozens of missing informants. A global task force was formed that included agents from just about every agency with initials.

Because officer William Bracket of the LAPD Missing Persons Department initially discovered the missing informants and was the only person to be contacted by email by someone who obviously had inside information, Will was included in the task force. When agent Daniels told Will that they all decided to include him in the federal task force, Will's response was that Daniels should be thankful that Will decided to include him. It could have turned into a pissing contest but Will turned his back on agent Daniels and told the CIA's SAC that he would participate in the task force on the condition that his partner, Gloria Holiday (Doc), be included, as well. The Special Agent in Charge agreed with a smile and handshake. FBI agent Daniels didn't like it and that made Will that much happier. Will was certain that there would be some traveling involved and he didn't want to be away from Doc. He knew he could trust Doc in a tight spot and it would be a lot more fun having Doc there to share a bed with.

Agent Daniels had never been around someone that actually considered other people and not simply their own personal career advancements. Daniels was convinced that Will had some underlying motive and Daniels intended to keep an eye on Will and get to the bottom of it.

With the email pointing to Nevada and the six dead informants being discovered in Nevada, the FBI and CIA decided to set-up a field office at the FBI headquarters in Reno. The members of the task force flew in from Washington, D.C., New York, Los Angeles and other venues for the initial briefing. During the meeting, the SAC was assigning teams to different aspects of the investigation breaking up the grunt work. When the SAC came to Will and assigned him and Doc the job of compiling a list of known local criminals Will didn't object. He knew he could print out a list of local criminals in about ten minutes then he and Doc could move on to his own investigative work.

After the briefing Doc asked Will why he was smiling. She had assumed Will would be mad with the menial assignment. Will held one of his fingers to his lips in that all too well known "shhs" fashion and beckoned Doc to follow. He quietly said, "We've got them right where we want them," and smiled. They went to their rental car, drove to the sheriff's office, showed the sweet little gal at the desk their badges and asked for a printout of all the known local criminals. In less than five minutes the young lady returned with a four page list of the local bad guys that included last known addresses. At the end of the day Will would fax or email a copy of the list to the SAC.

"Now what are we going to do?" asked Doc.

"Haven't you watched Rush Hour, II?"

Doc shook her head Yes, but it was clear she didn't understand what Will was getting at.

"Remember the part where Chris Tucker says his theory of investigation is to 'follow the rich white man?' That's what we're going to do. These kidnappings are about some serious money. Money being lost, money being made, or both. If it was simply vengeance we would be finding dead informants laying all over the place. So I think they are picking informants because they are the cause of losing money and they are kidnapping them, rather than just killing them, in order to make money. We find out who lost money and who is making money and we find the bad guys. Yesterday the FBI in Los Angeles lost another informant. Our friend agent Daniels just happened to have neglected to mention that fact at today's meeting. That tells me that agent Daniels is being somewhat less than honest with us and that includes his FBI and CIA cohorts. We are not going to get much assistance from that group."

"That makes Daniels a bastard and you a shit for not telling me sooner," said Doc.

"Yes, but the difference is, I always intended to include you, Daniels didn't. I was waiting on Daniels to tell us, but since he didn't, I figured that he just didn't want us to know. Now why would he do that? Could it be because he doesn't trust us or because two FBI agents were killed during the kidnapping? Two agents that were assigned to protect the informant while the FBI and DEA conducted a raid on a dock side warehouse looking for a suspected shipment of heroin."

"How the hell did you find out all this?" Doc asked.

"That, sweet lips is the interesting part. I had to find out long distance from my old friend at the NYPD who found out from his friend in the New York FBI office. The good part is, I did a quick check on the informant, Harald Butkus, if you can believe it and found out that he worked for Sarcosie International.

Guess who owns the freighter, the freight containers and the warehouse that was raided by the FBI and DEA?"

"First, I can't believe you called me 'sweet lips' and if I had to guess I would say Sarcosie International," said Doc with a smile.

"You do have sweet lips and you win the kewpie doll."

"I don't want an ugly, fat, little, naked, pink haired doll, I want sex. Sex is a lot better prize. So take me back to the motel and do me," commanded Doc.

On the way back to the motel Will told Doc that he was certain that the raid on the warehouse had to be part of an elaborate set-up to flush out Butkus. When they arrived at the motel they all but ran to their room. Shoes bounced off the walls, guns dropped to the floor and clothes were slung across the room. The first time around was so hot, hard and frantic that Will and Doc fucked right off the bed, on to the floor without missing a stroke. When they came together they both collapsed for a moment before Doc got on her knees with her upper body on the bed using both hands to spread her cheeks apart as Will entered her from behind. Doing Doc from behind was one of the greatest pleasures Will had ever known. It was pure ecstasy. Will started slow with long deep strokes until Doc said "Fuck me," then Will took off like a man possessed. When they came the second time they were sweating and breathing so hard that all they could do was gasp for air as they crawled onto the bed and flopped down next to each other.

When Doc could finally speak she said, "That's the kind of prize I want every time."

Will said, "I don't know who was the winner, me or you, but I feel like I won. That was the best pre-lunch lovin' I've ever had and I'm not sure I have the strength to go eat, but I sure worked up an appetite. I never thought I could enjoy sex that much and I didn't know it could make me so hungry. Let's eat."

Doc just smiled, thinking how lucky she was to have Will by her side and didn't say anything as they showered and dressed. Staying in the room and ordering out pizza wasn't going to work because they couldn't keep their hands off each other so they decided to go out. They had seen a pizzeria that had an outdoor picnic area with romantic umbrellas over each table. A four foot wall with flowers growing on top separated the picnic area from the street and cars driving by and the music almost drowned out the noise. Not bad for being in the middle of a city like Reno and the supreme pizza was the best ever. Thick with meat, cheese, onion and bell pepper.

After lunch Will checked his emails while Doc did a background search on Sarcosie International.

"Okay," announced Doc, "Sarcosie International is owned by Antonio Sarcosie. The name sounds a little mobish. He founded the company about fifty years ago and still owns twenty-eight percent of the public stock and is acting president of the very profitable company. The company is primarily into shipping and storage of wholesale goods from around the world. They have warehouses in just about every major port in the world and container ships on the move at all times. Over the years, Mr. Sarcosie's company has been the subject of several State and federal investigations but has always come out clean. He has no criminal record and looks to be a model tax paying citizen.

"My question is," said Will, "if the company is only into shipping and storage why did it buy a container full of hand-made wool blankets in Afghanistan and then ship them to the United States? The company doesn't own any retail blanket stores. The whole thing stinks of a set-up."

Will got back on his computer and Doc started making calls. When they finally concluded their inquiries they had determined that the authorization to purchase, ship and store the blankets was signed by A. Sarcosie.

After a brief discussion, Will picked-up the phone and called Sarcosie International. He identified himself as a police officer, said it was important and asked to speak with Mr. Sarcosie. He was placed on hold and a moment later a pleasant female voice came on the line.

"I'm sorry, but Mr. Sarcosie is in a meeting. I'm his daughter, is there something I can help you with?"

"I hope so. I'm looking at a shipping invoice for a container load of wool blankets from Afghanistan. The purchase order and invoice indicate that they were authorized by A. Sarcosie. I'm wondering why Mr. Sarcosie bought a shipment of blankets and where they were going."

"I can answer that. The A stands for Angela. I authorized the purchase and shipment of the blankets. It is part of a good will program to help promote trade with Afghanistan and stimulate their economy," Angela Sarcosie stated.

"But, correct me if I'm wrong, Sarcosie International doesn't have any retail stores," said Will.

"That is correct. The blankets are designated as tax deductible contributions. They will all be given to local homeless shelters and in turn be given to the homeless. We are always doing our part to help and looking for ways to better America," exclaimed Angela. "Is there anything else I can help you with?"

"No. That will be it, for now. I appreciate your help and cooperation."

"Always glad to help the boys in blue. Have a nice day."

As Will recited the conversation to Doc they both felt it was a little too perfect. They decided to take a closer look at Angela and the Sarcosie holdings. There had to be something to tie them to Nevada. At the conclusion of their research it was clear that Sarcosie International owned huge warehouses in most every State. Two of those warehouses were in Nevada, one in Reno, and the other in Las Vegas. A closer inspection of Angela Sarcosie revealed no criminal record, but there was an unusual influx of money coming in to her personal account on a regular basis. Of course, that alone was certainly not illegal. The bank only showed the deposits, not where the money came from. Her taxes were in order, but the additional income was substantially more than she earned at her father's company. It warranted a deeper look. Will decided to change his theory to "Follow the rich white girl," and to shake a few trees. The first stop would be the Reno warehouse.

Even living in New York and now Los Angeles, Will had never seen a warehouse so large. It took up a huge chunk of desert. Just the parking area for the trucks and trailers was a quarter of a mile long and at least that wide. There were trucks loading and unloading at sixteen docks. Forklifts were going in and out of the warehouse at a dizzying rate. One of the first things Will and Doc noticed was five white cargo vans parked beside the warehouse that matched the description of the van that dropped off the bodies. As they walked to the front office, which looked tiny attached to the massive warehouse, Will paused next to one of the vans and used his cell phone to take a close-up picture of its tire tread. All the vans were new and had the same brand and style of tires. Will just wanted to know if the tread matched the tread prints left at the scene where the bodies were buried.

The lobby area was spacious and cool. The horseshoe shaped receptionist desk looked like a command center for the Starship Enterprise. Will identified himself as a police officer and asked to speak to whoever was in charge. The receptionist was sweet and professional. In a few moments an older man in a nice suit appeared and introduced himself as Keith Fuller, head hancho of the Sarcosie Reno branch.

After the introductions and handshakes, Fuller asked, "What can I do for you?"

"We would like to ask you a few questions," Doc said, taking the lead. "Is there some place we can talk?"

"Sure, let's go to my office. Would you like something to drink? Coffee, soda?"

Will and Doc said "No thank you," and followed Mr. Fuller down a hallway to a large office. The office was decorated with pictures and models of ships and trucks. The atmosphere produced a nice effect for an office of a shipping and storage company.

Will and Doc had an agreement that if the interviewee was a man Doc would take the lead and if it was a woman Will would take the lead. People tended to open-up and talk freer to the opposite sex. The practice had been working good so far.

"We won't take much of your time," Doc started. "I'm sure you've seen on the news about the six bodies that were discovered up State. We are interviewing everyone that owns a van like the one spotted at the scene. How many of those white vans do you have?"

"We have ten, but surely you don't think we had anything to do with that." Fuller made it a statement, not a question.

"Mr. Fuller, this visit is routine leg work. It's process of elimination. There are agents inquiring about white vans all over the State. I'm sure you have logs and records of who checked out the vans, where they went, complete with odometer readings. For now, all we need is the records on those vans for the last thirty days."

"Okay," Fuller said. "That's easy. I'll have my secretary get that information for you right now." Mr. Fuller picked up the phone and placed the order for the records, then hung up the phone with a smile.

While Fuller was still smiling, Doc asked, "How well do you know Angela Sarcosie?"

The smile instantly vanished from Fuller's face. He recovered quickly and stated, "I've known Angela most of her life."

"When was the last time you saw her?"

"Just a few days ago. We had a company meeting and little party."

"What date was that?" asked Doc.

"That was the 26th," answered Fuller.

"Was her father with her?"

"No, Angela travels with Kera, her secretary," replied Fuller.

At that moment Fuller's secretary knocked on the door and entered the room holding a computer disk in a clear plastic case. She gave the case to Fuller and left the room.

"Here's the information you requested. If there is nothing else, I need to prepare for a teleconference. Let me know if there is anything else I can do for you," said Fuller.

"One last thing," Will interjected, "we need the names of the people who attended the meeting and party on the 26th."

Fuller was visibly upset, but he held his cool. "That will take some time. I'll have my secretary put it together for you and you can pick it up tomorrow," Fuller said as he stood. He was wishing he hadn't come into the office.

Will handed Fuller a business card and requested that the list of names be emailed to his email address on the card, then Will and Doc left.

As soon as his office door closed Fuller picked up the phone. He was pissed. When the phone was picked up on the other end Fuller instructed his man, Tony, to follow the two cops that just left, because he wanted to know every place they went and who they talked to.

As Will and Doc drove out of the warehouse parking lot they noticed that many of the semitrailers had Thompson's Trucking, Inc., on the side, with Reno, Nevada in smaller print below the name. Will believed in following the signs. He pulled out his phone and called information for Thompson's Trucking. After obtaining the address Will headed in that direction.

The trucking company was large, but not in comparison to the Sarcosie warehouse. Repeating the same process Will identified himself as a police officer and asked to speak with the owner. The secretary got on the phone and a short time later a big brawny man wearing Levi's and a denim work shirt with the sleeves rolled up came to greet them. His defined muscular physique, huge callous hands and deep tan were reminiscent of a man who worked his way to the top. With his hand extended the man stated, "I'm Troy Thompson, owner of this fine establishment. How can I help you?"

Doc asked, "Is there some place we can talk in private? We need to ask you a few questions, but we won't take much of your time."

"Sure," said Thompson. "I've got an office right back here."

Once inside Thompson's small office, Doc asked, "How long have you been doing business with Sarcosie International?"

"Better than twenty-years. Why? What's wrong?"

Ignoring his questions, Doc asked, "Did you attend a meeting and party at the Sarcosie warehouse on the 26th?"

After some contemplation, Thompson said, "Yes, I did."

"How well do you know Keith Fuller?"

"I know him as good as anyone, I guess. He's a flamboyant pencil pusher. A little full of himself, but an alright guy."

"Angela Sarcosie," Doc continued, "How well do you know her?"

"I've seen her and she is a looker. Always has her personal secretary with here. Tera or Kara, something like that," said Thompson.

"Kera?" asked Doc.

"I think that's it, Kera. It sounds right."

"Do you have any plain white vans that you use for shipping or deliveries?"

"No, all our shipping is done by semi-trucks and trailers. We do have several large box trucks for local deliveries but they are big tan trucks with the company name on the sides."

"Last question, do you know anything about the six bodies that were recently discovered in up State Nevada?" asked Doc.

"No, is that what this is all about? Jesus! I don't know and I don't want to know."

"Thank you for your time, Mr. Thompson."

When Will and Doc left his office Troy Thompson picked up the phone and called Keith Fuller. After returning to the car, Will asked, "Doesn't it feel like everyone we talked to, Angela Sarcosie, Keith Fuller and this Thompson fellow, knew we were coming? Their answers seemed rehearsed, almost practiced and they were all so nice and helpful. It seemed wrong."

"You might be reading too much into things. Maybe they are just good people with nothing to hide."

"Right, and I'm Prince Charming," Will stated.

"Will, you are Prince Charming. You're my Prince Charming, anyway."

Will and Doc stopped at the motel desk and faxed a copy of the known local criminal list to the task force office. Then they walked next door to a diner for dinner of chicken fried steak, which was the recommended house special.

Back in their room they updated their field files and typed up their daily progress reports on their computers. At bed time they took turns using the bathroom, brushed their teeth, then watched a little news before they turned out the lights and enjoyed a little one-on-one. The lovin' was slow, steady and passionate. They fell asleep in each other's arms, sated and content.

Sometime during the night Will woke with an uneasy feeling. He looked around the room, just as a shadow crossed in front of the motel window. Will was still looking at the window when the figure came back and stopped in front of the window. Will's sixth sense kicked in and he grabbed Doc and rolled with her off the bed away from the window. A burst of machinegun fire blasted in the window and the curtains jumped and twisted as slugs slammed into the bed and walls.

Will snatched his pistol off the night stand and fired three quick shots through the window into the gunman. After the deafening roar of the machinegun the sudden quiet was almost disorienting. It was like the whole world stopped. Will sprang to his feet, rolled across the bed, fumbled with the door chain, then jerked the door open and jumped out on the walkway in a crouch, gun ready. The gunman was laying on his back in a growing pool of dark blood. Will surveyed the parking area then stood looking down into the blank stare of a dead man he didn't recognize.

Doc had called 911. Will could hear the rapidly approaching sirens. Doc stepped out of the room wearing nothing but Will's dress shirt and carrying her gun. Everything had happened so fast that neither had time to really think, only react.

Doc said, "Son-of-a-bitch. That was a hit and he almost got us."

Will used his hand to raise Doc's chin so she wasn't looking at the dead guy, then looked her in the eyes and said, "Better get some clothes on. It's going to be a long morning." He then kissed her lightly on the lips and smiled. That's when Doc noticed Will's shoulder bleeding.

"Oh shit, the bastard shot you," Doc said. Then she kicked the dead man in the side before running inside for a towel. After taking a closer look at Will's shoulder Doc went inside to dress.

Will would need stitches, again, but he was otherwise okay. After the police arrived with wailing sirens and flashing lights, the paramedics cleaned and placed a temporary bandage on Will's arm to hold him until he could get to the emergency room for stitches. Will managed to get his pants and shoes on before agent Daniels and half a dozen other FBI and CIA guys showed up.

Agent Daniels actually seemed concerned. He asked Will how he was doing then told him that the SAC would meet him at the hospital. Protocol required Will to ride in the ambulance and Doc followed in their rental. About the time the emergency room doctor finished cleaning and stitching Will's arm the SAC showed up. He was obviously relieved to see that Will was okay. Daylight was approaching. They all agreed to meet at the office at 7:00 a.m. so Will would have time to change out of his bloody clothes and get some breakfast.

During breakfast of scrambled eggs, ham with biscuits and gravy, orange juice and coffee, Doc said, "You saved our lives. I'm changing your name from cowboy to superman."

"It looks like we got someone's attention yesterday," said Will. "That can only mean that we are closer than we thought."

"Too damn close, I'm thinking," Doc stated. "It looks like we may get our asses shot off before we get to the bottom of things."

"Stick with me kid. When this is over we'll be dancing together under the pale moonlight."

"Will, your pain medication is taking effect. You sound full of shit. Tonight, I realized that I'm falling in love with you and I don't want to lose you."

"Since we are on a truth telling kick, I've been falling in love with you since the first day we met. I don't want to lose you either. So let's find these bad guys and get back to finding missing people."

The meeting at FBI headquarters started off really well. Will and Doc gave their statements to investigators, but it was clear the shooting was justified. Because Will's previous ballistic tests were on file there was no reason to impound his sidearm. That was a good sign. Will was getting a lot of pats on the back and compliments. He was doing pretty good until agent Daniels told him they were having another task force meeting.

Daniels took the lead. "We still don't know who the shooter is. He didn't have identification and his prints aren't on file. It looks like a professional hit. My question is what brought it on? It's not every day that someone puts a hit out on a cop. Give us a run-down on what you did yesterday after you left the task force meeting."

Will stood, walked to the front of the room and got right to the point. "First, I would like to say thank you for including me and my partner in this task force. As you know, yesterday we were assigned the task of compiling a list on known local criminals. After completing our assignment, I decided that our time would be best spent gathering as much information as possible on the latest missing informant, Harald Butkus."

"Hold on. How did you find out about Butkus?" asked Daniels.

"You told me, agent Daniels," said Will.

Before he realized his mistake, Daniels blurted, "I certainly did not."

"Well, if you didn't, then you certainly should have. We are working as a team. Withholding vital information impedes the investigation so what were you thinking?" Will asked.

When it was clear that Daniels had lost his wind, Will continued. "My partner and I, whose job is to investigate missing persons in Los Angeles, especially the ones related to this case, quickly determined that Butkus was abducted and two FBI agents were shot and killed while the FBI and DEA raided a warehouse looking for drugs. The tip that the drugs were in the warehouse came from Butkus who worked for Sarcosie International. The freighter, the shipping container, which contained blankets from Afghanistan by the way, and the warehouse all belonged to Sarcosie International. Because there were no drugs found I believed that the whole thing was an elaborate set-up to flush out Butkus as the informant. Based on my belief, my partner and I conducted some additional research and determined that the purchase, shipment and storage of the blankets was authorized by A. Sarcosie "

"Antonio Sarcosie," stated Daniels.

"No, actually it was his daughter Angela. I called Sarcosie International and spoke with Angela Sarcosie."

"I can't believe this," said Daniels. "You actually called Angela Sarcosie without authorization?" asked Daniels.

"I have authorization to conduct a proper, full and thorough investigation into these missing informants. Especially the ones from Los Angeles, since that is my jurisdiction. And furthermore, I don't appreciate you interrupting me or you withholding information concerning said investigation. It makes me wonder what other areas you weren't truthful in and what other information you are withholding. In my opinion, you can't be trusted and should be removed from this task force and investigation."

"Hold on," said the SAC. "Agent Daniels, don't say another word. This is my investigation and I decide who is on the task force. Officer Bracket, please continue with your recitation of the facts and we'll go from there."

"Yes, sir," answered Will. "Angela Sarcosie explained that buying the blankets from Afghanistan was to promote trade and stimulate their economy. She further explained that the blankets were a tax deductible donation to homeless shelters. This sounded a little too perfect to me, so my partner and I conducted some additional background searches and discovered that Angela Sarcosie has some very large deposits coming into her personal account from an unknown source and Sarcosie International owns warehouses in Reno and Las Vegas. We paid a visit to the Reno warehouse and talked to Keith Fuller. We discovered that the Reno warehouse has ten vans that match the description of the van at the burial site. We got copies of the logs for those vans for the last thirty days. We also found out that Angela Sarcosie attended a meeting and party at the Sarcosie warehouse on the 26th. As you know, the Medical Examiner confirmed time of death on two of the six recovered bodies as sometime on the evening of the 26th. Based on that revelation we requested the names of the people who attended the meeting and party. Mr. Fuller agreed to email me that list today.

"As we were leaving the warehouse we notice that many of the trucks and trailers had Thompson's Trucking on the side. Conducting an interview with the owner of Thompson's Trucking seemed like the next logical step, so I decided to interview the owner of the trucking company. After all, both companies are related as far as they are shipping companies. The owner of the company, Troy Thompson, confirmed that he was at the meeting and party on the 26th and that he knows Keith Fuller and Angela Sarcosie.

"Then agent Holiday and I faxed the list of known criminals to this office, had dinner and updated our field reports and daily progress reports, which include all the information I just explained. The rest you know. Last night some guy tried to kill us. Did I leave anything out agent Holiday?"

"That about covers it," said Doc. "Other than the part where you got shot then took out the bad guy and went to the hospital for stitches. I would say that's about it. Our field reports and progress reports have a more detailed description of the interviews with Angela Sarcosie, Keith Fuller and Troy Thompson. They were emailed to everyone last night and we can print them out for everyone just as soon as we can retrieve our computers from the motel room, if you like"

The Sac said, "Okay, so let's keep up the good work," and the meeting ended.

Chapter 16

Angela Sarcosie was fuming with rage. "Who the fuck did those nosy cops think they were?" She was convinced that there was no way those damn clowns could have stumbled on to her, Fuller and Thompson through dumb luck. Cops were fat and stupid. They couldn't find their car keys or gun if they weren't attached to their belts. They ate disgusting doughnuts and rode around in cars all day bothering people. She was a firm believer that cops couldn't find shit if it was on their shoes. Someone had to be feeding them information and when she got to the bottom of it, heads would roll.

"Angela, you shouldn't have went after those two police officers. What the hell were you thinking? All you did was confirm that they were looking in the right place. Panic is not becoming of you, Angela?" Big Eddie stated.

"Panic! Panic! This is not panic. I'm fucking irate and somebodies head is going to roll," replied Angela.

"In my opinion," said Big Eddie, "the cops were doing just what they said, checking out the owners of white vans and don't forget about Butkus."

Angela didn't trust Big Eddie's opinion on this one. "They weren't checking on vans when they called me. They were checking out blankets that were supposed to be a shipment of high grade heroin. That's just a little too convenient. Someone close to us has to be talking and I want to know who it is."

"The police are simply following logical leads and conclusions. If there was someone talking they would be arresting people, not merely talking to them," Eddie exclaimed. "I don't want you taking any more drastic measures without discussing it with me first. We can't afford to make mistakes and killing cops is a mistake. Your man blew it and got himself killed. Now we have to hope that he can't be traced back to you. That would certainly cause some additional and unnecessary complications.

"Right now we just need to watch how things progress and take precautions. I'm already moving the next fight to another location. We'll stay ahead of the law and if things get too crazy we'll go to plan B. Okay?"

"I still think that damn computer geek of yours needs to be taken out," declared Angela. "He could be behind this whole problem. We already know he's a loose cannon and he knows too much. You can tell by looking at him that if he gets in a pinch he'll squeal. You're treating him like a prince or something. If he turns he could take down the whole operation."

"Angela, Ray didn't know about the white van. He didn't know about Butkus and the heroin shipment. If there is a leak it certainly isn't Ray. And just for the record, I'm treating him no different than I'd treat you if you had an attack of bad conscious. I'm treating him as a son, just like I would treat you as a daughter. I am confident that our young Ray will work through things. He could be a very valuable asset in the future. The kid can hack into any computer in the world. Besides, I'm having him watched around the clock. He is starting his vacation right now with a week on my yacht. In fact, I was planning to ask you to fly out and check on him. You could give me an update on how he's doing. It would be good to take your mind off things for a day. Put on a bikini and show Ray that we're just a bunch of fun lovin' people."

Angela, always quick on her feet, recognized the opportunity this little visit presented so she gladly agreed, smiled and left his office.

Big Eddie was thankful that Angela was going with his suggestion. He needed a few days to shorten her leash. The next time Angela started giving orders he wanted to be notified before the orders were executed. Not after the act was over. Angela was a hot head who often used poor judgment. If not for Eddie's careful planning Angela would have become a liability long ago.

Eddie's first call was to Keith Fuller. He made it clear to Fuller and then to Troy Thompson that if Angela ordered another cowboy stunt that he was to be notified immediately and no actions were to be taken without his approval. Big Eddie didn't have to remind them that it was him and his money and pull that put them both where they were and that was long before Angela was old enough to even think she was running anything. She was still in grade school when Eddie proposed that her father build a warehouse in Reno and that Keith Fuller would be the man to run it. If it wasn't for Big Eddie they would both probably still be pushing brooms and loading trucks.

Angela's overactive, devious mind was running in overdrive. She was in the process of formulating a plan as she drove to the heliport. She called Kera, explained the situation and asked her to prepare for a late night dinner for two. A romantic evening and wild sex with Kera was just what Angela would need and want after this trip to spy on Ray.

The helicopter flight took forty minutes. The yacht was sitting on calm waters when the chopper landed on the helipad. Angela bounced out and the helicopter flew away. It would be back at dusk to pick her up.

Angela had her own private cabin on the yacht where she kept extra clothes and all the amenities of home. The crew was expecting Angela for lunch so she wasted no time changing into more appropriate attire before reporting to the dining room. To keep with the ocean atmosphere and theme the food that was served on Big Eddie's yacht was always sea food, naturally. The noon meal was lobster tail and deep-fried coconut shrimp with a raspberry hollandaise sauce, served with a fruity white wine from the local California winery that Big Eddie favored. The setting was rich, but tasteful. The more elegant meals were usually reserved for late night dinners under the stars.

Raymond was going to skip the fancy lunch and have a simple meal in his room until he was told that Angela was coming to have lunch with him.

That peeked his interest and got him out of bed and motivated. Ray thought Angela was the hottest woman he had ever seen. The way she walked across a room like she owned the world made her the most desirable woman imaginable. Ray was a computer geek. He hadn't really thought much about women until Eddie fixed him up with an escort, Lisa Monroe.

Ray didn't think that was her real name, but it was fitting because she looked a lot like Marilyn Monroe. Ray enjoyed being with her but he knew it was just for fun. Lisa worked for Big Eddie and was just keeping Ray company. The sex was great, but he kept thinking about Angela. Getting to see her again had Ray smiling for the first time in days.

Angela and Lisa were already seated and talking when Ray came into the room. The lights were dimmed, curtains were pulled across the portholes and candles flickered on the table. To Ray it looked romantic and enticing. To anyone who knew Angela, it looked like just what it was, a spider patiently waiting on the unsuspecting fly to tangle in the spider's web. Poor Ray didn't have a clue how treacherous Angela was or how precarious his position was.

Unbeknownst to Ray, his life was hanging in the balance and he was standing on the edge of an abyss. His answers to Angela's questions would determine if he'd be pushed into a metaphorical bottomless chasm or allowed to continue with his sad, meaningless little pathetic life.

With her fake happy face, Angela asked Ray how he was doing and explained that she'd been stressed lately so Eddie had suggested she come out and spend the afternoon with him.

"You've lost weight honey. Are you feeling okay?" Angela asked.

The macho part of Ray had him answering, "Oh yeah, I feel great. I've just been spending a lot of time on a new game I'm working on. I get all involved in my work and forget to eat or sleep. Eddie fixed me up with a month vacation so I can rest up. That was pretty cool of him. He understands how important my work is and has been very supportive," said Ray.

That was the most Lisa or Angela had ever heard Ray Speak. Mostly Ray didn't talk much and when he did it was about computers. It was obvious that Ray was nervous and excited. He was talking fast and stumbling on his words. Angela despised men. They were as predictable as Pavlov's dog. They started salivating at the sight of a woman's tit. Men were weak. They could be led around by their dicks with sex, which gave women all the power, Angela believed. All a woman had to do was learn how to use that power to her advantage and they could have and do anything they wanted.

Angela and Lisa were being overly nice to Ray and flirting with him openly. It was fun to watch him blush. After they finished their meal they retired to the stern observation deck to sit in the sun and drink martinis.

While Lisa and Angela were nicely tanned, Ray was so white they could see his blue veins. Ray spent almost all of his time in a room lighted only with a computer screen. When he did come out it was usually at night to visit his few friends and play computer games. Not being use to sunlight, Ray was forced to wear sunglasses and sit in the shade. Ray didn't want a suntan or a sunburn, but he did want to watch Lisa and Angela laying almost naked in the sun. When both women took their tops off Ray had to sit with a towel in his lap to hide his erection. When Lisa went to the rest room, Angela moved over next to Ray in the shade.

"These gladiator fights," Angela said, "have me so stressed out. I don't know what to do. I don't like seeing those guys get killed. It freaks me out."

Angela had underestimated Ray's built in bullshit meter. Ray's internal warning signals came to life. He was born at night, but not last night. He could see a train wreck coming and he wasn't about to lie down in the tracks.

"Maybe you should do what I'm doing," Ray said. "I decided to just forget about it and never talk about it, ever. Maybe you should discuss it with Eddie. He might send you on vacation with me."

Angela's plan hadn't worked. The kid wasn't as dumb as he looked. Angela had failed to lure Ray into her trap and it made her regret coming out to the yacht. For a moment her temper flared and she thought about killing Ray and throwing him overboard. She then regained her composure and decided to let Eddie do things his way. The assignment was also good experience for Lisa while they groomed her for bigger and better things. As Angela was flying away from the yacht that evening she silently vowed to bide her time until she had proof that Ray was a threat then she would make him suffer before she killed him.

Ray's initial excitement of seeing Angela had faded quickly when he realized that she only came to try and trick him into incriminating himself. Angela was nothing more than a modern day Trojan horse. The Mexicans called women like Angela Plastica, because they were fake. Once Ray saw past his infatuation he could see that her visit was just a trick. Before Angela showed up Ray was thinking that Eddie was sincere. Ray's fear came back tenfold when the reality hit him. He was nothing more than a prisoner on yacht arrest, under heavy watch. When Ray realized that when his usefulness wore out he was dead, the paranoia rolled back in in a sickening wave. Ray was convinced that it was only a matter of time before Eddie decided he didn't need him anymore and now that Ray had completed the programs for the fights and betting that time was surely close at hand. Then Ray's paranoia and imagination kicked in and he thought they were already going to kill him. That's why they sent him on vacation. To do away with him some place his body would never be found or it would look like an accident.

Angela had only shown up to try and find out if he'd talked to anyone already. Right then Ray would have jumped off the yacht if he could have seen the shore, but being fifty miles out left poor Ray with no place to run. Ray knew he couldn't just call the police without implicating himself and running the risk of getting caught by Big Eddie. He didn't want to end up in prison or in a gladiator fight to the death like those informants. If Eddie and Angela got caught it had to look like it was coming from another direction.

In order to escape Ray needed money and a lot of it to be able to hide. Eddie had paid him a lot to write the programs, but that money was in his bank account and could be traced. He laid awake half the night formulating a plan.

The following morning Ray woke with a mission. Assuming the phones and onboard computers would be monitored, Ray used his personal laptop with a satellite internet link to open a business account at a bank in France where he transferred all the money from his savings account. He left his checking account intact to help throw off anyone that might be looking. The business account was under the name of Computer Connection, Incorporated (CCI), which was a company that Ray had created in his mind while lying awake that night. It sounded good and Ray could make it official later if he wanted to.

One of the things Ray did when he wrote the betting programs was to setup a master account at a bank in Zurich to manage the money. The master account included wiring instructions to subaccounts. Ray didn't know who the subaccounts belonged to and he didn't care. Ray still had all the bank account numbers and pass codes on disk. Ray accessed the master account and entered his account as an additional subaccount with instructions to divert ten percent of the gross incoming money to his new account before the money was divided and disbursed into the other accounts. By the time Ray arrived in France on his vacation the next fight would be over and ten percent of the betting proceeds would be in his account. As long as the regular deposits were made it would be months before anyone noticed the new account, because the statements came out quarterly. Even then it might be a year before someone actually paid enough attention to the account information to notice the new account. By then Ray would have moved the money several times and they would never be able to find it, because Ray would hack into the bank's computers and hide the transfer data with the help of a friend who worked at a bank.

Ray had lunch with Lisa then spent all afternoon on the ship's computer looking at vacation information on France, Rome and Italy. He wanted anyone monitoring the computer to see him looking at tourist locations. Knowing that Lisa was probably spying on him too, Ray acted excited about some of the tourist locations they would visit. He felt better now that he had a plan and that brought back his appetite and sex drive. Ray had sex with Lisa before dinner and three times after dinner. Might as well take advantage of it while he could and it seemed to make Lisa happier too.

Ray knew that Eddie and Angela were dangerous, but Ray was smarter than both of them. He was about to show them that the computer was mightier than the sword. Later that evening on the phone with Big Eddie Ray was showing his excitement about Angela coming to see him. He told Eddie thanks again for the vacation. "It's just what I needed," Ray stated. It made Eddie feel better about not killing young Ray, which was a decision he would soon regret.

After Lisa went to sleep Ray sent another cryptic email to officer William Bracket of the LAPD using a pre-paid Verizon Mobile Broadband Card that could not be traced back to him. The email would look like it came from the warehouse in Reno where the fights were taking place. He was giving the police just enough information to make it look like someone at the warehouse sent the email out of desperation and fear while trying to remain anonymous.

Ray didn't know that Eddie moved the next fight to a new location and he did not know that the money from the fights in China and Russia was also being sent to Zurich and deposited in the master account, as would be the proceeds from the fights in other countries when they started. Ray was in for a few surprises. For now, all Ray could do was relax, enjoy the ride and make plans. He had already informed the bank that he needed a debit card upon his arrival at the bank. From there everything he paid for would be in his new company's name which would make it close to impossible to trace back to him. It would at least slow things down for anyone looking and give him time to make his escape. If he used his personal credit cards it would only be to lead a false trail. Ray was actually starting to have fun. It was like playing James Bond or a reality computer game where the ultimate goal was to avoid detection, relocate and live. It gave Ray an idea for a new computer game. He would write the game as he went. It would be better than any other game on the market. Most games were basically the same. A lot of fighting, shooting and blowing things up during car chases. Ray's new game would give things a whole new twist. It would be more of an intellectual game for adults. Ray was excited about the possibilities. He was already past the thought of being caught and killed. He moved on to the thought of fame and fortune under a new name.

Chapter 17

It had been a long day. Will was sore and sullen. Being shot, for the second time, had Will hurting. His side still hurt from the first wound and now he couldn't lay on his freshly wounded shoulder. The pain was enough to piss Will off, but combined with the thought of killing yet another person in his short time with the LAPD had Will somewhat depressed. He was so worried about how to explain things to his mother that he'd forgotten to check his emails.

The attempt on their lives and Will being shot had Doc testy. The helpless feeling had Doc rather mad. They procured a new room on the other side of the motel and when they were finally allowed back in their old room it took two trips to move all their gear. The sight of the demolished room gave them both a new wave of anger. Even though there were still officers present looking for the shooter's vehicle, Will and Doc were on high alert as they moved their things. It wasn't likely that there would be another attempt on their lives, but they weren't taking any chances.

The day's events had them both in a foul mood. Will's phone and computer had been in the room that was shot to shit so Will had been unable to check his voice mail or emails. He decided to check his twelve missed calls first. His first few calls were from colleagues reminding Will to check his emails. The message from his mother simply stated: "My son got shot and I have to find out on the news. Nobody calls. I have to call the hospital to find out if you're okay. Then I call your boss and find out this is the second time you got shot. He then tells me that you shot three criminals. What's going on out there? You never shot anyone when you worked for the New York Police Department. You better call me right away. You're worrying me to death."

Will felt terrible about upsetting his mother. He called her and spent thirty minutes trying to explain things and calm her down. He told her all about each shooting and convinced her that his wounds were very minor. His father got on the phone and told him to stop worrying his mother and to please be careful. To change the subject, Will started telling his mother about the wonderful woman he was dating, Gloria Holiday. Will told his mother that Gloria was also his new partner at work and that her friends called her Doc.

"You're dating a doctor, how nice," said Will's mother.

Will had to explain why everyone called Gloria Doc: because of her doctorate in behavioral science and because she carried a gun and her last name was Holiday like the legendary gambling cowboy. Mom finally understood and thought Gloria sounded nice, but she didn't understand why Will was on vacation in Nevada.

"Are you gambling?" mother asked, "Because I always wanted to see the gambling."

Will assured her that he was in Nevada for work and that no, he wasn't gambling but he'd seen some people gambling and it looked like fun. She told him not to spend his money on gambling and they said their good-byes.

Doc had been listening to Will's side of the conversation and she was smiling. "That was so sweet. I would roll you over and do you if you weren't so cranky and hurting right now," said Doc with a kiss.

Will felt much better after explaining everything to his mother.

Somehow it didn't all sound so bad. It was a load off his mind and it put him in a much better mood. He felt so much better that he used his good arm to pull Doc on top where they enjoyed a little easy lovin' before getting back to work. Will started systematically going through his emails. The first one of interest was from the investigating officer in the Silvestre Deveraux case. Deveraux was cooperating. He claimed that he didn't know about the body in the barrel that was found in the apartment above the garage with the meth lab. After the woman in the barrel was identified by her prints, Deveraux told the officers her boyfriend's name and said he was a meth cook who also used the apartment. The officers then asked Deveraux why his name and phone number was found in Derick Jerome Aguilar's house and on his cell phone. Deveraux told them that he'd been selling methamphetamine, "crank," to Derick for about a year. When asked about Derick's girlfriend Kanesha and the kidnapped informants Deveraux didn't know who was behind it, but he'd heard from Derick that the kidnapped informants were being taken to Nevada and being forced to fight to the death in gladiator fights. That bit of news was consistent with the stab wounds and cuts on some of the bodies and the autopsy reports. It was also apparent from the autopsy reports that the winners, after being stitched up and fed a nice dinner, were then being killed with large doses of barbiturates.

Will's heart leaped with excitement when he got to an email from deadserious. The email simply read: "The informants are being forced to fight to the death in a warehouse near Reno, Nevada."

Will quickly sent an email to deadserious requesting additional information and promising protection even though he didn't really expect an answer.

Will and Doc couldn't believe their luck. The email was also a good indicator of who ordered the hit on them. Will put together a memo and sent a copy of the memo and email from deadserious to the other officers on the task force, a copy to his boss at the LAPD and one to his friend at the NYPD. Then Will contacted the computer specialist in the FBI and asked for an email trace. It was a little late to be making requests, but Will wanted to get a jump start on things.

The next morning Will invested considerable time on preparing his search affidavit. He laid out the facts of the case then walked through each step of why he believed he had probable cause for a search. The first email pointed them to Nevada. The Butkus kidnapping had alerted them to Sarcosie International, then to Angela Sarcosie and Keith Fuller who were both at the warehouse on the 26th when two of the informants died. The white van that disposed of at least two of the bodies had tire tread patterns that matched those of the vans at the Sarcosie warehouse. Will explained that three of the ten white vans were not in the lot, but the logs showed them in the lot and never checked out. Will added the part about his and Doc's attempted assassination just hours after talking to Keith Fuller and leaving the warehouse. He capped it off with the facts in the email from the anonymous deadserious that pointed to a warehouse near Reno, Nevada.

Will was quite proud of his detailed handiwork in the search warrant affidavit. While Doc proof read the affidavit, Will worked on the actual search warrant. A search warrant requires the name, address and description of the location to be searched and the things to be seized. To meet Fourth Amendment requirements a search warrant had to be particular and specific about the things to be seized. To cover all the bases Will was careful to start his description of what was to be seized with, "including but not limited to the following," just in case they came across something they didn't expect.

After completing the search warrant and getting Doc's approval of the search warrant affidavit Will was ready to see the task force SAC and go to a judge for a signature. It was still early, but before they could get out the motel room door Will's phone chirped out a little tune. It was the FBI computer tech informing Will that the latest email from deadserious originated at the Sarcosie International Reno Warehouse. Will took the time to add the new information into his search warrant affidavit before leaving for the morning task force meeting at FBI headquarters.

People were buzzing around FBI headquarters when Will and Doc arrived. The meeting hadn't started yet, but several agents were already there, including agent Daniels. As Will and Doc walked into the room Daniels said, "We've got an ID on the shooter. His name was Hector Montalvo from Los Angeles. We found his SUV this morning as many of the motel guests were checking out. His vehicle was in the side parking lot of the motel next to yours. We did a license plate check on the vehicles in the lot then checked the motel registration. We then printed the vehicle and matched them to the shooter. We have officers sitting on his residence waiting on a warrant." Daniels looked quite proud of himself.

"Have you found any ties to Sarcosie, Fuller or Thompson?" asked Will.

"Not yet," replied Daniels, "but we hope to."

"I assume you received the email I sent you last night that included a copy of the new email from deadserious. This morning your computer guy confirmed that the email came from the Sarcosie warehouse. Doc and I put together a search warrant and search warrant affidavit for the warehouse and would like to get moving on that first thing."

"A search may be premature," said Daniels, "but we'll run it by the SAC at this morning's meeting."

Will knew better than to say anything to agent Daniels. What's the point when dealing with a bureaucratic idiot. It would be like speaking to a jackass and expecting an intelligent conversation. It's just not going to happen, so Will was saving his speech for the boss.

After the SAC opened the task force meeting, rather than turn things over to agent Daniels for a progress report, he turned the meeting over to Will. The shocked expression on Daniels face was priceless and wouldn't have been any worse if someone had reached across the table and slapped him.

Will, favoring his left arm and shoulder, stood and walked to the front of the room like it was perfectly natural that he should give the morning briefing. Will didn't smile or rub it in he just got right to the point. He recapped the previous night's events and gave an update on where they were at on the investigation. Will explained that officers were about to search the residence of the shooter, Hector Montalvo, and that he and Doc had prepared a search warrant and search warrant affidavit for the Sarcosie warehouse. Will laid out his and Doc's plan for the search of the warehouse and the interviews of all Sarcosie employees.

Since he and Doc had already spoken with Keith Fuller, Will requested permission for him and Doc to be allowed to bring Fuller in for an on-the-record interview. The SAC approved Will and Doc's plan and left to get the search warrant signed while the search teams were assembled.

The search would be a tactical surprise in full force where every employee would be taken into custody and interviewed. The warehouse would be shut down until the extensive search and interviews were complete. Over twenty marked and unmarked vehicles and more than fifty agents and officers converged on the warehouse shortly after lunch.

After all employees were detained, cuffed, searched and secured, the agents commenced their meticulous search of the warehouse and white vans. One of their primary concerns was to locate the three unaccounted for vans. Determining which three vans were missing didn't take long, but nobody seemed to know where the three missing vans were and there was no record of anyone checking them out. They were simply gone. The task force commander had the Reno Police Department send out an All Point Bulletin (APB) on all three missing vans with instructions to assume the vans stolen and detain the vans and drivers.

While the search was underway Will and Doc transported the protesting Keith Fuller to task force headquarters where they placed him in an interview room and read him his rights in front of a video camera. Fuller was threatening to file a lawsuit and demanding his attorney. Will had a phone brought in while Doc took time to explain to Fuller that calling his attorney, even though he had a Sixth Amendment right to do so, would result in a considerable delay.

"We probably could have had you out of here in less than an hour if you would have cooperated," Doc explained to Fuller.

It took almost an hour for Fuller's attorney to arrive at task force headquarters. Fuller's attorney, Charles B. Weinstein, III, was one of the top three criminal attorney's in Reno, Nevada and probably the whole State. His friends called him C.W. and he didn't like to be kept waiting. Forty-five minutes later C.W. was escorted to the interview room where he had to wait with his client for another twenty minutes before Will and Doc walked into the interview room smiling with fake apologies. Before anyone could say anything Doc asked, "Do y'all need some more time together? We can start the interview later if you like."

C.W. chastised Will and Doc for holding his client and for keeping them waiting. He then demanded that his client either be charged or released.

"Just so I'm clear on this," said Will, "rather than answer a few questions so we can clear up a few matters you want us to go ahead and charge Mr. Fuller with conspiracy to kidnap and murder federal informants?"

"No," yelled C.W., "I want you to release him immediately. You have nothing on him."

"Sir, we do not arbitrarily and capriciously bring people in for questioning," Will exclaimed. "If we didn't have something he wouldn't be here and a federal judge certainly would not have issued a search warrant for his warehouse. You Sir, of all people, know very well that we can hold your client as a material witness or suspect for seventy-two hours before we have to charge him or release him. By the way, there is no bond for that seventy-two hours."

"This is outrageous," C.W. professed. "I want to speak to whoever is in charge."

Will said calmly, "That would be me. If you like, you are welcome to leave and go contact anyone you want about the matter, but I have six dead informants and unless I get some good answers I'm holding your client for the entire seventy- two hours, which is fine with me because the way things are progressing I will likely request formal charges anyway. So it's your call."

After a short conference with his client, C.W. said, "Ask your questions. But if I don't like where things are heading I'm terminating the interview."

Will thought it was funny how lawyers always wanted to impress their clients by making them think the attorney was in charge. It was just grandstanding to help milk more money from their clients. Now that Will had put them both in their place he turned the interview over to Doc so she could verbally slap Fuller around a little. Will and Doc knew that a confession wasn't likely, but they hoped to get a few incriminating answers.

Doc: "Mr. Fuller, I doubt very seriously that you are behind the kidnapping of these informants."

Fuller: "You're damn right, I'm not."

Doc: "Whose idea was it to hold gladiator fights at your warehouse?"

Fuller: "I don't know what the hell you're talking about."

Doc: "Mr. Fuller, do you know what forensic evidence is?"

Fuller: "Sure, I watch television."

Doc: "So, if I have forensic evidence linking one or more of the dead informants to your warehouse, how would you explain that?"

Fuller: "I - I - I, well, I don't know how to explain it."

With Fuller's attorney interrupting often, Doc was able to get Fuller to admit that he didn't know three vans were missing from his own lot and that Angela and Troy Thompson were at the meeting and party on the 26th. Fuller stated for the record that he didn't know a Hector Montalvo. The task force was in the process of cross checking Montalvo's, Fuller's, Thompson's and Angela Sarcosie's home and business computers and their cell phone records. They hoped to tie Montalvo to someone soon.

Doc's final question was more of a statement. "Mr. Fuller this interview is your opportunity to cooperate and avoid prison. If you will provide us with the names of the people who are behind the kidnappings and fights, provide all the details you are aware of and agree to testify, we'll bargain with you. Before you decide on your next course of action you should be aware that the first person to cooperate gets the deal. When you walk out of this office the dealing is over. We move on to our next interview. Someone will cooperate to avoid prosecution. So what's it going to be?"

Fuller, as nervous as a cat crossing a four lane highway on a hot afternoon during rush hour traffic, conferred with his attorney.

"If there was something going on at the warehouse," said Fuller, "it was after regular business hours and without my knowledge."

"After 'regular business' hours," said Will, "like during the afterhours meeting and party that took place at the warehouse on the 26th? The party you attended?"

Fuller didn't respond. Doc said, "Okay, Mr. Fuller, you are free to go. But you cannot return to the warehouse until after the search is completed and the officers leave. Speaking of leaving, we've checked and you do not have a passport, but I am formally advising you Sir, for the record, not to leave the State and we still need the names of the people at the meeting and party on the 26th."

Chapter 18

Big Eddie was at his desk when Fuller called to inform him about the search and his interview with the police. Fuller used a public payphone to make the call because he figured his private phone was tapped. Eddie, being wise in these matters, merely listened to what Fuller had to say, then told Fuller to be sure and follow the advice of his attorney.

Eddie wasn't surprised. Fuller's attorney called Eddie immediately after the interview with a run-down of the afternoon's events. That is the kind of service big money gets. Everyone jumps at the sound of money. It's only a matter of how high.

Eddie wanted to see Angela's reaction to the news, so he called her and invited her to dinner. Angela knew that a request for dinner meant that Big Eddie had something important to discuss. Being in a wheelchair prevented Eddie from going out much. His legs were just too weak. Eddie had a live-in maid and butler who cooked most of his favorite meals right there in the comfort of his own home while also looking out for Eddie's health. It was far better to sit at his own spacious table where he could listen to his own music, take his time and enjoy a meal. It was also more private. Being in a busy restaurant increased the risk of some busybody eavesdropping on their conversation.

Over dinner Eddie told Angela about the raid on the Reno warehouse and about Fuller being taken in for an interview. He further explained that Fuller's attorney had called with the news and he informed Eddie that, although Fuller was shaken, he was not stirred into admitting anything. Angela took the news well.

"Angela," said Big Eddie, "Fuller doesn't know how the informants are being located or abducted. He doesn't know where they are being kept or where I had all the equipment moved to for the next fight. What concerns me is, you called Fuller and told him to have the two cops hit. Fuller contacted that crazy-ass Montalvo who got himself killed. The cops have identified Montalvo. It is only a matter of time before the feds tie Montalvo to Fuller. The question we must consider is, what will Fuller do when he is faced with the attempted contract killings of two police officers that have the death of Montalvo as an aggravating factor? I've made the white van disappear, but there is still the possibility that the feds will turn up some evidence and charge Fuller with kidnapping and killing the informants. What will Fuller do?"

"That leaves us with two options," said Big Eddie. "We either do nothing and trust Fuller to keep his mouth shut or we take affirmative steps to eliminate the problem. In my opinion, once Fuller is charged and they hold him without bond and whisk him away to a safe-house with promises of a new identity he will tell them everything he knows and hope to live happily ever after."

"The first thing Fuller will tell them," stated Angela, "is that I sanctioned the hit on the two cops. Fuller's got to go and the sooner the better."

"You should prepare for plan B just in case. I have everything in place on my end," said Big Eddie. "We could give Fuller the option of disappearing, but he's not a partner. He's only a peon and he doesn't have the money or the imagination to disappear without getting himself caught. Our best bet is to initiate damage control before things get out of hand and too tough to manage. I'll take care of it."

This new development took their minds off any problem young Ray presented. The thought of more immediate danger took precedence. It would be a few days before their attention shifted back to the computer geek.

Eddie, using an untraceable cell phone, called his man Bob with instructions on how to take care of the Fuller situation. It would be best if it at least looked like an accident.

As instructed, Bob paid cash for a disposable pre-paid cell phone, then had a hot-shot delivery service deliver the phone to Fuller with a post-it-note stuck to it with a phone number written on it.

Fuller called the number. When Big Eddie answered Fuller didn't know whether to be relieved or scared. Trusting Big Eddie was not an easy thing. Fuller had seen Eddie do many crazy things over the years, including these damn gladiator fights. However, Fuller hadn't done anything to incur Eddie's wrath, so he didn't really feel the need to worry. The conversation went well. Eddie seemed genuinely concerned and willing to help. Eddie suggested that Fuller get a good night's sleep then take care switching vehicles with the one he kept in an underground parking garage at a casino. Make sure he wasn't being followed, then drive down to Eddie's place and spend a few days.

"The cops told me not to leave the State."

"They won't know you left unless they are looking to arrest you," said Big Eddie. "If that's the case, you sure as hell don't want to be there. They will call your attorney looking for you if they can't find you and if that's the way things go we'll work on a solution. If they are looking for you it would probably be to arrest you. If that happens, and it probably won't, it would be better for you to be here where we can make plans to relocate you to some place warm and sunny."

Fuller agreed with Big Eddie that it would be best to make himself unavailable until they determine what the police were going to do. When Fuller got up the next morning he took a shower, dressed then went to the restaurant in the casino where his other vehicle was parked. He kept an overnight bag in the trunk that contained not only clothes and toiletries, but some cash and a .9mm pistol for emergencies. He planned to keep his pistol handy while around Big Eddie, just in case something went wrong. Fuller drove around Reno just long enough to figure out if he was being followed. When he felt comfortable that no one was tailing him he headed for the highway that would take him over and down the mountain into California. It was a beautiful morning for a drive with the sun at his back.

He was enjoying zig-zagging down the mountain when a large four wheel drive truck slowly came up behind him. Fuller didn't think much about it. There were a lot of four wheel drive trucks in the mountains and they all seemed to be in a hurry. The truck was following a little too close, but Fuller thought the driver was just looking for an opportunity to pass. He'd slowed down some for a fairly sharp bend and was three quarters of the way through the curve when the truck accelerated. Its powerful engine roared to life and the truck slammed into the rear-end of Fuller's car. The impact was hard enough and just at the right angle to spin Fuller's car like a top. The car spun across the other lane, just missed the end of the guardrail and shot off the road into open space. As the car fell out of sight it clipped the tree-tops, flipped over and crashed to the ground up-side down next to a small creek two-hundred feet below the road. As the wheels stopped spinning the car's stereo droned on playing the Eagles song, Hotel California.

Two hours later a Highway Patrolman who patrolled that stretch of road saw the skid marks on the highway and stopped to investigate. He could see the car resting on its top with its four wheels sticking up like a dead animal on its back with its lifeless feet in the air. The procession of emergency vehicles, ambulance, fire truck and wrecker all arrived at the same time. They came from Reno which was the closest town to the scene. The car's top was smashed so flat that the wrecker driver had to run a cable down and roll the car back over before the rescue team could cut the top off to remove the body. Much to their surprise, the man was still alive. Other than a bunch of minor cuts he had no broken bones, but he was unconscious because of a head injury.

When Fuller's name was broadcast over the police radio one of the task force officers heard it and alerted the other task force members. By the time Fuller arrived at the hospital in the ambulance Will and Doc were there to evaluate the situation. After figuring out that Fuller wasn't going anywhere soon an officer was stationed at the hospital and advised that Fuller was under arrest. They instructed the officer to contact them if there was any change in Fuller's condition, then left to talk with the Highway Patrolman who found the car. At first it sounded like a simple accident. There was only one set of skid marks on the highway, but there were black marks and scratches on the rear bumper of Fuller's car that were consistent with the type of marks that could have been left by someone hitting the back of Fuller's car. The car was new so they didn't think the marks were there before the wreck.

The Highway Patrolman gave Will and Doc a copy of the inventory list of Mr. Fuller's vehicle, which included the overnight bag and its content. The .9mm pistol and fifty-thousand in cash were circled on the list as points of interest. It looked like Fuller was running. Will's main concern was an address book and pre-paid cell phone that were listed on the inventory. They quickly signed a transfer of custody form for Fuller's property, then left for task force headquarters to follow up on the leads in the address book and to find out who Fuller called on the cell phone.

The cell phone was a dead end. Fuller had only called one number and it was to another pre-paid phone. There was no record of who bought either phone and no one answered when Will tried to call the number Fuller called.

The address book, however, looked a lot more promising. The numbers of interest only had initials by them. A.S. turned out to be Angela Sarcosie. H.M. was Hector Montalvo, who they would soon learn had a past connection with Fuller. The H.M. entry gave them the connection they needed to charge Fuller with the attempted hit. Will and Doc ran the information they had by the prosecutor who agreed with their position and filed a Criminal Complaint against Fuller for two counts of attempted murder. That would be enough to hold Fuller without bond until the prosecutor could present the case to the grand jury. Hopefully, by that time they would locate the three missing vans and have the forensic evidence from the warehouse search analyzed. The only other number in Fuller's address book that was of interest was for a B.E. and it matched the number Fuller called on his pre-paid cell phone the day before his accident. If it was an accident. Will didn't believe there was any such thing as coincidences. The fact that the mysterious B.E.'s phone was sold in Los Angeles gave them another tentative connection between Reno and Los Angeles.

Even though Angela Sarcosie was clearly connected to Fuller and the Reno warehouse there was nothing to indicate that she was anything other than what she seemed: a young woman from an influential family with a lot of money. There was certainly nothing that would warrant bringing her in for questioning, but they did have enough to justify stopping by her office with a few questions. Hopefully, Miss Sarcosie would have some idea of the identity of B.E. Finding out the identity of B.E. was one of their top priorities.

Generally, the investigation work in most cases progresses rapidly. This wasn't one of those cases. Will had already shot and killed two of their lead witnesses and now another one was lying in a hospital in a coma. With six dead informants, they needed some quick closure. Finding the bad guy isn't as easy in real life as it was for Sherlock Holmes, Dick Tracy, and Phillip Marlow. Will was discovering that it was not as glamorous either. It was a down right bloody mess.

Chapter 19

Big Eddie was enjoying a fine veal cutlet that was sautéed with scallions and garlic chives then smothered in a thick mushroom gravy when his phone vibrated in his pocket. He kept it on vibrate because he didn't like the annoying little tune the sales-girl had programmed into the phone. Beautiful Girl was not what Big Eddie wanted to hear every time someone called him. What ever happened to good old fashion phones that simply rang? It was Bob on the other end of the tiniest phone Eddie had ever held in his rather large hand, which was another annoying factor about newfangled phones.

"We've got a problem," announced Bob, without any preamble.

"That's wonderful. It is becoming a regular occurrence. I wouldn't know how to get through my day without a problem. Should I dare ask what it is or would you like to keep me in suspense a while longer?"

"Fuller was taken to a Reno hospital where he's in a coma. The lucky bastard's condition isn't even serious. They are calling it guarded and they claim he could wake-up at any time."

"Making it look like an accident is no longer an option. I don't believe that I need to stress how crucial it is that he does not regain consciousness. Take care of it please. It seems that damage control is becoming a full time project."

When they disconnected Big Eddie looked at his unfinished dinner with a sigh. It was getting harder and harder to enjoy a meal without some type of interruption.

Based on how the staged accident turned out Bob decided to take care of Fuller personally. He waited until after the midnight shift made its rounds then he walked into the hospital through the emergency entrance wearing a white lab coat. The trauma unit and staff were busy with some traffic accident injuries and didn't notice him walk in. Fuller had been moved from ICU to a room on the third floor.

Bob walked up to the third floor nurses station and asked for the chart on Keith Fuller. It didn't work like in the movies where the nurse flirts with the killer and hands him the chart. The chubby little nurse with an upturned nose looked up from her work and said, "you're not a doctor here. You don't have an identification badge. I'm calling security."

As she reached for the phone Bob pulled out his silenced .380 and shot her once in the side of her head. Just behind the temple. The nurse flopped out of her chair with a backwards jerk and fell to the floor. Her roll-around chair shot backwards as she fell and crashed into a file cabinet with a loud bang. So much for going in unnoticed. Fortunately, there was an admissions board on the wall with the patient's names and room assignment written neatly across it.

When Bob walked around the corner looking for the correct room he spotted an empty chair next to the door of Fuller's room. He thought that maybe his luck was changing. It took only a few seconds to step into the room and shoot Fuller with one well-placed bullet to the head then he turned around to make his exit. Just as he was turning to leave the bathroom door opened to a grinning cop buttoning his pants and a sexy little nurse applying more lipstick.

Without hesitation Bob shot them both before they could raise an alarm. The nurse almost got a scream out when the cop went down, but a bullet tore the scream right out of her throat in a spray of blood.

As Bob was walking out of Fuller's room thinking that his luck couldn't get any worse a scream erupted from the direction of the nurses station. So much for a leisurely exit. Bob ran for the stairs. When Bob emerged from the stairwell on the ground floor, emergency medical personnel were hurrying to the elevators. Walking out of the emergency room doors Bob was engulfed by a cool breath of fresh night air. He could hear approaching sirens nearing the hospital. The entire hit had taken less than three minutes, but it seemed like an hour. Not much more could have went wrong. Bob removed the white lab coat as he walked, wiped his pistol, rolled it up in the lab coat then dropped the small bundle into a trash dumpster on the way to his vehicle. He was fishing his keys out of his pocket as he arrived at his car door when a police car pulled in behind him blocking him in. The young officer jumped out of his patrol car, not realizing the full gravity of the situation and yelled, "freeze! Get your hands in the air."

Bob rolled his eyes and raised his hands then started walking towards the officer. "I'm a doctor here, officer. What's the problem? I have identification right here."

The officer lowered his weapon some as Bob calmly walked over to him and slowly reached for his billfold. His mannerisms were friendly and disarming. When he was close enough to strike, in a flash, Bob struck the officer in the throat and grabbed his firearm before the officer could raise it all the way back up again. Bob kicked the officer in the groin as he wrenched the pistol from his grip and hit him in the head with it three times before the officer hit the ground. Quickly, Bob broke the officer's neck, moved the police car, then got in his car and drove away.

Before daylight the hospital was crawling with cops and media. One news hound was reporting that "Sources inside the Reno General Hospital have confirmed that two police officers, two nurses and one patient were brutally murdered here last night. The names of the victims are being withheld pending notification. It is unclear at this time what the motive might be or what exactly happened, but we are being told that at least four of the victims were apparently shot at close range. More details should be forthcoming as the morning unfolds."

Big Eddie liked to watch the news while he ate breakfast. He paused with a fork full of food halfway to his mouth when he heard the news flash. Lately, most every time he ate a meal he got bad news. It was starting to give him a complex about eating. He couldn't help but wonder what kind of problem he would be facing for lunch. When the newscaster announced that the police were investigating, but currently had no leads or suspects, Eddie was relieved. If Bob or one of his men would have been jailed it would have been another mess to untangle.

Bob called before lunch to let Big Eddie know that things were handled with Fuller and to verify that the weekend fight would proceed as scheduled. Eddie confirmed that the fight was a definite go then asked Bob if he'd seen the news. Bob had slept in after his long night and hadn't turned on the television. Eddie suggested that Bob watch the Reno news at noon. Without seeing the news Bob had a pretty good idea what would be the hot topic of the day.

"Emergency rush jobs don't always go as planned and things can get messy when a guy has to improvise," Bob responded.

"That was quite a bit of improvisation. I am aware that difficult situations often call for drastic measures. However, when possible it would be prudent to exhibit a little discretion."

"Actually, discretion was my top priority going in, but based on unforeseeable circumstances my priority changed when the situation became less manageable."

"That's one of the things I like about you Bob. No matter how difficult a project may be, you handle it with flair and never complain."

"I'll take that as a complement, Boss," said Bob as he disconnected.

Chapter 20

It was a long morning for Will and Doc. Hanging around the hospital hoping that a lead would develop had proven to be futile. There were a lot of people moving about in a hospital at night. Other than the nurse that discovered the first body, no one reported seeing anyone or anything out of the ordinary. With all the regular activity in progress it would have taken something pretty spectacular, like multiple homicides, to get a person's attention. The killer had killed everyone that noticed him so there were no witnesses.

They lost another witness, turned suspect, when Fuller was executed. It was time to regroup. Will and Doc went to lunch to put together a new game plan and think about their next move. During lunch they both came to the logical, sound conclusion that their only good lead to discovering the identity of B.E. was Angela Sarcosie. They didn't know for sure if finding B.E. would be helpful, but they both felt it would be and Angela Sarcosie was the only direction left to go.

Rather than fly back to Los Angeles for a surprise visit with Miss Sarcosie Will and Doc drove their rental. They left on Friday afternoon so they could stop and examine Fuller's crash site and then drive home and spend the weekend together catching up on things. Their plan was to rouse Miss Sarcosie bright and early Monday morning. Depending on how things went with the interview they would check in with their boss at police headquarters then drive back to Reno in Will's personal vehicle. They were ready to get out of the rental and into something with a little more class and comfort.

Arriving in Los Angeles well after dark they stopped at an all-night Wal-Mart super store for groceries before going to Doc's house for late night

Mexican ranchero omelets. After their hunger was sated it was time to satisfy their sexual appetites. Their newfound relationship had advanced from hot, clumsy and cautious to passionate, experimental and adventurous. They were examining the depth and breadth of their sexual proclivities. It was fun and exciting to try new things together, but it required a certain level of trust that many people can never achieve. Will and Doc trusted each other with their lives on a daily basis. It was only natural to trust each other in the bedroom. Wild sex was quickly becoming Will and Doc's favorite pastime and they were sleeping soundly because of it.

The following morning Will and Doc shared a leisurely run together around a small park about a half mile from Doc's house. After sweaty sex, a shower and breakfast they went to Will's apartment to water his plants and check his mail. They were spending so much time together that they agreed that it was pointless for Will to keep his apartment. When Will's one-year lease ran out they agreed that he should move in with Doc.

"I have always thought about building a large den off the rear of the house with a stone fireplace. That would give you room to put all your things. It would be romantic laying in front of the fireplace, naked, with a bottle of baby oil and a glass of wine," said Doc with a smile.

"Maybe we should consider buying something bigger and closer to the ocean. You could keep your house as a rental property. Another house would be a good investment for us." Will exclaimed.

"I love my little house, but buying a bigger one close to the beach sounds fun. Even if it was twice as far away from work as my house we would still break even on gas because we would be car-pooling. I don't care for the idea of being in debt again, but if we find the right place for the right price I'm game."

Saturday evening they went to dinner at an upscale, trendy restaurant that was quickly becoming popular for its soft music and dance floor. The general dining area was in the front of the establishment and it featured a romantic setting with moderate lighting. The bar area was in the rear with the lights so low it was almost in the dark. The dance floor was a common area in the middle where everyone mingled and danced the night away. On weekends the restaurant featured a jazz and blues band that was heavy on the saxophone. The young lady singing had a smooth sultry voice that went perfect with the atmosphere. It was a classy, romantic evening that ended in slow lovin' in a wine haze. Remarkably, Will didn't shoot anyone.

The next morning they took a drive down the coast highway and spent the morning on the beach. Lunch was at a little crab shack on the beach where the food was hot and spicy and the beer cold as ice. A perfect combination. On the way back up the coast they looked at several homes that Doc knew were way out of their price range. They came to one that was vacant. The grass and flower beds were un-kept, but there was no for sale sign. To get an idea of the view they stopped and walked around the place. The evening sun was just above the water, a huge radiant fire-ball. The house and deck needed some work, but it was in good order.

"This is wonderful," Doc proclaimed. "I would give anything to live here."

They stayed for a few minutes enjoying the spectacular sunset. Will noticed that the home wasn't much further from work than Doc's place.

Back at Doc's house they both checked and answered their emails then took a shower together where they made love standing up until the water started to get cold. While Doc started dinner, Will got back on his laptop and emailed the gun shop where he'd placed an order for a pair of custom made Smith & Wesson thirteen shot .9mm pistols. They came in a mahogany, blue velvet lined collector's case. He also bought the custom leather shoulder holster. The compact pistols would fit under each arm, both with two additional clips for a total of "seventy-eight" ready rounds. The custom pistols were left and right handers, which made them very unique. The left handed gun ejected the shell casing to the left. The right handed gun ejected the shell casing to the right like most traditional automatics. That way the shell casing from the "left" handed gun didn't cross over the center and interfere with the shooter's line of sight on the right gun. It was some seriously cool, modern day cowboy shit. Will was excited and could hardly wait to get them so he could show them off to Doc.

Will also emailed his attorney who was handling the sale of his home in New York. He gave his attorney the address of the beach front home that he and Doc liked and asked him to find out who owned the home and if it was for sale. It would save him some capital gains tax if he reinvested the money in another property. He hadn't mentioned to Doc that he had owned a home in New York. The subject had never come up. Now he didn't tell Doc about his inquiry into the beach house because he wanted it to be a surprise if he could pull it off.

Monday morning came early. Will and Doc were excited about rushing in to see Miss Sarcosie until they discovered that she would not arrive at her office until 9:00a.m., and she wasn't answering her home phone. Since they were dressed and ready to go by 7:00a.m., they decided to hit a coffee shop downtown so they would miss most of the rush hour traffic.

It was 9:30 when Will and Doc walked into the lobby and asked the nice receptionist to inform Miss Sarcosie that two police officers were there to see her. The receptionist called Miss Sarcosie and sent them right in. As they walked into her office Angela stood and boldly and confidently came around her desk to greet them. Will and Doc introduced themselves and they shook hands. Angela had a firm handshake and a pleasant smile.

"How may I help you?" Angela asked.

Will took the lead. "We would like to ask you some questions about your Reno warehouse and Keith Fuller."

"Certainly, but I don't know if I can tell you any more than I told you on the phone."

Miss Sarcosie's attitude seemed a little arrogant and she didn't seem the least bit phased or disturbed by their presence. Just another day at the office.

"Do you visit the Reno Warehouse often?"

"No. Just on special occasions."

"What kind of special occasion was the meeting and party on the 26th?"

"Customer appreciation mostly. The Reno operation exceeded its yearly productivity quota. Growth involves talk of expansion, promotions and some bonuses for innovative ideas that save the company money. For instances, one of our employees suggested that we install wind generators and solar panels to help curve the cost of overhead and for a substantial tax write off. Everyone is going green and we want to do our part to help the economy."

"How well did you know Keith Fuller?"

"I have known him for a long time, but I didn't know him well. He was an employee of my father's company. We weren't close if that is what you are asking. I'm sorry to hear that he was murdered and I hope his death in no way reflects poorly on the company. I am confident that your investigation will show that Sarcosie International is spotless. If Mr. Fuller was doing something illegal it was without our knowledge, of course."

"I know you are very busy so I won't keep you much longer. I called B.E. this morning and he didn't answer. Do you have any idea where he might be?"

After a slight pause, Angela stated, "I don't recall knowing a B.E. Do you have a full name? I'll check my records."

"We were hoping you could help us with that. Mr. Fuller had a small day planner with him that had the initials H.M. and a number for Hector Montalvo. Mr. Montalvo tried to assassinate both of us in our sleep the other night. He's dead now. The fact that his initials and number were in Mr. Fuller's day planner connects Montalvo to Fuller, which indicates that Fuller was involved in our attempted murders. Your initials and number were in Fuller's day planner, as well and so were the initials and number of B.E. You don't seem to know anything so we were hoping B.E. might."

"To think that Keith Fuller was connected to a potential murder is just ghastly. In fact, shocking. I don't see how I could have been so wrong about someone. I wish I could help you, but I don't know anyone with the initials B.E."

"Did you know that Mr. Fuller was suspected of kidnapping federal informants and forcing them to fight to the death in gladiator fights at your Reno warehouse?"

"Of course not and how absolutely absurd. That sounds like something out of a bad movie," said Angela Sarcosie, without a bit of shock or indignation.

"Yes, it does sound like a bad movie, only it's reality and people are being murdered. Your name keeps popping up in our investigation, which leads us to believe that you must know something. One of the kidnapped informants died of knife wounds on the 26th. The day you had your meeting and party at the Reno Warehouse. Another was poisoned the next day. We found them buried next to four other dead informants in Northern Nevada. The witnesses saw two men in a white van disposing of the most recent informants. The description of the white van and the tire imprints match those of the three missing white vans from the Reno warehouse. We are getting close and the closer we get people are dying. If you know anything now would be the time to speak up, before even more people die. Someone is making a drastic effort to kill people to shut them up. You could be next."

"Your theory would be alarming if I was involved and knew something. I'm not and I do understand your concern, but I resent the implication. I have nothing further to say about the matter. Good luck with your investigation and good-day."

With that Angela Sarcosie walked around her desk and opened her office door in a gesture of dismissal.

"Thank you for your time Miss Sarcosie," Will said politely as they walked out.

During the entire interview Doc had remained silent. In the elevator she said, "The two-faced bitch is lying."

"How do you know she's two-faced? We've only seen one," Will asked with a smile.

Doc laughed, "Oh, it's in there, cleverly hidden. I've seen her type before. She's mixed up in all this, all the way up to her lying eyes."

Will wanted to say that it looked like Doc was jealous of Miss Sarcosie's long sexy legs and well defined cleavage, but he knew better than to play in that area. He didn't want kicked in the leg, so he just smiled.

Will and Doc went to their office and gave their boss written and oral reports on their progress or lack thereof. They took the time to sort through their mail, make some calls and check their emails. Will's new guns were in so they went by the gun shop on the way out of town. When Doc saw the custom made, engraved Smith & Wesson .9mm pistols in their collectors case her eyes lit up with admiration. It's not every day that a person spends close to three thousand on a pair of custom pistols. Will bought extra ammunition and they stopped in the desert and took turns target practicing with them using water bottles for targets. The gunfire and smell of cordite got them so aroused that they had sex on the hood of Will's car before resuming their journey back to Reno.

After avoiding agent Daniels and meeting with the SAC they read a few field reports then left to check into their new motel. Once settled in they ordered a large, thin crust supreme pizza, hold the anchovies. While they ate they discussed their strategy for the interviews they were planning for the next day.

As they finished their pizza and were cleaning up the mess, both of their cell phones started playing little ditties. They answered to a conference call from their boss in L.A. He was not a happy man. Angela Sarcosie told her father that two LAPD officers had practically accused her of being involved with kidnapping and multiple homicides. She had left the office early in a state of distress, went home and committed suicide by overdosing on her prescription medication. While dying, she knocked over a candle and was burned beyond recognition in her living-room apartment. Her father was screaming lawsuit and on the verge of hospitalization himself. His only child was lying in a cold morgue awaiting an autopsy and dental record check. Their boss told them to keep a low profile and not to come back to Los Angeles until they had some answers. He further advised them that internal affairs would be conducting their interview by phone.

Not a great way to end the day, but Will and Doc were convinced that she was murdered. They refused to believe that the woman they met would ever commit suicide. At the rate they were losing leads they wouldn't have anything to go on in a few days.

Chapter 21

Big Eddie's accountant came into Eddie's office in a ragged state of despair, wiping sweat from his face. He knew he had a serious problem and he was very concerned about Eddie's possible reaction.

"What's the problem?" Big Eddie asked.

"I was verifying account deposits and discovered a new account that was recently opened. I wanted to check with you to make sure it was authorized."

"A new account? What the hell are you talking about?" Eddie demanded.

"There were ten partner accounts. Now there seems to be eleven. It is a ten percent diversion that only equals one percent from each partner, but it totals a substantial amount and it's growing significantly. It is a new company account called Computer Connections opened at a bank in France."

When all the dots connected Big Eddie said, "That little sonofabitch. Cancel the account and retrieve the money. Change all access codes and set-up any firewalls you can to prevent this from happening again. How much did he get?"

"Right now twenty-six million and change."

When the accountant left Big Eddie placed a call to France to the man baby-sitting young Ray. Eddie instructed the man to secure Ray and escort him back to America on Eddie's private jet.

"We can't find him boss. We've been looking all afternoon. He left this morning and we expected him back for lunch, but he never showed. Miss Monroe didn't go with him this morning because she didn't feel well. He has been acting fine, just going to museums and tourist attractions. We had no reason to believe that he might go AWOL on us. I thought everything was fine."

"So did I, but it's not fine. Find him and quick."

While Big Eddie was fuming with silent rage in his office, Raymond was sitting in a comfortable little furnished apartment, sipping a Coke while diligently opening new accounts, transferring money and covering his tracks.

It helped that he had a friend who was a fellow hacker who worked at the bank the money was now being transferred through. For a price his friend was covering the money trial. Ray was actually having fun. It was like a seriously advanced interactive video game where his life was at stake.

From the first day of his arrival in France Ray had been planning his escape, with his trollop Lisa and his watchdog right under his feet. Ray took them every place he went to make things look normal and so they wouldn't suspect anything. When Ray went to the bank he picked up his debit card that was set-up for one hundred thousand. Ray almost panicked when he checked his account balance and discovered it was over twenty-six million. He was expecting a fourth of that. He quickly recovered and informed the bank attendant that he would be transferring the bulk of the account to other investment accounts, while still maintaining an account balance in excess of one million. The attendant was pleased and happy to accommodate the young computer mogul. Ray's actions didn't appear out of the ordinary. Lisa and the watchdog waiting in the lobby area actually added to the look of Ray's importance and supported his credibility.

Later that afternoon Ray went on line and rented a furnished apartment using the new company account. He wasn't planning on staying there long, only two days, while he covered his tracks. He was laying a false trail. Ray used his personal credit card to purchase a one-way first class airline ticket back to the United States. He wasn't going that direction, but the more false trails he had the better he felt.

After transferring twenty-one million to the bank where his friend worked he opened four new accounts in four other countries and four different banks with five million in each account. His friend kept one million for his trouble. It was his job to hide the transfers to the other banks, including his own one million. The money trail would stop there. There would be a record of the deposit and a twenty-one million withdraw, but no record of where the money went from there. The bank would get its percentage and that would be that. Because the money was split between five new accounts they couldn't trace the money by looking for a twenty-one million deposit. Ray wasn't greedy, twenty million would last him a lifetime. He was going to use part of the money in his original Computer Connections account to lay more false trails.

When Ray first accessed Big Eddie's accounts he changed the original access codes for the master account without altering or interrupting the money flow into the ten original accounts. When Big Eddie's people noticed the addition of an eleventh account it would take days to unravel the problem. When the problem of an unauthorized account was brought to the banks attention they would immediately suspend all outgoing transfers until they arrived at a solution. However, without the new access code Big Eddie and his partners attorneys would have to meet at the bank to correct the error. The bank would not be liable for what amounted to employee embezzlement, but they would readily cooperate with an attempt to recover the money and find the responsible party.

The other problem was, Big Eddie could not provide the bank with young Raymond's name. Ray knew far too much to end up in police custody. Eddie had to act like he had no idea who could possibly do such a thing. If Ray fell into the wrong hands it could cost Eddie and his partners far more than a mere twenty-one million. Eddie had other ways of dealing with Raymond. It was only a matter of time before Eddie's people found him. Ray didn't turn out to be a rat, but he did become a clever thief. Eddie even admired Ray for having the guts to pull it off. It was too bad that Ray had to die for being a dumbass.

Ray used the money in his Computer Connections account to rent apartments in three other countries. He used the company debit card to buy inexpensive furniture on line and have it delivered to each apartment. He then purchased one-way first class airline tickets to each of the three countries using the company debit card. He had no intentions of going to any of those locations. It was just more false trails and dead ends for Big Eddie's people to follow.

Being a computer nerd opened a lot of doors in the electronic underworld. One trip to the right computer chat room led Ray to a cyber bar where he met a sweet girl who was also a cyber nerd. Her name was Kimberly, but her friends called her Kim. She knew the right people to get Ray French identification and passport. Once Ray had his new identification, he transferred one million into an account he opened in his new name and requested another one-hundred thousand dollar debit card and twenty-thousand Francs in cash. With his new name, Raynard Francois Chauvigny, his initials would remain the same, but he would be able to go places without detection.

He rented a nicer apartment under his new name and Kimberly helped him pick new modest furniture, which he paid for with his new debit card and had delivered. He took Kim on a shopping spree where he had fun buying her some new clothes and clothes for himself. He changed his image. In no time he looked like a young French college student with a sweet little girlfriend. He fit right in with the regular crowd. He was only planning to stay in France for about ten months before he moved on. Depending on how things progressed he would either give Kim everything when he left or take Kim with him and simply walk away. He wanted to live in a more tropical environment where English was the primary language. He didn't feel comfortable not being able to communicate well with the locals, but for now having Kim there solved that dilemma.

Ray didn't know that he had missed being caught by Big Eddie by only hours, but he did realize that once he pulled his disappearing act the hunt would be on. He didn't think that Eddie would discover the missing money until after he was long gone. He knew he was smarter than Big Eddie and all his friends and he knew that they would not dare turn him into the police. They couldn't risk it. He knew too much.

Kim stayed with him a lot in his new apartment. They played video games, searched the web, watched movies, ate popcorn and ordered take-out delivery food. Pizza and Chinese was their favorite. They were becoming good friends and their sexual relationship was just taking off. Ray had more experience than Kim, but she was an eager learner. They were both enjoying each other's company and having fun. It had been a long time since Ray could relax and enjoy himself.

The only thing Ray felt bad about was having to put ipecac in Lisa's orange juice to induce vomiting on the morning he took off. By the time she finished her breakfast she was in the bathroom hugging the toilet. He knew it made her terribly sick and he hated to do that to her. To make it look good Ray had offered to stay there with her, but she was so embarrassed she practically ran him out of the motel suite. Ray was gone in minutes.

It took several days for Big Eddie's people to get a copy of the account transaction information for the Computer Connections account. The first apartment they searched was the closest one there in France. All they found was a note on the table that said: "It would be in your best interest if nothing happened to me. Stop wasting your time. You'll never find me." It was signed, "E=MC2."

Big Eddie was pissed. He had people checking the other three apartments and looking for Ray in New York, where his plane ticket indicated he'd arrived. Eddie didn't think Raymond would be on that plane because the ticket was in his real name, but every lead was being checked. The twenty-one million had vanished along with Ray. Computers were supposed to make it easier to keep track of things, but with Ray's knowledge and ability, hiding things was nothing more than a game. It was only a matter of time before they all saw who the winner of the game would be: Ray with his computer skills or Eddie with his man power and good luck.

With as many problems as Big Eddie was dealing with, he was starting to think his luck was running short.

Chapter 22

The FBI and Marshal's Service were in the hot seat over the missing informants. Only one of the informants had been in the witness protection program, but had absconded from the program before he was kidnapped. Nonetheless, the negative media attention was making them look bad and incompetent so they were scrambling to resolve the matter with the help of the newly formed Task Force. That's where Will and Doc came into the picture. It helped that they had started on the ground level of the case, so to speak, when the case was only a missing persons problem. They were also the ones who were having the most luck at uncovering useful facts and evidence. Everyone was still hoping that Will would receive another email from deadserious that would solve the case.

Although they were gathering solid information and evidence that would help with the future prosecution of the case, they had no solid lead on who was behind the conspiracy. Obviously, the person or persons behind the kidnappings and fights was no amateur and had spared no expense to cover his tracks. Finding the culprit was proving to be a much more difficult task than Will and Doc had figured.

After they returned to their Reno base of operations Will parked his car and started using a regulation FBI SUV. They would be driving on country roads near the site where the six informants were buried interviewing the locals as they worked their way back towards Reno in a logical route. So far they were encountering a lot of resistance. People either didn't know anything, didn't want involved or were offended at being questioned.

Will and Doc had already been to one small ranch they suspected was harboring a meth lab. The prevalent odor in the air smelled like the garage apartment they'd busted towards the beginning of their investigation back in LA. Damn meth labs were popping up all over the place. They reported their suspicions to the Sheriff's Department and moved on. They would let the locals investigate and do the necessary environmental clean-up.

The good part was there were very few homes in that part of the State. It wouldn't take long to visit and interview the people in the area that were most likely to be of interest. A lot of that part of the State was wide open and empty of most everything but rocks, cactus and tumbleweeds. The foot hills of the Sierra Nevada mountains were largely National Parks and Reservations.

At noon they stopped at a roadside diner for lunch. The place was busy and the food was better than they expected. The waitress came right out and stated that it was pretty far off the beaten path for a couple of FBI agents and asked them what they were doing in these parts. Will explained that they were part of the Task Force investigating the missing informants.

"You mean dead informants, don't you?" the waitress exclaimed.

Before Will could answer a man at the next table said, "It sounds to me like they brought it on themselves. People should take more care to mind their own business. Then maybe they wouldn't get themselves killed."

"It takes concerned citizens to make this world a better place," said Doc. "We all have to work together to stop crime and keep everyone safe from killers and thieves."

"From what I heard on the news those missing informants weren't concerned citizens. They were criminals turned rat, trying to get themselves out of trouble. The world's a better place without them, you ask me," said the man at the next table.

Will and Doc paid their bill and left. There wasn't any point continuing the conversation with the man. The kidnappings and fights did amount to criminals killing criminals. Many people simply didn't care. They said good riddance.

Throughout the day Will had played the game of "if" with Doc. "If we owned the beach house what color carpet would you like?"

"Champagne shag in the living room, den, hallways and bed rooms. Tile in the kitchen, dining area and in the bathrooms. I'd want light colored curtains with white shams and decorative rods. I don't like cornice boards."

Will asked a lot of questions and committed Doc's answers to memory. The owner of the beach house had accepted Will's offer and Will's attorney was taking care of the details. Including hiring a contractor and decorator for the repairs and remodeling. The next time Doc saw the house Will wanted it to be her dream home. He was having fun. The beach house was not near as large as his previous home in New York and it wouldn't even amount to a guest cottage on his mother and father's estate, but it was sunny and cozy. Just what he and Doc needed to start a life together. Will was saving so much money buying the smaller home that he was planning on buying Doc a shiny new sports car for an engagement present. He would put the rest of the money from the sale of his home in New York into his investment portfolio and watch it grow. Will could actually make substantially more money working for his father, but he wanted to work at a fulfilling job that was rewarding in different ways, other than just financially. Will needed real life experiences in order to grow. Will's mother and father agreed that Will should spread his wings and fly around a bit before settling down at the family business.

The breakup with his ex was hard on Will and his parents encouraged him to take his time and not rush into any commitments. Will's parents were in their late 60s and very healthy. It would be ten-years before Will was actually needed at home and to take over the family investment firm. He planned to enjoy that ten-years doing something and someone he loved. He wasn't like most spoiled rotten rich kids. He was down to earth and responsible. Will fancied himself as Bruce Wayne. He'd had a Batman fixation since he was a kid.

They spent the better part of the week going from ranch to ranch asking questions and looking for the three missing vans. Other agents and detectives were interviewing people who were involved with the Reno Warehouse and the late Keith Fuller. Agents were also investigating Troy Thompson from Thompson's Trucking, Inc., because he was one of the major shippers to the warehouse in Reno. Will and Doc were still on "keep out of sight" field duty.

Friday evening at dusk they were headed back to Reno when they spotted a suspicious dark green van. Will knew it wasn't a factory paint job because the bumpers were painted the same color as the van and there was over-spray on the tires. The van was stopped at a 4-way intersection, headed east, when Will and Doc pulled up to the intersection heading south. That put the van on their left and they got a good look at the two big guys wearing matching black shirts and sunglasses as the van accelerated across the intersection in front of them.

Will decided to follow them and investigate. Doc hit the lights and siren and the driver of the freshly painted van hit the gas. The chase was on. Doc radioed in their location and asked for backup. At speeds in excess of one hundred miles an hour they followed the van around curves and over hills while Doc talked on the radio giving up-dates on their ever changing location. They were informed that a road-block had been established at a bridge two miles ahead of them. There was no other place for the van to go unless it turned around or tried to take off into the desert.

The bridge spanned a canyon with a river running wildly beneath it. When they shot around a bend in the road and the bridge came into view the driver of the van tapped the brakes like he was going to stop. There was nowhere to go. Instead of stopping the driver changed his mind and accelerated. It looked like the driver was going to ram the roadblock, but when it reached the center of the bridge it locked up its brakes, slid sideways to a stop and the driver and passenger jumped out with guns blazing. The passenger side was facing Will and Doc. As the passenger took off running he was firing in Will and Doc's direction, then he dove over the bridge rail. Will and Doc took cover until the gunfire that had erupted on the other side of the van subsided.

Doc had seen the passenger hit the shallow water about a hundred feet below the bridge and knew he was dead on impact because of the way he crumpled when he hit the water and started floating down stream in water that was quickly turning red. Will had seen the driver fall down in a hail of bullets at the rear of the van and figured he was dead or dying. They waited for the other officers to secure the scene and wave them over before they approached the van. Sure enough, the driver was shot to hell and couldn't have been any deader. They discovered two men in cages in the van. One was dead from bullets that went through the side of the van and the other was wounded. The guy who jumped over the side was lodged in some rocks under the bridge. There was no question of whether he was dead. He was faced down in a red pool of water next to a bridge piling and he was not moving.

Two officers were in the progress of working their way down to get him out of the water before he washed down stream. Life-flight was on the way to pick-up the wounded guy, who was probably one of the missing informants. The coroner was on the way to pick-up the bodies.

As they were looking in the van, Will asked, “What's that smell?"

"Horse shit," Doc answered.

One of the officers stuck his nose in the van and said, "Yeah, that's horse shit, alright. There's some on the front mats. It must have come off their shoes."

"How do you know it's not some other kind of shit?" Will asked.

"It's like smelling a can of Dr. Pepper and Coca-Cola. You just know. Horse shit has a distinct odor, different than cows or dogs," replied Doc.

"I can't believe we are standing here talking about shit and that you know so much about shit," Will laughed.

Doc laughed too and said, "I can't believe you didn't shoot someone. It's almost a first for you. I can't take you any place without you shooting someone," Doc said teasingly. On a more serious note she said, "These other guys are going to catch hell for shooting the place up like this."

Will didn't say anything because he knew Doc was right and he was silently thankful that he didn't fire his weapon. They were both hoping that the wounded guy made it and was able to provide them with some useful information.

By the time they had the wounded guy on the chopper and Will had cautioned the two deputies flying with him to stay on their guard, the Task Force Commander, agent Daniels, and several other Task Force agents had arrived with the SAC right behind them.

The first thing agent Daniels said was, "Hey Will, who'd you shoot this time?"

"I'm sure you'll be happy to know that I didn't fire a shot this time, but I certainly would have if I'd had a clear shot."

The crime scene crew started processing and collecting evidence while they took their usual thousand pictures. The van would be taken to Task Force headquarters for a detailed examination just as soon as the bridge scene was cleared. It was a mess.

What they didn't know was, while they were all standing around that van in the middle of the bridge, two more informants had been loaded in the back of a truck and were on their way to the new fight location. They also didn't know that one of the deputies flying in the helicopter was on Bob's payroll and he'd placed a call to Bob using his cell phone from the air. The fight would go on without delay, and if possible, the informant in the helicopter wouldn't live long enough to say a word. The news traveled fast that it was the same two agents who had visited Miss Sarcosie who had discovered the van and found the two informants after a harrowing chase.

It was late when Will and Doc got back to their motel room. They took turns taking hot showers so one of them would be ready when their pizza arrived. This assignment had them eating a lot of late night pizza. While they ate they were working on their daily reports. They only had time for a quickie before they both passed out from exhaustion. It was amazing how much paperwork was involved with being a cop and if you skipped a day on updating reports then you had twice as much to take care of the next day.

The next morning agent Daniels pounded on their motel room door. He just relished the opportunity to let Will and Doc know that he knew they were sleeping together. Of course, he apologized for the bother and requested the keys to the Task Force SUV that Will had checked out. Daniels' partner had left early for a meeting, so Daniels needed a vehicle, probably to go to breakfast. He promised to have it back in time for Will and Doc to make it to the mornings Task Force meeting.

Will had no sooner laid back down next to Doc and glanced at the clock, it was 5:37a.m., when he heard the SUV's alarm chirp, the door slam shut and the engine start to crank over, then an explosion rocked the building and shattered the room's windows. Will jumped up, grabbed his gun and ran out the door as debris was crashing to the ground and agent Daniels was burning-up in what was left of the SUV. A stroke of luck, fate or simply Daniels sorry disposition had prevented Will and Doc from being the intended victims. It was one of those moments when nothing was right. You're sad, shocked and at the same time damn thankful that it wasn't you. It was like one of those times when the dad stays home pretending to be sick, rather than going on a drive with his family, because he really just wanted to spend some time alone at home by himself on his day off. Then a police officer shows up to inform him that his entire family was killed in a car accident. You blame yourself and feel like shit because of the way you treated your family before they died. That's how Will and Doc were feeling. It was a sorry way to start a morning.

Doc was beside herself and openly crying. All Will could do was hold her as the SUV burned. Daniels may have been an asshole, but no one deserved to die like that. Bush-wacked without a chance to fight and defend yourself, leaving children and a wife behind. Doc and Daniels had a history and he was a fellow officer. It was just plain wrong and a horrible send off. It was going to be a long day.

It was obvious that someone had been following Will and Doc with the intent to kill them. They would have to take extreme caution from this point forward if they were even allowed to stay on the case. Will was already working on his argument to justify him and Doc remaining on the case. In his mind he was thinking that he would either be working the case with the team or he would quit his job and work it on his own. He didn't really think it would go that far, but he was ready if it did. It wasn't just him these nuts were trying to kill it was also the woman he loved. Will knew that whether they actively worked the case or not their lives would be in danger until the case was concluded. It was time to fight, not run and Will planned to fight.

Chapter 23

While one of the informants laid in the morgue and the recently rescued kidnap victim was undergoing emergency surgery to remove one bullet from his liver and a fragment that nicked his left lung, two other kidnapped informants were fighting for their lives in an old airplane hangar. The new fight location was privately owned and perfect because small planes could land without anyone noticing. It was so far out in the desert that cars could be seen coming for miles. There would be plenty of time to fly away if they saw the cavalry coming. Unlike the other fights that had lasted mere moments, this fight gave the bettors what they'd been looking for. It was almost ten minutes of slashing and stabbing.

Both opponents were covered in blood and almost bled out before one got lucky with a fatal stab to the neck and his adversary started spraying copious amounts of blood from the side of his neck in unbelievable spurts. He was bleeding profusely, but for obvious reasons it didn't last long. The man dropped to his knees, give completely out and as the last two small spurts poured from his gaping neck wound he fell face down, dead.

The winner was short lived, literally. He had a wound high in his side that was spitting foaming blood from a ruptured lung. He fell to the mat and the officiator pronounced him the winner and a moment later the doctor pronounced him dead. The few bettors who took the long shot, "Double Death," just got one hell of a payoff and everyone watching the fight got one hell of a show. The fight clip would be played over and over for years to come.

The next morning while firemen were diligently working to put the fire out so they could recover agent Daniels' charred body from what was left of the

SUV, two men loaded the bodies of the unfortunate gladiators into the back of a truck and drove them to a remote location deep in the desert where they buried the gladiators in their final resting place in the cool morning sand. It would be months before their bones were discovered.

This time Will and Doc were forced to change motels. Not only did they not want to stay in the same motel, the owner had refused them another room before anyone had even asked. They quickly packed their bags and gathered their guns and equipment, then had one of the Task Force members take them to headquarters where Will's personal car was parked. They both felt better just being out of sight of the burned SUV. Knowing that the fire department was waiting for the SUV to cool before they could remove Daniels body gave Will and Doc a sick feeling. After retrieving Will's car and checking into a motel that offered a secured underground parking area, they typed up their morning reports on the incident and emailed them to the required parties then they tried to eat a few bites before the morning meeting that had been postponed until 10:00 a.m.

In a penthouse apartment several thousand miles away in Moscow, Russia, Angela Sarcosie was screaming something about incompetence and stupidity into a phone. How the hell hard could it be to kill two meddling cops. She didn't give a damn if Big Eddie liked it or not. Angela had used her new found friendship with Carmine (Pierre) Antonellie and his body guard Hammer to put a contract out on the two cops, Holiday and Bracket, who had confronted her at her office. These Russians were supposed to be professionals, but they couldn't even orchestrate a simple hit on two sleeping cops. Angela was madder than mad. She was irate.

Angela's plan B, her exit from the United States, had been perfectly executed, in more ways than one. First, those pestersome cops had laid the foundation for her exit by coming to her office and questioning her about the kidnapping and murder of the informants. Angela put on a show for her daddy and explained how distressed she was about the accusations. Then Angela told her secretary that she was going home because she was depressed. When she got back to her apartment she spiked Kera's drink with liquid diazepam. As customary during oral sex with Kera, Angela slipped a morphine suppository into Kera's tight little ass, just as she licked Kera into a climax. Her very last climax. Minutes later, as Kera lie on the couch passed out from drugs and pleasure, Angela, as frigid as an artic wind, traded jewelry with Kera and set the stage for her suicide. The last thing Angela did was carefully knock some candles over and made sure they caught the carpet and couch on fire before she walked out of the apartment like nothing happened. Angela was walking out of the side entrance of the building when the fire alarm started blaring. She had known this day was coming, so she had switched her dental records with Kera's weeks before. It wasn't difficult to switch the dental x-rays when she was fucking the cute little married dentist in his office after hours.

Angela didn't enjoy killing Kera, but it was a necessary part of plan B. It was still like killing a part of herself. Angela and Kera could have passed for twins. That was one of the reasons that Kera often died her hair red so people could tell them apart. That was exactly why Angela had picked Kera for a lover. It was all about plan B. That and Angela just liked to eat pussy.

Along with her new name and home in Moscow, Angela had already acquired a new lover. Angela's new name was Nicole and her hot, sexy, blonde haired, long legged companion's name was Joanna. They called each other Jo and Nic. Angela knew they were a match the first night she'd met Jo in a Moscow night club. She took Jo back to her penthouse apartment and as Jo fucked her hard and fast with a fat eight inch dildo, she grabbed a handful of Angela's hair, jerked her head back, and said, "Come for me, bitch," with a thick, sexy, Russian accent that triggered an orgasm so intense that Angela almost passed out with pleasure. Afterwards, as they both lay next to each other sweating and catching their breath, Angela (Nic) knew she had discovered what she had been looking for, for a long time. Living in Russia was going to be a blast.

Joanna told Nicole that, "When you go to clubs in Russia you must always carry knife. Russian men are very aggressive. You must teach them that their aggression will not be tolerated. Men are pigs who think with their dicks."

Nicole, being the cold hearted bitch that she was, was thinking that even pigs have their uses.

When Big Eddie got the news later that day, when he was having lunch again, that Angela had ordered a hit on the same two cops, that failed, he was so mad at the stupid bitch he could have choked her to death with his bare hands. What the hell was she thinking going after the same two cops, again.

On top of that she had missed them, again. Eddie knew that, even though the wrong agent was killed, the heat had just gotten turned to high. Cops would be all over the place harassing people and bringing them in for questioning. It would be like in his favorite Humphrey Bogart movie, Casablanca, where the French policemen said, "Round up the usual suspects." Things were going from bad to worse real fast. Big Eddie knew that with Fuller gone and Angela out of the immediate picture there was no one to connect him to Reno other than Bob and young Ray of course, who had certainly proved to be elusive.

Eddie pulled Bob out of the fray for the time being. One of Bob's subordinates, who didn't know Eddie, would stand by and monitor things in Reno and do a little damage control when the situation arose.

The hospital where the kidnap victim was being held was on high alert. There had already been a fire in the basement laundry room that morning that may or may not have been intentional. The informant currently laying in a hospital bed in ICU was Wu Tran from New York City. He had absconded from witness protection only to be nabbed by the bad guys. Tran was lucky to be alive. He'd been in surgery until after 4:00 a.m. Will and Doc were hoping to talk with him by noon. The other less fortunate kidnapped informant, Jose Sanches, who died in the "van shoot-out," as the event had been dubbed, was certainly not so lucky. One of the officers at the road block had been firing an M-16 that had ripped through the side of the van like it was a thin aluminum soda can.

Rather than sit and wait, Will and Doc went to talk with Eugine Dawlrimple, the Crime Scene Unit SAC there in Reno who was going over the van and other evidence. There was so much blood in the van from the dead and wounded guys that it would be days before they finished processing the inside of the van. They'd verified that the van was one of the three missing vans from the Reno warehouse that had recently been painted green in a poor attempt to disguise it. The two dead kidnappers had not been identified, as of yet, which was certainly odd, because criminals, military personnel, casino employees and even cops had their prints on file in Nevada. Neither of the dead guys had identification so it would probably take days to identify them, if they ever did. Agents were taking pictures of the two dead men around hoping that someone would recognize them and put names with the faces. Will and Doc wanted their names and where they lived so they could gather more information and evidence that would help them find who was responsible for the kidnappings and gladiator fights. They needed more leads to follow.

The SCU techs had positively identified horse shit on the two dead guys boots, in the van, under the wheel-wells and on the tires of the van. Clearly, the two guys and the van had been some place with a lot of horse shit. The agents agreed that the horses the shit came from where grain fed, which was indicative of well-kept horse stables. Maybe the race track one agent suggested. That would certainly fit with the betting angle of the fights. There were literally hundreds of buildings, barns and stables in and around the race track they were referring to. Will and Doc ran this information by the Task Force Commander who immediately dispatched agents to the horse races to start asking questions and showing pictures of the two dead guys.

However, after looking at a map to see where the horse track was located, in relation to where they encountered the van and the body dump site, Will and Doc had another idea. A lot of horse shit required a lot of horses. Will called the Sheriff's office and arranged for a small plane to fly them around the area where they first spotted the van.

The staff meeting was short. Nobody wanted to talk about Daniels' death. It was all way to fresh. Several of the agents still smelled of smoke from the burning SUV. They were all mad, scared and in shock. The SAC gave a short speech and told the Task Force members to continue to follow all leads. Local law enforcement would become more heavily involved with the investigation and every effort would be made to ensure that no other Task Force members would die and the responsible party for Daniels' murder would pay and pay dearly.

Everyone left the Task Force meeting with a look of determination and despair on their faces. Will and Doc headed for the hospital to check on the status of Wu Tran. The nurse at the hospital advised them that, although Mr. Tran had opened his eyes a few times, he was heavily medicated and probably wouldn't be able to provide any coherent answers to their questions until later that evening or the next morning. With that in mind, Will and Doc looked in on Wu Tran then decided to have lunch before they started flying all over the country side looking at horse ranches from the air.

To keep from thinking or talking about agent Daniels and how close they both came to death that morning, during lunch, Will continued his game of "if" with Doc. "If we owned that beach house do you think we should put a hot tub on the back deck?" asked Will.

"A hot tub built into the deck would be cool. I would want it flush with the deck so we'd have to step down into it. We could box in the sides of the deck and keep the lights off so people on the beach couldn't see us naked and making love in the hot tub."

Will kept filing away Doc's answers and every chance he got he would pick-out designs on the internet and email them to his attorney so the changes could be made without Doc knowing. He was going through his family attorney because he didn't want the contractors bothering him. It cost a little more, but it was worth it in the long run. He didn't want Doc to discover what he was doing because it would spoil the surprise.

After lunch, which they couldn't eat much of, they went back to their new motel room to check their emails and make a few calls before they had to meet the pilot at the airport. Will also looked on line at decks and hot tubs then sent another email to his attorney. The decorator had been through the house, made a list of the needed improvements and ordered the changes to be done by a local contractor. Will wanted everything done as soon as possible, because he planned to ask Doc to marry him on the back deck of the beach house as the sun dropped below the horizon. Will wanted everything so perfect that Doc would have no choice but to say yes.

From the motel they went to a small airport and climbed into a tiny single engine prop plane that would take them on a tour of the area. The plane only held four people and with just three of them in the plane it was crowded. The pilot looked at the map Will brought with him and they decided on an idea for a search pattern using the main road and the intersection where they first came into contact with the van as a central starting point.

Neither Will nor Doc had considered how hot it would be in the small plane flying over the desert in the afternoon summer sun. The plane didn't have air conditioning, which was a fact that Will and Doc had a hard time comprehending. Why would anyone want to fly around in a little plane in the oppressive heat with no air conditioner. As far as Will and Doc were concerned it was boarder line crazy. The small amount of air that was coming through the vents and windows was hot enough to take their breath away. The heat was stifling and they'd just gotten started. It only took them a few minutes to decide that one fly-over was all they wanted in that heat.

The pilot flew alongside the main road leading to the intersection in question then flew five miles past it before turning around and heading back. Between wiping off the sweat Doc made notes and marked the locations of three large farms that had barns, corrals and horses on her map. On the return trip they flew further east of the road and spotted four more possibilities they planned to check-out the following day.

Back at the airport the pilot was barely sweating and looked fine. He smiled and laughed when Will and Doc almost fell out of the plane in a heavy sweat. They had been in the plane just over one hour, but it felt like a week. Neither could recall ever being that hot in their lives. After thanking the pilot they both hurried to Will's car and the comfort of its air conditioner. Once they cooled off and had something to drink the whole event became funny and they both agreed that it was a lesson well learned. They vowed to stay out of small planes. Will and Doc agreed that the flight was generally miserable and less productive than they had hoped. They'd been primarily looking for the other two missing vans and maybe a large sign that said: "The missing informants are being held here."

On the way back to their new motel room they picked up Chinese take-out. The sesame chicken, sweet and sour pork, fried rice and egg rolls were just what they needed after such a long, hot, shitty day. The entire day had been shadowed with thoughts of agent Daniels being blown-up and burnt. They both went to sleep, exhausted, hoping the next day would be better and more productive.

Chapter 24

Harry Butkus had watched the guards take out two prisoners. A short time later two different guards had taken out two more prisoners. It was pretty obvious to Harry that something had went wrong with moving the first two prisoners. He didn't know what was happening, but it must have been bad for two new guards to show up in a hurry and hustle two more prisoners out so soon after the first two were pulled out. Harry was excited and was hoping that whatever the problem was that it would lead to his rescue.

Usually the two women who brought the food didn't come back after the evening meal and tray pickup, but they had both been up and down the hallway several times pulling loaded carts and carrying boxes of what looked to be food and supplies.

After the second set of guards picked up two more prisoners the women running the ranch were advised to cover the rear exit of the barn and prepare in case the cops came around asking questions. They took their time moving over three hundred, fifth pound bags of horse feed into the room that had a stairway leading to the underground hidden prison. When they were done it looked like nothing more than a room for storing feed. The adjacent part of the barn where the van backed into to load the prisoners was raked to cover up tire tracks then a small tractor was parked in there to help disguise the purpose of that portion of the barn.

Most of the supplies for the prison were moved from the ranch house basement down the hidden underground passageway that led from the house to the prison under the barn. The basement contained the laundry for the ranch and the small prison. All the bedding, towels and extra clothing were moved into the prison area. The door leading into the passageway was cleverly built as a solid retracting wall of concrete. It had to be well designed to avoid detection and to last because it was opened at least six times a day for the prisoners' food cart and to pick up food trays. The last thing they did was sweep the basement floor and roll out a rubber mat to help cover scuff marks. Then they went to bed with each other.

The following day was uneventful. They didn't have many prisoners to cook for so meals didn't take long. The hardest part was carrying the food trays down the basement stairs. They wheeled the food cart in and delivered the food and came back thirty minutes later for the trays and trash. They were careful to burn their trash every day in burn barrels behind the barn.

About three that afternoon, while the two rather beautiful women who ran the ranch were out at the corral working with a couple of high strung sorrel mares they were preparing for a show, a small plane, flying too low, flew by just west of the ranch. They suspected what it might mean and worked on getting their stories straight. It looked like a shit storm was coming and they were ready for it.

It was the next afternoon when Will and Doc showed up with a note book full of questions. There were a total of five women there at the ranch when Will and Doc arrived. The scene reminded Will of that ZZ Top song "Planet of Women." Three of the women just came during the day to work with the horses and they weren't involved with the prison end of things. The two women who managed the ranch introduced themselves and the other girls and took Will and Doc on a tour of the stables, barn and corral as Will and Doc asked their questions.

"Where are the men?" Will asked.

"Honey, we only need men for recreation. We do all the workin'," said the sexy redhead with a smile.

"We need to ask you some questions about some missing informants," said Will.

"You mean you're not here to look at the horses?" asked the blonde.

"That's why we showed you our badges, told you we are police officers and said we would like to ask you a few questions," Doc replied.

"Oh, I thought you wanted to ask us some questions about the horses," the woman countered.

The redhead said, "I was wondering why you were asking us about a van. We use pickups here. We don't have a van."

Will said, "We are wondering if you've seen a white or dark green van around, either here or at other ranches?"

“We haven't seen one here and we don't get out much. The ranch and horses require a lot of care and attention," answered the blonde.

"Ma'am--" Will started.

"Just call me Cindy and call her Red, on account she has red hair. Everyone calls her Red. I call her Kitty. You should hear her purr."

"Okay Cindy. We are part of the Task Force that's investigating the death of the six informants that were discovered buried not far from here," said Will.

"Not far from here?" Cindy asked. "I thought that was way up by the Indian reservation. That's like sixty miles or something. We don't know anything about that."

With that answered, Will asked, "I'm curious how you two got into the horse ranching business, if you don't mind me asking?"

"Oh, honey, we don't own it, we just manage the place and train the horses. We were both showgirls at the Mirage. Then as we got older we were floor girls. Then we were replaced by new and younger talent with tighter asses. One of the co-owners started this ranch to give us retired showgirls a nice home and a good job. It's nice out here and we see a lot of girls come and go. Some stay awhile, others move on to better places and things," said Cindy.

"It looks like a good setup," said Doc. "He must be a nice man."

"Oh hon, he's great. He's just an old horn-dog who loves beautiful women and high dollar horses," said Cindy. "Hon, as pretty as you are, when you retire you can come out here and stay with us if you like."

"Well, thank you," Doc responded timidly.

Will quickly interjected with, "Thank you ladies for your time and for showing us around. This is a nice place and those are some fine horses."

Red spoke up and said, "Come back and see me. I've got some other things I can show you."

Will and Doc drove away with uncertain smiles on their faces.

"That was awkward, but interesting," Doc stated. "I think we both could have had a romp in the hay if we'd wanted one."

"I wanted one, but with you," Will said quickly.

"Right answer big boy," Doc said. "If you do any romping it better be with me. You're too far out in the stream to change horses now. You might drown, if you catch my drift."

"I love it when you talk that cowgirl slang to me," replied Will with a smile. "So is it okay if, when I'm doing you from behind, I slap you on the rump and say giddyup?"

"Baby, you can slap me on the ass anytime, but if you say giddyup I may turn around and bite you," Doc said teasingly.

They stopped at two other ranches and asked their questions. With no luck they headed back to Reno. They had no idea how close they'd been to the kidnapped captive informants. At one point they had walked right over the prisoners on their tour of the barn.

When they got back to their motel room they went through their evening ritual of eating take-out, writing field reports, reading and answering emails. They noted that a church service had been scheduled for 10:00 a.m. the following morning for Daniels before his body was transported to his home town where his parents would bury him close to other relatives, right next to their own plots, where they would take their final rest one day.

Lust overrode thoughts of Daniels and their investigation. They didn't make love, they fucked hard and fast, right into exhaustion where they fell asleep in each-other's arms. Good, intense sex is better than a sleeping pill and just as addictive. The truth of the matter was, Will and Doc had both been real horny ever since visiting Cindy and Red at the horse ranch. They were very sexy women and the whole encounter had a sexual overtone to it.

Chapter 25

The services were closed casket, or course. There was no need to delay the memorial service. An autopsy certainly wasn't necessary. The cause of death was obvious. The forensic portion of the investigation was concentrated on the bomb fragments and residue. The service was not large. It was mostly for the Task Force members that knew Daniels. A few other agents, officers and local dignitaries were present, as well. After a minister delivered a moving service and touching eulogy the SAC and the Task Force commander spoke briefly of the tragic loss and the importance of catching and punishing the responsible party. There would be another service held by the family when Daniels' body arrived back home.

Most everyone was silently thankful that they didn't have to see the wife, children and parents in their grief stricken state. Several of the agents that knew Daniels well were flying back with his body to attend the additional service and burial and to comfort the family. Will was not going because he'd only known Daniels a short time. Doc wasn't going because too many people, including Daniels' wife, knew about her affair with Daniels. The last thing Doc wanted was to be the reason for a scene at Daniels' funeral. She figured she would do Daniels a better service by finding his killer.

After the service, most of the Task Force personnel just wanted to immerse themselves in work so they didn't have to think about Daniels and his fiery death. Finding the person responsible was far more important and rewarding then dwelling on something that they couldn't change and was so depressing. The dead were past caring and now it was all about retribution.

Doc knew that Daniels wouldn't want her crying about his death. He would want her to avenge his murder. Doc kept picturing the flames pouring out of the SUV through the holes that use to be windows. While the flames were reaching up like bloody demonic fingers to the sky, thick black smoke was boiling away from the shattered SUV in an angry cloud that was racing towards the heavens. Doc remembered feeling the heat on her face, knowing it was Daniels burning, with that song running through her mind, "All we are is dust in the wind," over and over. She hoped it was a long time before she heard that song again, because she knew it would remind her of Daniels and the awful stench of him burning for the rest of her life.

"You want to talk about it?" asked Will.

"Thank you, but no. I'm trying my best not to think about it."

"If you change your mind we'll take a break and find a park where we can talk."

"I sure got lucky when I found you, Will."

"You sure did," Will said with a smile. "But not half as lucky as I did. Let's go get some lunch then find some bad guy ass to kick."

Doc just smiled and Will drove them to a popular Italian restaurant where they beat the noon rush hour by thirty minutes. As they were finishing their meal Will's cell phone vibrated in his pocket. It was the Task Force Commander advising Will that a waitress in a club had identified the men in the van as two guys who lived in her apartment building. The waitress thought they must be gay because they wouldn't give her a second look and she'd never seen them with women. She gave them the apartment number. The SAC was on his way to get a warrant signed and an agent was talking with the building super to ascertain the names of the two dead men.

By the time Will and Doc arrived at the apartment complex the agent on scene had identified, through the superintendent, the names of the two bad guys, Jerry Blackmon and Dennis Stevens. The superintendent didn't believe anyone else was staying in the apartment. A few minutes later four additional agents showed up in tactical gear with the warrant in hand. The superintendent, deducing what was about to transpire, advised Will that there was no need to break down the door because he had a key. At the door of the apartment one of the agents slid a small flexible fiber-optic camera lens under the door. It was a tight fit, but he found just enough space in a corner where the weather stripping's rubber seal didn't go all the way to the corner. The agent quietly said the place looked empty.

Will knocked while the agent watched the room on his monitor. When no one answered and nothing moved, Will inserted the key and opened the door. The tactical team went in fast and hard to secure the apartment.

The entire apartment was completely empty and it had been painted and cleaned. The smell of fresh paint and pine scented cleaner was cloying. It was obvious that the apartment itself was another dead end, but now they at least had the names of the two dead guys to work with. If the names were real then it was likely they would be able to check tax and employment records to find out more about the two dead guys. Something would turn up. However, Will wasn't real hopeful, because the apartment rent had been paid in cash, in advance, for a year's rent. In a place like Reno, Nevada a man throwing cash around didn't raise any red flags. If a person had a lot of cash places like Reno and Las Vegas, where cash was the primary commodity, were the best places to spend it. Paying cash for a new vehicle, or most anything, didn't even raise an eyebrow in Reno. Cash was expected in a city that thrived on gambling proceeds. Will assigned officers to interview the neighbors and start record checks before he and Doc left the building. The wheels were turning, but turning too slow for Will's taste. He had no doubt that something would break loose, it was just a matter of when and where.

As they were pulling away from the apartment building Will's cell phone started vibrating again. It was the computer tech that was running traces on the deadserious emails, advising Will that another email had just popped up. Will and Doc drove back to Task Force headquarters to check it out. The tech was attempting to trace the origin of the new email, which was short and cryptic. It simply read: "Mr. Big and his dark Angel are running things from Los Angeles. Now they are holding fights in China, Russia, England and Mexico."

"The email originated in France, but I don't know exactly where in France. It was transmitted by satellite. All I have is a general location of Paris," said the computer tech.

Will took his time formulating an email to deadserious in hopes that he would provide them with more information. Will's previous emails had gone unanswered, but he had to at least try.

The Task Force was already aware that informants were being reported missing in Russia, China, England and Mexico. They had come to the conclusion that death matches were probably being held in those countries, as well. So far no bodies of dead informants had surfaced in those countries.

However, the information that was being gathered indicated that organized crime families were sponsoring gladiator fights at clandestine locations where people could bet on the fights. Several raids had been conducted but no additional leads had been forthcoming.

Unbeknownst to Will and Doc, later that evening the DEA executed a search warrant on a club belonging to one Carmine Antonellie. The DEA, working on a tip from a reliable informant, had sent undercover officers into the club to make controlled buys of cocaine, methamphetamine, ecstasy and LSD. The drugs were being stored and sold at the club, although they were only sold in small quantities.

When the DEA went in they interrupted a private party in the back where the people present were drinking and having a great time while they viewed a fight on a huge big screen television. Much to their astonishment, the DEA arrived in time to witness the ending of a live gladiator fight. One of the DEA agents happened to recognize the significance of the fight and used the video camera he was carrying to videotape the bust to film the last part of the fight. It was a bloody ordeal that stopped the agent in his tracks. He was stunned and could not believe what he was seeing. The people in the room didn't even get excited at the sight of the DEA and their guns. They were just drinking and talking and enjoying an evening at the club. When questioned many of the people said they weren't paying attention to the fight and didn't know who changed the channel to the fight. None of the people there would admit to betting on the fight and only one person in the room had a small amount of cocaine in his pocket that he claimed was for personal use.

The agent who filmed the bloody ending of the fight later told Will and Doc that "That damn football player and his dog fights ain't got shit on this."

Mr. Antonellie was not present when his club was raided. He was at another location viewing the fight. Some of the key personnel at the club that was raided, who ran the drugs and gambling, had fled through a hidden door that the DEA didn't know until later existed, into a row of adjacent warehouses. By the time the door was discovered those key players were long gone with most of the dope and money. The one thing they didn't manage to take was the computer hard-drive that contained the descrambling program. But without the password the computer program was pretty much useless.

Will and Doc learned of the fight footage the next morning at the Task Force meeting where they had to, once again, justify the reason why they should be allowed to remain on the case after two attempts on their lives. A valid argument had been made that it was not only Will and Doc's lives that were in danger, but other officers, as well. Evident by agent Daniels' fiery murder. In the end, because the email from deadserious said that "Mr. Big and his dark Angel are running things from Los Angeles," the SAC used that fact as an excuse to send Will and Doc back to Los Angeles. Everyone knew it was just to get Will and Doc out of the hot zone.

At first it pissed Doc off to be sent away from what she considered a fight. Then Will, with his usual smile, took Doc aside and explained that the fight would likely follow them back to Los Angeles and it was better to go after the head of the snake rather than the tail. With Mr. Big in Los Angeles and Carmine Antonellie's club being busted, the logical conclusion was to get back to

Los Angeles and track down Antonellie, who had yet to be found, because he might lead them to Mr. Big.

Antonellie was hiding behind a team of lawyers that were claiming Antonellie merely owned the club, he didn't run it and certainly wasn't responsible if one of his employees or a customer did something illegal. The controlled drug buys had been made from people who were not even on Antonellie's payroll. So far there wasn't even enough evidence to justify an arrest warrant for Antonellie. He was only wanted for questioning. Finding and questioning Mr. Antonellie would be one of Will and Doc's first priorities when they got back to Los Angeles.

Will was excited. They had exhausted most of their good leads in Reno. Other than Wu Tran, who was still in the hospital and didn't know who had kidnapped him or where he was held, most of the other leads were dead. Wu Tran would be handled by other agents while Will and Doc went on the hunt for Carmine, Mr. Big and the dark Angel.

Chapter 26

Ray hadn't been planning to send officer Bracket any more emails under his deadserious pseudonym until his live in girlfriend, Kim, received a call from one of her friends at the cyber cafe where she'd met Ray. Her friend told her that two rough looking men had been to the cafe showing around Ray's picture, asking questions and offering a reward for information on Ray's whereabouts.

When Ray heard the news he was pissed, but also thankful that computer geeks stick together and help each other when in a jam. Ray had warned Big Eddie to leave him alone. Ray knew he had to be very careful, because he didn't want to do anything that would look like he was the one informing the police. He would give them just enough information to point them in the right direction and not draw any attention to himself. Ray knew that if he sent an email to Big Eddie warning him off, again, it would tip Eddie off that he was still in France and that he knew Eddie's men were looking for him. Ray had some other ideas that would probably work a lot better and would help point the police in the right direction while pointing the blame on someone else.

When Ray first discovered that over twenty-six million had been transferred into the account he initially opened he knew it was far more money than would have come in just from the fights in America. Before Big Eddie changed the account access code, Ray had accessed the account and traced where the money came from. Ray found that large deposits into the master account were also coming in from China, Russia, Mexico and England. That's when it dawned on Ray that things were a lot bigger than he'd anticipated. Ray knew that Big Eddie had started new fighting operations in these other countries. The kicker was, Big Eddie didn't know that Ray had figured it out.

Therefore, if heat got drawn to these other locations Big Eddie would have no reason to believe that it came from Ray. Ray decided to send another deadserious email sharing this information with officer Bracket. He didn't know that Angela Sarcosie had faked her suicide or that the Task Force was already aware that informants were missing in these other countries. He'd been sitting in his nice cozy little apartment with Kim playing video games and enjoying life. Ray had been hoping to stay in the apartment for a while, but it was looking like he needed to move quickly. He knew better than to panic, but he also knew that he should take caution and not linger. Ray had thought all this through already and had already made plans in case of an emergency. He rigged his computer with a motion detector so the camera would come on and the computer would record the movement and transmit the live feed to his laptop. Then he invited Kim to spend a few days at a bed and breakfast in Aigle, Switzerland near Lake Geneva. The Berner Alpen was supposed to be beautiful in the summer. Ray had already cultivated a new friendship in Vienna that could supply him and Kim with Austrian identification if need be.

The last thing he did before they left on their little vacation was to send officer Bracket another deadserious email that informed him that the fights were also being conducted in China, Russia, England and Mexico and that Mr. Big and his dark Angel were running the fights from Los Angeles. Ray pointed officer Bracket in the right direction and hoped he could figure out the rest. It would certainly be interesting to see how things progressed, but for now, it was time to make haste.

On the train Ray and Kim had a small private compartment and were traveling first class. There was something about sex in a traveling train with people in the next compartment and walking up and down the passage in front of their door that made it stimulating and exciting. Ray and Kim made love in rhythm with the slow rocking of the train. After the conductor came by they enjoyed a lunch of cheese, sausage, olives, crackers and a cool wine that Kim had packed in a small basket for the first part of the trip. It was romantic and fun.

When Ray's laptop started beeping he knew what to expect. It was the computer in his apartment calling to alert Ray of an intruder. Ray opened the security program that showed the live feed of the apartment living room. Two men were moving in and out of the frame obviously searching the apartment. The two big, tough looking men looked out of place rummaging around in Ray's small apartment. When they finally stopped searching and sat down on Ray's couch with a bottle of wine from Ray's cupboard it was clear that they intended to wait for Ray's return. One of the men picked up the remote and turned on the television. A few moments later the men were engrossed in a video game and having fun. They looked right at home as they jabbed the controls with intense expressions on their faces. Ray had seen enough. He pulled out his cell phone and called the French Gendarmes to report the break-in. The inspector Ray spoke with was outraged and he dispatched a car immediately. Ray explained where he was and how he knew his apartment had been broken into, told him that the would be burglars were still in the apartment playing video games and assured the inspector that the entire incident had been captured on his computer's security program. They both agreed that technology was a wonderful tool and the inspector agreed to return Ray's call once the crooks were apprehended. It was a great day for crime fighting in France.

Ray and Kim watched the video screen until the Gendarmes appeared with guns drawn, disarmed the bad guys and took them into custody. Ray watched as one of the uniformed policia sat down at the computer and proceeded to access the computer security program. Ray then turned on his camera so the officer could see his face and hear him talking, then he explained how to save the security file and copy it to disc.

A short time later the inspector returned Ray's call and informed Ray that the two men were not ordinary burglars. They were both armed and not carrying any identification, which led the inspector to believe that there was some serious skullduggery afoot. However, the inspector explained, the two men were known because they were ex-Interpol who had been discharged for suspicion of being involved with the French Mafia.

The inspector was very interested to know why the French Mafia would be interested in Ray. Ray assured him that he did not know and agreed that when he returned from his vacation, with the inspector's gracious assistance, they would try to figure it all out. Ray knew that his best option was to call the Gendarmes and report the break-in so he could discover who they were. He also knew that once he called them that he would not be able to go back to his nice little apartment or France. Ray liked France, but figured Austria would be a nice place too. Anyway, it didn't really matter what Ray wanted, he had to stay out of France. Not only had Big Eddie managed to find him, Ray sensed the inspector was not homme moyen sen-suel: the average non-intelligent man, who would easily believe Ray's total innocence of wrong doing. Not with an obvious Mafia connection in the mix. Ray and Kim decided that, rather than continue to Aigle, Switzerland, they would detour to Vienna, Austria where they would acquire new identification and start a new life. It was just another step towards his ultimate plan of disappearing into the blue, so to speak. The only trick was, everything they did required a passport, so there would be a record of them changing their plans and going to Vienna where they would then drop off the grid. Kim knew someone they could stay with until their new identification was ready, which would help them go undetected until Ray could setup a new account and get another apartment. This time he planned to open the account and lease the apartment in Kim's new name. That should help him drop further under the radar.

Once they decided on a plan they embarked on their new adventure by getting off the train at the next stop. Ray figured that it was probable that the inspector would have someone waiting for them in Aigle, under the pretext of taking their statements, so they could check Ray and Kim out further. Ray couldn't take that risk. Ray and Kim went to a bank where they withdrew more cash using Ray's debit card then they proceeded to a used car lot where Ray purchased a nice little economy car using his debit card. They then rented a motel room for two days using the debit card and had an excellent meal. Using the same debit card they bought some clothes, some jewelry and other items then took to the road. They intended to drive throughout the night heading for Vienna. If the inspector checked it would look like Ray decided to stay in that area and do some sight-seeing before proceeding with his vacation. Ray hoped to be well on his way by the time the inspector figured out what really happened.

With any luck Ray and Kim would be in a new cozy little apartment with new identities within the week where they could settle in for a while without being bothered.

Chapter 27

Will was excited. Not only was Carmine Antonellie a solid lead to follow they were headed back to Los Angeles where more kidnappings had recently taken place and the beach house was almost ready. Even though they were in the middle of a huge investigation, with someone trying to kill them, Ray was in the process of making everything ready so he could pop the question.

The drive from Reno to Los Angeles was more than Will could take. While driving down the highway at 80 mph Doc had unzipped Will's pants, carefully taken out Will's hard penis and wrapped her plump, soft lips around it then slowly worked them up and down his hard shaft until Will exploded.

Doc sucked every drop out of him then she raised her skirt, learned back against the passenger door with her left leg over the back of the seat so Will would have a wide open view of her hot, wet, pussy then she slid two fingers of her left hand inside her and started vigorously masturbating with the finger of her right hand as she moaned with delight.

Will pulled into the first motel he came to in Barstow and he and Doc did each other over and over, in every position they could think of, way into the night.

The next morning the remainder of the drive to Los Angeles was less sexually frantic and they were able to concentrate on what direction the investigation was headed and what their next steps would be. The first place they stopped was Doc's house to drop off her luggage. As soon as they walked through the door they knew the house had been searched. It wasn't wrecked, but everything had been moved around and obviously gone through. Whoever searched the place took care not to damage anything, but still made it known that everything had been touched and examined. The first thing Doc did was hurry into her bedroom where she discovered her gun case open on the bed with her guns laid out neatly on the bed. To add insult to injury, whoever searched the place had taken the time to lay out some of Doc's lingerie, three sexy teddies, on the bed before placing the firearms on top of them with some of Doc's sex toys, two dildos', cock rings, condoms, fish net stockings, handcuffs and a few other items, including a pair of black four inch stiletto heels that were artfully placed among the firearms. It was a display laid out to signify sex and violence. Doc was pissed beyond measure.

Will smiled and said, "That is the perfect picture of what I was thinking. Let's find these assholes and shoot 'em, then we can fuck like bunnies. I suggest that we load this stuff up and go to my apartment. Then we can get busy and figure all this out."

Doc pasted on a fake smile and agreed. They cleaned the place up a little and took the guns and play toys with them when they left.

Will jokingly said, "When we get to my place if there are any dildos lying on the bed we'll know something is seriously wrong."

Doc issued a strained laugh and asked Will to stop by the gun shop on the way to his apartment.

At the gun store the owner waved to them as they walked in. The owner said, "Hey, Doc. Your order is in. Just a minute, I'll get it." When he came back from the store room he placed a large box on the counter in front of Doc. On top of the Box, written in gold script, were the words "Schweizeriche

Industries Gesellcraft." Doc opened the cardboard box, removed a styrofoam insert then lifted out a hard plastic carrying case that had the initials "SIG" on top. She opened the carrying case to show off her new .45 caliber SIG-Sauer P220 semiautomatic with two extra clips. It had a custom, extra wide, combat hammer and trigger and modest accent engravings.

"I guess size does matter," said Will.

"It certainly does," replied Doc. "You may have more bullets in your new guns, but mine is bigger. I went with take down power, rather than volume."

"Are you talking about me, or the gun?" Will asked with a smile.

"Both!"

"Remind me never to piss you off," Will said.

"I just reminded you when I bought this gun," Doc answered with a serious expression. Will and Doc thanked the owner and left with Doc's new gun.

Will's apartment was just as he'd left it. No one had been through his things, making obscene displays, which was a good thing. The down side was, his plants were pretty much a goner. Thank goodness he didn't have a dog. Pets and plants don't go well with a cop's busy, unpredictable schedule. At least not Will's. He wouldn't have time for a relationship if the woman he loved didn't work with him every day.

Will and Doc got settled in, unpacked, started a load of laundry then went to lunch before reporting in to the office. They hadn't been there much lately so it took them all day to get caught up on all their paper work. It took Will a solid hour just to read and delete his emails that didn't require a response. Then it took another hour to reply to the emails that required an answer. Computers may be time savers in some ways, but in others they take up a lot of your time. The world is moving so fast that people aren't taking time to smell the roses. The world is quickly becoming impersonal. People are dealing with computers so much they are forgetting how to deal with each other.

Will read the file on Carmine Antonellie and made a list of addresses to start their search for him. Then he read eleven more missing person/informant reports from all over the United States, but concentrated on the four in the Los Angeles area. Will made another list of people to talk to in those cases. While the police were interviewing their families, Will and Doc would focus on known criminal associates. It was a lot of leg work, but it had to be done and it could pay off.

The next morning Will received a call from the Task Force Commander who informed him that the two guys who were driving the van were Russian. They had given fake names to the apartment manager. Based on the fact that the apartment superintendent of the building said the one who paid the lease had an accent the Task Force commander had the prints ran worldwide. They turned out to be Russian Mafia with records and "suspicion of" files a mile long. The Russians were glad to hear the two men were dead and said the world would be a safer place with them removed from it. No one knew how they managed to get out of Russia with the Russian authorities looking for them and into the United States. The driver of the van was Demetri Curtikov and the other one was Vladamir Sovinski, both wanted for murder and a shopping list of other crimes. Will was advised to keep that in mind as he was asking around, because it was looking like their might be a Russian connection and "Those guys are crazy," as the commander so tactfully put it.

Will thanked the commander and hung up then filled Doc in on the new development. Things were coming together, slowly. It was only a matter of time before everything broke wide open.

Armed with a copy of a material witness warrant Will and Doc decided to start the morning looking for the elusive Mr. Antonellie. They had a list of his personal vehicles, including his limo. They figured that if they could find the vehicles and the limo driver they would find Antonellie.

Knowing that Antonellie's clubs didn't open until 2:00p.m., they decided to check his apartment on the off chance someone might be there. Will stepped to the side while Doc knocked on the apartment door. There was a better chance of whoever was inside opening the door if they saw a pretty face when they looked out the peep hole.

When the door opened Will stepped into view with his gun drawn and said, "Carmine Antonellie, you're under arrest --"

"I am not Carmine --" the man tried to say.

"Shut-up and get down on the floor with your hands behind you head," Will commanded.

"I am not—"

"Shut-up. You don't speak unless I ask a question," Will stated as he put the cuffs on the guy he very well knew was not Antonellie and he motioned with his head for Doc to check the rest of the apartment.

In a few moments, Doc said, "Clear."

"So you thought you could get away with it, did you Carmine?" Will exclaimed.

"I am not Carmine. I am chauffeur."

"I suppose now you'll tell me that you don't really live here, that you're just watching the place?"

"That is correct," the man said from his place on the floor.

"I suppose now you want me to believe that you've never heard of Cinderella or Santa Claus·?"

"I do not understand--"

"Shut-up. That's what I thought you'd say." Will was having fun with the guy who he could tell was of low intelligence and not from America.

By that time Doc had finished her quick look around the apartment and she said, "Maybe he's telling the truth. Better check his ID."

"Yes. Yes. Check my ID, please," said the distressed man.

Will fished the man's billfold from his back pocket, flipped it open and examined the identification. "I'll be, if this is real--"

"Is real, is real," said the handcuffed man.

"Then you're not Carmine. You're Serge Molisnikov?"

"That is correct. I am not Carmine."

"Why didn't you tell me that when you opened the door?"

The man's head dropped to the floor and he let out a long breath. Will had succeeded in rattling the man's cage. He helped the man up and placed him in a kitchen chair and asked him, "Then where is Carmine?"

"I do not know."

"You just told us you're his chauffeur. Where did you pick him up last?"

"At his club on the Strip."

"Where did you take him?"

"I take him here."

"Then where is he?"

"I do not know. He left"

"Where did he go?"

"He does not tell me. I am only chauffeur."

"Who did he leave with?"

"No one. He just told me to stay here and left."

"That's a likely story."

"Yes."

Will removed the cuffs and told the man, "If I find out you lied to me I'll be back."

Will pulled the door closed as they left the apartment and told Doc that he wished they had a tap on the phone so they would know who the chauffeur called when they left.

When they stepped into the elevator Doc was still smiling from Will's banter with the chauffeur when she said, "The DEA probably does have the phone tapped. We could ask them who he called after we left."

Will's phone started vibrating before the elevator reached the bottom floor. It was the DEA calling to inform him that, not only was Carmine's phone tapped, his apartment and the elevator were bugged, as well. The DEA agent told Will that he'd be surprised how much information they'd gotten from conversations held in elevators. The crooks, thinking their apartments might be bugged, used the privacy of an elevator to have quick conversations about illegal business and the DEA didn't have to have a warrant to bug a public elevator.

Will thought that bugging the elevator was a great idea and made a mental note never to have sex in an elevator, again.

The DEA agent found Will's approach to questioning the chauffeur humorous and effective. He invited Will and Doc back up to the floor and apartment below Carmine's so they could visit about the case. When the elevator stopped on the bottom floor Will pushed the appropriate button to take them back up for a visit with the DEA. Doc was looking somewhat perplexed until Will briefly explained what was going on then she just smiled and followed Will down the hall to the room where the DEA agent was waiting.

DEA agent Elijah King was an intelligent black man with a pleasant disposition and an infectious smile that made you want to invite him over for a weekend barbecue. After introductions that all went very cordially, Agent King showed them to a room that was loaded with high tech surveillance equipment and personnel who were all busy monitoring computers and recording devices. It was a busy place, complete with coffee and a nice selection of doughnuts.

Will had been expecting a confrontation and was happy to discover that he'd been wrong. Will could see immediately that he'd made a new friend. Agent King was very professional, courteous and willing to explain the surveillance operation and its goal.

What Will didn't understand at first was, that the DEA already knew exactly where Carmine Antonellie was hiding. He wasn't going to get away. Everything was bugged, tapped and had GPS tracking devices on them, so Antonellie could not fart or go to the bathroom without the DEA knowing about it. They were just taking their time, applying some heat to increase the pressure and waiting to see if the lid would blow off the pot. Pardon the cooking metaphor and pun.

Through their surveillance the DEA had already located at least one of the individuals who fled the night club through the secret door the night of the raid who was suspected of running drugs for Antonellie. It was just a matter of time before the others felt comfortable enough to emerge from wherever they were hiding. The DEA was planning to wait a few days, then hit the club again, taking care to cover the secret exit.

One of the reasons agent King was being so cooperative was to gain Will and Doc's assistance. King wanted Will and Doc to put things on hold in regards to Antonellie for a few days while they gathered more evidence and built their case against him. King promised Will and Doc that they would get a crack at Antonellie as soon as he was brought in.

Will and Doc certainly didn't have a problem with that. It would save them a lot of looking. The DEA already had Antonellie under the gun and they could have kept that fact quiet, so they were going out of their way to fill Will and Doc in on their operation.

Agent King informed Will that he had been following the progress of the missing informant Task Force and explained that it had been one of his agents that had filmed the ending of an actual gladiator fight. He also let Will know that he'd heard some of the stories about Will's first month on the job with the LAPD and about the two attempts on Will and Doc's lives. Will couldn't decide if agent King was amused or impressed, so Will just played it off as part of the job.

In the interest of sharing information, Will explained to agent King that he had received a phone call from the informant Task Force commander that morning where he was told that two of the suspects that were killed in a shoot-out in Reno were identified as Russian Mafia who were wanted in Russia for murder, among other things. Because Antonellie's chauffeur was Russian Will thought there might be a connection and asked agent King to keep an eye out for any other Russian's that might be involved.

They thanked each other for sharing information and after customary handshakes Will and Doc left to get started on interviewing the known criminal associates of the four recently kidnapped informants from the Los Angeles area.

Antonellie was in the bag, so to speak, so focusing their attention in other areas just made good sense.

It was still early. Will and Doc didn't have any idea just how interesting and long the day would be.

Chapter 28

Big Eddie was not a happy man. He was wishing people would stop giving him bad news while he was trying to enjoy a meal. He was starting to get a complex about sitting down to the dinner table.

While trying to have a peaceful lunch Eddie received a call from his expensive connection in the FBI informing him that officer Bracket received another email from deadserious advising him that Mr. Big and his dark Angel were running gladiator fights in Russia, China, Mexico and the UK, from Los Angeles. Now Eddie had doubts that the emails were coming from young Ray, because Ray didn't know about the fights in those other countries. Big Eddie was thinking that someone may be trying to make it look like the emails were coming from Ray. Eddie figured that if Ray flipped he wouldn't play games, he would just spill the beans and in that case the cops would already be there knocking on Eddie's door.

Eddie was in the process of taking out Ray anyway, but if there was another rat in the mix then he needed to know who it was. The FBI man also told Eddie that based on the email and the situation with Carmine Antonellie and the two failed attempts on their lives, the two meddlesome cops, Bracket and Holiday, were back in Los Angeles. Eddie was starting to wish he'd supported Angela in her quest to take them out. These two cops were proving to be either very lucky or extremely smart. Either way, Eddie was wishing they were out of the picture.

The next round of disturbing news came while Big Eddie was having dinner. A representative of the noted Mafia don, Giovanni Antonellie, showed up at Eddie's home with a status report on the day's events and a message from the don.

Before Will and Doc started the task of locating and interviewing the known criminal associates of the four recently kidnapped informants from the LA area, Will got another interesting idea that he thought worthy of pursuit. Will intended to keep his promise to agent King to leave Carmine Antonellie alone, for the time being. However, Will decided that it wouldn't do any harm to shake the tree a little closer to home.

Will had closely read all the files on Carmine and knew who his father was. Will had Doc call one of her connections in the violent crime and racketeering task force to get an address on Giovanni Antonellie. They were advised that the reputed Mafia don spent his day at a small Italian restaurant he owned in Little Italy, of course, where he generally ate the noon meal.

When Will and Doc walked into the restaurant it seemed like all eyes were on them. They looked back at the crowd and started making their way to the rear of the establishment. Nobody tried to stop them. Will and Doc approached a table where a waiter was discussing an order with four men at a table.

To the waiter, Will said, "Excuse me, would you please tell Mr. Antonellie that were would like to speak with him."

Before the waiter could reply, one of the men at the table said, "Mr. Antonellie don't speak with law enforcement types."

"We're not here to ask questions. We have some news we would like to share with him about his son, Carmine," Will said.

All eyes turned to an old man who stood up at the next table and said, "Let's take this into my office."

Giovanni Antonellie had spoken. Giovanni held up his hand in that well known "Stay" position to indicate that his men were to wait. Will and Doc followed him through a door that led to the kitchen and on to a small back room office that smelled of stale cigar smoke and a perpetual aroma of excellent Italian cooking. It wasn't like in the movies, the retired don didn't ask them if they wanted something to eat. He simply pointed to two comfortable padded leather chairs and said, "Sit. What can I do for you?"

Will took the lead, because in the old Italian world men do the talking, women do the listening. That might seem a little chauvinistic, but it was the way of things and everyone respected that tradition.

"I'm sure you are aware that your son Carmine is under investigation by the DEA for drug trafficking."

"This I know. Drugs are a scourge upon America. A disease. I've discussed this with Carmine."

"We are part of the Task Force who are investigating the missing and dead informants. We have reason to believe that Carmine is involved or at least knows something about it. When Carmine's club was raided last week there was a fight playing in a back room. The fighters were two of the missing informants who were being forced to have a knife fight to the death. Also, the nickname 'Mr. Big' came up and I would like to know who Mr. Big is. I think your son knows the answer to that question."

"In my days if someone wanted to take out an informant it was just 'pop' and it was done. It was a lot less dramatic. Today everyone wants to be a big shot. If you're looking for 'Mr. Big' here you're in the wrong place. My days as Mr. Big are long gone."

"I'm not suggesting that you are behind any of this. I don't think Carmine is behind it either, but he may be close to the people who are. I'm sure that you would agree that it would be best if this matter could be resolved before someone makes Carmine out to be the fall guy. I want to know who Mr. Big is so he will be the target, not Carmine."

Mr. Antonellie stood and said, "I see your point. I'll convey this to my son. Thank you for coming by."

Clearly dismissed, Will and Doc stood and left Mr. Antonellie's office. Out on the sidewalk Doc said, "Damn. You are something. I guess you know that you may have started a war, or at a minimum, got Mr. Big snuffed?"

"You've got to shake the tree and watch were the nuts fall if you want to get fed," answered Will with a smile.

Giovanni's representative was telling Big Eddie about Will and Doc's visit to Mr. Antonellie during dinner and explaining the necessity of Big Eddie ending all business relations that he may have with Carmine. With one word, "Capisce," Giovanni's representative made the point that it was not simply a request it was an obvious command. The type you do not refuse without serious repercussions.

When the man left Big Eddie was so mad he couldn't finish his dinner. He didn't need a war with an old Mafia don, but who did the old fuck think he was sending someone by to threaten him. What nerve. If he took out the don he'd have to deal with Carmine. If he took out Carmine he'd have to deal with the don. So it was both or neither. Eddie was wishing that he'd helped Angela take out the two cops who were going around stirring up all this crap. Big Eddie was thinking about his own plan B. It was beginning to look like he might need to relocate. He'd been thinking about Cairo, Egypt, where he already had a high rise office complex with a penthouse apartment, all in another name that couldn't be traced back to him. He loved ancient Egyptian history and culture. Plus, it was closer to some of his business in the Middle East. Eddie wasn't sure if he wanted to leave or show all these smug bastards whose boss. After some careful thought he decided both would be appropriate. The decision was really a no brainer. Big Eddie was certain Carmine would rat to avoid prison just as soon as the DEA got him. From that point forward it would be a race to see who got Carmine first. Obviously, papa Antonellie would have to go too just to avoid additional complications. Going that far, Big Eddie figured he might as well take out the two cops, as well.

Big Eddie called Bob in and told him to hire a couple of Italians to hit the two cops and to make it sound like the hit was sanctioned by Giovanni Antonellie. He told Bob to work his magic and eliminate Carmine and daddy Antonellie. Bob thought it a bad and dangerous move, but did not question his boss. He simply left to take care of business.

Thanks to his connection in the DEA Bob knew exactly where Carmine was and that he was under twenty-four hour surveillance. Hitting Carmine wasn't going to be much trouble. Bob just had to get a little creative. Getting the old man might be more of a problem, but nothing a little careful, advance planning couldn't handle.

Bob contacted an independent Italian contractor he knew in Brooklyn and ask him to hire Italian hitters to go after the two cops, Bracket and his partner Holiday. Bob told the guy to discretely drop Giovanni Antonellie's name so it would look like the hit was coming from that direction. He also faxed all the information he had on the two cops to his guy. Bob then sent two of his guys to the garage where Giovanni Antonellie kept his personal Lincoln Town Car to wire it with a remote control explosive device. Then Bob gathered up the supplies he needed and went to the Hilton Hotel where Carmine was hiding. Bob knew Carmine's room number and that the DEA was set up in the room beneath Carmine's. Armed with that information Bob rented the room next to Carmine's room. He rented the room under an assumed name. When he got to the room it was early, so after putting on latex gloves to prevent leaving any prints, Bob sat down to enjoy the light meal he brought with him and to watch some local news.

Bob already knew the layout of the room Carmine was in. The bedroom of Carmine's suite was adjacent to Bob's sitting room. Judging the approximate position of the bed in Carmine's room Bob used a small hand drill to make a tiny hole in the wall down at floor level so he could see under the bed in Carmine's room with a flexible camera probe that was attached to his laptop. Sure enough, Bob had an unobstructed view from under the bed. Bob could see anyone walking towards or away from the bed and hear everything that went on in the room. With that done Bob settled in to wait.

Shortly after the ten o'clock news two pair of feet showed up on the video screen. A man and a woman, judging from the sound of things, approached the bed then climbed onto the bed. Carmine wasn't much for sexual marathons. There were a few grunts and moans and Carmine was soon snoring.

Bob removed the video probe and inserted a slender hose that was connected to a small canister that was about a foot long and six inches in diameter. He then put on a gas mask and slowly opened the valve on the canister. Bob could hear the lethal gas escaping from the bottle, filling the room next door with toxic fumes. The gas was odorless and clear so it would not set off smoke detectors. Soon Carmine and his unfortunate girlfriend would simply stop breathing. Hopefully the gas would dissipate enough as it was circulated through the air conditioning system that it would not kill other people in the hotel. For all apparent purposes the gas was the equivalent of a heroin overdose in its concentrated form. By the time the gas thinned out it would just help people have a good night's sleep and maybe give them a little hangover to boot.

When the canister ran out of gas Bob quickly removed the hose and plugged the hole with putty. He then removed the gas mask, picked up his suitcase and the bag he had his trash in and left the hotel room. He took the stairs and left the building through the staff exit. It was only a short walk to the parking garage where he left his car.

Bob figured it would take some time for the DEA or someone to figure out that Carmine was dead. He slept in until 8:00 a.m., which was late for him, then had a thirty minute workout before he showered and took a taxi to Little Italy where he stopped by a coffee shop near Giovanni Antonellie's restaurant. Bob read the morning paper and enjoyed a cup of coffee and a croissant while he waited on the lunch crowd to start arriving at the restaurant.

Just before the lunch crowd started arriving the don came walking up the sidewalk with two of his bodyguards. He was shaking hands and saying hello to almost everyone he passed like some greasy politician. Bob actually hated to see the old man go, but he knew it was necessary. Giovanni only looked like he was harmless. There was no telling how he might react to news of his son's death.

After Mr. Antonellie went inside the restaurant Bob got up and slowly walked over to the establishment and went in. He picked a small table that faced the window, but was far enough away from the glass to make sure he didn't get cut from the shattered window. The food was marvelous. It was the best Italian cooking Bob had ever tasted. Generally, Bob stayed away from heavy, fattening foods, but he wanted a front row seat for the occasion.

Bob was in the middle of his meal when two men in suits hurried in and approached the don. After a short conversation Giovanni threw down his napkin and told two other men to go get his car. Giovanni was visibly shaken. He sat there until his car pulled up out front then the two new arrivals escorted him to his car. As soon as the door closed with Giovanni inside Bob pushed the button on his remote detonator and the car blew up in a fiery ball of flames. The restaurant window blew in, just as Bob expected and people started screaming and running out of the building. It was chaos. Bob got up and left without paying for his meal.

Chapter 29

At 9:00a.m. a maid knocked on Carmine's hotel room door. When she did not receive a response, she let herself in to clean the room, as was her general practice. She always started in the bedroom then the bathroom, then worked her way out cleaning the sitting room and wet bar as she left the room.

When she walked into the bedroom she was startled when she discovered two naked people laying in the bed. She quickly turned away and said, "Oh, excuse me. I'm sorry." Then she realized that something was terribly wrong. The room was too quiet. The people weren't moving and as she turned

back around to take a closer look she noticed how pale the people were. That's when the smell of feces and urine hit her and she screamed. She managed to call the front desk to report the problem just before she passed out, clutching the phone in the sitting room area.

The DEA surveillance team heard the scream and were monitoring the call. DEA agents were on the scene when the hotel manager and security arrived. The first two DEA agents who entered the bedroom realized something was wrong when they started getting dizzy. They told everyone to clear the hotel room and opened the sliding glass door that led to the balcony to help vent the room while they waited on the homicide detectives to show up. They carried the maid into the hallway to wait on an ambulance.

Elijah King, the DEA agent in charge of the surveillance team, called Will and Doc and told them the news. It was pretty obvious, and likely, that Carmine and his girlfriend were murdered. They just didn't know how yet, but they suspected it was some type of gas or poison.

Will and Doc arrived at the hotel room by 10:30 a.m. to ask agent King if there was any documentation or computers discovered in the hotel room that would assist them with their investigation. While they were talking with agent King, Carmine's Russian bodyguard showed up asking what was going on. When the officer assigned to the elevator realized the significance of the bodyguard's presence he told agent King that the bodyguard was there.

Will and Doc went with agent King to inform the bodyguard that Carmine was dead. The bodyguard was visibly upset because it was his job to watch after Carmine. Agent King explained that they didn't know what killed Carmine and his girlfriend. However, they expected foul play, but wouldn't know more until the autopsy and toxicology reports came back.

Serge Molisnikov, AKA the Hammer, was a known killer in Russia. He'd gotten soft being Carmine's bodyguard. Carmine liked to party and all Serge did was follow Carmine around and eat and drink. He had no idea that someone was out to kill Carmine. Had he known he would have stayed closer. Now he had to tell Carmine's father that he'd failed and Carmine was dead.

Serge left the hotel and called the emergency number he'd been given. He was thankful that Carmine's father did not answer the phone. It was one of Mr. Antonellie's bodyguards, Serge, who wasn't feeling much like the Hammer these days, explained the situation to Mr. Antonellie's man then went back to Carmine's apartment to clean out the safe before he left California. He had a job offer in New York and he'd always wanted to visit the East Coast. One thing for sure, he didn't want to be anywhere around when the old Mafia don found out his son was dead.

Giovanni Antonellie's apartment was just a short walk from the restaurant. The man who took Serge's call hurried down the sidewalk to the restaurant to give his boss the tragic news. That's when Mr. Antonellie ordered his car and was blown to bits before he could pull away from the curb.

Big Eddie's man, Bob, left the damaged restaurant and went back to the coffee shop across the street where he could watch the commotion from a safe distance.

While Will and Doc were still at Carmine's hotel room when agent King received a call about the Giovanni car bombing. "This just keeps getting better and better," said agent King to Will and Doc. Then he proceeded to tell them the news.

When agent King finished telling them what happened, before Doc could say anything, Will said, "We'll head over there and check it out and get back with you this afternoon."

Will didn't want Doc telling agent King that they'd been to see the old Mafia don the day before, because it was looking like their visit to him may have caused or inadvertently triggered the whole thing. For now, Will thought it best to keep their visit to the don to themselves. Will made it a point not to say anything in the hotel elevator, he knew it was bugged, but when they got to the lobby Will explained his reasoning to Doc. She agreed that it was a sound decision and hoped they could keep the matter between them.

The charred bodies were just being removed from the smoking car when Will and Doc showed up on the scene. It reminded them both of agent Daniels' fiery death. The smell and atmosphere were the same. Cops and fire department personnel were walking around the scene, talking to people, gathering evidence and putting away their emergency gear. Some of the restaurant's patrons were being treated by EMS technicians for minor cuts caused by flying debris from the explosion and some had already been taken away by ambulance to area hospitals to be treated for more extensive injuries.

The place looked like a war zone in Bosnia. The blast had shattered windows in store fronts next to the restaurant and across the road from it. Several vehicles that were close to the explosion were also damaged. It was a mess.

Will and Doc talked with one of the officers on scene and verified that witnesses had confirmed that Giovanni Antonellie had just gotten into the car when it erupted into a fiery ball of death. There was nothing else they could do, so they decided to take a late lunch.

Sitting at a table in the coffee shop that featured a partial view of the mayhem across the street in front of the late Giovanni's restaurant, Bob noticed Will and Doc arrive and talk with one of the officers. Bob knew it was the two meddlesome cops as soon as he saw them. Bob thought of Matthew 7:13: "Wide is the gate, and broad is the way, that leadeth to destruction." Bob laughed. He liked that verse because it could be taken several ways.

By making an appearance the two cops had stepped right through the gate, paving the way to their own destruction. It was perfect. Bob placed a call to his man that hired the Italian shooters to take out Will and Doc. He told his man that he had located the two cops. Bob then left the coffee shop and walked in the direction the two cops had to go when they left. The street was blocked off so they were forced to leave the same way they came from. Bob was watching from the closest intersection when he saw Will and Doc heading for their unmarked car. Cabs were in abundance so as soon as it was obvious which direction the cops were headed Bob hailed a cab so he could follow them.

It was before the lunch rush-hour crowd so Will and Doc didn't have a problem finding a curb-side parking place close to the sea food restaurant they liked. Will ordered boiled shrimp and Doc ordered the lobster tail. Because they were working they ordered ice tea to drink.

Bob went into the restaurant and took a place at the bar where he could watch Will and Doc while he had a drink. He then called his man to report the location of Will and Doc's car. The car bomb had worked so well with the old don that Bob was tempted to try it again with these cops, but he'd already hired out the hit and he didn't have another bomb ready. The first two attempted hits on the two cops had failed, but as the saying goes, "The third times a charm."

Bob's two man hit team had gotten in place while Will and Doc were eating. When they walked out of the restaurant heading towards their car Will noticed a man standing on the sidewalk near their car looking in the store front window of an electronics store. How odd, the man was wearing a full length tan duster in the heat. Because Doc liked to drive she was walking behind the car on her way to the driver's side door when another man walked out of the electronics store wearing a long black over-coat. Something snapped in Will's mind and alerted him to the danger just as he saw the glint of steel coming out from under the black over-coat and the man in the tan duster started turning his way.

Will yelled, "Down, down, gun, gun," as he fumbled for his weapon.

The man in the black over-coat let go with both barrels of a sawed off 12 gauge shotgun. The blast took out the windshield and driver's window, just as Doc was dropping to the ground. Had that gunman been going for Will he would likely be dead, because he was out in the open on the sidewalk.

By the time Will got his gun up the man in the tan duster had tuned and was bringing up an AK-47. Will's first shot was too soon and too low. It hit the man with the AK-47 in his right thigh, which caused the man to pull the trigger on the AK-47 and bullets started stitching a line on the sidewalk in Will's direction as the fully automatic rifle came up. The noise was deafening as it reverberated off the store front windows and gun smoke filled the air as Will shot the man in the chest three times. The AK-47 kept firing just like in the movies, even when the man hit the ground and Will dove behind their car.

By the time Will worked his way around the car to Doc the firing had stopped. Will and Doc chanced a quick glance to determine where the other gunman was. He was gone. He'd dropped his shotgun and ran for the far end of the block.

Will and Doc were too shook-up to chase him. They checked the guy on the sidewalk, looked each other over then called it in. They gave dispatch their location and a description of the other shooter and the direction he was headed.

Shortly after the responding officers arrived on scene DEA agent King showed up. The hotel Carmine had died in was just a few blocks from the restaurant. Now that Carmine was dead agent King's surveillance team was packing up all of their equipment when King heard the call for backup.

King walked up to Will and said, "I had to see this for myself. It looks like those stories I heard about you are true. Trouble seems to follow you around. I'm glad to see that you came out on top. I'd hate to lose a new found friend."

"I hate to think what might happen when my luck runs out," replied Will. "I'm more worried about Doc than I am myself."

"That's one of the things I admire about you Will," said agent King. "You have a heart."

Doc walked up just then smiling, with six or seven tiny bloody spots on her face from where the shotgun blast blew glass into her face.

"What?" Doc said with a smile as she looked at Will and agent King.

Agent King said, "I was just complementing Will on his extraordinary abilities."

"Oh, you don't know the half of it," replied Doc, with a smile.

They all shared a laugh as the Internal Affairs Division (IAD) man came up to Will to collect his firearm, again. They were all now on a first name basis. After Will surrendered his firearm he opened the trunk of their car, got out his gym bag and removed his duel shoulder holsters and his matching left and right hand collector .9mm pistols and started strapping them on.

Agent King was impressed. He said, "Are you planning to start a war?"

"I didn't start this war," said Will, "and I am not going to lose it."

As with the previous shootings Will and Doc went on immediate investigative suspension, with pay, pending an IAD board review. They went back to the station, did their required interviews and typed up their reports.

They had a mandatory week off whether they liked it or not. Will intended to take full advantage of that week. The contractors were finished with the repairs and improvements to the beach house and Will hadn't even seen it yet. He was going to ask Doc to marry him over dinner at their new home, before he ended up getting himself killed over the crazy case they were working. With everything that was happening it was time they took a few extra days off to get married and for their honeymoon.

Chapter 30

Moscow, Russia was an exciting place for Angela Sarcosie, AKA Nic. In the past, working for her father's company had taken a lot of her time and kept her from getting board. With all the extra time on her hands "Nic" was dreaming up all kinds of mischievous things for her and her new lesbian lover "Jo" to get into. Hitting the clubs and enjoying the night life had been fun, at first. Nic and Jo loved to tease the men while they drank and danced the night away.

During the day Nic was on the phone and computer authorizing wire transfers to pay for large shipments of drugs, weapons and anything else she could purchase on the black market that she could make a profit on, including gold, precious gems and art work. She was directing the movement of these items all over the world through her well established connections and monitoring their delivery and the deposits. It was a full-time job, but she still found time to run her legitimate businesses and play with Jo.

Even though her office was in her penthouse apartment Nic ran it professionally and dressed the part, just in case they had to entertain visitors. Appearance was everything. Nic painted a perfect picture of a powerful corporate executive. It was an image she loved to maintain. In order to cover-up all the large amounts of money moving all over the world Nic had to run legitimate businesses, as well, in order to legitimize the transactions. She was buying products from all over the world and having them shipped and distributed anywhere there was a market and money to pay for the goods. It wasn't as lucrative as the illegal market, but it was less risky and made substantial amounts of money. She was moving millions back and forth every day and taking great care not to commingle the legal profits with her illegal income.

All of the partners had agreed on a ten-year dead line on their illegal activities. By that time they planned to have made their money and legitimized it properly and moved on with completely legal businesses. They would simply shut down all questionable practices. So far, even with the expected losses in the drug trade and the problems they were experiencing with getting the gladiator fights up and running things were progressing well.

During working hours Jo dressed the part and acted as Nic's secretary and personal assistant. She answered the phones, scheduled appointments and even made great coffee. Jo was enjoying her position in the office and in the bedroom, even though some of the people coming to see her boss/lover were known, dangerous criminals. Some of them made her nervous, but she took care not to let it show.

There were only two appointments scheduled for the day. The first appointment was to be at 10:00 a.m. and the name on Jo's planner simply read "Otto." The significance of the name did not register to Jo when the lobby called to announce his arrival. However, Jo knew exactly who he was the moment she buzzed him through the door. Jo had seen his face on television and in the newspapers many times. He was escorted by two beautiful women, one on each arm, dressed tastefully, but provocatively and two well dressed and armed bodyguards.

Jo tried not to show her surprise when they came in. She remained seated and said, "Good morning. I'll let Nicole know you're here." Then she pressed her intercom button and announced, "Nicole, your ten o'clock is here." Jo had been instructed to use only their first names in a professional setting.

After Jo announced Otto's and his entourage's presence, Nicole buzzed them through her office door. Nic had four stages of security. A person coming to visit had to have an appointment that was pre-arranged and verified at the lobby before the elevator would bring them to the penthouse. Then Jo could view them on a security camera before she buzzed them into the outer office. After that, Nic had the only control to release the security door leading into her office. The final and fourth stage was the firearms Nic and Jo kept in their desks and in other areas.

Nic released the inner door and Jo escorted the visitors into the office. Nic stood, but remained behind her desk, and said, "Good morning Otto. Thank you for coming. Joanna, would you please bring us coffee."

"Hello, Nicole," Otto replied curtly as he seated himself across the table from Nicole. Otto's arrogant demeanor was exuding contempt. "I've been wanting to meet you. Are you enjoying Russia?"

"Very much so and thank you for asking. The weather here is cooler than I expected and some of my business partners have turned out to be not quite what I expected, but I'm working that out just fine," replied Nicole.

Joanna came back into the room with a tray laden with a carafe and two small delicate china cups with matching saucers. She carefully filled the cups with the steaming hot coffee and placed one before Nicole and then one before Otto. The order of placement was designed to show company who the boss is.

"Is there anything else?" asked Joanna.

"Yes, please have a seat with us and I'll be with you in a moment," Nicole said.

Joanna dutifully took a seat next to Nicole's desk, facing Otto and sat there prim and proper, with her back straight, looking professional.

"One of the problems I am experiencing," continued Nicole, "is a lack of loyalty and greed here in Russia. How do you deal with that?" It was a trick question.

"In Russia, punishment for disloyalty and greed is swift and harsh. Often permanent. Loyalty is rewarded and in Russia, only the strong survive," Otto said. It was an implied threat.

"I appreciate that insight Otto. So what am I to do with you? Your greed has interfered with your loyalty. You are stealing far more than your share."

Joanna was having difficulty maintaining her composure. She could see where this was heading and knew something bad was about to happen.

"My solution, if you are not pleased with the current arrangements, would be to kill you and take all the profits," Otto stated with a grim expression.

"Otto, I don't believe you have the man power to kill everyone you're stealing from."

"Nicole, surely you realize that I can eliminate them one at a time, starting with you, right now," Otto stated.

"I've discussed this matter with some of our other associates and they share my opinion that you are a thief and a threat and it would be best for you to resign your position," Nicole declared.

Otto sat forward in his chair, and yelled, "You crazy bitch. Who the fuck you think you are? You and 'our other associates,' as you put it are only alive because I haven't tired of you yet. I will take what I please and you all be damned."

"Thank you for clearly stating your position for us, Otto," said a voice from the intercom.

Otto knew that voice and his fear was evident from his expression. Nicole pressed the disconnect button. Otto glared at her with hatred in his eyes. He had been out foxed by a woman.

"Kill her," Otto commanded of his bodyguards, who just stood their quietly.

Nicole stated, "These two gentlemen, whom you have treated so poorly, are now running what used to be your operations and the two lovely ladies will be their escorts. Your time is up."

Nicole raised a silenced .9mm pistol and shot Otto twice in the chest. Joanna was the only one shaken. The others knew what was coming. Nicole had already discussed all the details with them and made them the best offers they ever had. Offers that were non-negotiable and certainly not wise to refuse.

"Joanna, be a doll and get the maid's laundry cart so these gentlemen can use it to haul out this trash," ask Nicole.

Joanna was no stranger to death. She obeyed without question. When she returned with the cart the two men had already wrapped Otto's body in a blanket. They lifted the body and dropped it in the cart.

As the men were pushing the cart towards the door, with their new girlfriends beside them, Nicole said, "Let me know when my private booth is ready."

"It will be ready for tomorrow night's fight, boss. Should I have champagne on ice?" asked one of the men.

"Yes, I'd like that. I'll see you around six."

The two men, who were now the supervisors of a huge underground criminal network, would drop the laundry cart off with a man waiting at the building's loading dock, who would in turn dispose of the body properly.

Nicole was excited and Joanna was apprehensive. She didn't know quite what to think of this new development.

"Come," Nic said, taking Jo by the hand. "We don't have another appointment until 2:00 p.m. I want to fuck you, take a shower and have lunch before they arrive."

Nic walked hand-in-hand with Jo through the penthouse to the bedroom where they would start their lunch break. By the time they had their clothes off Nic was wet with excitement and Jo was over her inhibitions and was enjoying the side of Nic she hadn't seen before. Jo had been living under the incorrect assumption that Nic was only a spoiled rotten little rich girl. It was a pleasant illusion and it would take some mental adjustments to adapt to the reality of things. In order to survive in Russia Jo had become a quick learner. It wouldn't take her long to get use to her new boss, friend and lover being the most powerful woman in Russia. In fact, she absolutely loved the idea.

After hot, sweaty sex they showered, taking their time to lather each other up with soap, then after rinsing, rubbing each other down with scented body oil. It was a sight fit for a scene in an x-rated movie. Then they enjoyed a light lunch and got back to work. Nicole had to clean a tiny spot of blood off the carpet where Otto had fallen out of his chair after she shot him twice. Once a person's heart is stopped by a bullet very little blood leaks out of the body. In Otto's case, most of the blood that did seep out was trapped in Otto's clothing. Seeing a lot of blood is usually only in movies where it is used for dramatic effects. The two slugs did not penetrate through Otto's body, so there were no messy exist wounds.

Laughing at the pun, Nic thought it was a clean kill, in more ways than one.

Nic's next appointment was with the Russian Minister of Defense. It was good to have friends in high places. He was bringing a computer disc that contained a list of the military arms and equipment that were currently available, complete with a cost breakdown. Very convenient and professional for a black market operation.

After the Minister arrived, introductions were completed and certain solid guarantees were made clear, Nic placed the disc in her computer, reviewed the list, tagged the items she desired to purchase, totaled the cost and with the Minister's approval transferred the money to the Minister's account. It was handled through a Dutch holding company Nic owned. She in turn would sell the munitions to a company in Africa, labeled farm equipment, who would then trade it to the rebels for gold and uncut diamonds. The profit margin was staggering. Not as good as the drug market, but substantial.

With the day's business concluded Nic and Jo retired to the apartment to watch the news and prepare dinner. All in all it was a very satisfying and productive day.

The following evening Nic and Jo dressed for a night out on the town, but rather than go to the clubs Nic took Jo to watch her first gladiator fight. Jo had never been to a live fight before. She wasn't really interested in seeing a fight, but if it pleased Nic Jo was happy to go along. Nic enjoyed seeing the shocked expression on Jo's face when something big happened that got her excited or nervous. The first time was when she gave Jo a diamond necklace and asked her to move into the penthouse apartment and be her personal secretary and lover. The next time was when Jo was scanning invoices into a computer filing program and storing the original hard copies in files. Jo was seeing the names of several corporations and very large amounts of money moving around.

Jo said, "It would be nice to own these companies."

"I do own them," replied Nic, with a hint of a smile.

When she shot Otto the look on Jo's face was absolutely priceless. Nic couldn't wait to see Jo's reaction when she saw this fight.

Nic's private box was very plush and comfortable. There were four private boxes owned by influential people or companies that were used to view regular boxing matches, each would seat six and contained a small wet bar.

There was a computer in each box where the fighter statistics would be viewed and bets placed. Things were done different in Russia. A regular boxing ring and nice auditorium was used on a day when no regular scheduled events were taking place.

On these off days only certain members were welcome by invitation only. The police were paid off and the bodies taken directly to a morgue for cremation. As Nic and Jo sipped champagne together they reviewed the information on the fighters who were only identified as "White" and "Black."

Jo said, "I don't understand how this works or why it discusses their crimes."

"Don't worry about that part. Just look at how big each man is, how much he weighs and whether he looks to be in good shape. Pick the one you like best and I'll place a bet on him for you. You pick one and I'll take the other guy. If you win not only do you get to keep the money, you get me any way you want me," said Nic.

Jo smiled and picked "White."

Nic placed their bets on the computer. When the fighters stepped into the ring two men assisted them with their shields while the ring master announced the fights.

"I never saw a fight where they have shields before," said Jo.

"You haven't seen anything yet," Nic exclaimed.

The two men were pumping their arms in the air and waving their shields as the crowd cheered. Jo hadn't noticed the men with the shotguns stationed around the ring. When the two men turned to their corners to have the knives strapped on their wrists Jo couldn't see what was happening. When the bell rang everything became crystal clear.

"They have knives," Jo said, surprised.

That's when Nic explained that the men in the ring were documented informants who were being forced to fight a gladiator fight to the death.

"We call it 'forced Attrition,"' explained Nic. Nic explained to Jo that the winner got to live, received an award and was absolved of his wrong doing. There was no point telling Jo that they later killed the winner too. Just seeing the fight would be enough shock for one night.

"So this was your idea?" asked Jo.

"That's right. This is my brain child. My baby, baby," Nic answered with an evil smile on her face. "I'm hosting these fights in other countries all over the world."

The fight didn't last long. The fighters circled each other jabbing and fainting in hopes of getting a lucky stab in. White raised his shield too high on a block and Black slashed White's ribs. Even though the knives had been dulled some the cut was long and deep. White was losing a substantial amount of blood, rather quickly.

The pain and fear caused White to go crazy and rush Black. When Black raised his shield to block as he retreated he stumbled, lost his footing and fell backwards with White pressing him hard. Before Black hit the mat White stabbed him twice in the stomach. Black pulled his shield down to protect his stomach leaving his upper chest and neck exposed. White pinned Black's shield down low with his knee and started stabbing Black in the chest, neck and face. Black managed to get in a few more cuts to White's left hip and thigh before he died. The blood was thick and covered both fighters and most of one corner of the ring. When White stood, Black's shield fell away from his stomach giving the crowd a view of his exposed intestines.

Jo just stared at the bloody mess as the announcer came into the ring to announce the winner and the medics started patching up White. Two more men came into the ring with a plastic boat shaped litter to carry out the body.

Jo couldn't believe what she'd just seen was real, but she knew it was, even though it was un-fucking-believable. What was even more un-believable was the cheering of the crowd. It seemed like even the losers were cheering as they got up to leave.

"You won," Nic shouted. "Now you get me any way you want me and the money." There was a knock on the door and a man stepped in with a tray that had fifty thousand that was freshly banded in stacks of ten thousand laying on it for Jo.

"Here are your winnings, ma'am," said the attendant.

Jo tipped the man with a hundred and said, "Thank you."

The money was all it took to get Jo past her initial shock. It was more money than she'd ever had. Nic had bought her a complete new wardrobe, now she had the money to go with it. It put a big smile on her face. She was so excited that she put the fight out of her mind in about two seconds. By the time the night of sex with Nic was over, not only had Jo gotten over the shock of seeing the first fight, she was ready to see another one.

Nic knew that she had Jo right where she wanted her. Russia wasn't so bad. She missed the sunny California weather and the fresh fruits and vegetables, but other than that Russia would do just fine.

Chapter 31

While Doc slept in Will drove out to the beach house to meet with the lady decorator. The contractor had done a marvelous job on the repairs and the few improvements. The hot tub looked inviting and the flowers around the new trellis work that were put in by the landscaper not only looked great, but mixed with the smell of the ocean they smelled great too. The outside corners that faced the ocean had been cut off and angled so the rear deck could be made to resemble a gazebo with a partially open roof. All the wood had been bleached then re-stained so it would match. It was beautiful with a new walkway leading to the beach.

Will left the beach house and went to meet a party planner who specialized in weddings and any size parties and functions. He explained what he wanted, picked the place settings, flowers and meal, then decided on a date and left to visit a BMW dealership.

Will knew what he was looking for. He'd saved an enormous amount of money by purchasing a smaller home. Just the land that his home in New York sat on was worth more than he paid for the beach house and the improvements. The money he was saving on insurance and taxes, for just one year, by selling his New York home far exceeded the amount he was spending to splurge on an extravagant engagement gift for Doc and it was fun. He certainly wasn't going to tell Doc that by finding her he'd saved a few million. He didn't want her to think she was a cheap date.

Will told the sale's clerk that he'd already visited the dealership web-site and knew they had exactly what he was looking for. Will told the clerk what it was and the clerk had an electric blue BMW M3, with a 414 hp, 4.0 liter V-8 engine and a six speed manual transmission brought around. It was fully loaded, complete with spoiler and ground affects. Will opened the door and smelled the new black leather interior, and said, "I'll take it."

The clerk was pleased when Will whipped out his check book and paid for the car in full. While the paperwork was being taken care of Will called his agent and added the new car and Doc to his insurance plan. Will made arrangements to have the car delivered and backed into the garage at the beach house. It was a productive morning.

When Will got back to the apartment Doc was just coming out of the shower, smelling like peaches.

"I'll start breakfast," Will stated.

"You left awful early this morning."

"I was out planning a party."

"Right," Doc said, with a smile as she hugged Will, kissed him lightly on the lips and said, "Good morning cowboy."

Every time Doc called him cowboy, with her sexy voice and those seductive eyes, it drove Will nuts. It was all he could do to keep his hands off of her while they ate. While they were playing in the kitchen putting away the dishes Will got a call on his cell phone. It was Stanly Hall, the Humboldt County Sheriff, calling from Reno to advise Will that he came down to interview their witness, Wu Tran, but he was too late. Someone had permanently silenced Mr. Tran while he slept in his hospital bed the night before he was scheduled for transfer to a safe-house.

Because there was no sign of a struggle and no obvious new wounds they were assuming that someone snuck into the room and injected something into Wu Tran's IV line. As in all cases, they would know more after some tests were ran. He was recovering well and they were fairly certain that he didn't die of natural causes. The nurse had changed his IV bag shortly after the midnight shift change and Wu Tran was alive then, but he was dead two hours later when she made her routine rounds. It was possible that something could have been in the IV solution before the nurse connected it to Wu Tran's IV line. It was too soon to tell.

The Sheriff also wanted to tell Will that he'd located one of the missing Sarcosie warehouse vans. It was being used by one of Sarcosie's subsidiary delivery companies in Las Vegas. Other than that they were still doing some interviews and following leads.

Will thanked the Sheriff for calling and relayed the news to Doc. Will was a little put out that someone from the Task Force hadn't called with the news. Then he remembered that he hadn't checked his emails.

Wu Tran hadn't provided much useful information. He'd been on pain medication since his surgery and he was unable to give them a good description of the man he called the "face," but he was certain he could identify him. The guards wore masks and the people doing the feeding and picking up trays may or may not have been women. The hallway outside his cell was somewhat dark and the light in his cell reflected off the small window in the door and obstructed his view, so he couldn't see out clearly. He was sure he was held under ground, because they brought him up cement steps when they brought him out and put him in the van. However, he didn't know how he got in the cell.

He'd simply woke-up there. He had no idea even what State he was in, care less a location of the prison he was in.

The one thing Wu Tran did describe, in great detail, was the execution on the autopsy table, the fights and the rewards to the winners that had been played over and over again while he was held captive. Wu Tran's murder made the Task Force look inept and Will didn't like it. It also looked like there was someone in the Task Force, or other closely related law enforcement agency, working with the bad guys. Will and Doc had thought that all along and the death of Wu Tran made it pretty evident. He had been moved four times within the hospital and was under guard. This was obviously more than a mere slip-up. Someone close to the operation was working against them. Will had some ideas on how he might flush out the trader. He would work on that when he got back to the job, but for now he was going to get married.

After three days of rest and relaxation Will and Doc were more than ready to get back to work, but Will had other plans.

"We're going someplace special tonight, so don't make any plans," Will told Doc.

"Okay, but where are we going? I need to know how to dress," asked Doc.

"I would say something sexy and formal would be appropriate. I'm not going to tell you where we are going because it would ruin the surprise and when we get there you can't ask questions. It will be more fun if you don't know and I fill you in as we go along. Okay?"

"Okay, cowboy. I trust you," replied Doc.

That evening Will dressed in a black suit with a black bow tie. Doc wore her hair up, with pearls and a royal blue satin spaghetti strap dress that came to well above her knees and three inch heels.

"This is driving me crazy. Tell me where we're going, please?" pleaded Doc.

"You'll see soon enough. Just hold your horses partner," Will said.

When they turned into the driveway of the beach house, Doc said, "What are we doing here?"

"No questions. From this point on you don't say anything. Got it?"

"Okay, but I'm not sure I like this," replied Doc.

As they approached the door, Doc said, "Oh, all these new flowers are nice."

"You're not supposed to be talking," Will said.

"You're not supposed to be talking," Doc mocked him under her breath in a high pitched sarcastic voice then gave him an ornery little flirtatious smile. Will couldn't have loved her any more than he did at that moment.

The door to the beach house opened when Will and Doc came on to the porch and a man dressed like a waiter, complete with a black tux and a white linen cloth draped over his arm, said, "Good evening. Please come in. Your table is ready and waiting."

Doc was about to say something, but Will was quicker, "No questions and no talking."

It was hard for Doc to look exasperated while she was smiling, but she managed.

"You're not breaking up with me, are you?" Doc asked. "Because, if you are, you need to wait because I didn't bring my gun."

Will just smiled and said, "shhh."

“Oh, my God, you shhhused me.”

The waiter seated them at a table set for two, poured them wine and left to the kitchen area where Doc could see an actual chef dressed in kitchen whites and tall white hat, busily preparing their meal. Doc was looking the place over and taking in her surroundings. The house had been remodeled. It was gorgeous. Heavy drapes were drawn to cover the sliding glass doors leading to the deck. The chef and waiter served the salads with fresh baked bread. Then came the main course. Will had decided to keep is simple. They had New York strip steaks, baked potatoes, steamed asparagus and brussel sprouts with a light cheese sauce. For color and spice, a small bowl of red beans and rice was included next to their plates. Dessert was fresh sliced peaches and strawberries moistened with cream and sprinkled with sugar. It was perfect. After dessert was served Will thanked and tipped the chef and waiter, who promptly left Will and Doc alone for the evening.

The small stereo provided by the caterer was softly playing classical music in the background creating a romantic atmosphere.

"This is wonderful," Doc said. "Now when do I get to ask questions?"

"Soon. But for now be patient. I have something I want to ask you first. You have made it very easy for me. You're perfect in every way I can imagine. We complement each other and we have like interests. The only problem I've been struggling with is whether I should address you as 'Doc' or 'Gloria' when I ask you to marry me. I finally decided on 'Gloria,' because I'm sure my mother will call you 'Gloria.' I hope you don't mind. So that brings me to the big question. Gloria, will you marry me?" Will handed her a tasteful engagement ring.

"I can't believe you catered our dinner and borrowed this house just to ask me to marry you," Doc said, as she smiled at the ring.

Will raised his eyebrows and Doc said, "Oh, my God. You bought it didn't you? Wholly shit. This must have cost a fortune. I would have said 'yes' without any of this. As long as I have you."

"So, that's a yes?"

"Hell, yes," Doc said loudly, as she placed the ring on her finger.

"Then let's take off our clothes and I'll show you to our new hot tub." Will kissed her then and they removed their clothes, turned out the lights and then opened the drapes to a view of the new deck and ocean beyond. The deck lighting was very low and subtle. When Will slid open the sliding glass door the sound of the hot tub bubbling was mixed with the constant sound of the surf and the smell of the ocean breeze. Will carried their wine glasses and an open bottle of wine to the hot tub, then stepped down into the hot water and helped Doc step in behind him. Will opened the hot tub air inlet to get the bubbles really flowing and sank down into the water. Doc slid in next to him and they just sat there enjoying each other.

Doc said, "I'm having a hard time with this. Well, not the marrying part, but the house thing. You really brought the house for us and had it remodeled?"

"That's correct. Do you like it?"

"What's not to like. I love it, but just when I thought I was really getting to know you, I realize that I don't know much about you. Who are you, Bruce Wayne?" asked Doc with a laugh.

"Sort of, Batman was my hero," replied Will.

Will had Doc sit on the side of the hot tub and spread her legs wide while he used his tongue to pleasure her. Then they traded places and Will sat on the side of the hot tub while Doc slowly sucked him into an orgasm. While he was still hard they stood in the hot tub and Doc bent over and held on to the side while Will entered her from behind and slowly worked them both into sexual frenzy. By that time they were both overheated and had to spread towels out on the deck and lay down, catching their breath, looking up at the stars.

"Damn, I'm going to enjoy this hot tub and this house and that ocean and you. Not necessarily in that order," said Doc. "So is this house like a wedding present to ourselves or what?"

"No, this is more like our starter home. Your wedding present is in the garage," Will declared.

"You've got to be shitting me. Like the house isn't enough. What did you do, buy me a dog?" Doc said, laughingly.

"Come on, I'll show you." There were matching robes folded next to where the towels had been placed. Will helped Doc into her robe.

"You sure planned this out well," said Doc. "I'm going to have to keep an eye on you."

Will led Doc into the house and down a hallway to the interior door of the garage. He then opened the door and flipped on the garage light. The new BMW looked like it was glowing under the florescent lighting. The car was so sleek it looked like it was going a hundred miles an hour just sitting there.

"Wholly shit. No way. That sure isn't a dog," Doc said laughing and crying at the same time. She jumped into Will arms and planted kisses all over his face. Then Doc squealed, jumped up and down, turned around, and said, "Wholly shit Batman, you are Bruce Wayne. Please tell me we are not going to be in debt for all this for the rest of our lives."

"It's all yours, baby. Paid for and insured," Will informed her. "Do you feel like taking me for a ride?"

"A ride in that car is not all you're going to get buster," Doc said as she kissed Will again.

Will road quietly as Doc drove her new BMW down the coast highway. She had to stop several times just so she could start all over again, shifting gears. Will enjoyed seeing her smile like a kid with a new toy, which in effect, she was. He loved to hear her excited voice.

When they got back to the beach house Doc backed her new car into the garage then kissed Will and helped him get blankets and pillows out of Will's trunk so they could spend their first night in their new home.

The next morning a little stiff from sleeping on the floor, they dressed in casual clothes that Will had the forethought to bring, then drove Will's car to a pancake house for breakfast. That's when Will told Doc they were taking a trip and that he had everything arranged. They just needed to go back to his apartment to pack overnight bags and get to the airport.

"It seems like you were presuming a lot," said Doc.

"I've got you all figured out," Will replied.

"Have not and you wish," said Doc. "I haven't gotten you figured out yet so I know I'm still a mystery to you. Men aren't capable of figuring women out. We are far too clever and complex for the male mind."

They packed their bags with Will, once again, being elusive about where they were going then they headed for the airport. When they got to the airport Will turned onto an access road that led to private terminals. Doc held her tongue and didn't say anything, but it was very obvious that she wanted to. Will pulled into a charter service that specialized in service and maintenance of private planes.

"You chartered a plane?" asked Doc.

"No."

"Don't tell me you own your own plane."

"On a cop's salary. Not me," replied Will. "You're not very patient. I'm guessing that 'shhhs' thing won't work again, so come on, I'll show you," Will said. They walked into the charter service with their bags and went up to the counter where Will stated, "I'm William Bracket. I believe you're expecting me."

"Yes, Mr. Bracket. Your plane has arrived and is ready for you," said the smiling clerk. "Our attendant will shuttle you and your luggage to the plane." The attendant took their bags, escorted them to the waiting shuttle then drove them to a sleek new Lear Jet.

The pilot met them as they stepped off the shuttle and said, "Hello Mr. Bracket. It's nice to see you again."

"Good to see you too, Brandon. Meet my future wife, Gloria Holiday," Will said.

"Please to meet you Miss Holiday. I have everything ready for us to embark on our journey. Shall we go?" stated Brandon, as he picked up their bags. "The weather looks great for our flight."

Doc waited until they were seated with drinks before she said, "I thought you said you didn't own the plane. It's kind of looking like you do and it's huge."

"I don't own it. It belongs to my father's company and it's not that big. It only seats ten people and is only used here in the United States. Father has a customized 747 that he uses for international flights."

"Okay, okay. I can deal with this, but at least tell me where we're going?"

"To get married of course. I thought we'd fly to Lake Tahoe. Get married. Then go to this place I know that serves the best sole you will ever taste. We can do a little gambling then turn in early so we can fly to New York to meet my mother and father. That about sums it up."

"Wholly shit Batman. You don't give a girl much time to prepare. Since yesterday I got engaged, got a new house with an ocean view and a hot tub I might add and you gave me a car that's worth more than my house. Today we're getting married and tomorrow I'm meeting the family. Sounds a little backwards. After saying it all out loud it even sounds a little crazy, but I do crazy pretty good."

"I think I know you well enough to know that you don't want the kind of wedding my mother would put on if we gave her the chance. It would take six months to plan. It would involve about three hundred people that you don't know, a church cathedral, a park and a huge reception in the garden at my parents' estate. Not to mention the bachelor party my old friends would want to throw that would probably make you shoot them. I was trying to spare us both all that discomfort. However, now would be the time to tell me if you would rather have a big wedding. My mother would love nothing more than to plan the whole thing while you stood there with your mouth open in shock and awe. I apologize if I was wrong. I hope you can see that all I care about is your happiness."

"Oh, Will, my sexy cowboy. I'm overwhelmed and a little jealous that you could manage all of this without me knowing. That blows me away. With that said, I'm so happy I'm at a loss for words, which is unusual for me. All I want to do is marry you and get back to our new home where we can start our life together and I can show you how much I love you."

"I'll do the best I can to make the rest of our lives a honeymoon," Will stated.

They landed at Lake Tahoe where a car was waiting, then drove to the Touch of Love Wedding Chapel where they were married. Doc got tickled at the thought of them being Mr. and Mrs. Bracket and kept laughing from time to time. The Dover Sole was as excellent as Will had described. They did a little shopping, had fun gambling then turned in early so they could consummate their marriage.

The next morning, as planned, they flew to New York to meet Will's parents.

Chapter 32

New York was magnificent. Hundreds of Taxis were zipping around. Millions of people were walking up and down the sidewalks and the buildings were so tall they looked like they were touching the clouds. Now Doc could really understand why they called them skyscrapers. She couldn't even imagine what type of men it would take to build structures that huge. It was breathtakingly beautiful, in a scary way. Thinking about all that concrete and steel towering above you was a little unsettling.

A limo picked Will and Doc up at the airport. Will knew the driver and he asked him to take this particular rout through downtown New York so he could point out some of the historical sites and see the look on Doc's face when she looked up at the buildings around her. It took over an hour to drive through downtown New York and out to what Will called "the country" to Will's parents' home. On the drive they passed many large estates and Doc commented on how large, pretty and old they were.

When the limo turned onto a private brick road and passed through enormous, ornate iron gates Doc could see a sprawling mansion, complete with gate house, guest house, carriage house and stables.

In her mind she knew, but asked anyway, "Where are we?"

"Home," Will, answered.

"Wholly shit Batman. You did it to me again. My God, it's bigger than the White House."

"Not quite. Its three stories, not including the attic and wine cellar. Father has one of the oldest and extensive wine collections on the Eastern seaboard. I could always tell what my father thought of a guest by what vintage wine he had brought up for dinner. The place has forty-six rooms and I don't believe I've seen them all. The old servant quarters are in the rear, but now we call them domestic help, which is considered politically correct and they live in the residence now. The older structures are maintained for historical purposes," Will explained.

A butler was walking down the steps as the limo came around the drive. He arrived just as the car stopped and opened the rear door for Will. Doc expected Will to call him "Alfred," but to her surprise, the butler said, "Master William, how delightful to see you."

"And you, Wilfred. It's good to be home. I trust you've been taking great care of mother and father?"

"Of course, and they are in good health. You did give your mother quite a fright by getting shot, twice. If you would have seen her face and felt her distress, as I did, you would surely rethink your profession," Wilfred said.

It was obvious that Will and Wilfred were very comfortable with each other. Will laughed and they both followed Wilfred into the manor. Doc could tell that the friendly banter between Will and the butler was more like father and son. It must have been nice being raised in a household with so many loving people looking after you, Doc thought.

Will's mother was waiting in the library where hundreds of old leather bound books lined the walls in hand carved book shelves. Doc could see all kinds of mythical creatures carved into the woodwork: lions, griffins, unicorns, dragons, angels, gargoyles and more. It was beautiful. Will's mother stood as they entered the room and said, "Gloria, how delightful to meet you." She crossed the room and hugged Doc then held her at arms-length and looked at her closely. "I'm a little put out with my son right now for not allowing me to plan your wedding and for getting shot and worrying me so, but I am very happy you are both here."

Doc simply smiled as Will's mother turned to him and gave Will a warm embrace. "Your father will be here for dinner. He had some pressing business matter to tend to, as usual," Will's mother said.

Will kissed his mother's cheek, told her how lovely she looked then hugged her again. Both had tears in their eyes. It was a very moving moment that almost had Doc crying too. She had to wipe a tear from her eye, as well.

"Your room is ready. Why don't you and Gloria take a few minutes to freshen up then meet me in the dining room for lunch."

What Will's mother really meant by giving Will and Doc "a few minutes to freshen up," was that she needed a few minutes to compose herself and freshen up. Her grieving son had left for California on an adventure to help him get past his heartache and come back a married man, full of love and hope. She could see the happiness in Will and Gloria's faces and it brought joy to her heart. She had to call Will's father at the office and give him the wonderful news.

Doc was amazed at the size of the place. Will explained that the common rooms, sitting room, dining room, kitchen, library, solarium, and domestic help quarters were on the lower floor. Will's mother and father occupied the second floor along with a host of guest rooms that were used for any overnight guests. The guest house was used for any long term guests. Will's room was on the third floor, along with other rooms that could be used for housing family. Will's room overlooked the front of the property. As a child, Will explained, he dreamed of being a knight and played like he was watching over the castle keep from his towering room. Will's room was huge and filled with childhood memories.

One of the many pictures on the walls was one of Will dressed in a Batman costume for Halloween.

"You are Bruce Wayne," said Doc. "You made a wonderful Batman."

"I'm your Batman, baby and you don't even have to put on a yellow cape to be my sidekick. We can fight crime together and we don't even need a bat cave," Will declared.

"I bet you have a bat cave around here some place. If not, then I have a little bat cave that can accommodate you lover boy," Doc said with a mischievous smile. She was enjoying being Mrs. Bracket.

Because the mansion had been built in the days when people still used a pitcher of water and a washbasin to freshen up and chamber pots to relieve themselves in, the advent of running water and plumbing resulted in entire rooms being converted to "bathrooms." Following suit and keeping with the times, the carriage house had been remodeled into a garage.

After lunch with Will's mother, Will took Doc on a tour of the grounds. He walked her through the garden and behind a wall of tall hedges into a wooded area where he pointed out the old servant quarters that were built in the early 1800s out of red brick. The roof was sagging in the middle and the brick was crumbling with age. It looked sad and Doc wondered that, if it could talk, what kind of wild stories it could tell. They walked deeper into the woods where Will played as a child. Will's tree house looked like something out of Daniel Defoe's Robinson Crusoe, only all grown over and abandoned. Reduced to a childhood memory. Gone but not forgotten. Reclaimed by the forest where it once thrived with excitement and dreams. Doc could only imagine what a wonderful life Will lived as a child. Long before he experienced heartbreak and sorrow.

Will showed Doc the converted carriage house where his first car was still parked. A Triumph Spitfire, covered in dust. They walked through the stables and Will told her that the horses were before his time. His mother had horses as a child, but had lost interest in them. His father didn't have the time or the passion for them and Will had grown-up in a time where go-carts and mini-bikes were the craze. Horses were slow and more for girls. Will wanted to go fast. He'd known some girls who had horses, but he'd never been riding. The closest he'd come to a horse was seeing them in movies and in fields on the side of roads. More recently he'd experienced some closer looks when they'd visited the horse ranches in Nevada where Will confirmed that, where there are horses, there is horse shit. Which resulted in an unpleasant odor that he could gladly do without. Will was more suited for big cities with modern conveyances.

As they walked hand-in-hand back towards the main house Doc asked Will where his house was located. All she really knew was that he'd sold his home and bought the beach house. She wanted to see what kind of house Will was going to live in before they'd met. Rather than simply explain Will got the keys to one of his father's cars and drove Doc back towards New York City.

As they neared the city the homes became smaller and closer together. Will told Doc that they used to be huge estates that were sold, broken-up and subdivided into five acre plots, each walled in with privacy gates and enormous trees. Where Will's parents' home and property was valued at over one-hundred million, these newer homes on smaller parcels of land built in the 40s and 50s, were valued in the twenty to twenty-five million range. They were very nice and exclusive.

Will turned off the main road onto a picturesque tree lined country lane. The trees arched up over the road giving it a shaded tunnel affect. Will pulled into a driveway, stopped at an electronic gate and pointed to a beautiful fourteen room mansion, complete with Roman colonnade supporting the front upper floor above the entrance. It was far more than Doc expected.

"My father helped me with some very good investments when I was in high school. While in college I played the stock market during the dot com era and did well on various tech stocks. Unlike some, I was lucky and picked the right companies," Will said.

"You gave this up for a house on the beach?" asked Doc.

"No. I gave this up for a new life with the woman I love more than the moon and the stars and the beach house," Will replied smiling, “a very hot and sexy woman with a sexy butt, I must add."

"Right answer," Doc stated.

"Don't you want to know who she is," Will said teasingly.

"It better be your new wife buster or I'm going home to get my gun," Doc said as she leaned over and kissed Will. "I think your butt is sexy too, my sweet Batman."

Doc loved Will's father from the moment she met him. He was warm and affectionate and commanded an air of aristocracy. Doc could see where Will got his charm.

Before dinner Will and Doc were in the library visiting with Will's parents when Wilfred came in and asked which wine to serve. The wine needed time to chill and breath before the evening meal. "Tonight, we'll have two bottles of the 1920 burgundy," stated Will's father.

Then, as Wilfred left to retrieve the wine, Will's father, who was a substantial wine enthusiast and connoisseur explained the history of the wine.

"Gloria, in 1907, the French had an exceptional growing year. They were blessed with an overabundance of fine grapes. They were not prepared for such a windfall, so they were short of wine casks. To remedy the problem, they resorted to filling one hundred empty brandy casks. Those casks were set aside until 1920 when the owner of the winery had a bad year for grapes and was forced to bottle the wine. To his delight the wine had a heavy bouquet and was much sharper than the other wines he produced. The flavor and the aroma alone are intoxicating, which caused a stir in the wine community. People from all over wanted to purchase the wine, but due to its limited supply and high quality, the cost was exorbitant.

“My grandfather, who happened to be visiting France at the time was invited to a social gathering of the French elite where he sampled the extraordinary wine. He bought twenty cases and had it secretly shipped to America during the height of prohibition. Wine cellars back then were not only for keeping wine at a favorable constant temperature, but were also used to secret away the ill-gotten, forbidden spirits. A whole section of our wine cellar is hidden behind a movable brick wall. It is quite ingenuous, actually. William used to play down there when he was a child and we had an awful time finding him," Will's father stated with a laugh.

Doc thought, "Will does have his own bat cave." She smiled at Will and he smiled back, knowing what she was thinking. Will must have spent many hours in his make-believe bat cave playing Batman, saving his parents from the evil deeds of the Joker and the Riddler.

The main course for dinner was lamb, which Doc usually didn't care for, but had to admit that it was prepared with just the right amount of herbs and spices to make it delicious. It was still difficult for Doc to get the picture of a tiny little white lamb out of her mind while eating. She wondered why she did not think of cows that way. The wine was as excellent as Will's father claimed it would be. Dessert was strawberry cheesecake, which was one of Doc's all-time favorites and it was delightful.

After dinner Will and Doc retired to their room and Doc said, "I take it that your father must approve of me. He broke out the good wine, right?"

"He 'broke out,' as you put it, not only the best wine but two bottles of the best wine. I can only remember that wine coming out for company twice. Once when Bush senior and his wife came to dinner when their son was running for President and once when Bill Gates and his wife came to dinner. It is a short 'A' list, for certain. I should point out that neither my graduation from college nor my first engagement warranted the 1920 burgundy," Will exclaimed. "It appears that my father is as taken with you as I am."

The next morning Will and Doc had a long leisurely breakfast with Will's parents. They discussed vacationing in Europe and Rome as a belated honeymoon for Will and Doc. After breakfast and hugs all around, Will and Doc climbed into the limo and were driven back to the airport and the waiting Lear Jet. It is more fun flying from the East coast to the West coast, because of the time change and the slow but steady rotation of the earth. As fast as the Lear Jet was traveling it appeared that you arrived in Los Angeles not long after you left New York. Even though the flying time was the same, flying the other direction gave the appearance of taking twice as long. It was an interesting illusion, because you could fly out of New York after breakfast and be in Los Angeles for a late lunch. Of course, that didn't stop a person from being completely give out from jet lag.

They arrived back in Los Angeles early enough to make arrangements to have a moving company move all of Will's belongings from his apartment to the beach house. They brought boxes back to Will's apartment and packed some of his more personal things to help the moving process along.

Then they went to Doc's house to check on things before they went to the beach house for the night. There was no need to get in a hurry about moving Doc's things. They would take their time deciding what furniture they were going to keep and or replace. Will sold his home in New York with part of the furnishings, but some of his prize pieces were stored at his parents' home. Will had some items, such as his matching Eames changes that he would not dream of parting with, but they were so unique and unusual that it would take a special room just to display them in and there wasn't such a room in the beach house. Will knew that he would live with Doc in his parents' home some day and he would put his Eames chairs in his father's study where they would be the topic of many conversations. They may even open the stables again so their children could learn to ride. But for now, they would spend their time looking at wondrous sunsets from their hot tub overlooking the ocean. Will was already thinking that it would be best for him and Doc to get out of the hazardous law enforcement profession. He enjoyed his work and he knew Doc did too, but with the recent attempts on their lives he didn't want to risk losing Doc. He certainly didn't want to raise children in that type of environment.

They were both young. In a year or two they could reevaluate what they wanted and which direction best to take to get there and plan things accordingly. There was no need to hurry. They were right in the middle of a huge case that they both wanted to see closed so they could get back to the simple task of finding missing persons. They were currently focusing on areas way outside their job description. If they wanted excitement and danger they would have went into a different department such as narcotics or a gang unit. Working in missing persons was a calling not just a job. Will and Doc were like two sides of the same coin. They both wanted to help find people that were lost or needed help. Even though they were both enjoying their assignment they were ready to bring it to a close so their lives could get back to normal. All the running around from State to State was taking away from their home life and now that it was going to be the two of them they were seriously ready to spend more time at home, doing things like, each other.

Chapter 33

While Will and Doc were getting married and jet setting around Big Eddie relocated to Cairo. Egypt was hot, sandy and dry, but that wouldn't affect Big Eddie much because he would be spending most of his time in his penthouse suite that was climate controlled with all the comforts a man could ask for.

Big Eddie, formally known as Edward Freeman, wasn't concerned about being traced to Cairo. Edward Freemen was an alias he'd used for over twenty years. When American law enforcement finely uncovered his alias, and they would soon, it would lead them to a commodities company that Big Eddie had used as a front for his vast smuggling operations that had recently been diverted through yet another recently developed company. The old commodities company was now only involved with legitimate commodities. Big Eddie had transferred ownership of the company to another person who was buying the company on credit making the monthly deposits to an account in the name of Edward Freemen that would just sit there and draw interest while Big Eddie lived in Cairo under another assumed name.

The new owner was left with instructions to tell anyone who asked that Mr. Freeman retired and moved away. He'd never actually met Mr. Freeman because he purchased the company through his attorney and made the monthly deposits directly to an account that was set up to receive his monthly mortgage payments. That was the story he was given and he was sticking to it. In reality, the man who bought the company was the son of a trusted friend. The young man was intelligent and had a business degree, and most importantly, he was not involved in anything even remotely shady. It was a perfect setup.

All of Big Eddie's other holdings had been in corporate names. The only other item that Big Eddie was concerned about was his yacht. Too many people could associate him with the yacht so it was on its way to Japan where it would be re-outfitted, complete with new serial numbers, title and name, then brought down to Australia, across the Indian Ocean and up through the Red Sea where it would be taken through the Suez Canal into the Mediterranean Sea to its new home at Port Said. The Yacht was worth the trouble. It was far too luxurious to abandon or part with. Men need their toys.

Big Eddie's new combined penthouse apartment and office was a testament to men and their toys. He had the best of the old and new worlds. While tastefully decorated with ancient museum quality Egyptian artifacts, it was equipped with the latest modern technology. The entire top floor was devoted to Big Eddie's needs. His apartment/office occupied one corner and was large enough to host a party of fifty, comfortably. The computer and communications department managed most of Eddie's investments and business transactions from another corner and was staffed with over twenty lawyers, clerks and secretaries. The security department occupied another corner with twelve full time guards, ten part-time guards and two pilots to fly the Bell Jet Ranger that was parked on the roof. The final corner was the kitchen, cafeteria and Big Eddie's private dining room that employed a large variety of waiters, waitresses, two chefs and other support staff. It was a private city in the sky and Eddie had the option of never touching the ground. When his yacht arrived in Port Said he would be able to fly from his roof-top heliport directly to the helipad on his yacht. It was actually a far better situation than he'd created in America.

Eddie's new Egyptian secretary, with her silky dark skin, green eyes like a cat, long sexy legs, tight, short skirts and her straight raven hair cut across the front into perfect bangs that gave her an exotic look did more than simply turn heads, she stopped men in their tracks. Eddie was enjoying the thought of his yacht arriving next summer so he could fly his new secretary out to the yacht for a week or two and watch her walk around in a bikini.

Eddie was pleased with the way the Antonellie father and son hit went down. He knew he could always count on his man Bob to handle things with a flare. But, Eddie was pissed about the "third" botched hit on the two cops. Although killing the cops was no longer pressing, because he and Angela were now out of the country with new identities, it was still a matter left unfinished. Three failed attempts made them look incompetent and it was a matter of professional pride that drove Big Eddie to see the situation through. He would have Bob handle it personally, but only after letting things cool off for a bit, which would give Bob time to plan the newlywed's demise. Eddie had no doubt that Bob could manage it in some spectacular fashion. Crime fighters who lie together can die together Big Eddie thought, jokingly.

Because of Big Eddie's move, young Raymond the computer program designer was no longer a pressing issue. That certainly didn't negate the fact that Ray knew too much and he'd stolen from Eddie and the other partners, even after Eddie went out of his way to protect the kid and teach him how to be a man. Eddie thought the kid was so smart he could have made himself a millionaire. The thought made Eddie laugh, because the kid did make himself a millionaire, only he went about it wrong. Being a millionaire for Ray was going to be short lived, literally. Eddie couldn't have Ray telling what he knew or getting away with ripping off the largest crime syndicate in the world. The only other organization that equaled Big Eddie's and Angela's operation was the Chinese Triad. Even the Triad did a large part of its business with Big Eddie's organization.

Currently, Eddie had teams scouring Europe looking for Ray. He had hackers working the computers trying to trace the money Ray took and trying to monitor and track the origin of the deadserious emails. It would take some time, but he would find Ray and then the little bastard would die slowly and painfully. The more Big Eddie thought about it, the more he wanted to feed Ray to the sharks piece by piece as Ray watched. He might even hold a special gladiator event, just for Ray. Of course, all his murderous thoughts were on hold because he had to find Ray first. For now, Eddie would enjoy watching his fine new Egyptian secretary walk around the office in heels and a mini-skirt and savor the thought of catching and killing Ray, while he relished the thought of seeing his new secretary in a bikini. Both thoughts gave him great pleasure.

Another great advantage of relocating to Cairo was, other people in America were now taking care of the day to day problems there and Eddie could enjoy his food without suffering meal interruptis. All of his staff had strict instructions not to disturb his meals for any reason.

After lunch, Eddie's goddess of a secretary gave him a message to call Nicole in Moscow. Eddie was a little put out with Angela/Nicole because she often did not listen and tended to jump the gun. He was careful with her because she was text book insane. One minute she was daddy's little rich girl and the next minute she could go psycho killer bitch from hell in an instant. The way she killed her long time lover, Kara, proved that she wasn't just cold-blooded she was sub-zero, but that was what Eddie loved about her. She could switch from good to bad in the blink of an eye. Eddie returned her call and was put through immediately.

"Hello, Edward," Nicole stated. "I wanted to call and ask how you like Cairo?"

"I absolutely adore it. It is a welcome and long overdue change. You'll have to come visit soon," stated Eddie. "How are things progressing in Moscow?"

"Wonderful. I've had to do a little restructuring, but things are progressing rather well, thank you. Some of these uneducated cretins seem to have watched too many of those old black-and-white gangster movies. They all want to be the big chief, when most of them are barely qualified to be little Indians. It is typical and quite tiring, but I'll have them all towing the line in no time. I see you received the file I sent you on the available equipment. That was such a nice find. The Minister of Defense is a very amicable and charming man. We got along splendidly. He has personally guaranteed that all purchases will be delivered with the required export documentation. All he asks is that the items not linger in Russia," Nicole explained.

"I have a container ship in route," Eddie said. "Part of making money revolves around being able and ready to capitalize on good deals when they are available. Some of the larger items I don't have buyers for yet, but I should have by the time we take possession of them. The smaller items, as you know, like the AK-47s, RPGs, mortars and plastic explosives I could sell by the train loads. Those desert rats in Iraq love to blow shit up. I was happy to see that you purchased what you needed for Africa."

Eddie was just making conversation until Nicole got to what she wanted to discuss and it didn't take long. The arms trade was a very small thing in comparison to the Afghani opium and heroin trade, but they used the armaments to trade for opium, heroin and even hashish. Any time he could trade ten million in weapons for one hundred million in drugs Eddie had to be ready to make the trade. The good things about weapons and drugs was, they got used and had to be replaced. Obviously, this ensured a continual market with a high profit margin. It was a never ending cycle and someone had to make the profit and it might as well be them. The fact that it was illegal added to the risk and excitement.

"Thank you for calling me back so promptly," Nicole stated professionally. "I wanted to give you an update on how things are progressing here. I took care of that problem with Otto we discussed. He wasn't receptive of my retirement suggestion, so I was forced to replace him. Also, I wanted to complement you on the way you handled Carmine and ask about your progress with those two damn cops. Are we having any luck yet?"

Nicole's comments made it clear that she still had eyes and ears in America checking up on things. Eddie hoped that didn't create additional problems.

"The wheels of progress are turning a little slow in that regard, but I assure you it is being taken care of," replied Eddie. "Amazingly, the two married each other recently in Lake Tahoe and took a trip to New York in a private jet, no less. I have arranged for them to get a final wedding gift from us. I knew you would approve."

"I certainly do. Exterminating them won't stop the investigation, but it will send a strong message to the rest of them. They need to know that if they mess with the bull they get the horns," said Nic, laughing.

"That's an interesting an unusual metaphor and it fits my girth. But for you my darling, a more fitting metaphor would be, if you play with the devil, you pay for the deed," Big Eddie stated.

"Oh, I like that. I hadn't heard that one. But enough with the metaphors. This wasn't just a social call and an update on Russian diplomacy. I wanted to let you know that our new fighting operations in Milan and Saudi Arabia are opening next week. I plan to attend the grand opening in Saudi. I know you don't attend any of the fights yourself, but I was hoping that you would consider meeting Joanna and I afterwards for a late dinner. We could get a suite and have dinner catered. It will be like old times. I miss you, Edward."

"I think that is a delightful idea. I'm looking forward to meeting your new friend, Joanna. It will give me a chance to show off my new personal secretary, Hecate. She's named after the Egyptian goddess of wisdom. She is a wonder. I have some other pressing business I should attend to in Saudi, as well. This will be a perfect opportunity to address those matters. I'll have Hecate make the necessary arrangements and fax you the details. Until then, hugs and kisses," Eddie said.

Big Eddie hung up thinking that he liked Angela, but he certainly wasn't going to let liking her influence the fact that she was one crazy bitch and he just couldn't really trust her. Not completely. He would take all the necessary precautions when they met in Saudi and her fate and future would depend on how she acted. Any meetings would be on his turf, not hers. Eddie knew that she loved money, but she wasn't really greedy. For her it was more of a power trip. Eddie dealt with that by giving her more control. There was no doubt that she was a brilliant business strategist. The main problem was, as Eddie saw it, she was a blood thirsty nut. She enjoyed seeing blood more than a vampire. He had miscalculated with Ray and it made him hope he wasn't miscalculating Angela. Eddie laughed. It made him think of the prayer: "God, please protect me from my friends, I can take care of my enemies myself." Eddie knew who his enemies were and he kept them on a short leash and watched them carefully. He didn't really expect any trouble out of Angela, but usually, that's when the sleeping dog spun around and bit you. Beware the sleeping dog. He'll bite you when you least expect it.

"I'm getting too old for this shit," Eddie said to himself as he picked up the phone to put together another deal.

Chapter 34

Because they had to break the news to everyone some time, Will and Doc got on their phones and starting inviting all their friends and coworkers to a Sunday brunch. Will called the caterer, thanked her for making their engagement dinner perfect, apologized for the short notice and asked her to cater the Sunday brunch for thirty. She was delighted and exclaimed that short notices were her forte.

Will and Doc agreed that brunch would be best. That way there wouldn't be any drinking and a lot of drunk cops hanging around until late. They purposely did not tell anyone what the get together was about because they wanted to surprise everyone and they didn't want everyone running out at the last minute buying a lot of unnecessary gifts. It was a perfect time to throw a party because they didn't have all their furniture in yet. The caterer would bring some fold-out tables and chairs. Perfect.

On Sunday, the caterer and her crew arrived at 8 o'clock and everything was setup and looking beautiful by 9:30. The guests started pouring in at 10:00 as prearranged. By 11:30 all the guests had arrived and had eaten their fill. Most of the guests thought they had a pretty good idea what the big announcement would be. Some thought it was a house warming, retirement, wedding or maybe a baby.

After giving everyone plenty of time to eat Will asked the crowd if he could please have their attention, then he turned the announcement over to Doc.

"First, thank you all for coming on such short notice. Everything for me lately has been a little short notice," Doc said to some laughs. "Getting to the point, I'm sure many of you have noticed that Will and I have been spending a lot of time together—"

"Closing cases and shooting up the town," someone said from the back and everyone laughed.

"That too. I'm certain that to most of you it was obvious that Will and I are quite taken with each other. Last week we were married in Lake Tahoe (cheers and applause) at the Touch of Love Wedding Chapel (laughs and applause) then we flew to New York so I could meet Will's wonderful parents."

"Weren't you guys supposed to have this party and meet the parents before the wedding?" asked a coworker. (everyone laughed and clapped).

"You think that's backwards, Will was so sure of himself that he bought us this new home before he asked me to marry him," Doc said with a laugh.

"Atta boy Will," came a cheer from the crowd and they all laughed.

Doc was on a roll. "I'll tell you how cocky our sweet little gunslinger is, he bought me a new BMW for an engagement present, before we were engaged and we were only engaged one day before we got married."

"You go boy," said the heckler and everyone joined in for a laugh.

Will just stood back with a smile and enjoyed seeing Doc have fun. Doc had motioned for everyone to follow her and the entire crowd paraded through the hallway to the garage to see her shiny blue engagement present sitting there looking fantastic. Doc opened the garage door to let in the light and make it easy for her friends to admire her new car.

At one point Will and Doc's unit commander walked up to Doc and said, "I knew your boy was loaded, but damn. All this had to set him back some."

"Trust me, Boss. This didn't make a dent," relied Doc.

Everyone was gone by 3:00 p.m. Will and Doc decided to take a drive up the coast to find some new place for dinner while the caterer cleaned up the mess.

Doc absolutely loved driving her new car and Will loved seeing her smile. They stopped at a pleasant looking sea food restaurant that featured a nice picturesque view of the ocean, where they both ordered shrimp platters and shared a light, white, sweet local chardonnay that was recommended by their waiter. It was almost midnight before they got home to share each other. A lot had taken place in a very short time and Doc was a little overwhelmed and overjoyed.

The next morning Will and Doc went into the office early hoping to avoid some of the jeers and sneers, but they weren't early enough. A few people were already in and a simple "congratulations" sign was on the wall behind Will's desk. They both gave a sigh of relief and were halfway to their desks when some clever cop hit the play button on a boom box and "Love Shack" started blaring across the room.

Will smiled and Doc held her hands up in surrender. The music was turned off and Doc said, "Okay, okay, I knew we weren't going to get off too easy."

Just then their commander walked in and said, "Well, if it isn't the newlyweds, Wyatt Earp and Doc Holiday. You're both starting the week off good. You're early to work and ol' Wyatt here hasn't shot anyone yet."

"Not yet, but the week is young Boss," Will stated with a smile.

As he turned to leave the commander stated, "Will, you and your partner and I mean that in more ways than one, have been officially cleared on that last shoot. Come by my office when you have a free moment and pick-up your sidearm. Now get to work you slackers, we've got missing people to find."

As Will was clearing and answering his emails he came to one from the Assistant District Attorney (ADA) regarding the Silvertre Deveraux case. Mr. Deveraux had cooperated and been cleared on the homicide and was looking at a reduced sentence on the meth manufacturing charges because of his cooperation. The ADA wanted to know if Will had any comments or objections. This gave Will an idea, so he emailed the ADA, stating that he had no objections and asked if he could interview Mr. Deveraux about another matter. Within the hour Will's computer announced, "You've got mail," with the accompanying "Bing." It was a response from the ADA okaying Will's request and asking for an update after the interview.

Will called lock-up and asked the duty officer to have Deveraux brought out of Protective Custody (PC) to an interview room. Deveraux was nervously waiting when Will and Doc came into the interview room. If Deveraux recognized them there was no sign of it.

"Mr. Deveraux, I'm officer Bracket and this is detective Holiday."

They had decided to use Doc's maiden name at work and in a professional capacity to avoid confusion, explanations and jokes.

After introductions Doc took the lead. "I see you got lucky, avoiding that murder rap. You did the right thing by helping us solve it and helping yourself. Rather than life, now you're looking at a ten on the meth manufacturing and distributing charges. How would you like to turn it into a five?"

"I'd like to turn it into a zero," said Deveraux. "What do you want to know?"

"We're looking for someone referred to as Mr. Big."

"Hell, everyone selling dope in LA thinks he's Mr. Big. I need more than that."

Doc said, "This Mr. Big is supposed to be running worldwide kidnapping and gladiator fights from here in LA and he might have the initials B.E. Does that help?"

Will and Doc saw Deveraux's expression change when he realized who they were referring to.

"Shit-fuck. That's 'The Mr. Big.' He is seriously untouchable. You'd have a better chance of going after the President of the U.S. of A. He's like, worth zillions. He's got his hand in everything illegal around the world. Word is, he's having informants kidnapped and killed and from what I hear he did the Antonellie hits. I tell you who he is and I'll be dead before I get back to PC."

Doc told Deveraux to hold on a moment while she stepped into the hall to place a call. She ran what she had by the ADA who agreed to let her make a deal. Then she called the federal Task Force SAC and ran it by him, told him what she wanted and got his okay.

Back in the interview room, Doc said, "Here's the gig Deveraux, you give me a name and make me believe it, my partner and I will escort you out of here and you will be taken to a federal safe-house where you'll have a steak dinner tonight. If what you tell us is true, your charges will be dismissed and we'll put you in the witness protection program."

"Shit-fuck. Hell, I don't think you'll be able to protect me, but I'd rather take my chances in the witness protection program then spend the next ten years in prison. Your Mr. Big - or B.E. - is Big Eddie Freeman. He has a commodities company based here in LA. As a front he buys, sells and ships food and farm equipment to third world countries. He has a big mansion on the beach in Long Beach and a huge fancy yacht. I hear he's in a wheelchair."

They spent over an hour getting all the details. The name and location of the business the mansion and the yacht and the details on how Deveraux knew all this information. Will and Doc got on their phones and got people working on verifying the information and got a team on the way to transport Deveraux to the safe-house.

It was just chance that Deveraux knew anything. When Harry Butkus ratted on the container ship and the dock was raided, coming up empty of course, because Big Eddie was tipped, then Butkus came up missing, a guy who knew the deal on Butkus told the whole story to a friend. The reason for that transgression was the guy needed help ripping off a warehouse where Butkus had some very valuable merchandise stored. The friend enlisted Deveraux's help to liberate the items from the warehouse and in doing so told Deveraux the whole story. Deveraux made ten grand for his help with the warehouse job and the information he gleaned turned out to be priceless. Things were looking better for Deveraux.

The ADA came to the interview room with the necessary transfer of custody papers and assured Deveraux that he was the luckiest person on the planet and that the charges would be dismissed if the information he provided was true. It was all stated on the record as part of the formal interview. When the FBI team arrived to transport Deveraux Will and Doc escorted him to the waiting van without going through processing. Deveraux would get his steak dinner.

Will and Doc spent the rest of the afternoon and evening doing research until the key members of the Task Force arrived from Reno. They didn't have enough for an arrest, but they had a direction and they were headed that way. The information Deveraux had given them was proving to be correct. At least on the surface.

The first question they had was, how could Mr. Big Eddie Freeman, who was only showing a taxable personal income, according to the IRS, of about five million a year, afford a yacht valued at over twenty million and a mansion in Long Beach that was valued at over twenty million? What they didn't know yet was that the yacht was gone, the home and business were sold and Mr. Freeman was missing without a trace. These were facts they would soon learn, but all the sales transactions were so fresh those facts weren't known yet. Will and Doc were researching last year's records.

At the Task Force meeting Will gave Doc the lead. He loved to watch her enthusiastic approach to laying all the new facts out for the Team. That and he knew it pissed off some of the career driven men in the room to see a woman doing so well stealing their thunder. Doc broke-up the grunt work: find the yacht, get more info on the home and business and locate Mr. Freeman. They would have people working on it throughout the night. Tomorrow the foot work and interviews would begin.

With the briefing done and after a few pats on the back saying great job, Will and Doc headed home for a few hours of much needed sleep before their big day tomorrow. They planned to take the lead on the Big Eddie Freeman interview as soon as things got rolling in the morning.

At 5:00 a.m. the beeping of the phone jarred Will awake. It was the Task Force commander telling Will and Doc to get their butts to headquarters, because someone had blown Deveraux to bits.

The early morning meeting was a heated one. Pictures of the suburban safe-house, with one entire corner missing, looking like a huge fire breathing dragon had bitten it off, still smoking, were being passed around the room.

The team members were reduced to the simple vocabulary of, "Shit," "Son-of-a-bitch," and "Fuck."

The commander stated that it was without question that someone very close to the investigation was working with the enemy. Losing a witness after only a few hours in a safe-house was unacceptable. He explained that a separate and full investigation was already under way to find the person or persons responsible for the leak and murder of Deveraux. He made it clear that he expected everyone to fully cooperate and informed them that everyone would be subjected to a lie detector test by the end of the day. However, he added, he knew that most of the people in the room didn't even know the location of the safe-house. That part of the operation, the witness protection end, was taken care of by another branch for the very purpose of isolating the number of people who know where the witness was being held.

"It appears," the commander stated, "that the perpetrator even knew what corner of the safe-house that Mr. Deveraux was sleeping in. Based on the blast patterns we believe that shape charges were placed on both sides of the corner on the outside of the house. This would be the corner where Mr. Deveraux was so conveniently resting. Both bombs went off simultaneously, which, combined with the degree of planning and the swiftness of the hit shows an obvious degree of sophistication. My point is, it matches the degree of sophistication that we saw in the Antonellie hits, which leads me to believe that they may very well be related. Keep that in mind."

The meeting went on for another thirty minutes then the polygraph tests began. Each person took about ten minutes while the other team members used that time to conduct more research. The first agent to speak up was the man assigned to the yacht.

The agent cleared his throat to get everyone's attention then said, "I have confirmed that the yacht was in harbor two weeks ago fueling and taking on some provisions, but it left with destination unknown and hasn't been seen since."

Shortly thereafter, another agent who was researching the mansion on Long Beach stated that, "We've got more bad news folks. The mansion was sold two weeks ago. The new owner bought the place through a real estate company and he never met Mr. Freeman. He said that he was told that Mr. Freeman moved to the Cayman Islands. It looks like our chicken has flown the coop."

As Will and Doc watched all their hard work fall apart around them, the agent researching the commodities business stepped into the room and said, "Guess what?"

"The business was sold two weeks ago," replied Will.

"What are you, psychic?" the agent asked.

"Did the new owner happen to tell you that Mr. Freeman moved to the Cayman Islands?" Will asked.

"Hello, if you already knew, why did you have me do all this research?" the agent replied as he turned and walked out of the room.

"This tells us that he knew we were coming. Okay, guys," said Will, "let's follow the money and find that yacht. If we find the yacht, we find the man. He didn't take on fuel and provisions for nothing. Alert all ports that yacht can possibly reach and notify the Coast Guard to be on the lookout for that yacht."

"Okay team," the commander announced, "let's get this show on the road. I want to know everything about Mr. Freeman by the end of the day. I want to know where he was born, where he went to school and what he eats for dinner. Get me a list of family, friends and business associates. Let's take this guy's life apart. He can run, but he can't hide. Finding assholes is our job people. So let's find this asshole."

The energy in the room was electrifying. Everyone had a task and they were going at it with gusto, hence the name Task Force. They didn't know it yet, but they were about to discover that Big Eddie was really good at long term planning.

A short time later the polygraph examiner provided the commander and SAC a copy of his polygraph testing results. Every member of the Task Force had passed with flying colors. This meant that the agents conducting the investigation into the leak could concentrate on the witness protection agents, rather than waist time and energy with Task Force members. The polygraph examiner and the SAC were headed over to the witness protection branch to start lie detector tests there. They would find the person responsible, and with a little luck, that person would lead them up the food chain. It was going to be a long week.

Chapter 35

Before Deveraux was moved to the safe-house, Bob's connection in the FBI, the same man who was providing him with background information on the high profile informants in the United States, called Bob with the scoop on Deveraux and the location of the safe-house he was about to be moved to on the condition that Bob would not kill the two FBI agents that were assigned to watch over and protect him. Bob didn't like being given conditions, but he agreed. Everybody always wanted something, but for the amount of money this FBI clown was being paid, Bob thought that the least he could do was what he was paid for without more damn conditions.

When Bob called with the news that the same two cops had found themselves an informant who put them on the trail of Big Eddie Freeman, Eddie wasn't surprised. He'd been expecting it and was well prepared for it. The fact that it was the same two annoying cops that uncovered his Edward Freeman alias was disturbing, because that particular problem should have been eliminated long ago.

It was fitting and understandable that it would be someone affiliated with that piece of shit Harry Butkus that would spill the beans. Eddie never really liked Butkus, because he talked through his nose and whined and complained a lot. The only reason Butkus even acted tough was that he had bodyguards standing next to him all the time. Without those bodyguards Butkus was just another sniveling punk. One consolation was, Mr. Butkus was still in the underground prison waiting his turn at a gladiator fight. His time to die was rolling around soon enough.

But the new rat, Deveraux, had to be made an example of so the FBI Task Force and those two damn cops would know who they were dealing with. Big Eddie gave Bob the order to take out Deveraux and quick. Less than two hours after Deveraux arrived at the safe-house Bob completed his reconnaissance. Using a tranquilizer dart Bob neutralized the neighbor's dog. There wasn't any point in killing some kid's pet just to get at a rat. Then using infrared, heat detecting goggles he watched the activity within the safe-house. While the two agents watched television in the front room, his target, Deveraux, watched television in a rear corner bedroom all relaxed in a prostrate position on a bed. He looked very comfortable. Bob could see him picking up a cold drink from time to time.

The address matched so Bob was relatively certain that he had the correct house, because it was the only one with security bars on the windows. Bob could never understand why people felt secure in a wooden house, simply because it has security bars covering the windows. On one occasion Bob had used a chain saw to cut a hole in the side of a house that had security bars so he could pull a safe out that was on the other side of the wall. It took less than two minutes and he was able to simply reach in and tip the safe over into the back of his truck. It was a fast and easy job that made him over a million. All he had to do was wait for the people to leave so he could cut the hole and not be disturbed.

Based on the fact that the heat signatures of the two people in the front room looked like they were wearing side arms (guns get warm after being worn all day), logic and reason said it was Deveraux in the corner room. Bob carefully approached the house from the rear, then placed his explosive charges just under the barred windows on each side of the corner room, flipped on the timers and left as silently as he came. Ironically, Bob hung the explosives from the security bars. It was only fitting. Bob was driving away on the next block over when the enormous explosion shot fire into the air and likely blew out the windows on all the nearby houses. The people in that neighborhood would have something to talk about for a long time.

Big Eddie was watching the world news from his office/apartment in Cairo when breaking news showed an aerial view of a moderate size suburban home with a back corner of the house blown away and debris scattered all over the back yard. It looked a mess. Fire trucks and police cars were parked in front of the house and crime scene tape had been strung up to keep the gawkers at bay.

A pretty reporter was informing the public that sources say that the damaged home behind her was reportedly a safe-house used to house witnesses, that turned out not to be too safe for the occupant who was reportedly dead and the two FBI agents who were reportedly injured as a result of a tremendous blast that rocked this tiny peaceful suburban community.

She went on to state that windows were shattered for at least one hundred yards in every direction and the blast was heard and felt up to a half mile away. Short interviews with some of the neighbors who thought it was a terrorist attack were interesting. Some people were appalled and even outraged that the FBI would put a safe-house in a neighborhood full of innocent, unsuspecting children. The FBI was getting hammered by the press and neighbors. They now had a perfectly good example of how dangerous it was to have safe-houses close to innocent people and they were demanding an in-depth investigation. The reporter managed to get a shot of a couple of crying kids being herded into a car by their frantic mother so they could escape the chaos.

It was a perfect opportunity for a clever exit line. The reporter closed with a question: "Is the government putting the safety of your family at risk by placing safe-houses in your neighborhood?" Then they showed a dramatic close-up of the mangled corner of the blown-up safe-house. Then the news shifted back to the familiar rhetoric about hurricanes and floods.

Big Eddie laughed. He didn't need Bob to call him with a status report. The world news provided a nice one. When Bob did finally call, all he had to say was, "Did you see the news?" He was like a proud child showing off one of his greatest accomplishments. A very dangerous child. Big Eddie congratulated Bob on a job well done, explained that there was no hurry or real rush on the two cops, but he ordered Bob to, "Make it happen, number one." They were both Star Trek Next Generation fans. Eddie figured that the cops would be a little busy for a while trying to cover their asses.

The next phone call Eddie received was no less interesting. It was a status report on the progress of the new gladiator fights that were about to start in Milan and Saudi Arabia. For good reason, these countries, unlike America, did not have a lot of readily available informants. In America law enforcement agencies cultivated informants. The entire, so called, American justice system was reliant on informants. They literally paid informants to make statement and testify in cases the informants knew nothing about until the cops gave them the information. It was an easy fix. They often let killers go so they could arrest and imprison other people based on the killer's unreliable statements without any real evidence of whether the people did or didn't commit the alleged crime.

It was a sweet deal for everyone but the guy getting accused. That way America could lock-away anyone it wanted to, without real evidence and justify it with informant testimony. The sad part was that American jury members weren't smart enough to see and understand they were being manipulated by the government. The prosecution can say that, "I didn't convict the person, the jury did. All I did was present the evidence." It is nothing more than a glorified racket.

When you have an admitted killer or drug dealer on the witness stand saying, "Yes, I did it," but then trying to shift the blame to another person by simply stating that the other person hired him to do it or sold him the drugs, the very first question should be: "Where's the proof?" Why would anyone believe an admitted criminal whose only motivation is to get out of trouble?

Why? Because the American people at large are stupid and the government knows that and exploits and takes advantage of their ignorance. In other countries criminals aren't so fortunate. Their statements without any supporting evidence are only sufficient to start an investigation, if that. In Europe they don't even have drug "conspiracy" laws because they know how unreliable the statements and testimony of drug dealers and users can be.

To think that a criminal would not lie to get a shorter sentence would be to bathe the criminal element in more nobility than they deserve. Clearly, statements and testimony from drug dealers and users is suspect, at best.

Some informants don't fare very well in foreign countries because of the wide spread corruption in law enforcement agencies. It is easy for a cop on the take to tell his supervisors that a certain criminal didn't provide any useful or helpful information, then either hang him in his cell or release him to a worse fate. In other words, informants in Milan and Saudi Arabia have a short life span and are usually dead before there was any possibility of a gladiator fight. Letting them live long enough to fight was almost more trouble than it was worth, but Big Eddie's people were getting systems in place to help manage the change. There was a lot of money to be made and when people were making money they accepted change.

The gladiator fights consisted of a very small portion of the illegal activity that Big Eddie was involved with. Sure, the fights generated a pretty good chunk of money, but they were more for fun and sport and to send a message to all the informants in the world. It was really no different than when a rat sneaks into your pantry and starts eating your food. As soon as you discover the nasty little rat's existence you have to make a game out of killing the rat. It becomes a mission to exterminate the rat in order to protect your assets. The gladiator fights were the same thing. There would always be rats, but Big Eddie was going to do his best to thin them out and capitalize on it at the same time.

After lunch Eddie's new computer jockey came in with the news that the FBI had managed to trace the transmission of the last fight in America back to the communications company's massive computer system. When the alarm alerted them to the breach Eddie's people deleted the program from the system and routed the next transmissions through a different location. Now they would be using a computer at a medical research facility in Wisconsin. Ray had hidden the program on their system long ago and on the computer systems of five large colleges in the United States. With the fail-safe program they would know when someone was looking at the system and they would simply delete it and move on to the next location. They could move it around forever. These huge corporations spent millions on security and password protecting their sensitive information and for the most part their efforts kept the hackers out of secure information. However, that didn't stop anyone with access to the mainframe from using a simple utilities program and installing an entirely new program on the system.

The new program was also password protected and did not interfere with the existing programs. It merely broadcast a scrambled signal for just a few hours every other week. Of course, there were other scrambled signals being broadcast from other countries during the intervals which should work to their advantage by keeping interested law enforcement officials busy all over the world. It was another thing that Big Eddie expected and he already had contingency plans in place to manage things. He was used to it, the drug and weapons business was the same way. You always had to be ready to change things at a moment's notice.

This new development, which was obviously foreseeable, didn't bother Big Eddie, but it did remind him that young Raymond was still out there. Another loose cannon that could go off unexpectedly causing all kinds of additional trouble. Eddie had a pretty good idea that Ray was probably still in France or close to there.

While Ray was on his mind Big Eddie picked up the phone and called his connection in Paris for a status report. Getting Deveraux out of the way so quickly and effectively had Eddie wondering what kind of incompetent assholes were running things in France. Every time Big Eddie thought of France he laughed because the first thing that popped into his mind was Inspector Clouseau from the Pink Panther movie. Eddie knew his people had a solid lead and that two French operatives had been arrested after breaking into an apartment they believed to be young Raymond's. Someone at the Internet cafe had identified Ray's picture and told them who Ray was seen with. They ran a check on the girl and discovered a recently rented apartment in her name. The building attendant assured the two men that Kimberly and her nice boyfriend, Raynard Chauvigny, were very good people. They were quiet, respectful and never made trouble. She identified the picture of Ray as being Raynard Chauvigny.

Big Eddie thought that Ray's arrogance in picking a new name with the same initials as his old name would undoubtedly be his downfall in the long run. Ray was so smart that he did dumb things thinking no one would notice. Eddie's guys in France had run a check on Raynard Chauvigny and determined that the identity was new. That was another mistake Ray made, by not creating a history for himself. Eddie now had Ray's new bank account information and a long list of all his debit card expenditures. Eddie's people were working on tracing the original money transfer but hadn't had any luck, so far. Ray was covering his tracks well. It was obvious that someone had tipped Ray off. Within one day of visiting the Internet cafe and discovering the apartment Ray and his girlfriend got on a train and were gone. Eddie had a list of everything that Ray used his debit card on after he left the train.

It was obvious to Eddie, by the account transactions, that Ray knew they found out his new name and he was leading them to that small town for a reason. Big Eddie was certain Ray wouldn't be there, but he also knew that given a little time they would pick up another lead and maybe Ray wouldn't be so lucky next time. Ray's luck would run out and Big Eddie would be there when it hit rock bottom.

Eddie hung up the phone with the satisfaction of knowing Ray was running for his life like a scared rabbit. They forced him out from under one rock and Ray was looking for another rock to crawl under.

Ray's train tickets and reservations indicated that Ray was headed for a resort in Switzerland. Then after his apartment was broken into Ray and his girlfriend got off the train. Ray must have figured that the risk of someone waiting on him at his destination was too great. The big question was, where would he go from there and how would he get there? Eddie looked at a map of that part of the world and decided that Ray basically had two choices: Austria or Italy. Big Eddie guessed Austria because it was closer and figured large city because it would be better for Ray to hide in. The largest city in Austria was Vienna, with a population of almost eight million Ray could find a place to hold up.

It took Big Eddie ten minutes on the phone to explain what he wanted and to get pictures and basic information sent to a source in Vienna that would hire the right people to start canvassing the libraries and Internet cafes with pictures of Ray and his girlfriend. It was as good a place to start as any.

Eddie was pretty sure that the deadserious emails were coming from Ray. On one hand, Eddie wanted to send an email to deadserious letting Ray know that he knew and was coming for him. On the other hand, Eddie didn't want Ray to know that he knew about the deadserious emails. That way Eddie could monitor the emails and have a heads-up on what Ray might try to accomplish. It was almost like a chess game where Eddie was moving around his pawns and trying to pin down the King and Queen.

When Hecate tapped on his office door, then walked into the office with her brisk purposeful stride, it was certainly a welcome distraction. Visions of Hecate in a bikini walking across the deck of his yacht ran through Big Eddie's head. It was a lovely picture. She quickly approached his desk and handed him a copy of the itinerary for his trip to Saudi. Eddie was happy to see that the hotel where he'd be staying for four days had a heliport, which would grant him easy access and enable him to avoid riding in a limo. Cars and traffic were not things Eddie endured well. Hecate would be traveling with him and he hoped they could expand their professional relationship into something more personal. Hopefully, more of a sexual nature.

Eddie was being careful because the customs in Egypt were quite different from those in America and he did not wish to offend anyone. Eddie was going to have a mistress and he liked the idea of it being Hecate. It would be interesting to see Angela's and Hecate's reaction to each other. This trip would be a perfect time to let Hecate know how he felt and what he wanted. Just the thought of having her had Eddie hard half the time. It was mind numbing to think that a woman could stimulate him so completely without even touching him. Their relationship was definitely going to the next level. Whatever it cost.

Chapter 36

The new kidnapping Task Force was working round the clock investigating every aspect of the life of Edward Freeman, AKA Big Eddie. His company had been under investigation a couple of times for suspicion of drug smuggling but nothing ever panned out. Will and Doc called in their new friend Elijah King, the DEA agent who was working the Antonellie case, so they could compare notes and share what information they had on Edward Freeman. It was tedious and time consuming. Every new lead turned up another dead end. Elijah agreed that finding the yacht should be a high priority. There was no record of the yacht being sold. That didn't mean much. What did matter was, by all indications, it looked like Mr. Freeman was keeping the yacht, because he took on fuel and provisions. Sadly, by the end of the day they were no closer to locating Mr. Freeman or his yacht.

It was not like they were looking for a little rowboat that could be easily hidden. The yacht was a huge luxury item that would draw a lot of notice and attention. It couldn't just disappear. Yet, nobody had seen it or had a clue where it was. Surely it would turn up at some point.

Will and Doc invited Elijah to a nearby bar and grill for dinner so they could further discuss the case. With a smoking ban in public buildings a person could go to a bar and grill and actually enjoy the environment and the food without the stink of cigarette smoke. The place was a little crowded, but they found a booth and ordered the old fashion flame grilled cheese burgers, onion rings and an appetizer platter that consisted of battered and deep fried things: zucchini, pickles, cheese sticks and mushrooms with cold Ice House beer. A fattening feast made for kings and a queen. They talked and ate for over an hour. After promising to get together again soon they left the bar and headed home.

On the ride home Will enjoyed watching Doc maneuver her new car through the evening traffic. He was also thinking about their conversation with agent King. King believed that the informant kidnappings and gladiator fights were like the drug trade. They would never be able to completely stop them, because it was going on worldwide and the best they could hope for was to slow them down. They would save a few informants and lock-up a few bad guys, but King didn't believe that they would ever catch the people who were actually behind the whole thing. People like Big Eddie Freeman even if he was responsible. They had no evidence to suggest he was, other than Deveraux's hearsay, uncorroborated and unsubstantiated statements that were worth absolutely nothing with Deveraux dead. Looking at Doc smiling made Will forget all about work and start thinking about how Doc responded when he kissed her neck just below her ear.

Doc noticed Will looking at her and she wondered how she got so lucky to find such a great looking, wonderful man. She pulled into the driveway of their new home and whipped her new BMW around and backed it into the garage.

"I think I'm still in shock," Doc said as she cut the engine off. "All this really hasn't sunk in yet. I'm still wondering what I did to deserve you and such a wonderful life. I keep hoping that, if it is a dream, I never wake up. I feel like it had to be divine intervention that brought us together. I've been so long just living for the job, thinking that there must not be anyone out there for me. I wasn't happy. Now I'm so happy I can't stop smiling."

"I thought I knew what love was," said Will. "Then I met you and discovered a whole new sensation that I didn't know existed. I love you Doc."

"Are you sure it's not just gas?" Doc said laughing, as she leaned over to kiss him softly on the lips and play her hand across his crotch. They both shared a laugh and got out of the car. Judging by the hardness of Will's pistol Doc was pretty sure it wasn't gas that had him motivated.

After a fierce kiss in the doorway leading into the house they left a long line of shoes, guns and clothes all the way to the bedroom. Doc was a whole other person in bed. She let all her inhibitions go wild. Will was always careful to follow her mood and lead. Standing next to the bed Will embraced Doc, pulling her smooth, hot body tight against his as he kissed her neck and grabbed a handful of her hair, tugging her head to the side forcefully so he could expose more of her neck to kiss and suck on. Doc moaned with pleasure and they both fell sideways together on to the bed.

Doc rolled so Will would be on top, then she used both hands to spread herself wide open so Will could enter her with ease. Will quickly worked his way in her and slid in as deep as he could, then he raised up on his arms so they had an unobstructed view of him sliding all the way in and out to the very tip, progressively getting faster. Finally, Doc had to have it. She drew her knees almost up to her shoulders, forced her legs apart as far as she could with her arms, pulling her knees further up and growled "Fuck me," in a deep, low, husky whisper that drove Will crazy. They groaned and moaned as their sweaty skin slapped together in a familiar rhythm. When they both came, Doc let go of her shaky legs, wrapped them around Will and held him tight inside her.

They knew each other well. There was no need to say anything. When Doc released her grip with her legs Will pulled out, still hard and Doc quickly rolled over and got on her knees so Will could enter her from behind. As Will drove into her as hard and fast as humanly possible Doc met every thrust. When they came together it was earthshaking tremors of pleasure. They collapsed next to each other on the bed, satiated and spent. Sleep came easy. They were both too tired and give out to get up and get a towel.

The next morning Doc looked at Will and said, "Do you need to pee or are you horny again?"

Will said, "Come here and I'll show you what I need."

After a quickie, a hot shower and breakfast they headed for the office. The moment they walked in they could tell by the buzz of activity that something was happening. Two Task Force members were there talking with their commander.

"What's going on?" asked Doc.

Agent Cyrus Clauson stated, "I was just explaining to Commander Lewis that we caught a break on the kidnapping case. We have a location where a gladiator fight will take place tonight. The SAC wants you both on scene and you'll be briefed on the way. Let's get your gear. We have a jet standing by to fly us back to Reno."

With that said they left to retrieve their war bags and vests from the trunk of Doc's BMW. They stayed ready for just this type of event. Forty minutes later they were climbing aboard a jet with other key Task Force members.

During the flight the Task Force SAC passed out copies of a hastily prepared memorandum that outlined what they had learned so far. They had only received the new information late the previous evening and had little time to get ready for a raid on the old airplane hangar where the fight was scheduled to take place.

After giving the other members time to read the memorandum, the SAC stood up and said, "Now you know what I know. We don't have much. We have the location, which is way out in the middle of nowheresville. We are in the process of running all the usual background checks on who owns the property. We have a guy watching the property and videoing everything, but he is so far away that it isn't doing much good. There is some activity on the property and a guard at the entrance gate leading to the hangar. It is the only road in. We tried sending a guy in and he was told that no one gets in without being on a pre-approved list."

"How did we come by this information?" asked Doc.

"Yesterday a small time dope dealer was busted in Reno selling crack to a minor and soliciting lewd sexual acts from that minor. It turns out his day job is driving a delivery truck for Thompson's Trucking. Yesterday he was sent to the old airplane hangar to deliver refreshment stands and all the refreshments. He spent half his day helping set of the stands on each end of a boxing ring that was placed in the center of the hangar. It just so happens that the police and sheriff's departments are asking everyone they arrest if they have any information about the kidnappings or gladiator fights. This guy overheard one of the other workers mention a gladiator fight while they were working, but he was out of there by noon and never gave it another thought."

Will said, "From what I see here there is only one road running in front of the property where the hangar is located. They will be able to see us coming for miles in either direction. How are we going to get in there?"

"Unless you have some better idea," said the SAC, "we will drive in fast from the Reno direction and crash the gate. One team will hold the gate and the rest of us will converge on the hangar. We'll use one chopper to keep any planes on the ground and to help spot any runners. I have the warrants in progress and they will cover a night time raid. Our spotter will let us know when the spectators have arrived and we will try to time the raid before the fight starts so we can save the kidnapped informants. We don't have time to walk a team in and there is not enough ground cover close to the hangar to allow us to get close enough on foot to be effective. We'll just have to come in fast and crash the gate. Then seal off the hangar exits and start the arrests. Another team of marked cars, ambulances and paramedics will come in behind us when we give them the all clear signal."

Agent Clauson said, "So we go in hot, neutralize any resistance, secure the area and then have a cold beer on them. I like it."

Everyone clapped and cheered agreement. Because there was no scheduled sporting event for that location and no liquor license issued to the hangar address, it was easy to get a warrant for the hangar and all modes of transportation at that location at the time of the raid. The Task Force spent the remainder of the day prepping their gear and going over the aerial photos of the old airport and hangar. They formulated a plan, assigning each Task Force member a specific duty, then sent out for pizza. Everyone was charged and ready when they got the call from their spotter informing them that people were starting to arrive by cars, limos, SUVs and small planes.

The Task Force loaded up and drove to within five miles of the location and held there for a further update. A short time later their spotter called with the news that it looked like all or most of the guests had arrived. The five black SUVs and four black cars with their lights off, except for the lead car, took off towards the hangar at one hundred miles an hour with the chopper following close overheard with its lights off. It was just after dark and the sky was still showing color to the West so they had plenty of light for their surprise raid.

There was a low spot in the road about a mile from the target, a small valley about a half mile across that the Task Force came flying through. As they crested the small rise beginning the last mile of straightaway leading to the old hangar all hell broke loose. From the rock formation on the North side of the road came heavy gun fire. Bullets ripped into the grills, windows and tires of the Task Force caravan.

The lead car turned sideways and flipped in a cloud of dust and steam from the ruptured radiator and sand, then it burst into flames. The next two SUVs swerved and rolled. Two more SUVs crashed into the first two flipped SUVs with a horrendous crash that sent glass and metal flying every direction. The last SUV and three cars were barely able to avoid the wreck. At one hundred miles an hour things happen in an instant. Nobody had anticipated an ambush. When the helicopter turned around to investigate the crash the pilot turned on his search light, which drew the gunmen's attention to the chopper. The chopper was low and almost directly over the crash when a rain of bullets hailed into the cockpit and the side of the chopper. The search light blew out and the helicopter tried to turn and pull away from the onslaught. The pilot managed to crash about two hundred yards off in the desert and get out, wounded, before the chopper blew.

The snipers continued to fire on and disable the last few vehicles then they climbed onto dirt bikes and took off across the desert. They had already notified the hangar, which was being evacuated as they rode away. Small planes were taking off and an assortment of about fifty vehicles were speeding away in the opposite direction. The Task Force was so confident that they would be able to contain everyone by quickly sealing the gate that they didn't set up road blocks on the main road east of the hangar. There wasn't anything in that direction for fifty miles.

Will and Doc had been in one of the two SUVs that had crashed into the first two that flipped. They had some cuts and abrasions and were pretty shook up, but otherwise okay. They radioed for backup and ambulances and started trying to help the injured. The hangar raid and gladiator fight was forgotten during the pandemonium and the main objective became survival.

By the time the dead and injured were taken care of and another team was assembled the old airfield and hangar were completely abandoned. Not even the gate guard remained. They raided a hangar empty of people, but full of all kinds of other evidence. There was the ring, bleachers, refreshment stands complete with alcoholic beverages and a fancy lighting system, but no computers. The monitors and key boards were still there but the towers and hard drives were all gone. Their first real solid break turned into a disaster.

Will and Doc left the hangar to the forensic guys and went to check on their injured friends and coworkers. One of the agents that were killed in the lead car was Cyrus Clauson. A man who Will and Doc both liked and admired. It was a sad night. They were going to have to wait until daylight to follow the motorcycle tracks across the desert, because they no longer had a readily available helicopter. It was some pretty rough terrain and there was no way they could track those dirt bikes at night.

The only consolation in the whole mess was, now they had some new leads to follow. Thompson's Trucking was back in the mix and so was the owner of the old airfield and hangar. Several people had been identified, including the gate guard, which should help expand their investigation.

The assault on the Task Force would draw national attention and more funding would be allocated to the Task Force. The heat had been turned up to high and the people in charge were boiling mad.

Will and Doc didn't get any sleep that night. It was noon the next day before they were able to drag their tired, dirty asses to a motel to get cleaned up and sleep. They called the motel office and got a wake-up call for eight o'clock so they could have a late dinner before checking in with the Task Force commander. It had been one fucked up day and they knew that tomorrow would be a crazy mixed up mess. There would be a lot to answer for and Will was glad he was one of the people following orders instead of giving them. In a situation like this, no matter what they would have done, it had the potential to turn into shit storm and it certainly did. Will never would have expected it to be this bad, but from here on out they would have to expect the worst and try to anticipate the unexpected. They certainly couldn't just sit back and let the bad guys win this one. From the looks of things war had been declared and now all they had to do was identify and find the enemy.

Chapter 37

It was the first time that a fight had to be postponed and rescheduled. Big Eddie was pleased to hear that their contingency plan worked okay and not one person was arrested. What he didn't like was they didn't know the raid was coming. With as many cops as he had on the payroll one of them should have known something and alerted his people to the raid. Either the new Task Force was getting better or his people were not paying attention and were getting sloppy.

When his phone buzzed Eddie expected it to be Angela, but he was wrong. It was Troy Thompson calling. Troy didn't know that the call was being forwarded from Los Angeles to Egypt. Eddie kept the connection open for Bob and other emergencies taking place in the States. Troy was calm, cool and collected. He called to tell Eddie about the attempted raid on the fight and about one of his drivers being arrested the day before the raid. Using a little foresight Troy had left town on vacation as soon as he got the call about the raid and ambush on the officers conducting the raid. The police had already been to his office looking for him and he knew they did not have a warrant for his arrest. Troy notified his attorney that he would not be available for a week. Then he called Eddie.

"You have worked your ass off for over thirty years, Troy," said Big Eddie. "Why don't you hang it up and relax. Money is not an issue. You have a good crew there running your trucking company or you can sell the company. Cut your losses and go have some fun."

They talked about old times for a while and laughed some. It was a good talk between old friends.

"You're right Ed. My business there in Nevada is clean. But if the cops find something they want to arrest me for or question me about they will have to find me and come a long way to get me. Maybe Antigua or Antilles. I might even grow some grapes and start a small winery. It would give me something to do."

With that they said their goodbyes and wished each other luck. Whatever Troy decided to do, Big Eddie was confident that he would do it quickly, quietly and efficiently. They had both planned well for this moment for many years. A person who went into anything without a long-term contingency plan was not a wise person. Eddie and the other partners had not come this far by being stupid. Troy had so much money put away that he could walk away from his trucking company and not bat an eye.

The next call Big Eddie received was from Angela, AKA Nicole. She was excited. She'd seen the news about the ambush and foiled raid on the airfield. She thought it was delightfully funny that during the assault, not one of the cops got off a shot and six of them were dead. It happened so fast and was so intense that all they could do was scramble for cover. Then it was over and there was no one to shoot at. It was a short conversation. They would see each other soon in Saudi.

After talking with Angela and once again confirming, in his own mind, that she was as crazy as a shit house mouse, Big Eddie called his man Bob in L.A. Eddie had to relay the name of the likely informant that caused the evacuation and postponement of last night's gladiator fight. What Eddie really wanted to know was, why did he not have the information sooner. Were his people in the Reno Sheriff's Office sleeping on the job or just plain incompetent? Eddie knew that the rat was nothing more than a driver and delivery boy and he did not possess any sensitive information. It was just a fluke that he was arrested on unrelated drug charges and knew the location of the fight. None of that mattered. The rat, punk still had to be taught a lesson and made an example of. Eddie gave Bob the order to either kill or kidnap the rat for the fights. Whichever came easiest. It was just another step in the clean-up process.

"I'm on it Boss," Bob stated.

Big Eddie liked and appreciated Bob more every day. He was a real man of ability and he had a creative imagination. Just what a guy needs in an evil henchman.

Bob was still in L.A. taking care of some other urgent business, so he called his man in Reno and put him on the informant. It was about an hour later when Bob got a call back with a status report. The informant had been moved to a federal holding facility and was in protective custody, being held without bail on drug conspiracy charges. He had opened his mouth trying to get himself out of trouble and made matters worse by telling about a large scale drug operation. An indictment was expected the following day, several arrests had already been made and more were coming. It was typical for druggies to get busted for something relatively small then incriminate themselves and others on something larger that was often not even true. The rat thought the bigger the lie the better deal he would get and it generally backfired. The rat ended up getting more time than he would have received if he kept his mouth shut. People who use and deal drugs aren't generally known for their intelligence. There is a good reason why lawyers tell their clients to never say anything. It's because the police will use it against you in a Court of law, just like the Miranda warning says. That's why they call it a warning. They should probably revise the Miranda warning to say: You have the right to remain silent (Unless we can trick, threaten or beat it out of you). Anything you say can and will be used against you in a Court of law (or might get you killed).

The guy was under heavy guard and in a place where they could not get at him easily. A little patience would be necessary, but they would get their man.

The attempted raid had bought Harry Butkus another day of living. Eddie smiled as he thought about ol' Harry. They already had another alternate location ready for the fight. It would be a little crude and hastily thrown together, but it would suffice and the fight would go on. It would be another day for Harry Butkus to sweat. Eddie was a little surprised that Butkus hadn't keeled over from the stress. Butkus was a coward at heart and Eddie didn't really expect him to put up much of a fight. Butkus had been in the underground prison for a while because they had to find an opponent of the same stature and ability. Eddie wanted the fighters to be matched as fair as possible to help with the odds. He certainly didn't want it to be too easy to pick the winner.

Most of Eddie's thoughts now days were interrupted by visions of his sexitary setting on his face and riding him like a wild horse. He could picture himself laying there with Hecate on top of him. His cock deep insider her while she rocks back and forth, squeezing her breast, pinching and pulling her nipples. He used to have these visions of Angela. Then later they included Angela's lover, Kera. It was nice to think about. That is, until Angela killed Kera and Eddie started seeing just how crazy she really was.

Eddie had loved watching Angela grow into a gorgeous young lady, then into a seductive woman. What made him nervous was seeing her turn into a cold blooded killer with absolutely no compunction. He remembered when Angela was very young and had first come to him with ideas of using her father's shipping company to move illegal items. She had unfettered access to the computers and could move shipping containers to and from any place in the world with no way to trace the source of the transaction. That's how she made her first million, in less than a year. Then, through Eddie, she invested that million in illegal goods and had been making big money ever since. She was seriously intelligent and was soon making deals on her own. By the time she was twenty-one years old she was worth over fifty million and had her own connections all over the world.

The rest of Eddie's day was fairly normal. He had no complaints about his new life in Egypt. He had a great view of the city and with the building's windows being tinted it helped mask the true color of his desert surroundings everything looked pretty and green. Normally, the entire city looked covered in a cloud of sandy dust. The window tint softened things and made it look cooler. It kind of covered up the hard reality. There was a lot of poverty in Egypt, but things were slowly getting better.

That evening Big Eddie asked Hecate to have dinner with him. She gladly accepted. It made Eddie smile. During dinner Eddie told Hecate how lovely she was and explained that he was becoming romantically inclined towards her. Hecate did not shy away from the compliment or the advancement so Big Eddie continued.

"I like having you close to me," Eddie exclaimed. "If you will accept, I would like you to move into one of the executive apartments. I'll have it furnished to your liking and you'll have your own company car with no strings attached."

The company maintained eight apartments on the next floor down, two of which were unoccupied at the moment. The company cars were all champagne colored Mercedes two door sports coupes.

"I am delighted that you would make such a generous offer. I am not very experienced in romantic matters. I think, perhaps a woman would feel more secure if there were some strings attached to responsibilities," Hecate said.

"It was never my intention to place demands or responsibilities on our relationship. I want you to feel comfortable. I am an older man and I don't want you to think that I am trying to take advantage of you. I enjoy looking at you and watching you, but I have also developed a desire to touch you and make love to you."

"I assumed, because you are in a wheelchair, that you may have lost the ability for a sexual relationship," Hecate stated bluntly.

"The wheelchair is deceiving. My legs are weak, but I can walk and my desire is as strong as ever. More so when I look at you. I function fine in that regard and so do my hands. I can satisfy you in many ways," Eddie said.

Hecate came around the table and kissed Big Eddie softly on the lips and said, "I have grown to like and respect you. I can tell you are a kind and gentle man. I know you would never hurt me. I accept your offer and I look forward to satisfying you, as well. Tonight, I go home to pack my things and to prepare myself for this new change."

With that Hecate left with a seductive expression on her face and a little finger wave. Eddie was elated. These Egyptian women sure knew how to speak their mind. Eddie could not believe things had worked out so well. What he thought started out an awkward moment had turned into a dream come true. After what took place, Eddie didn't know who was in control him or her, but it really didn't matter. He didn't care as long as they both got what they wanted. He was going to go to great lengths to please her. Damn he loved Egypt.

Eddie slept well that night. The next morning Hecate was acting in her usual professional manner in her secretarial duties. Eddie called her into his office, first thing and handed her a folder that contained her new car and apartment keys, insurance verification forms and authorization letters that would cover the expenses of whatever Hecate wanted, from redecorating and furnishing the apartment to a complete new wardrobe.

Eddie said, "If you like you can use the company decorator. Spare no expense and bill everything to me."

"Thank you," Hecate said with an enthusiastic expression then with a slight bow she turned to exit his office with a little more bounce in her step.

She stopped at the door and asked, "Are we having dinner again this evening?"

"Most assuredly. Dinner is a 7:00. I look forward to your company."

The day went slow for Eddie. Thinking about what the night might bring had time crawling along at a snail's pace. Eddie had a feeling that his quality of life was about to get a whole lot better and more satisfying. It was nice being worth a couple of billion. Being able to have what you want, when you want it, was a pretty powerful feeling.

Eddie picked up the phone and put a call through to his personal chef and explained what he would like for dinner and that he would be dining with a guest. He then opened one of his desk drawers and took out a small black case that contained a tear drop diamond necklace. It would certainly look nice on Hecate's long, slender neck. Eddie was enjoying doing nice things for her and he had no doubt that she would be doing some nice things for him that very night.

Chapter 38

At noon, two days after the ambush and assault on the Task Force, Will and Doc were standing at their second grave side service of the day and another one was scheduled for three o'clock at another cemetery. They'd lost six Task Force members in the ambush. Five men and a woman, between the crashed vehicles and downed helicopter, had died unnecessary and tragic deaths. Three of the dead had been sent to their home towns for burial. Inside, most of the remaining Task Force members were secretly thankful that they didn't have to attend the three additional funerals. Three was too many and six would have been just about unbearable.

After a tearful eulogy from a close friend, the well-respected agent Cyrus Clauson was lowered into the ground as family and fellow agents and officers stood watching solemnly. Two funerals in one day was more than anyone should have to bear, but they still had one more to attend. When the casket reached the bottom, a few people bent and picked up a handful of dirt and threw it in, along with a few flowers as people started walking away. There's not many things sadder than walking away from a grave while the grave men are throwing shovels of dirt on a coffin. It is a lonely, depressing sound.

It was a hot day, but even in the heat the cemetery was beautiful with its tall trees and the mild breeze blowing. It made the heat bearable. Will and Doc slowly walked to Doc's car, taking their time so some of the other cars could thin out before they joined the throng of vehicles leaving the cemetery. They had two hours to kill before the next church service and their third drive to another cemetery. The air conditioner was a huge relief. Doc turned the air on high so the cold air would help dry them out.

They'd eaten breakfast at home before the first funeral. They'd eaten light and both were hungry now that the second funeral was over. Rather than go to the grieving family's home to eat like some people were, Will and Doc decided to skip that step in the funeral process and go someplace nice to eat.

Even taking their time with a long lunch they arrived at the church ahead of the others. They decided to burn up some time by walking around a small park across the road from the church, giving some of the other people time to arrive. They got back to the church with five minutes to spare before the service was scheduled to start. It turned out to be the hardest funeral ever. The widow was crying for her husband and the children were crying for their daddy. There wasn't a dry eye in the place. At the burial, the wife collapsed and had to be carried away with her crying children in tow.

It was after five by the time Will and Doc got home. They heated up leftover roast beef and made sandwiches and margaritas to take with them outside so they could eat and relax in the much needed hot tub. By the time they finished their meal and the first round of margaritas the tension had been massaged away by the powerful hot tub jets.

"This is the best way I can think of to end such a crappy day," Doc said. "This whole day just pretty much sucked. I hope we don't have to go through that again for a long time, or ever."

"I could definitely do without multiple funerals and crying widows and children," Will replied.

A couple of margaritas and some slow lovin' later, Will and Doc both fell into a dreamless, alcohol and sex induced sleep.

The next morning, they were both jarred awake bright and early by their cell phones. One making an annoying chirping sound and the other playing a little ditty. Will was starting to dislike cell phones, immensely. Next they would invent a cell phone that administered a small electric shock to get your attention. It wouldn't be much more intrusive. It was command calling to advise them that they had a Task Force meeting at 9:00 a.m. Why did they call at 6:00 to tell you that you had a nine o'clock meeting. What's wrong with 8:00, Will thought.

There were a lot of people at Task Force headquarters when Will and Doc arrived. A few new faces. There was a noticeable absence of the six dead Task Force members, not only in the room, but in their hearts, as well. Even though they were expecting it, they were all somewhat surprised when a new suit walked in the room and asked for their attention. Everyone in the room tensed and got quiet. They could tell by the look on the new suit's face and his demeanor that it was not going to be a pleasant meeting. They all sat, waiting for the fallout.

The man surveyed the room and stated, "My name is Royce Lamberth. I am the new Special Agent in Charge of Task Force operations. I was sent in from Washington, D.C. to get things back on track and to try and clean up this mess.

I'm sure you all understand that the heat is on, so I am not going to waste time playing the blame game. Your SAC was relieved, I'm here, so let's deal with it like professionals. Just so you know where you stand, because of that stunt that got six of your team members killed, you are all on the verge of being transferred to positions of lesser responsibility. This is my thin ice pitch and I want you all to know that we're all walking on thin ice here. Including me, because I stuck my neck out and went to bat for you without even knowing you personally. I convinced the powers that be that you guys and gals have been on this since the beginning and it would take too long to bring a new team up to speed. Under my supervision there will not be any more reckless hundred mile an hour raids. If it would have worked you'd be innovative heroes, but since it didn't work, consider yourselves villains on probation. Maybe villains is the wrong word, but I'm sure you get my point. It made you all into bad guys. The quickest way to lose a government job is to generate bad publicity. Last week's publicity could not be much worse. Until we make some progress we'll all be suffering from the fallout.

"You see some new faces. These are your new team members. I brought a few of the best with me and I am looking at background information on some other agents. We will have at least four more agents immediately. Get together after this meeting and introduce yourselves. Bring these new people into the loop. Consider this your get acquainted time, but by noon I want everyone working on something. Tomorrow morning I want a short status report from each of you. One or two pages consisting of what aspect of the investigation you are working on and your opinions and ideas on what needs to be done and what directions you think we need to take. If you have a complaint, put it on a separate page marked complaint and turn it in with your status report. All complaints will be kept confidential.

"The final point I would like to make is, I was very pleased to hear that you all passed polygraph test in the Deveraux matter. That fact, plus the fact that two agents at witness protection didn't pass, was a contributing factor to you people remaining on this Task Force. The two agents that did not pass are suspended pending investigation. Failing a lie detector test is obviously not enough for criminal charges. The preliminary investigation indicates that both agents were living above their means. That's not criminal either, so we have to wait and see where the investigation leads. I will not tolerate crooked cops. I look forward to working with you. Now get busy and make me proud." With that said he nodded his head and exited the conference room.

When the door closed the room came alive with the buzz of conversation and the introductions began.

Will looked at Doc and said, "Well baby, that wasn't so bad. I didn't believe that part about him going to bat for us. The way I'm reading it, he tried to get us all canned so he could bring in his own team. Somebody up top put the kibosh on it and made him work with us. I don't think he liked it, or had a choice. This may have even been a demotion for him. It makes me wonder who he pissed off on Capitol Hill. I don't think anyone would step into this mess willingly. A transfer from Washington, D.C. to Los Angeles was surely not a position upgrade."

"Hell, who cares," Doc said. "As long as he stays out of the way and lets us do our job, I don't care who he is or what he does. I've been seeing that look in your eyes. Either you have some new idea about the case rolling around in your pretty head or you're plotting and planning something. Talk to me, honey."

"So I have a look in my eyes and a pretty head," replied Will with a smile. "Maybe I just want to get you back in bed."

"I'm always game for that, cowboy."

"Let's get our minds back on work. Obviously, we need to find the yacht, which I hope will lead us to Big Eddie Freeman. We need to find Troy Thompson, who is missing in action. He may be able to lead us to Freeman. We need to cross-reference the owner of the airfield with other properties and talk to the owner, whoever that turns out to be. The airfield is a corporation, but that will lead us to some person or persons of interest and probably additional properties. We know that the fight broadcasts were coming through a communications company and that the program was deleted after it was discovered. We have guys working those areas. Let's try sending deadserious an email to rattle his cage. Maybe we can scare him and he'll provide us with more information."

"Yes, let's do it. I was hoping for something a little more proactive, but rattling cages is good," said Doc.

"Oh, that's just what we do before lunch. I'll think of something a lot more fun after lunch. We can probably work in a quickie if we play our cards right," Will said with a smile.

They both started writing ideas for an email to deadserious. They compared notes and thoughts on the best approach and in the end came up with:

“Deadserious: Your situation is far more serious than you believe. Mr. Big, i.e., Big Eddie Freeman knew we were coming. He vanished without a trace. I'm thinking that Mr. Big and his Dark Angel know all about you. They are coming for you. The only chance you have is to help me get them before they get you. Either point us in the right direction or come in and I will see to it that you are protected. Willbrac@hotmail.com”

They sent the email out onto the electronic highway in hopes that deadserious would at least contact them with more information. Then they went to lunch. During lunch, pizza, they talked about the two agents that failed the polygraph tests. Will and Doc knew that every aspect of the agents' lives were being dissected by a separate team of FBI agents. There was little they could do to help with that part of the investigation.

As they were leaving the pizzeria Will's phone sounded an incoming call. It was the computer tech who was monitoring the deadserious email account. Will received a response from deadserious. The tech sent a copy of the email to Will's phone. The message said:

Willbrac@hotmail.com: If he knew you were coming then he's been watching you. It is you who has a serious problem. He knows where to find you. If he knew where to find me I'd be dead. Look for his lickspittle Bob (Robert Rynalds.) Use caution. deadserious :-).

Will was excited. He had a new lead. He called back the tech and asked for a full search on Robert (Bob) Rynalds starting with the L.A. area. He then called his LAPD office and asked for an address on Robert Rynalds. In less than a minute they had an address and were hurrying to Doc's car. They knew they should probably wait for a background check and request backup, but they were already out and Will was sure they could find the house without much trouble. Will and Doc agreed that they needed to work fast in case this Bob fellow got tipped off about the email. They didn't even know if they had the correct Robert Rynalds, but someone had to go check it out. It may as well be them.

Forty-five minutes after getting the email and last known address for Robert (Bob) Rynalds, Will and Doc were approaching a nice three bedroom brick home with a two car garage in a middle class neighborhood where the homes were valued at about a quarter million. All the lawns and shrubs, including Bob's, were perfect. There was very little traffic and the home they were observing certainly did not look like the home of a criminal. All the drapes were drawn, there was no activity and all was quiet. The children that lived on the block were probably still in school. If there was a vehicle it was in the garage.

Will and Doc parked half-a-block away and walked to within sight of the house. Since nobody had called and told them not to approach the house, Will and Doc walked across the front lawn together, stepped up onto the porch and Will calmly rang the doorbell. When the doorbell ding-donged, Will heard a "snap" on the other side of the door that his brain instantly identified as a fuse for a satchel charge, just as Doc said, "I smell natural gas."

"Run," Will said as he pushed Doc ahead of him off the porch. They had time to reach the sidewalk at a dead run when they were knocked to the ground by a tremendous explosion. They kept scrambling away from the burning house as flaming chunks of debris came slamming back to earth all around them.

When Will was pulling out his phone to call 911, they heard the sound of an engine and then tires screeching to a halt at the intersection half-a-block away where they'd parked. It was a black Cadillac Escalade with the passenger side window down. They saw the man wave with his left hand, then his right hand came up with a pistol in it and he started methodically firing shots in their direction. Doc was nicked in the leg and fell to the pavement. Will turned and stood between Doc and the gunman and started firing at the open window of the Escalade with both guns as the SUV sped away.

"You're hit," Will stated, more to himself, because Doc was surely aware of it. He holstered his weapons and knelt beside her in one smooth motion, picking up his cell phone to call for backup and an ambulance. He took off his jacket to make Doc a pillow, then pulled his belt off to make a tourniquet.

Doc was bleeding bad, but was not a bloody mess. The bullet missed the artery. Thank God. Will used the silk handkerchief that he'd taken from his suit coat pocket and his belt to stanch the bleeding until the ambulance arrived.

"You lied to me." Doc said. "You told me it didn't hurt when you got shot. This hurts like a son-of-a-bitch."

Will was so thankful she was alive he was almost in tears. When their eyes met, Will smiled and said, "Candy-ass."

Doc playfully hit Will on the arm, but even though the movement hurt, she said, "I've got your candy-ass right here, baby." They both laughed.

Doc said, "Boy are we in trouble now. The boss just told us this morning, 'no more cowboy stunts,' and we blow-up a house and you must have literally gotten off twenty rounds at that sucker before he got away."

"Technically," Will stated, "we didn't blow-up the house and even though I wanted to I didn't kill anyone, so the SAC shouldn't be too upset."

Doc was in shock and rambling a little. Will let her talk as they listened to the sirens in the distances getting closer. Some of the neighbors had ventured out to examine the damage. Will just sat there looking at Doc and listening to her. Silently he was hoping they'd both be fired. He was tired of this shit.

"I wish you'd have got him," said Doc.

"I wish he'd have been a little closer," Will stated.

Police cars, fire trucks and an ambulance all arrived at the same time. A short time later some of the Task Force members showed up trying to suppress their smiles. The place was a smoldering mess. The new SAC came striding around the ambulance with a scowl on his face. He was seriously pissed.

He looked at Will and said, "What part of no cowboy shit did you not understand? What the hell happened here, Bracket?"

"A routine knock-and-talk boss. I guess it got a little out of hand. We--"

"You guess? I've got an officer down and a house blown all over the block and you guess."

"There is a silver lining sir. Technically, we didn't blow up the house. No one's dead and we've got a positive ID on the bad guy. We almost got him. He'll think twice before he pulls that again."

Several of the other agents snickered and turned away so the SAC wouldn't see them smiling.

"From what I understand, not killing someone is almost a first for you. Hell, maybe you should get a medal for showing such great restraint. If I had my way you'd be off this Task Force, but somebody up top thinks you are a rising star. A wonder boy. They believe that, if it wasn't for you, we wouldn't have made much progress on this case. I'm of a different opinion. Go with your partner to the hospital. Type up your report and have it for me in the morning. We have a Task Force meeting at 9:00 a.m. The one thing I do like about you Bracket is, you never complain."

Will said, "I thought it would be my charming personality."

The SAC shook his head at Will, then smiled when he looked at Doc and said, "For someone whose just been shot you look remarkably well and jovial. Now get out of here and avoid the press. We'll clean up this mess."

Doc grimaced when the paramedics lifted her onto the gurney then slid her into the ambulance. Will followed the ambulance in Doc's car.

At the hospital emergency room, when Will walked into the room, Doc said, "Hi sweetie," in a little drug induced voice that brought a smile to Will's face. "You were right. This doesn't hurt at all. Did you get that guy? He shot me. You must be royally pissed."

"Royally pissed," Will agreed with a smile as Doc slipped into oblivion.

The nurses and doctor were smiling and laughing a little, too. "She'll be fine sir. I'll have her patched up in no time. She'll spend the night and you can have her back in the morning. You must be her partner."

"Partner and husband. We were married recently," Will explained.

"You're a lucky man. This gal has some seriously nice legs. I've seen a lot of gunshot wounds. This one is from a fully jacketed bullet. Not a hollow point. It didn't hit bone so it didn't mushroom much. That means the exit wound is clean. She'll have a tiny scar on both sides and will be sore for a week. Other than that, she'll be fine. Muscle hits are painful, but not near as bad as bone hits," the doctor stated.

"I hope she stays asleep until morning. She will want to walk out of here the moment she wakes."

"I know how you macho cops are. I've learned that you're easier to deal with when you're sleeping. She'll be out until morning," said the doctor with a smile. He looked much too young to be a doctor or to have very much experience at anything. Including Doc's fine looking legs.

After some thought, Will said, "If you're sure she'll be out all night, then I'm going to go try and catch the man who shot her."

Will went back to headquarters and requested all available information on Robert (Bob) Rynalds, then quickly wrote his daily report and incident report. He then emailed the reports to the SAC and started researching Mr. Rynalds.

Will had been ready to quit and spend all his time with Doc in their new home and seeing the world together. Now he was mad. These jackasses had been trying to kill him and his wife, now they actually shot her. That was way over the line and Will was going to see to it that Mr. Rynalds paid for his evil deeds. Will went home and cleaned up, fixed himself something to eat, then cleaned his guns. He would get a few hours' sleep then be back at the hospital before the woman he loves wakes up.

Chapter 39

Big Eddie was on a health kick. He wasn't huge, but he was a big man. Losing fifty pounds would be a good start. He wanted to be in better shape for Hecate. It had been a long time since he'd felt this way about a woman. He brought in a physical therapist who had him doing water exercises in the hot tub and he was walking in the pool downstairs. He could already see the benefit of walking in chest deep water. Floating took a lot of the pressure off his legs and allowed him to do a cardiovascular workout. He should have started water workouts a long time ago.

Eddie changed his entire diet. He'd been eating a lot of heavy, fatty foods and drinking too much, which had his sugar high all the time. Now he was eating healthy things and drinking fruit juices and a lot of water. He started eating crab salads for lunch, which were a lot tastier than he would have believed possible.

Hecate knew that she was the reason for the sudden change. She was complimenting him on his choices and encouraging him. Truth be known, Hecate was growing quiet found of this gentle bear of a man. Sex was a little awkward the first few times. Until they worked out a method that gave them both plenty of gratification. They were both feeling more relaxed and comfortable with each other and were starting to have a lot of fun. Oral sex was something that Hecate didn't have much experience at, until she met Eddie. Now she was enjoying it with a fervor that was boarder line ferocious.

Eddie had been in a real good mood. He was planning some cosmetic surgery, starting with liposuction and a tummy tuck. By the time his yacht arrived in a few months he'd be a new man. His mood changed early the next morning when an "alert" warning started flashing on his computer screen. He clicked his mouse on the "alert" icon and saw that willbrac@hotmail.com had sent an email to deadserious soliciting additional information. It was a clever message, designed to instill fear in deadserious. Big Eddie didn't expect deadserious to respond. That's why he was surprised a short time later when his computer indicated another "alert." This one was far more disturbing. It was a response from deadserious pointing the cops at Bob.

Eddie snatched up the phone and called Bob's emergency number. When Bob answered Eddie simply stated, "You've been compromised," and hung up.

Bob kept his gear and bag ready at all times. He emptied his safe, turned on his defense system, disconnected the gas line on his kitchen stove then he quickly left through the garage. He climbed into his Cadillac SUV and drove away from his home for the last time. He didn't go far. There was a small park two blocks from his house where he parked his vehicle on the opposite side of the park. He then walked across the park towards his home until he came to an empty house a block away from his. It had had a for sale sign in the front yard for two months. It was only a few houses away from his on the other side of the intersection and on the opposite side of the street. Bob walked up the sidewalk and sat down on the front porch steps. He could see his front yard and a small portion of the front of his home.

Bob didn't have to wait long for the excitement to get started. He saw a dark blue BMW M3 slow down and stop at the intersection, then turn away from him and park close to the intersection. Then those two cops, Bracket and Holiday, got out of the car and started walking towards his house. There was no doubt in Bob's mind what would happen next. Everything was already set in motion.

He jogged back to his SUV and drove back around the park to see the explosion that he hoped would kill the two cops. Bob was sadly disappointed when he saw the cops getting up off the ground in the midst of burning pieces of his house. It was surreal. Like something you'd see in a Die Hard or Lethal Weapon movie. In a silent rage Bob grabbed his thirteen shot .9mm Berretta from the passenger seat and started firing at the cops through the open passenger side window. He hit the woman, knocking her down and the man, Bracket, jumped in front of her and started firing shots at him with two guns literally blazing. The bullets were coming so fast and were so close that Bob was forced to flee. That damn cop was crazy. A sane man would have ducked for cover, but Bracket just stood up, with a gun in each hand and started blasting away. The guy had balls. Bob could feel and hear bullets zipping past his face and bullet holes were appearing in the windows close to him. He had to run, so he drove away as fast as he could.

Bob went straight to a parking garage where he kept another vehicle and switched rides. Then he left L.A. heading for Reno. He was pretty sure he only wounded the female cop. He would give them a few days then come back to finish them off. For now, he had some other business to take care of in Reno.

Bob was in the mood for some soothing jazz, so he popped in a Miles Davis CD for the drive to Reno. It was a long drive, so it was late when Bob got to the ranch house. Cindy and Red answered the door together, as usual. They did everything together.

"Oh, look Cindy, a big pretty man," said Red.

Cindy smiled and said, "Come on in Bob. We'll do our very best to make you as comfortable as possible."

With a woman on each arm, Bob was led into the ranch house for a night of fun and pleasure. He thought the world of Cindy and Red and always looked forward to an opportunity to visit them. Bob kept some of his equipment in a small storage room that was located in the long underground hallway leading from the house to the hidden prison where the kidnapped informants were kept.

After a couple of fun loving hours of wild sex with Cindy and Red, who were the two most amazing and accommodating women Bob had even known, Bob slept well. Still, his internal clock had him awake at 6:00 a.m. Bob had breakfast alone because the girls were busy cleaning up after feeding their few prisoners. They only had seven at the moment. Bob liked the look of Cindy and Red in the kitchen, laughing and smiling as they worked. They were both excellent cooks. The kitchen had the wonderful smell that came with long term use and of baking and preparing exquisite foods. Bob could picture living there with Cindy and Red. He could even help with the horses. Working for Big Eddie paid great, but he was getting tired of killing people he didn't even know and cleaning up Eddie's messes. Bob was a little surprised at himself. He looked around and thought, "Maybe it's time to retire."

Bob called his man in Reno and found out as much as he could about the driver that had informed on the gladiator fight at the old airfield. Bob learned that the informant was scheduled to testify in front of a grand jury at one o'clock that afternoon. That didn't give him much time. The only place Bob could ambush the rat was at the holding facility when they brought the guy out to put him in a vehicle or in route to the federal courthouse. He didn't have time to devise an explosive charge and then place it in a likely place to take out the vehicle carrying the informant. His only real option was to snipe the guy. That way he could manage it on his own, taking out only the target and not a whole car load of FBI agents.

Bob retrieved a sniper rifle from his storage area. It was in a nice hard plastic carrying case that ensured that the sights would not get bumped and knocked off a little. He knew the gun well. He'd practiced out in the desert with it many times. All he needed was a target and he could hit it.

The way things were positioned at the jail Bob could not get a clear shot at anyone coming out of the building. But when the vehicle pulled out of the parking lot into the alley it had to turn one of two directions that would take it to one of the two main roads that led to the courthouse. Bob found a spot a block and a half away in the alley. He parked behind a dumpster and got out to wait. One of the deputies would call him as the informant was being loaded into the transport vehicle. If there was more than one vehicle the deputy would tell him which one to target.

At 12:30 Bob saw a single black SUV with two marshals in it pull into the parking area. The rat's ride had arrived. Ten minutes later his phone beeped and the deputy told Bob that the package was on its way. Bob used the dumpster for a gun rest and waited for the SUV to appear. When the SUV pulled into the alley it was less than two hundred yards away. The driver turned away from Bob, giving him a full view of the rear of the SUV. Even with the tinted windows Bob could easily identify the silhouette of a man's shoulders and head through the rear window. It was an easy shot. The bullet proof vests that the marshals made their witnesses wear didn't help with head shots. Bob carefully applied pressure and slowly squeezed the trigger as the SUV drove away from him until the rifle bucked and a tiny hole appeared in the rear window if the SUV. The SUV's brake lights flared and Bob was back in his vehicle and gone before the driver of the SUV could get his shit together enough to radio for assistance.

Bob didn't know it at the time, but the bullet went through the informant's head, which deformed the bullet before it blew the marshal's head apart who was sitting in the front passenger seat directly in front of the rat. The high velocity bullet literally blew a large chunk of blood, bone and brain matter through the front windshield, the suddenness of which threw the driver into momentary shock. It was a mess that would cause quite a stir in Reno, Nevada.

Bob backed out of the alley and drove down the main strip to a casino that featured a five star restaurant. It was best not to be driving right after the shooting because the cops might throw up road blocks and search all vehicles. Bob enjoyed a late lunch, then did some gambling and drove back to the ranch during five o'clock rush hour traffic so he could spend some more time with Cindy and Red. He planned to stay at the ranch a few days than go back to L.A. and finish off those two cops before he left the country.

Even though Big Eddie was bothered by the fact that the cops now had Bob's name, he was pleased with Bob's status report and plans. After Bob took care of the two cops he would go to Japan and wait for the yacht to be finished, then enjoy a leisurely cruise to Port Said. It would be a good and well deserved vacation for Bob.

However, for the moment Eddie was more concerned about his impending trip to Saudi to meet with Angela/Nic. If he didn't have other business interests there he would not be making the trip. It was good for relations to go visit Saudi princes. It would help open up all kinds of doors for business opportunities. He also wanted to show Hecate a good time before he had his surgery. The trip should prove to be interesting and enlightening.

Chapter 40

When Doc woke-up the next morning bright light was streaming through her hospital room window, casting rays of sunshine all over the room and Will was sitting in a chair reading. He was clean and refreshed. He looked up and smiled when he heard Doc stirring. She loved to see his smile. What she didn't love was the pain and tightness she felt in her leg. As the memories of the previous day came flooding back to her, she was dismayed at the thought and realization of what happened. Getting shot made you feel helpless and it sucked.

Will saw Doc's expression change and asked, "What's wrong, baby?"

A single tear leaked out of Doc's eye and she said, "I want to go home."

Will stood and kissed the tear away and said, "I'll go hustle up the doctor."

But before Will could leave the room a nurse walked in with a tray and said, "I'm glad to see you're awake. I was coming to wake you for breakfast. The doctor said you had to eat something before he let you out of here."

Doc was real hungry so eating certainly wasn't a problem. She was more than ready to eat and get the hell out of there. The doctor came in a few minutes later, as Doc was finishing her meager meal, with discharge papers and a short list of prescriptions. He handed everything to Will and the nurse removed the IV from Doc's arm and helped her get into the sweats Will had brought from home. The man was so thoughtful and considerate that it brought tears to Doc's eyes, again.

Will had emailed his daily report and incident report to Task Force headquarters the night before with a note to the SAC apologizing for not being at this morning's Task Force meeting. He briefly explained that he would be bringing Doc home from the hospital and taking the day off.

The slightest movement of her injured leg hurt like hell, but Doc was determined not to let it show. The wheelchair ride to the parking lot wasn't too bad, but getting into the car required her to bend her leg more. On the drive home Will pulled through a drive through mom and pop doughnut place and got sugar glazed doughnuts and little cartons of chocolate milk for the ride home. Sugar and chocolate was all that Doc needed to put a smile on her pretty face. It helped take Doc's mind off the fact that her hair was wiped out.

Will helped Doc into the house, then cut up a trash bag and used white medical tape to tape a small section of the bag around Doc's wounded thigh so she could take a long overdue shower and wash her hair. After the shower, the loss of blood and medication had her tired, so she laid down for a nap.

Will got on his computer and accessed the Task Force investigation file on Robert (Bob) Rynalds. The first thing that popped up was a fairly recent DMV photo taken from Mr. Rynalds California driver's license.It was the same guy that waved at them and shot Doc in the leg. Born in 1968. Sandy blond hair, blue eyes, 5' 11", 178 lbs. He was average everything, probably even shoe size, from what Will could see.

Except for his military background, it was far from average. The man had been an intelligence officer in the Special Forces. He was an expert marksman and was trained in explosives, chemical warfare and antiterrorism. He spent several years running around all over the Middle East. He was suspected of stealing arms shipments and selling them to rebels. Before he could be arrested and court-martialed the only witness disappeared. With no tangible evidence and no witness, the government could not pursue charges, but forced him to retire. Rynalds military ID photo showed a hard, fierce looking soldier and tough adversary. That's just like our great government, train these young men in warfare, then when one of them crosses the line and goes too far, just kick him out of the military and send him back to America with no supervision so he can utilize all his Special Forces training on American citizens. It was definitely a flaw in the system. The only up-side was, not many military personnel went bad, so the statistics were manageable. Most military people were unsung heroes. There were only a few bad apples, but when they went bad, people usually died.

Rynalds income tax records showed that Mr. Rynalds no sooner than landed back in the States and he was working for Big Eddie Freeman's commodities company making $250k a year as a consultant. There was the connection between Freeman and Rynalds. The man had no criminal record and property searches were still under way. Things were starting to come together and were pointing at Big Eddie Freeman.

Will put his research on hold and made lunch for himself and Doc. Lunch in bed was kind of fun. Will brought Doc up-to-speed on his research. After they ate, Will cleared the dishes, took off his clothes and slid into bed beside Doc. She rolled onto her side, with her wounded leg facing up and Will entered her from behind. They made slow passionate love until they both shuttered in ecstasy. Will got up and retrieved a warm wet washrag and a towel for Doc.

After making sure Doc was comfortable, Will took a shower then left Doc in bed watching an old movie on the bedroom flat screen. The commodities company that used to belong to Mr. Freeman was located in a string of warehouses that took up an entire city block. The first thing Will noticed when he pulled into the vast parking area was two semi-trucks and trailers belonging to Thompson's Trucking backed up to loading docks. Then he saw several shipping containers with Sarcosie International logos on their sides. More connections were falling into place and all leading to Big Eddie Freeman.

The secretary who politely welcomed Will to the commodities company apologized for not being there long enough to be able to answer his questions. Will wasn't ready to talk to the new owner yet. He was still hiding behind a team of lawyers who maintained innocent ownership and was refusing to grant an interview or cooperate. His official statement was that he did not personally known Mr. Freeman and had purchased the company through his attorneys. They had nothing on him, yet.

Will's next question was, "Who has been here long enough to help me?"

"Maybe Reba, in accounting," the secretary explained and pointed Will in the direction of her office.

Reba was an elderly woman who actually supervised many other people who were secretaries and accountants. She was nice, but in a hurry to get back to business. Just the type of employee most companies were looking for.

As soon as Will knocked on her office door, which stood open, Reba looked up and said, "Hey, good-lookin', what do you need?"

"I would like some background information on the company and on one of its ex-employees, a Robert Rynalds. Can you help me with that?"

"Sure, be happy to," she offered. As she turned and came into better view Will noticed that she was a very attractive older woman who still had a nice body for her age. It was only the wrinkles around her eyes and mouth that gave her age away. She was probably sixty, but didn't really look fifty. "Robert Rynalds was a consultant until the company sold. He was a field man. I never met him, but I wrote his checks and direct deposited them. Apparently, he was good at his job, whatever that was, or Mr. Freeman would have fired him."

"Do you have any idea where Mr. Freeman or Mr. Rynalds could be located?"

"No," she replied. "I just know that Mr. Freeman sold the company and moved away. Mr. Rynalds quit at that time. The new owner replaced some of the support staff, but kept me on because of my experience and long-standing with the company and for that I'm thankful. I don't know what I would do if I didn't have my work to keep me busy."

"Can you tell me how long Mr. Freeman used Sarcosie International and Thompson's Trucking?" Will asked.

"As long as I can remember. Almost everyone who does international shipping will use some branch of Sarcosie International. Thompson's Trucking has been doing a large portion of our interstate shipping for years. They are very reliable and reasonable," she answered.

"Can you check your records and give me a date on when Mr. Freeman started using Sarcosie International and Thompson's Trucking?"

"By law we are only required to maintain business records for five years. But I can tell you that we have been using those companies since we opened about twenty years ago. Thompson's Trucking was just starting at that time and has been with us from day one. Sarcosie International has been around a lot longer and we have used them from day one."

Will talked to the flirtatious lady for several minutes, but got little more useful information. One of the things he was looking for was a picture of Mr. Freeman, which she didn't have. Will thanked her and left. Will liked doing personal interviews and visiting actual locations, rather than doing everything with a computer. He could get a better feeling of things talking to real people. He could examine things with his own eyes and formulate a better opinion on the situation at hand.

Will went by his LAPD office and talked with Commander Lewis. Then checked his emails, wrote some responses and drove over to Task Force headquarters where he and Doc were still on loan. He spoke with the new SAC to make sure that he and Doc were not on his shit list, then wrote a quick daily report on his interview with the accountant, Reba.

That's when the report from Reno came in about the airfield informant and marshal being shot by a sniper. Will figured that if Rynalds left L.A. right after shooting Doc he had plenty of time to drive to Reno, get some rest, then shoot the informant. It fit Rynalds MO and it was just likely. From all indications Bob was Big Eddie's clean up man. The way Deveraux was taken out and now this airfield informant and even the Antonellie father and son hits, pointed to a highly trained professional, Rynalds. Even the Keith Fuller and Wu Tran hits, as sloppy as they were, screamed professional hits by a trained expert. Rynalds fit that mold.

Will took time to notify the Reno field office to be on the lookout for Robert (Bob) Rynalds and indicated that he should be considered armed and dangerous and a suspect in the airfield informant shooting. Reno P.D. and the Sheriff's Office would be notified, as well.

Having done everything he could Will went home to his wife. On the way he picked-up their favorite Chinese take-out for dinner. He even got fortune cookies. Back home, Doc was rested and feeling better. She got excited about the Chinese food. Will coaxed her out of bed so they could have candle light take-out. It was fun and romantic even though it was take-out.

Doc smiled when she read her fortune. It said: "You are on the road to happiness."

"That's right," Doc exclaimed. "In my new car with my honey."

Will's fortune made him smile too. It said: "You will find love."

"I already have," Will said as he showed Doc the little paper with his fortune written on it.

"That's right buster," said Doc, "and you better not find another one as long as I'm around." She smiled and poked Will in the ribs with her chopstick.

Will forced a smile. He couldn't imagine not having her around. He pushed the thought from his mind and helped Doc back to bed where he tenderly made love to her until they both fell into a peaceful sleep.

Chapter 41

Over the recent years, Saudi Arabia had transformed into a veritable thriving metropolis. The days of the camel had long past. Expensive cars lined the roads and the age of the high-rise palace hotels had arrived. Big Eddie's private jet flew him, Hecate and his security detail to the Saudi airport, where a helicopter was waiting to ferry them to the most luxurious and plush hotel in Saudi Arabia. All the rooms and furniture were trimmed in hand carved gilded wood. Everything was designed to convey the importance of power and money. These Arabian's wanted their guests to know that they were in the midst of wealth beyond belief. The place was created to impress and it certainly did. There was nothing small about it. Arabian's liked their space and the view was spectacular.

Eddie arrived the day before Angela and her new lover Joanna were scheduled to arrive. He had to keep reminding himself to call her Nicole in front of Hecate and others. Eddie spent the day entertaining a few important guests that were high up in the Arabian political stratum. In order to prosper a man must cultivate new and meaningful relationships in unusual places. In Arabia, the powers that be were in a constant state of flux. If a person carefully chose his business partners early in the game and choose wisely, the financial benefits could be almost limitless. By starting on the ground floor and making the right connections a person could get on top with the help of friends. Big Eddie had picked the party he thought would win and was now giving the proper assistance to make sure it happened as planned. His guests left happy. Eddie was helping to start a coup and he felt pretty good about the prospects.

After the men left Hecate came into the room and said, "Those men are very dangerous."

"I agree," Eddie replied. "That's why I didn't invite them to stay for dinner."

That evening Big Eddie and Hecate enjoyed freshly flown in Alaskan snow crab for dinner. Eddie was eating more sea food and fowl and less red meats in order to improve his digestive system and lose weight. After dinner, Big Eddie enjoyed watching Hecate practice her oral sex technique on his rock hard erection while she experimented with playing with herself. With a few instructions, she was doing a fine job of it, just the way he liked it and she would do anything he wanted. She caught on quick and was obviously enjoying the learning experience. Their relationship was working out even better than he expected.

Eddie pulled out the black velvet lined case that contained the diamond tear drop necklace he'd been saving and handed the case to Hecate. She opened the case and sucked in an audible intake of breath and her eyes lit up with excitement. There was no need to tell her it was a quarter million dollar diamond. That part was evident. Hecate's smile was electrifying. Eddie helped her put it on and the diamond sparkled nicely between her perfect, ample breasts. The black push-up teddy she wore with tiny hot pink and teal green bows with her shaved vagina below made a perfect picture. She sat on the edge of the table while Eddie licked her into an orgasm. Then she enthusiastically took Eddie's swollen cock into her mouth and showed him how much she appreciated his generosity.

"I would like you to wear it tomorrow when Nicole and Joanna come for lunch," Big Eddie stated. "Will you do that for me?"

"Of course. I would do anything for you," Hecate replied.

Nicole and Joanna flew in early the next day. Big Eddie had a banquet catered to his suite, complete with flowers and a live four piece band playing 1920s jazz softly in one corner of the room. Nicole and Joanna arrived promptly at 12:00 and were shown to the dining area.

Eddie was already seated at the head of the table with Hecate on his right. The arrangement, combined with Hecate's cool demeanor and the huge diamond that rested between her breasts made it clear that Big Eddie now considered the gorgeous Hecate the most important woman in the room.

For an instant Nicole had a flash of psychotic madness, boarder line unjustified jealously, then she quickly brought herself under control. Nicole notice that the opposite end of the table was set for her, directly across from Eddie which made her his equal and a place for Joanna was set to Nicole's right. Eddie had played that cool, as usual.

Eddie introduced Hecate and Nicole introduced Joanna. Things were very civil and polite. There was never any mention of business, which was the usual practice in mixed company and during meals. Mixed company meaning Hecate and Joanna who didn't need to know their business details. Nicole talked of things that impressed her about Russia and Eddie talked about Cairo.

There was a moment when Nicole talked about her excitement of taking Joanna to the premier fight that evening. There was no mention of what type of fight it was and Big Eddie quickly changed the subject to his yacht. It was due to arrive in the mail in a few months and Big Eddie was planning a party that he wanted Nicole and Joanna to attend. It would be a top notch celebration with some of the other partners in attendance.

After lunch and an hour of reminiscing and hugs all around, Nicole and Joanna excused themselves to go relax before their evening out.

When they left Hecate said, "It seems you know a lot of dangerous people." There was no doubt who she was referring to.

"That one especially," Big Eddie stated. "I would rather piss off ten raging Arabian princes than that one crazy woman."

They didn't say anything more about it, just enjoyed a nice afternoon and evening together.

Nicole had taken Joanna to gladiator fights in Russia and they both loved the fights and sight of blood. There was something very primitive and stimulating about watching men fight to the death. It was intense and sexually arousing. Nic had finally told Jo how things really worked behind the scene. Jo now knew that the men were motivated by the prospect and promise of a reward, which the winner actually received just before he was murdered for his misdeeds in order to prevent him from informing on the fights. Nicole had shown Joanna the video of what happened to the informants if they refused to fight. The video was so vivid and bizarre that it was hard to believe it was real. It was a sick, sadistic way to die. It was no wonder the men fought, they didn't want to end up on that table. There couldn't be a much crueler way to die.

Jo thought the whole thing was perfectly deceptive and crazy, but she absolutely loved it. That is, until Nic told her that she had arranged for the two of them to give the winner of tonight's fight his reward and his death. It didn't sound so amusing then.

At first Jo thought Nic was kidding, until Nic produced two beautiful and exotic feather masks that flared up and out to the sides, adding accent to the eyes, while leaving the mouth uncovered. They would wear the masks with bright red lipstick while fucking and killing the winner. Jo became apprehensive when Nic explained how things were going to go down, until she took two valium and had a glass of wine. Whatever Nic wanted, Jo was relaxed and ready to go along with it. She had already seen Nic shoot one man in her office without blinking an eye. It would take a lot to surprise her at this point.

At the fight, they shared a private box with the sponsor of the fight. He was a very wealthy Arabian who also dabbled in drugs, prostitution, weapons and other illegal items such as stolen high-end sports cars. If it was illegal, like the fights and money was to be made, he had his hands in it. He'd met with Nicole recently when he expressed his interest in the gladiator fights. They'd come to an agreement for him to provide the fighters and location and she would provide the world wide betting that would net him a very satisfactory percentage.

Part of the agreement was that, in order to ensure uniformity, the betting and fighting would be conducted in the same manner, with the same rules as in other countries around the world that were sponsoring fights. The other little concession was, after the first fight Nic and Jo would give the winner his much-deserved reward and death. Until that moment the new sponsor romantic inclinations towards Nicole. Her cheerfully stated condition/requirement that she and her mate Jo be the ones to fuck and kill the winner gave him second thoughts. She stated her terms in such a cool manner that it made it sound like she did it every day and it made the man nervous to be in the same room with her.

She was a praying mantis about to bite the head off her unwitting partner. He was thankful it wouldn't be his head. He shuddered at the idea but gladly agreed. One day he might regret it, but the money was too great to ignore. That and someday he might need support for an unusual request and his acquiesce in this matter would surely garner him favor. At the most he would just have to clean up her mess.

Just before the fight started Nic and Jo placed their bets then each took an ecstasy pill, at Nicole's insistence. Nic had recently introduced Jo to the morphine suppositories that her and her former lover, Kera, used to enjoy together. It was fun having sex in a drugged haze until you passed out from the pleasure of it.

The crowd was very loud and enthusiastic. The smell of cigar smoke and alcohol was heavy in the air and mixed with the sound of laughter. The area the ring was in was small, which made the room compacted with people who were shoulder to shoulder waiting on the event. Ring side bets were taking place, drinks were being passed around and hookers were plying their trade. It was a smorgasbord of activity and corruption.

As the fighters approached the ring cheers rang out from around the arena. The fighters climbed into the ring, one outfitted in gold the other in silver trunks and matching boots. They looked impressive and past the point of fear, even though you could clearly see the fear in their eyes. The ring master introduced each fighter as "Gold" and "Silver" as he explained their crimes and statistics, then he stepped out of the ring while the attendants strapped the shields and knives on the fighters.

The fighters, as instructed, stood in their corners facing each other until the bell rang, then they advanced and started circling each other looking for an opening. Their skin glistened with nervous sweat and Gold could be seen shaking with fear and anticipation. When Silver rushed in for the kill he went high in an attempt to force Gold's shield down so he could get at Gold's neck. Gold ducked and slashed Silver across his leg. Silver backed up screaming and trying to regain his balance. When Gold rushed in he lost his footing in Silver's blood trail and stumbled, which gave Silver a momentary advantage.

He jumped towards Gold and tried to stab at his stomach but Gold blocked the move with a downward movement of his shield, which left his upper body open. Seizing the advantage Silver stabbed Gold three times in the shoulder, neck and face before Gold could get his shield back up to protect himself. Gold was in pain and shock but he managed to stab Silver in the side as he raised his shield to ward off his attacker. Blood was flowing from both fighters and the ring was a mess of bloody footprints. The stab to Silver's side was deep and judging by the way he was bent over and favoring his side it was very deep and painful.

Gold saw the opening and the opportunity and came in for the final and fatal assault. He was stabbing for Silver's throat, but when Silver saw the thrust coming, he pulled his head back and tried to duck under the knife, but he didn't drop quite far enough and Gold rammed the knife into Silver's eye and on into his brain. Silver went instantly limp and fell to the mat, pulling Gold with him, because the knife was lodged in the bone and strapped to Gold's wrist.

The Attendants had to come into the ring and remove the knife strap from Gold's wrist so they could separate the two fighters and the doctor could start patching up the winner.

The ring master hurried back into the ring and announced Gold the winner as Silver's body was being dragged from the ring. Until that time there had been a hushed stillness throughout the arena. People were in awed shock until the announcer's voice boomed over the speaker system and snapped them back to the reality of the fact that some of them had just won a bunch of money. Cheers went up and in a moment the din of voices started to rise as people collected their bets and filed out of the area where the fight was held.

The winner was taken to a room that was prepared just for him. As instructed, the doctor only used local anesthetic for the pain while he stitched up Gold's wounds. Gold was handed a glass of wine that he gulped down greedily. He was starting to feel pretty good and cocky about his win and the prospects of his future. By the time the doctor finished sewing him up he was on his third glass of wine and was sitting back comfortably with an IV in his arm. For the moment, he was feeling no pain. The doctor quickly gathered all of his instruments, tossed the bloody items in a trash bag and left.

The fighter known as Gold was relaxing on a brown leather couch when the door opened and a cart with food on it was pushed through the door by a woman wearing a mask and a full length black leather duster. Gold smiled at the sight. He really got excited when another woman with identical mask and duster followed the first one into the room. Both women were smiling, which helped put Gold even more at ease. When the door closed both woman removed their coats to reveal their naked bodies. All they had on were garter belts, black stockings with a seam running up the back of their legs, spike heels and their masks. Two absolute visions of loveliness.

The women took their time putting on a show for the camera by wheeling the food laden cart over to the wounded winner. Jo picked up a stack of money and fanned it for the camera then handed it to the winner. Nic removed a cover from a plate of food, cut off a piece of steak and fed it to the happy winner. Gold was smiling so big that it was about to pull the stitches lose on his cheek, but he couldn't feel the pain because the local pain killer hadn't worn off.

Because of the IV line he couldn't move around much. He was pretty much stuck to the couch. The women, being mindful of this intentional dilemma and his stitches, cuddled up close on each side of him and fed him bites of food as they touched him and told him how great the fight was. He'd had a lot to drink and was feeling the effects. All he wanted was sex with these two gorgeous women, which was evident by his erection.

The ecstasy was kicking in and Nic and Jo were feeling hot and sexy. They took turns fondling, kissing and licking on the winner and each other. Jo straddled the man while Nic moved the cart so the camera would have a better shot. Then Jo raised up and guided Gold's member insider her. She slid up and down his shaft for the camera and ground her pelvis into his as hard as she possibly could. Nic saw that Jo was getting close to an orgasm so she carefully laid one of their coats over the camera then walked behind the couch. She then took an antique ivory handled straight razor out of the back of her garter belt and opened the blade down low out of sight behind the coach.

Nic waited until Jo's breathing became wildly erratic and she was fucking the man as hard and fast as she could and when Jo gasp for breath through her gritted teeth Nic knew it was time. She reached around the man's neck from behind and with a flourish that would have made Sweeney Todd proud, quickly dragged the razor from under Gold's left ear, around the front cutting into his wind pipe, to just below the right ear and stepped back with the razor raised high in her right hand.

Jo was in the heat of passion as hot, thick blood sprayed across her breasts and coated her stomach as the man thrashed in pain and shock beneath her. Jo instantly had another orgasm and couldn't help but grind down harder on the dying man until he stopped moving and she saw the life go out of his eyes. Nic folded up the razor as she came around the coach and tossed it on the floor next to her coat. The realization was just sinking in and Jo was staring at Nic with a blank expression on her face. Nic leaned over and kissed Jo on the lips then helped her off the dead man, who was still sporting a hefty hard-on. Nic embraced Jo so the blood was smeared all over her, as well and kissed her deep and long. Jo gave into the passion and held Nic tight.

Nic said, "Next time I fuck the winner and you slit his throat. Let's take a shower and get out of here."

Jo nodded and Nic took her by the hand and led her into the adjoining bathroom where they bagged up their bloody garter belts and stockings and took a shower together. When they left they didn't look back. They both knew they had just taken their relationship to another level.

Chapter 42

It only took the young doctor a few minutes to remove Doc's stitches and to pronounce that she was healing well. To Will's annoyance the doctor smiled and complimented doc on her nice legs, again. Doc thought the doctor was cute and sweet. Will just grumbled under this breath, which Doc and the doctor both thought was rather funny.

It was early Friday morning when Will and Doc left the hospital after getting Doc's stitches removed. It had been four days since she'd been shot in the leg. She refused to use a crutch or cane so she was limping like Festus on Gunsmoke. In a way her stubborn determination was comical, but every time Will saw Doc grimace with pain his anger was renewed. Doc laughed it off, but Will silently boiled. Saying that he was simply hot would be a serious understatement.

From the hospital they went to their office at the LAPD to talk with Commander Lewis and do paper work. Commander Lewis was openly sympathetic about Doc's injury. He congratulated Doc on her quick recovery, then looked at Will and said, "Get him." Everyone loved Doc.

The few people that were in when they walked into the squad room clapped and cheered Doc when she came limping in with Will trailing close behind. The greetings were short and Doc went back to her office where she discovered balloons, flowers and a get well card signed by the whole department. It was sweet.

Lunch came quickly and because Doc had been cooped up most of the week Will took Doc to her favorite little Italian restaurant where they enjoyed a meaty three cheese pasta. The meal was heavy, but excellent.

From the restaurant they went to Task Force headquarters and met with SAC Lamberth who was actually happy to see them because the fallout from the Rynalds' home being blown-up and Doc getting wounded had been relatively minor. The media rightfully attributed the explosion to Rynalds who was a murder suspect and made Doc out to be an officer wounded in the line of duty, i.e., attempting to arrest Rynalds.

Doc got more cheers, balloons, flowers and another very nice get well card signed by everyone. It was a moment of fun before she sat down to work and to another round of paper work and answering emails. Those people who thought cops spent most of their time in doughnut shops had been misinformed. They spent most of their time doing paper work and research.

While Will was reading all the daily progress reports he came to one from the Reno field office concerning the airfield informant shooting. The crime scene team had found the place where the shooter had been positioned for his killing shot. They found a shell casing in the dumpster, gunshot residue on the edge of the dumpster where the gun had been fired from and fingerprints belonging to one Robert Rynalds. They got the fingerprint match from the military data base. Either Rynalds was getting sloppy or he just didn't care any longer, because he knew he'd already been identified. It was probably the later. Anyway, you looked at it they were closing in on Rynalds and hopefully Mr. Freeman, as well.

They had discovered that Freeman was an alias that went back twenty years, which was as long as his commodities company had been in existence. They still had no clue who Freeman really was. They had no prints, no picture and no idea where he disappeared to. They had a general description of a big man that may be in a wheelchair and was approximately fifty years old. They knew he was apparently wealthy and owned a huge yacht they could not locate. Finding that yacht had proved to be a daunting task. Even Will didn't realize how many yachts were scattered about the world. By now Freemans' yacht could be anywhere.

By five o'clock Will and Doc were caught up on paper work and research so they headed home. Because they'd both over-done it at lunch they decided to have a late dinner of leftovers when they got home. The sun was bright and hanging low in the sky above the ocean, just starting to turn orange, when Will and Doc pulled into the driveway of their new beach home.

Will saw a twinkle of sunlight reflecting off glass, what he knew must be a rifle scope, to his left about fifty yards away up the beach in the sand dunes. Rather than slow down and wait for the garage door to open Will turned the car to the right, away from the gunman and drove across the front yard. He turned in beside the house, on the opposite side of the gunman, so they would have the house for cover.

"What are you doing?" asked Doc.

"There is someone with a rifle up the beach. Call for back-up and stay here," said Will as he opened the door.

"No, no, no, wait," Doc said as Will jumped out of the car and closed the door.

Doc fumbled with her cell phone as she watched Will run to the back corner of the house, then crouch and edge around the deck out of her line of sight.

Doc was cussing Will as she called 911 and then Task Force headquarters before she got out of the car and started slowly working her way around the front of the house with her gun drawn.

Bob was watching from the dunes south of Bracket and Holiday's nice little love nest. He was using the scope on his sniper rifle to look over every inch of the property. He wasn't planning on shooting them, because he knew he would probably only get one before the other took cover. His plan was to wait until the middle of the night, then slip-up to the house and place explosives on the wall outside where their bedroom was located like he did on the Deveraux hit. He would be back to his vehicle and driving away when Bracket and Holiday were blown into the next world, if there was a next world. Bob didn't believe in the hereafter, he believed in the here-and-now. Bob thought it odd that Bracket drove across the front yard and pulled around to the opposite side of the house. He didn't realize something was amiss until he saw Bracket's head peek around the corner of the rear deck looking in his direction. Before Bob could retrain his scope directly on Bracket's head, Bracket had ducked out of sight again. Bob's thought was, "Were these fucking cops psychic or just lucky beyond belief."

Bob decided to play the hand he was dealt and try to take out at least one of them then get the hell out.

Will had a mental fix on the shooter's location, who he was certain must be Rynalds. The wooden walkway stood two to three feet off the sand in places, so Will crawled down the side of the walkway towards the beach until he came to a spot with enough clearance for him to crawl under to the opposite side, where he would be hidden from the gunman's view by the sand dunes. He was closing the distance between him and the gunman, and at the same time, working his way around the side so he could come at him from the rear.

Bob was certain that Bracket was using the beach walkway for cover and was going to try and work his way around and behind. That's what he would do. He knew he didn't have much time to get into a better position to take out Bracket, but just as he was about to move, he noticed movement at the front corner of the house. To his surprise, it looked like Holiday was going to work her way around the dunes to the front. Only she had to cross an open space to get to the protection of the dunes.

Doc hobbled around the front of the house, cussing her injured leg and staying in the shadow of the house. She peeked around the corner and scanned the dunes but didn't see anything. She thought Will probably just saw a reflection off an old bottle. She decided, after only a moment's thought, that she would run over to the sand dunes, then work her way around the front. When she took her first step out, she saw the flash and felt the bullet tear into her chest and knock her to the ground. Things got fuzzy with pain and she didn't understand why she couldn't get up.

Bob saw Doc's indecision through his scope as she pulled her head back out of sight. But he saw her looking towards the sand dunes and knew she was about to make a run for them. When she stepped out he went for a moving chest shot, because it presented a target with the best odds and pulled the trigger.

When the rifle went off Will could tell by the sound that Rynalds was shooting towards the house. Will risked a quick look over the dunes and saw Doc laying on the driveway by the garage door and Rynalds swinging his rifle around in his direction. Will went instantly crazy with rage, jumped up and ran over the top of the dunes towards Rynalds firing at Rynalds with both guns. Will was thirty yards away and he saw Rynalds take a hit in the shoulder, drop the rifle and roll back as Will kept firing in Rynalds direction. Will stopped and crouched just long enough to slam in two fresh clips then he ran towards Rynalds position looking for a target.

Bob knew he was fucked. He was hit in the shoulder, neck and a graze on the side of his head. As he was rolling away he took one in the leg. He pulled out his pistol then pulled a ten second fuse on one of the explosive charges.

When Will ran over the dune where the rifle was laying Rynalds shot him in the hip as Will kept shooting at Rynalds with both guns, yelling like a wild man. A fraction of a second later an explosion blew Will up and back over the sand dune. Will was hurt and in shock, but all he knew was he had to get to Doc. He managed to stumble and fall the fifty yards back to Doc's side.

Will arrived just in time to see Doc smile and hear her say, "I love you," as the light went out of her eyes. Will collapsed beside her and never heard the sirens approaching or back-up arrive.

All the officer had to do to figure out what happened was follow Will's bloody foot prints in the sand to where what was left of Bob was scattered around the sand dunes.

Chapter 43

Four days later Will woke-up in the hospital with the light so bright it hurt his eyes. He looked around and saw his mother coming towards him with a bottle of water with a straw in it. He tried to smile but his mouth was so dry it hurt. His mother put the straw in his mouth and as he drank his mind cleared and realization hit him like a ton of shit.

He looked at his mother and asked, "Gloria?"

"She didn't make it, honey. I'm so sorry."

Tears welled-up in his eyes and the medication put him back into a drug induced, dreamless sleep. The next morning Will was too weak to do anything or even think much. He'd lost a lot of blood and the doctors were somewhat surprised that he regained consciousness as fast as he did.

Coworkers and friends came and went with their condolences. Will didn't say much. He uttered a few thank yous and laid there in stunned disbelief. At one point, between visitors, Will looked at his mother with tears running out of his eyes, and said, "I told her to stay in the car and call for back-up, but then I left here there, alone." He was blaming himself.

"Oh, honey it wasn't your fault. You did everything you could," his mother assured him.

"It wasn't enough," Will cried. "It was never enough."

Doc's funeral and burial had taken place the day before Will regained consciousness. People were telling him how beautiful it was. Some were congratulating him on getting Rynalds. The media was trying to get an interview. It was a madhouse for a few days.

The morning Will left the hospital all was quiet. Will and his mother were able to walk out to a waiting limo without being accosted by the press. Will's mother wanted to go directly to her hotel suite but Will had the driver take them to the cemetery. When they arrived things were a mess. The mortuary service was in the process of having the headstone set. Will, using a cane, slowly approached the grave site where the earth was still freshly dug. The workers brought sod to lay when they finished setting the marker. There was no doubt that it would be beautiful when it was done.

One of the workers looked-up, and said, "I'm sorry for your loss, sir." Then the workers stepped away to give Will some space and a moment alone.

The marker said, "Gloria Bracket, Loving Wife of William Bracket."

Will's parents had made all the arrangements. When Will thanked the workers and walked away he could barely see for the tears flowing from his eyes. He was thinking, "How could God be so cruel as to give him something so wonderful then allow it to be taken away."

Again, Will's mother wanted to take Will to her hotel suite to rest, but Will gave the driver instructions to take them to his home on the beach. During the ride Will and his mother cried together and talked of things long forgotten. It was safer to talk about the past than it was to discuss the present or future. The past held a lot of great memories.

When they turned into the driveway the house looked the same. How could anything look the same after such a tragedy. Some thoughtful person had tried to wash away the blood stain, but the porous concrete wouldn't give it all up. There was a darker spot on the cement where Doc's blood had slowly flowed from her body. Someone had moved Doc's car into the garage. That was nice of them. He would keep the car and think of Doc every time he drove it.

Will and his mother sat at the dining room table talking about not getting in a hurry about making any decisions about what to do with the house and his life. Mother was recommending a month of convalesce either back at home in New York or maybe a month in France where everything was absolutely beautiful that time of year when the doorbell rang.

Will was already standing up to get more coffee so he went to the door. He looked out to see a very attractive young woman who he knew to be a reporter. On impulse he opened the door because she had that look of determination he'd often seen in Doc's eyes. Then he stepped out on the porch, leaning on his cane to give his first and only interview.

"Mr. Bracket, I'm Cynthia Baylson with Today's News, I know how hard this must be for you--"

"I don't think you do or you wouldn't be here. But I'm glad you came. A large piece of my heart has been ripped away and I do have a comment."

Cynthia motioned for the camera man to come closer and said, "I was hoping you would Mr. Bracket. I know it's a bad time, but can you tell us what really happened?"

"My partner, Gloria Holiday and I were recently married. We were working as part of a Task Force that is investigating the kidnapping of federal informants. As we got closer to the truth there were three attempts on our lives. During our investigation we discovered that a Robert (Bob) Rynalds was involved and when we went to his home to question him he had the home rigged to explode. He shot and wounded my wife, Gloria, in the leg as he was getting away. Rynalds then went to Reno, Nevada where he shot and killed an informant and a federal Marshal. While Gloria was still recovering from her leg wound Rynalds setup an ambush here at our home. He was waiting about fifty yards south of here in the sand dunes. Rynalds shot my wife then he shot me before I could get him. After being shot I made it to my wife's side just in time to see her smile and hear her say, 'I love you,' before she died lying right over there in the driveway. We have reason to believe that Rynalds was working for a man known as Big Eddie Freeman. I want Big Eddie Freeman to know that I'm coming."

With that Will turned around and went back into the house. The camera man and reporter were crying as the door closed.

The next morning Will flew in his father's private jet back to New York with his mother. His plan was to spend a week in New York with his parents then fly to France for three weeks where he would take some time to think about what to do next and to heal. It was hard to believe that so much had taken place in the span of only one summer. He'd found true love and lost it and from there only had one goal in mind, retribution.

Afterward

The summer after Doc's tragic death there was a report of a luxurious private yacht exploding off the coast of Egypt near Port Said during a lavish party. All aboard were presumed dead and there wasn't enough of the yacht recovered to determine the cause of the accident.

Will was watching with binoculars from a fishing trawler a mile away when the yacht blew-up. The FBI had managed to locate the yacht and who they believed to be the elusive Big Eddie Freeman who they suspected was supporting terrorism through the illegal drug and arms trade. The problem was, they could not prove it, but there was more than one way to take out a suspected terrorist. It just so happened that the same day the yacht exploded with a party well in progress all of Big Eddie's corporate assets and holdings were seized by the United States Government under the Antiterrorism Act and now there was no one to contest the seizure.

Will knew that they would never be able to stop the drug and weapons trade but he meant to make a dent in it. The consolation prize was Big Eddie Freeman was no longer around to profit from the illegal activity that was infesting the world. Deadserious, whoever he was, could probably move on with his life without the worry of being killed and so could Will.

Will looked up towards the heaven and said, "That one was for you Doc. Batman doesn't have shit on me."

This is not the end.

Watch for the second Will Bracket novel “Forced Justice” coming soon.

Made in the USA
Middletown, DE
31 October 2022